To Bill and Betty Cole-for gifts I cannot repay.
To Brandon and David-my "boys."
To Nancy-the "fan" who has always encouraged/
supported/nourished.

RECOLLECTION

TIM COLE

ISBN-13:9780615532325

LCCN:2011909941

Pender House Publishing

Fear not for the future, weep not for the past.
—Percy Bysshe Shelley, "The Revolt of Islam"

RECOLLECTION

TIM COLE

PROLOGUE

July 7, 1981, was hot and humid in much of the southeastern United States. In the days after the celebration of the nation's independence, the drought that had begun in the dead of winter was strangling the land. Farmers who depended on the volatile temperament of the weather had begun to question their fate as their fields grew brown and dry, then began to die. But the clouds that had massed over the central part of the country had begun to move sluggishly to the east, threatening finally to spill over, like a great black cauldron of cool water onto a simmering frying pan. When they at last arrived, they carried the unbridled violence that only nature can muster.

In the town of Stacey, North Carolina, the storm finally came in the first wee hours and under the cover of darkness. Most citizens were asleep or listened from the safety of their beds as it swept over the tiny mill town like a great lion, its jaws hungrily gnashing on a helpless foe.

But it was the second beast, the one with a mind and a soul, the one that lurked under the cover of the gales that fed silently that night. So tucked away in the shadows that almost no one knew it had come at all. Except for the boys who bore witness.

And they were blades of grass in the path of the storm. Some twisted and torn, others left whole; to recover in time and to grow again.

Some were not so fortunate.

And even those left behind would not realize the depth of their wounds until the time came for the beast to stir again.

CHAPTER ONE

"Chew's old," Zeke rasped. He folded the pouch several times over before stuffing it deeply into his backpack. The tobacco tasted like he expected one of his old hunting boots might, full of the earth and the backwoods, with maybe just a hint of wet dog.

"I'm guessing Andy's lost...again," Jeb whispered. He sat Indian style, facing the first of the hulking black oaks that bordered the pasture. "Dumb shit." He waved a twisted sliver of a tree branch as he spoke, a symphony conductor looking out over a dark cacophony of field crickets and cicadas.

Zeke grinned and settled into the thick cushion of the deepest grass. He looked back over the rolling terraces of the pasture, trying to find a hint of the cattle trail they had followed. But the moon had already given way to the first of the mammoth clouds that had followed them from camp, and the fields had assumed the pale glow of the night.

"You got everything?" Jeb asked. "You checked it, right?"

"'Course I checked." Zeke patted the backpack as he spoke. He was shorter than Jeb, and younger. And whereas the older boy had begun to grow harder with adolescence, the nudges of baby fat still peeked out with Zeke, making him work hard to be like the other two boys. "Think I'm stupid or somethin'?"

Jeb poked the stick into ground and began to twist it. "You ain't scared, are you?"

Zeke grunted.

"Well?" Jeb waited.

"Ain't scared." But his voice trailed away, and he didn't look at Jeb, or up at the woods beyond.

"Fuckin' Andy." Jeb spat a long, dark stream of tobacco juice into the grass. He watched it trickle down a stalk, bleeding finally into the black dirt. Somewhere out there, the long, mournful cry of a hound lifted up and drifted over the hills.

"That Grady's dog?" Zeke asked. He strained to peer into the darkness.

"Betcha it's Leemore Williams's old Blue Tick."

"My pa says Leemore Williams's ain't worth a damn," Zeke said.

"He's a drunk for sure. But he can raise a hell of a hunting dog."

"Reckon he'll flush a rabbit?"

"If he don't get a raccoon...or maybe a fox, even."

"Think he's out hunting or drinking?" Zeke asked.

"Usually propped against that old radio listening to the Braves games with a pint of Jack. No baseball, so maybe he's hunting."

"My pa says the president ought to fix them major leaguers' tails for striking anyway. Says only a damn fool argues about getting paid a million dollars for playing a kid's game."

"Got a feeling President Reagan don't give a shit about major league baseball, Zeke."

"Well, he ought to, that's what I think anyway."

"When you're president you can take care of all that, I reckon," Jeb said. "President's got Russians to worry about. Cold war stuff."

"Why's he worried about coal anyway?"

"Not that kind of cold, Zeke. Cold like c-o-l-d. Like freezing to death cold."

"Sounds even stupider then," Zeke said. "Probably ninety degrees out here."

"Not the same thing. Not the same thing at all."

"You think you'll play in the majors someday, Jeb?"

"You kidding? Be lucky to play in high school."

"You could, you know. Play in the majors someday," Zeke said and he picked up a branch that lay in the tall grass and pretended to swing it like he might a baseball bat. "You could for sure."

As he spoke, the first hint of crimson bubbled over the western mountains, kissing them lightly then shrinking back into the night.

"You looking at that?" Zeke pointed.

Jeb did not turn.

"Clouds coming, Jeb."

"Going to give him another five. Then, we're going to have to go in and find him. Fuckin' Andy," Jeb repeated. He took aim with the stick and pretended to fire at the first of the oaks, pulling the "trigger" as he might if a panther was approaching in the gloom.

"Maybe Old Man Thompson done got him and ate him," Zeke giggled.

Jeb spat the wad of tobacco into his hand and flung it into the trees. It landed with a splat against something hard. They heard it slither into the undergrowth.

"You just make sure he don't get *you*," Jeb said, grinning.

Zeke did not return the smile. Instead, he turned back and gazed quietly at the mountains. Several seconds passed before the lightning flickered and died again. He waited for the low growl of thunder, but only the plaintive cry of a barn owl floated back. It was far off and headed toward cover, Zeke guessed.

"You know a lightning strike at night...it's like twice as deadly," Zeke said.

Jeb finally turned and scanned the sky.

"Yeah, maybe even three times," Zeke repeated.

"That right?" Jeb asked.

"'Course it's right."

"You study storms, do ya, Zeke?"

"Don't got to study 'em. It's a scientific fact."

"Scientific bullshit, you mean."

Jeb stood and grabbed a fistful of dry pasture grass, holding it high overhead. He released the blades into the night and they watched them float lifelessly back to the ground.

"If it's coming, gonna be a while," he announced and walked back to a nearby pine, propping up against it. "And who the hell told you about lightning?"

"Jeremy Ward."

"Jeremy Ward? That Yank's little brother?"

"He knows a lot of stuff, Jeb."

"Ain't he like...in the fourth grade?"

"Got held back on account of missing so much school, is what I heard."

"He the one that pulled the fire alarm last year?" Jeb plucked a long strand of grass and began to chew on it. The taste of the tobacco still lingered. "Got the school closed down for half the day?"

"Never owned up to it." Zeke's voice grew quieter. "Think it might have been a set-up or something."

The pine comb sailed past Zeke's ear and vanished into the tall grass beyond.

"You're such a dumb ass, Zeke."

• • •

Andy crouched under the low-hanging limb of a giant hemlock pine and waited. He was tall for his twelve years, but so painfully thin that he could still wear jeans that were a couple of years old, even if they rode high above his ankles. His tee shirt was a hand-me-down from his dad and it swallowed him. It smelled like his old man's sweat and Aqua Velva and reminded him he would be getting crap tomorrow afternoon about his paper route. His dad went ape shit when there were complaints about newspapers being tossed in the middle of begonia gardens or an occasional roof top landing. Old people were funny that way.

He swept his skinny fingers through his tangled mop of sandy brown hair in search of any remnants of the spider web. It was impossible to see so deep in the trees, and he'd walked face-first into it. Now the web and sweat mixed into a slimy gunk, and he was certain that somewhere in the deepest recesses of his scalp, a large black widow spider was dancing lightly; her jerky legs propelling her as she grimly searched for the place to insert her deadly fangs. He'd heard about that kid over in Stanly County that died from a spider bite a couple years back. Probably in woods just like these. He frantically swatted at his ears for a second time. Everyone knew black widows automatically sought out a victim's ears.

But this was as far as Andy was going to go, even with a damned spider crawling around on him. From this distance, he could make out the outline of the Thompson house, a brooding, looming giant that sat alone, framed in the street light just beyond. Three stories of it. It sat as far away as Grimley Park's center-field wall from home plate, maybe a little more, but close enough by Andy's reckoning. And he did not care to get beyond the infield by himself.

One dull window glared back at him, gazing vacantly into the trees like a Cyclops. He could feel its dead stare even as he crouched in the shadows.

A twig snapped somewhere off to his left, and he forgot about the spider, shrinking further back against the hemlock's trunk.

He waited. No sound, except those damn crickets. They bleated at him, mocking from the shadows.

Jeb said nobody would be out here this time of night, but Andy wasn't so sure. He half-expected a dark figure to suddenly emerge from the shadows, a hulking thing that melted with the blackness and could see him there.

He never asked for this duty, he told himself. Nobody needed to check this damned old house, anyway.

• • •

Zeke pulled the dented tin canteen out of the knapsack and took a long swig. They'd filled it when they crossed the river, but the cool stream water already tasted dry and hot, and it mixed with his sweat and the tobacco and rolled grudgingly down his throat.

"Should have brought more food," Zeke said, turning his attention back to the pack.

"We brought a dozen hotdogs and like forty million Snickers bars," Jeb said. "And don't you go losing all the stuff we got in there."

"Where are they? The hotdogs and the candy bars?"

"Judging from how much Andy and I got to eat, probably in your belly."

"I had maybe four 'dogs."

"You had maybe seven."

"Weren't seven," Zeke said, even as he dug further into the empty knapsack. There might be a Snickers bar that had escaped the carnage back at camp.

"Listen!" Jeb hissed.

Somewhere in the distance, the hound's howl grew louder and more insistent. But the pitch had changed. The rabbit was beginning to run out of time.

And somewhere up ahead, there was movement in the trees.

• • •

They were the same in many ways, the old man and the house. When he had been young, the house was new and freshly painted and impressive. But as the years passed, so too did the brilliance of youth, until finally the first signs of age began to seep in, coloring the corners and scraping away at the lines, tearing away the beauty until all that remained was the hint of what was. From a distance one might catch a glimpse of the past. It was only when you drew closer that the erosion of the years became more apparent.

The old man trudged slowly to each window, checking the same locks he had inspected since he was a boy. His father had insisted on it, and it had been his responsibility before the family retired each evening.

"Lot of meanness in the world, son. Sooner you learn that, the better off you'll be. People always going to want what they don't have. We don't want to make it easier for them". Then he had clapped his old pipe solidly on the cherry wood ashtray as he did every evening, rolled the newspaper up, and patted him on the head with it as he headed up to bed. "And check the backdoor too," he added as he trudged up the stairs.

Daddy was dead and buried some seventy years, but the admonition still lingered.

He fingered the last dusty lock and paused to gaze out over the garden. All was safe.

As he followed his father's footsteps up the rickety stairs, Franklin Thompson could not know that the danger on this night lay within the house, and he had just locked it inside.

• • •

"So, nobody's there. Right?" Jeb asked the question a third time.

Andy took the beginning of a long gulp from the canteen and then glared over at Zeke.

"Damn it, Zeke. You already drunk it all." But he continued to wave the canteen upside down, as if he might suddenly tap a fresh stream.

Zeke shrugged and they could feel his awkward grin, even through the darkness.

"It's clear." Andy's voice was harder now. "Make *him* carry the damn canteen back." He shoved it into Zeke's belly.

"We're going then," Jeb said. He looked at Zeke.

"That's right," Zeke whispered. "We're going."

They briefed the plan in the shadows of the trees. Zeke recited his assignment and showed the other two the contents of the knapsack. As he did, he discovered a final candy bar, but it was frazzled and worn, and none of them could be sure how long it had been stuffed underneath the army bayonet in the side pocket. They eyed it with some degree of interest, but no one seemed inclined to take the first bite.

They huddled there in those last minutes, watching the glimpses of light exploding against the distant hills with the same wonder as when they once crawled to the top of Crawford's Bluff and peered down on the field of car tops and teenagers making out in front of the towering movie screen, talking about serious subjects, like Judy Stroupe of eighth grade fame and Bolie Schenk's Dodge Charger and past campouts and the relative risks of lightning strikes after dusk.

A quarter-mile away, hidden in the recesses of the large ramshackle house and amid the quiet of night, death stirred. It wrapped quietly around its victim, like a great boa constrictor, growing tighter and tighter until its icy embrace began to choke the heart of its prey. It did so without witness and without conscience. It was not yet aware of the interlopers that were drawing closer. The house nurtured its malevolence. Shielded it. Gave it power.

CHAPTER TWO

"You hear it?" Andy crouched low behind the carcass of a crumbling stone wall. They could see their target clearly across the carefully tended garden and the courtyard beyond. A veiled whisper of music wafted through the air. It drifted lightly in the blackness, like the murmur of their imaginations.

"You telling me you *didn't* hear that before?" Jeb looked toward Andy.

"Wasn't playing before." Andy said. "Would have heard it."

Jeb groaned and looked toward Zeke. "Someone's there…we can't."

"Jeb, I got it," Zeke protested.

"We can't go with it like this. You know that."

"Come on, Jeb. We don't go tonight, it just means we got to come back tomorrow night. Or maybe the one after that."

"What do you think?" Jeb glanced over at Andy.

"Scrap it. That old man's up, we got problems," Andy answered.

"I ain't afraid," Zeke said. "It's the same deal. I'll be back in two minutes."

Jeb studied the outline of the house and the one single eye that stared lifelessly back. Dull and yellow, its glare reached across the deep purple of the gardens until it mixed with the dark and faded into the shadows. He searched again for signs of activity inside but found none.

"I don't know, Zeke," Jeb said.

"Relax, Chief. I got it." Zeke's tone suddenly took on a mocking seriousness.

"Can't kid around with this."

"I know that, Chief." Zeke saluted.

"Damn it, I'm serious, Zeke." Jeb glanced back at the house. "You see anybody, you run. You understand?"

"Yes sir!"

"You just stay out of the light, all right?" Andy grabbed Zeke by the shoulder. "You hear?"

Zeke broke into a big toothy grin. Andy shoved him, and he laughed louder.

"Make it quick, OK?" Andy said.

"Relax, will ya'? Jeb said it was okay."

"Zeke…"

"*Jeb said it was OK,*" Zeke repeated.

"Also OK to run if you see somebody, right?" Jeb whispered.

"Ten four, Chief."

Jeb tried to stifle the smile but couldn't. They all three giggled.

A wisp of wind brushed through the woods. It carried the smell of the rolling pastureland and mixed with a hint of the rain that lay somewhere beyond.

Jeb and Andy watched Zeke walk away.

He moved quickly, navigating around the thick foliage of the back-yard and gliding toward the shadows of Red Tips that ringed the court-yard. He tripped once, sprawling over a rake that lay hidden in one of the flower beds, his heart pounding as he stumbled to the ground.

But Zeke clambered to his feet, and in the dim light they watched him jump up and down, gesturing wildly with the rake he had tripped over. Raising it above his head like some tribal spear collected by an ancient chieftain, dancing about in a silent dance of celebration.

"Wish he wasn't such a smart ass," Andy growled. "Everything is a damn joke."

"Old Man Thompson hears him, he ain't gonna be laughing then," Jeb whispered as he crouched back down.

They watched him continue on, staying low as he lurched from one side of the courtyard to the other, until he made his way to the deep folds of darkness beside the window. Safety.

Somewhere in the distance, the first low rumble of thunder rolled toward them, finding them in their hiding place, where it mixed with the music of the trees and wrapped around them, gently at first, almost caressing them, moving closer.

Zeke fumbled with the knapsack even as he dropped below the large bay window. He slowly rose to a crouched position and reached toward the pane.

"Little son bitch's going to do it. Easy." Jeb grinned.

"How long you think it will take us to get back to camp?" Andy asked. He was looking back behind them, in the direction of the rain.

"Beat that storm, no time."

"I ain't staying in these woods tonight, Jeb."

"Nobody's asking you to."

"Well, that rain gets here when we're out in the pasture, gonna be a mess. You know that, don't cha?"

"Damn, Andy. You're such a baby."

"Ain't no baby. You want to be out there in the open with it lightning and everything?"

"Look, five minutes and we're headed back..."

"What's that?" Andy interrupted him. He had turned back to the house.

"Besides, you get wet, you get wet. So what?" Jeb went on.

"No...Jeb. *What's that?*" Andy's hand tightened around Jeb's arm. Jeb turned.

"Second floor," Andy said.

"What are you talking about?"

"Look at the second floor window."

Jeb scanned the row of darkened windows. Nothing.

Andy's grip tightened.

Then he saw it. The corner window of the second floor. The white curtain silhouetted there. But as he studied it, he began to see something else.

"What is that?" Andy whispered.

"Window shade, maybe."

"No window shade."

Jeb stepped forward, straining to make it out.

"I think...someone's standing there, Jeb." Andy's voice tightened.

They looked back toward Zeke.

The boy had slowed. For some reason, he was standing now, peering intently into the bay window.

"What's he doing?" Andy asked. "What's he *doing?*"

They watched Zeke suddenly drop to the ground, flattening out against the dry grass.

Jeb was up. He was moving toward the house. Something was wrong.

The flash of lightning that ripped through the trees suddenly bathed the house in a jagged scar of brilliance. It exploded around them at once, scorching the night and for a split second it seemed to be with them there, wrapping around them in a white hot cocoon. The ground rose up at the same time, and Jeb found himself rolling through thorny underbrush and pine needles, trying to make out where he was. He thought he could taste the simmering aftertaste of scorched earth but couldn't be sure.

In those few seconds, he found himself staring across the garden to the second floor window. It was as if the lightning had chosen to linger there, pulled to one dark corner of the house. Jeb could see it clearly; the faceless figure that stood looking down at them.

Neither boy heard the roll of thunder that followed. But they would both remember the screams.

• • •

Jeb awoke with the same name on his lips as before. A hot lather of sweat soaked the sheets where his legs lay hopelessly intertwined. He kicked them off, waiting for the sound of his own heart to slow.

Just another of the damn nightmares. But he scanned the room instinctively, searching the shadows. It was always the same, always the feeling that someone else was there when he awoke. He could feel the dark, oozing sensation that ran down his arms, and even in the night, knew the smell of the blood.

And he knew he was not alone.

The boy stood at the foot of his bed. A dim silhouette in the darkness. Unmoving.

Jeb Mason screamed as he madly clawed toward the headboard. He was still screaming when he finally awoke from the second of the nightmares.

He let the cool night air wash over him, begin to soothe his ragged breathing, bringing him back. He studied the dark ceiling of his condominium and waited for sleep's terror to slip away. Then padded quietly to the bathroom.

Seconds later, as he splashed the cool water over his face, he looked up into the mirror at the middle-aged man with day-long stubble of beard, the slightly bloodshot eyes that looked back at him.

Thirty damn years.

"We didn't kill anybody," he whispered. And in his heart he prayed it was true.

PRESENT DAY

CHAPTER THREE

Tony Delvechio longed for a doughnut. Not the standard grocery store issue you could pick up down on the corner, no, he wanted the hot, dripping kind that swam in a river of glazed sugar. The one you didn't just swallow, the one that soaked into you with a gooey warmth that made your insides kind of dance. That's what he wanted. Tatem's Bakery was probably taking their first batch out of the oven right about now. Still hot, still soft. Then a couple of cups of coffee to wash them down with would be just about right.

Tony glanced up at the clock. Fat chance of slipping out to get one. There was another hour before his last break, and there was no way to make it six blocks and still get back in time. A cigarette might be a nice substitute. But even that was a problem—even lighting up in the bathroom wasn't without risk anymore. Damn smoke detectors made sure of that. He leaned his three hundred pounds back in the blue swivel chair and gave a cursory glance at the row of television monitors that lined his desk here in the main atrium of the Chandler Building. Twenty-six years as a Chicago beat cop had taught him to stave off the urges when they came knocking. He could wait.

He saw the Audi as it pulled into the western entrance to the building's underground parking lot. Silver. Late model. It slowed as it approached the security gate, which would remain unmanned until 6:00 a.m. The driver sat there, slowly punching in a code. So slowly that one might wonder if the numbers had been poorly memorized or perhaps were being read off of a stolen ID card.

Delvechio had spent his last ten years of "retirement" here, as a security guard in the towering forty-seven story Chandler Building on

Chicago's North Side, working the midnight to 8:00 a.m. shift. It was slow work for the most part. Easy time, if you could learn to smile and nod your head at the corporate types who waltzed in and out the door, most only dimly aware of your presence, preferring to regard you like they might a potted plant or a piece of heavy furniture. Occasional vagrants had to be chased out. There'd been a couple of vandalism problems in one of the parking lots, and only two attempted break-ins during all that time. Not bad overall.

He watched the security gate rise, and the Audi pulled into underground parking. It circled the lower level slowly, the driver surveying the empty lot carefully. It finally rolled into the farthest corner, a darkened recess that was the greatest distance from the main surveillance camera.

The phone began to ring at the same time. Delvechio snatched it up, his attention still riveted on the monitor.

"You watching level one?" The voice was young and high-pitched.

"Got 'em."

"The first few times he punched in the code it was incorrect."

"Who is this, anyway?" Delvechio growled. He could never keep up with the succession of twenty-something-year-olds who paraded through the security director's office, each a graduate of some high-brow executive program and with no clue what real police work was like. There were always at least three of them on duty up on fifth floor, watching the various monitors and assuring themselves that they were the thin line between business as usual and panic in the streets.

"Hudson Daniels, Officer Delvechio."

"Well then, Hudson Daniels, I *have* him. Why don't we just watch for a while."

"Mr. Samuels is sending me down now, Officer Delvechio. Be advised."

Delvechio cursed quietly into the dead receiver and laid his stained Bears mug down. He shifted his sizable girth forward in the swivel chair and watched the man slowly climb out of the car, where he stood quietly in the shadows for several minutes. Waiting. Then he began walking toward the main bank of elevators and into the light. Medium height. Brown hair. Muscular. He had a quiet, confident air as he strolled forward, almost like he owned the place.

He stopped when he was about thirty feet from the elevators, seeming to notice the tiny camera that was just above the second elevator for the first time. He glanced up at it and then suddenly averted his gaze. Then he bolted to his left, in the direction of the stairwell at the back of the building.

Delvechio flinched, and then bounded out of his chair and away from the bank of monitors. He moved quickly for his size, covering the marble tile floor to the far stairwell in seconds. Then he suddenly skidded to a stop. Something was wrong. He walked back to the monitors. Waited there. The fourth monitor was focused on the far stairwell door. The man should be there by now. His eyes swept back to the central screen, the one focused on the elevator. Where was he?

No sign of the perp in the parking lot. He couldn't have just vanished. The elevator doors opened. No one walked inside. They slowly closed. Still empty. Delvechio broke for the far stairwell a second time just as the bell chimed the fourth elevator's arrival at the lobby. He was standing there, on his toes and in an offensive lineman's semi-crouch, when the doors opened and Jeb Mason nonchalantly strolled out.

"Morning, Tony."

"Damn, Mr. Mason." Delvechio straightened, a huge grin sweeping over him. "You 'bout got me that time."

"Figured so. What gave me away?"

"Hunch," Delvechio answered, his eyes twinkling with merriment. "You got tendencies, Mr. Mason. Tried the same maneuver one time last fall, remember?"

"You're old, Tony. You should have forgotten that by now."

"Maybe, maybe," Delvechio answered as they headed back toward the security desk. He reached below the tabletop and produced a second mug. He poured in the steaming coffee and pushed it toward Jeb. "When did you get the new car?"

"Loaner. Mine's in for a service. Like it?"

"I'm guessing the fifth floor boys are pissing all over themselves right about now." Delvechio smiled at the thought. "Let's see…5:50. That's kind of early, even for you, ain't it, Boss?"

"Rough night, Tony." Jeb tested the coffee and grimaced.

"Really?" Delvechio raised an eyebrow.

"Not that kind of rough night." Jeb frowned.

"None of my business. Course, a young healthy fella like you…"

"Tony, I can only hope that my love life someday matches what you think it is."

"Not what I'm hearing."

"Christ sakes, Tony, you're like an old woman!"

"Maybe…there's a story going around that you were down at Carmine's last week with a pretty fine lookin' young thing."

"Blonde or brunette?"

"Brunette."

"It was a blonde. Your sources are clearly misinformed."

Delvechio considered this new information seriously, running a thick paw through his thinning white hair. "Missus says we gotta get you married before you're forty-five."

"And why's that?"

"Read another Cosmo article about single male death rates."

"Thought you canceled that subscription."

"Newsstand."

Jeb studied the *Chicago Tribune* headline that was already spread across the desk as they talked. The taste buds not destroyed by the first gulp of coffee were showing the first signs of response.

"'Course I'm dead set against it anyway," Delvechio offered.

Jeb looked up and waited for the punch line.

"You getting married. You get hitched and all the adventure goes out of my life."

Jeb smiled and nodded to one of the monitors. "Here we go," he said.

A gangly young male in a crisp blue blazer was approaching the parked Audi. He was yelling into a radio and glancing nervously around the parking lot. A second man, older and with a soft potbelly, was rushing down the far stairwell. He was gesturing wildly and also barking into a handheld.

Delvechio clicked a button and the harried exchange of security officers Hudson Daniels and his supervisor filled the lobby. Jeb joined him in listening to the drama playing out below with quiet satisfaction.

"I'm thinking that one of these days you're gonna get shot with some of these shenanigans," Delvechio said, failing to hide his enjoyment.

"Shouldn't Field Marshall Samuels know me by now?" Mason asked.

"Yup," Delvechio said. "'Course, Samuels should know where he parked his car every day, too, but I've watched him walk three floors to find it."

"I feel much safer."

"You should. You should."

Jeb glanced down at the sports section that lay spread out underneath the "Da Bears" mug. It had several coffee-stained circular imprints left behind among the late night baseball box scores. He quietly groaned.

"Lankford let you down last night, Boss," Delvechio said.

"You got to him, didn't you, Tony?"

It was a deep laugh that started somewhere around his large belly and rolled up his diaphragm, exploding in a spasm that caused Delvechio's face to turn a deep crimson.

"Come on. You can tell me. I won't squeal on you. What was it, Tony? Money? Women? Unlimited buffet pass to Quincy's? Talk to me, Tony," Jeb said.

Delvechio roared with laughter. "I told you his slider was off and on," he stammered between gasps.

"You're ruining the sport, Tony. You and your other conspirators. Once I have the goods I'll be turning state's evidence on all of you."

Tony could only attempt an answer between rolls of laughter.

Jeb wrapped the ten-dollar bill into a tight cylinder and placed it quietly into the big man's front pocket, beside the beloved Cubs ballpoint and just above the glistening security badge. Delvechio made a show of unfolding and carefully examining it, though his eyes had grown so watery it was debatable he could make out the print. Jeb headed toward the elevator.

"Got a three-game series next week with the Mets!" Delvechio yelled after him, wiping his brow with the same blue handkerchief he'd carried for the last twenty years. "You're due, Boss."

"I'm not emotionally ready, Tony," Jeb answered as the elevator doors closed, leaving a thoroughly pleased Tony Delvechio behind.

CHAPTER FOUR

Twenty minutes later Jeb poured his second cup of coffee and glanced out the window of his thirty-eighth floor office. The Chandler Building offered an impressive view of Lake Michigan and the uptown business area. To the south, interstates 57 and 94 converged, and he paused to consider the ribbon of traffic already forming as Chicagoans poured into the city. July 15 would soon become a furnace. Barbara, the bouncy weather girl on channel seven predicted high nineties on last night's weather report.

He savored the calm of the early morning, and took the moment to glance over at the first few sailboats already on the lake, tiny dots of white atop a blue-green glass, the sun a magnificent crimson orb rising slowly behind them in greeting. This was the best time of the day; no phone calls, no meetings, no new emergencies requiring "your immediate attention"; just the tranquility of the city and the sky, thirty-eight floors above the rest of the world.

Jeb tore himself away, glanced down at the reports spread across his deep red mahogany desk, and plowed into the real world. By 7:30, the office would be at full gallop in preparation for the end of day Operating Team meeting.

The second-quarter figures had only barely hit target. Though it marked the seventh consecutive quarter, the natives would be restless. They were attracting more and more attention from the financial mavens in New York, the ones whose endorsement represented the lifeblood of the company's future.

As vice president of sales for Tolliver Medical, Inc., Jeb's responsibilities extended far beyond the prototypical sales role and into the areas of marketing, commercial development, managed care, and even research. Tolliver's sales of 750 million in North America made it a middle-of-the-road player in the medical equipment and supplies arena, but staying in the middle had become a daily battle. The confluence of factors dictating Tolliver's future had become a mind-numbing blur over the last three years, with no conclusion in sight.

Jeb scanned the proposal his colleague, Larry O'Grady, had e-mailed the evening before. They had started together, two of the few Maylor Med guys still around after all the bloodletting created by the Tolliver acquisition. Jeb and Larry had spent months privately discussing and debating the development of their national campaign for the fourth quarter. Brendon Tolliver was coming in for the presentations today. Jeb felt the acid churning in his stomach. Too many Tolliver visits would guarantee him his first ulcer.

He swept through the numbers again and checked his watch. It was 6:30. Still too early to call. He gulped down a second swig of coffee and then said, "To hell with it," and picked up the phone.

Larry O'Grady picked up the receiver on the second ring.

"Hi, Jeb. How are you this morning?" his voice cheery, upbeat.

"Great, great. Hey listen, if you got a minute, thought it might be worthwhile to go through the figures. Got an idea about the meeting…"

"Forget the numbers. Are you OK?" Larry suddenly sounded concerned.

"What…"

"Has something happened?"

"Larry, what are you talking about?"

"We've been worried, that's all. I mean, it's almost 6:35, and you still hadn't called. Margie wanted to call the police but I said no, let's wait. Maybe there's a problem with the phone…"

"All right, what's that supposed to mean?"

"Jeb, you've never called this late on the morning of one of our O.T. Meetings…you sure you're OK?"

Jeb could feel the gentle chiding even through the phone. "You're funny, Larry. You're killing me. You know that?"

"Margie says to remind you that you still haven't called her friend, Cindy. She wants to know if you're intimidated by her education."

Jeb groaned. "No, tell Margie I will call her, it's just been pretty busy, that's all…"

Muted voices on the other end. "Margie wants to know how you can call us three to four times a day but not have time to call Cindy."

"I promise I will call her."

"Margie says prove it."

"Can we talk about the numbers now?"

A long pause on the other end. "Margie's sending you a picture of her on e-mail...whoa...Jeb, if you don't call her, I'm going to..." A thump on the other side. "You're a witness, Jeb. I've got spousal abuse here."

"Larry, will you be in soon?"

"Seven-thirty on the nose. Just got to finish my coffee."

"See you then, Larry." Jeb quietly hung up the phone. Everyone was a marriage counselor these days.

Mason was days short of his forty-second birthday. Divorced, with no immediate prospects for a return match with matrimony. Happily single but with a crowd of well-meaning friends who had the singular goal, it seemed, of finding Mrs. Right for Jeb. The most avid seemed to be the wives. He was convinced there had been some type of clandestine meeting at which he had been voted Most Eligible. The possibility of marriage wasn't one that he lingered on. He contented himself with a third review of the numbers.

Margie O'Grady could drive him nuts sometimes.

CHAPTER FIVE

Walter watched the Learjet taxi down the runway and turn toward the terminal. He took one last long draw on his Winston and flicked the butt away. Then he hit "send" on his cell phone.

"Son of a bitch probably has binoculars on me," he muttered.

He got back into the sparkling black Lincoln Town Car and adjusted the rearview mirror to double- check himself. Tie straight. Hair combed, though the cowlick in the back threatened to defeat the pomade he'd used that morning to plaster it down. Teeth: acceptable. He could move the partial he had replaced the year before easily with his tongue and for a brief second he contemplated wiggling it for the benefit of his client. Sort of a brief form of insanity. He tried to rehearse his welcome smile again but no matter how many times he tried, it still came across like a football coach who just watched his team score their first touchdown late in the fourth quarter of a game in which the opponent had scored ten. Not quite pleasurable.

The captain opened the hatch and hustled down the plane's stairwell. He wore a crisp white dress shirt and an expression that was clearly more practiced than Walter's. He waited at the bottom of the stairs, at full attention, focused on the Lear's doorway.

His Excellency's arrival was imminent.

The lanky man that appeared there several minutes later ducked to avoid hitting his head. When he uncoiled to full height he greatly resembled a vulture, with deep-set eyes that paused to survey a distant landscape. Searching, perhaps, for the latest carcass on which to feed.

Walter watched him stride down the steps. He did not acknowledge the pilot who waited at the bottom and offered him a respectful nod and "good day" as the company founder passed. Walter knew it was the same pilot that had been his personal chauffeur on global jaunts for over eight years. And that he ranked with the stairwell and the plane— vehicles that carried him from point A to point B.

Walter involuntarily pressed his hand down the front of his tie and snapped to attention as Brendan Tolliver approached the car. He was about to become the connector to point C.

· · ·

"A.H. is on the ground." Bonnie Collins glanced at the text message from Walter and her fingers tightened around the phone. "Forty-five minutes and counting."

Elizabeth Collins was better known as "Bonnie" to most everyone in the office. She was a salt-and-pepper-haired veteran of thirty-one years with Tolliver and Maylor. Seasoned in the political wars of corporate life, she was the gatekeeper for sales, marketing, operations, and, specifically, Jeb Mason.

Jeb referred to her as the office "muscle"—no nonsense and not effected by corporate politics. Because of that, he went to great lengths to keep her out of the line of fire of Brendan Tolliver. She was not given to kissing ass and he was not accustomed to anything less.

Her announcement sent one of the coordinators into a dead run while another began to make hurried calls to alert remaining staff.

"A.H.?" Jeb raised his eyebrows. He was jotting personal notes in the margin of the presentation and standing at Bonnie's desk.

"You ever ask yourself why Mr. Tolliver insists on having operating team meetings at 5:00 p.m. on a Friday, Jeb?" Bonnie asked.

"Well, that's easy," Jeb answered. "Because he *can.*"

"And you're asking me about A.H.?"

"So I can assume..."

"Awfully handsome," Bonnie said. She kept her eyes on the keyboard in front of her.

"Please tell me you haven't made that a part of the office vernacular," Jeb said, stifling the beginning of a smile.

She hit "print" on her computer, whirled to grab another stack of pale blue manila files behind her. "OK, A, I don't have the faintest idea of what you're talking about, and, B, I'm not completely sure what a vernacular is."

"Though he is stunningly handsome," Jeb added. "I can see the attraction."

Bonnie glared back.

"And you probably are somewhat close in age…"

"If I ever—and I repeat—ever, suggest even a passing interest in Brendan Tolliver, you have my permission to sign commitment papers."

"But you just said…"

"We're at forty-four minutes and counting, Jeb Mason," Bonnie said. "Unless you want me to kill you, and I am prepared to do that, I suggest we get back to work."

Jeb grabbed the completed folders on Bonnie's side desk and marched deliberately toward the Board Room.

"Of course, we could still pray for a car crash," she called after him, and returned to her typing.

CHAPTER SIX

The call was not immediately noted by anyone in the office. It was rolled over to another secretary, who patched the outside caller into Mason's voice mail system. Standard protocol for the day of an Operating Team Meeting.

Bonnie was running a final check of the numbers for Jeb and O'Grady, the Vice President of National Accounts. The office was at DEFCON One-launch phase. *All* calls were redirected.

At 4:35 p.m., in the final moments before the meeting was to get underway, Jeb buzzed Bonnie and asked for an update on messages—a tension reliever before the main event.

She handed Jeb the pile of sticky notes. He thumbed through them quickly, his mind focused on the fireworks to come.

"Bonnie, this says I had a call from an Andy Gardner. No number. Did you talk to him?"

"No. Probably left a message with Linda…" She yanked another set of numbers off the printer and whisked them into a third folder. Twenty minutes and counting.

"No message?"

"Can't be sure," Bonnie had already dived back into her typing, "but I would guess she just automatically sent them into voicemail. That's how Linda always does it. Do you know him?"

"I used to know an Andy Gardner. Couple of lifetimes ago."

He picked up the speakerphone and punched in his voice mail number. Hurried through the benign introduction of Voice Mail Lady and his series of messages until he reached the first from an "outside caller."

There was a long pause. "Jeb...Jeb Mason...this is, damn, is this thing working? This is Andy...this is Andy Gardner from Stacey... Stacey, North Carolina. Jeb, I know it's been a long time. But I wanted to try and find you. It's about Zeke, Jeb. Zeke...sorry to have to tell you this...he's dead. I thought you might want to know that...I'll leave you my number, but...it's been a long time. It's 704-555-8417...I hope you're doing OK...I wanted you to know. See ya."

"You find out about your caller?" Bonnie wheeled around the corner and stopped.

Jeb stood staring out his window, blankly gazing into space. He seemed unaware of Bonnie or the telephone. As Voice Mail Lady stoically offered the option of deleting or skipping the last message, Bonnie quietly hung up the phone. Jeb did not notice.

• • •

"So you're telling me Jeb Mason is *not* going to be here?"

Brendan Tolliver stood at the front of the boardroom conference table. His question was directed to no one and everyone.

"Yes sir. Family crisis," Larry O'Grady said. He glanced quickly at the others gathered around the boardroom table. None established eye contact.

Tolliver looked down at the report that lay in front of him. He tossed it aside and poured a glass of water from one of the shimmering crystal carafes that were positioned strategically around the room. No one spoke. Tolliver walked to the flip chart on which the latest sales figures were posted. The AV team had spent the majority of the last two days in preparing a series of cardboard data charts for the operating team to work with. The last quarter's figures were posted there.

Tolliver thumped the trend lines once, then a second time. Then a third. He held one long, bony finger there. "How long will the 'family crisis' be?"

He gazed out the window as if he were searching for Mason, somewhere among the simmering heat waves that rose above the city.

O'Grady cleared his throat. "It involves a death, Mr. Tolliver, so I believe it may be several days." He wondered if his voice sounded two octaves higher or if it was his imagination.

Brendan Tolliver turned back to the Operating Team and smiled. "I see." He craned his long neck as if the purple Italian tie had begun to strangle him. He twisted and coiled until he found an acceptable comfort level. "Then we will proceed without him." He opened the report and pulled out his Mt. Blanc fountain pen.

Let the Inquisition begin.

CHAPTER SEVEN

"Arthur!"

The voice swam closer.

"Arthur Henry Patterson!" Sharper now.

"Arthur Henry Patterson. Get off your butt!" Jake Lamotta growled the words.

A trickle of blood streamed from Lamotta's left nostril and ran down over his mouthpiece. Patterson watched it pulse back and forth with each long, heaping breath Lamotta made. He glared at Arthur through the slit that was once his right eye and moved forward, his boxing gloves held high.

Arthur "Bump" Patterson struggled to get off the floor even as Lamotta laughed coldly. He glanced over at the referee, his shirt soaked with the same blood as he began his count.

"You good for nothing..." Lamotta's voice seemed strange, Bump thought. Somehow terribly out of place for the middleweight champion of the world.

"Arthur, will you wake up?"

Bump opened his eyes. Ilene Patterson stood over him, wiping cake batter on her bright turquoise-colored apron and laughing.

"You bobbing and weaving in your sleep, old man?"

Bump looked around groggily at the familiar confines of his living room.

"I thought you said you was going to watch that movie through for once." Ilene said.

Bumped pushed his TV tray and the last remnants of his Papa John's delivery back from his Lazy Boy and kicked the faded maroon chair

back up to an upright position. The pizza and the chair had started
Raging Bull with him, but the T.K.O. had gone down sometime earlier.
The specter of fighting the middleweight champion of the early fifties
had been replaced with the image of his wife, who appeared almost as
menacing at the moment. He glanced toward the old Panasonic and
watched a bloated Robert DeNiro get tossed into solitary.

"Old man, you are some sorry sight." Ilene put her hands on her
ample hips. "You going to clean up this mess, too. I'm going to tell you
that."

Bump wiped his eyes and returned, at last, to his living room.

"Mary Ruth called. You need to go over and pick up a couple of
grills at the school for the cookout."

Bump grunted. He picked up the last piece of pizza and took a bite.
It tasted as rough and dry as he felt.

"Did you hear me?" Ilene said.

"Why do I need to get a grill when William's s'posed to bring his
big gas job? Been hearing about it for a month."

"Cause William showed up without it, that's why."

"Good lord."

"I know, I know. But you know William."

"What time is it?"

"Time for you to get up off your sorry ass." Ilene handed him his car
keys and began to pull him from the warm nest of the Lazy Boy. "You
be there and back in twenty minutes."

"Ain't going tonight. That cookout's not 'til Sunday."

"And you fishing with Roy and Lee tomorrow and won't be back 'til
late. She needs that grill tomorrow morning. And we ain't going to be
running all over Stacey, North Carolina, to find one, either."

Bump moaned and clambered out of the chair.

Ilene studied his weathered face and smiled. "You'll be glad on
Sunday. You know your sister's making pork chops."

"I just wish Mr. William would remember his black ass from time
to time," Bump muttered. "Seems to me a college graduate ought to be
able to…"

"William took after his daddy and that's all there is to it," Ilene
shushed him, even as she hustled him in the general direction of the
front door.

"Don't you be throwing away that pizza," Bump said as he plodded out. "Man lays food down around here and it gets thrown away 'fore it's even cold."

"You don't look like you're gonna be starvin' anytime soon," Ilene scolded. "Just make sure you woke up enough to drive."

She watched her husband of the past forty-five years trudge down the driveway. "And you wear them eye glasses too, you old fool."

Bump dramatically placed the scratched spectacles on, adjusting the bent frames to a point that they sat evenly across his nose, and then smiled back at Ilene. She watched him from the front door step as he drove away in the faded blue pickup, turning just as the oven timer announced that the first of Ilene's two apple crumb cakes was ready to be introduced to the world.

CHAPTER EIGHT

The other car that approached Steadman Elementary that night moved quietly down Dekalb Street. It slowed as it passed the Stacey Police Department cruiser parked at the corner of Summit Boulevard. The lanky officer inside the Handy Dan's Convenience Store didn't bother to glance over. He was engaged in an animated conversation with Emily Debnam, the very unattached cashier. Emily was twice married and twice divorced, and rumors said she had once been a dancer somewhere up north. She was pushing forty now, but the lighting and the time of night made for interesting conversation.

Sgt. Arlo Pendleton had made Handy Dan's his favorite snack shop, but only on weekends. Emily worked weeknights over at the skating rink in Brayleyville, and Handy Dan Peabody was not nearly as appealing as Emily. When Sgt. Pendleton settled back into his cruiser, the other vehicle was almost two blocks away. There was no other traffic on the road.

By that time the car had pulled onto the grounds of Steadman Elementary, where it circled the school twice before settling into a darkened corner of the bus parking lot. It was not visible there from the street.

Eight minutes later, Bump Patterson turned his pickup into the gravel parking lot behind Steadman's Gymnasium. He was two months shy of his sixty-eighth birthday. As he did every summer, he spent only three days a week at Steadman, mopping the halls, checking on the air conditioning system, watering plants in the atrium—the general maintenance activities required to keep the school ready for the late August return of students. On this particular Friday, he'd spent half his day fixing the rusty piping in the girls' shower with washers he bought in town, and the other half mopping up the mess he had made. He would be damned before he would pay fifty dollars an hour for a plumber— even if it was school money.

"Boy's got to be the stupidest educated man I ever seen," Bump muttered to no one in particular as he entered the dark, musty gym. "Course, Mary Ruth's to blame. No doubt about that. I told her when he was a boy, you cannot expect a boy who you dress up in a shirt you button to the top and make carry a fountain pen from first grade on to be normal…" He didn't bother to feel his way down the wall to find a light switch. He knew this place in his sleep. The dark suited him just fine.

The sound of his worn loafers echoed across the vacant gymnasium floor as he ambled over to the north end, to the storage room that was situated to the left side of the bleachers. He kept that door unlocked during the summer months. He pushed it open slowly and peered into the blackness. The streetlights that stood opposite the gym could not reach into this far corner.

Bump paused for a few seconds and tried to make out the dim impressions of boxes and sporting equipment, then finally realized both cartons with the Hibachis sat only several feet away to his right. He stacked one on top of the other, grunted as he hoisted them up, and backed out the way he'd come in. Giving the door a nudge with his foot, he set out toward the rear of the gym.

It was a dull thump that first caught his attention, coming from the direction of the storage room he'd just left. Bump thought perhaps one of the boxes had shifted and fallen because of the rooting around. He waited, and he had just about convinced himself when he saw the brief flash of light through the far door of the gym, the one that led out to the main building. Bump froze, and then quietly laid down the boxes.

Someone was in the school building.

CHAPTER NINE

The north door of Steadman Gymnasium opened onto a long corridor that led directly to the administrative offices and the school nurse's center. If one entered that hallway from the gym, they would be able to see out the long window to the left into the teachers' parking lot and the back of the kitchen loading docks. To the right was the Wall of Fame, the pictorial history of many of Steadman's athletic exploits of the past, the framed photos of the '59 state basketball champions and the '64 baseball team. There was even a signed photograph of Jake Daniels, who had gone on to play pro football for the Vikings before his knee finally gave out on him.

Bump padded softly past each memory toward the administration offices. Cupping his keys to avoid jangling them, he slipped one into the lock and quietly pushed the door open.

He squinted to adjust his eyes as he entered the eerie, pale offices, which were bathed in the secondary glow from the streetlights outside. Bump remembered for the first time that he didn't much care for being here alone at this hour of night. He fingered the cell phone on his work belt. Maybe slipping out and calling the police might make more sense.

But instead, he was standing there in the doorway—hoping his eyes would finally acclimate to the darkness and considering the wisdom of investigating further—when he heard a faint noise, then a second "tha-dump" somewhere up ahead and to the right. Now he was certain. He was not alone.

There were two doors that led to the right from the main office. The far door accessed the main body of the school. The closer one was to a large storage room, once used as office space back in the school's early days, but for the past many years, it had become mostly just a junk hole. Bump still used it to occasionally stash a few mop pails and a squeegee for the schools two tennis courts, along with the two broken softball bats that he'd never gotten around to tacking.

He waited, heard nothing, and considered the value of arming himself. The bats were starting to seem like a real good idea.

Somewhere out front he heard a truck pass by, revving its big engine as it barreled up DeKalb. His mind flashed back to the Pabst that sat on the table beside his Lazy Boy. By now LaMotta and Robinson should have given way to the 11:00 news.

But the more he thought about it, the more convinced he became that the noise had come from the main lobby, and he was starting to have a good notion on the source. Twice in the last six months, teenagers had broken into Steadman, once rolling the auditorium with toilet paper and the last time smearing lard from the school's kitchen over the bronze bust of Captain Steadman in the atrium. P. Titus Steadman, the school's namesake, was a revolutionary war hero. Sheriff Yates had arrested one of the Lawson boys for the lard caper. Bump seemed to recall it was Lloyd, the most stupid of a generally stupid family. The Lloyd Lawson Lard case had attracted attention throughout the entire county.

Bump did not consider it nearly as funny as a number of citizens did. He believed degrading a local icon was nothing short of felonious assault, and if Sheriff Roy Yates hadn't been such an old friend, he would have written a letter to the newspaper.

He was chomping at the bit to put a little fear into the latest troublemakers. Bump figured an angry, old black man charging out of the darkness with a Louisville Slugger in hand ought to do the trick. He glided toward the storage room. "Here I come, Lloyd," he murmured.

Easing the unlocked door open, Bump edged into the darkness, and then cursed as he walked into a metal file folder. The bats were somewhere ahead, off to the right and propped against a barrel that contained Styrofoam canes for the school holiday cantata. School policy mandated that they drop the "Christmas" part years ago, but the decorations and music remained the same. He made his way in that direction, gingerly feeling his way around the years of clutter. He wasn't sure which he wanted more—to scare the hell out of the teenagers in the atrium or to tell his nephew William where to put the Hibachi.

The sound was so low that he wasn't sure he'd heard anything at all. He was now only feet from the barrel and the Louisville sluggers when the air suddenly changed. Even in the pitch blackness, Bump Patterson knew he was no longer alone in the room.

He felt the hairs on the back of his neck suddenly come to attention and the sense of dread starting in the back of his throat. It bubbled into fear just as a sudden, intense flash of light separated him from the conscious world and flung him into another place, far away from Steadman. A deep, black place.

He could feel waves of fog pour over him, muffling his mind and wrapping around him in a great sweeping current. Somewhere in the midst of the fog, there were voices. He imagined himself lying atop his bed, with thick heavy quilts piled over him. The weight was crushing him, taking away his breath. There was something burning on the stove outside his room. He could smell it and as the stench grew, so did the sound of it. It was raging now, and the voices were retreating. He called out to them, but the fog sucked his voice away and he began to choke. The quilts pushed him down further and began to swallow him. The burning thing outside his room was moving closer. He could smell its stench as it crept into the room.

In that last moment of life, Bump somehow sensed that the quilts and the smell were one.

Then the fire engulfed him.

CHAPTER TEN

Jeb Mason's plane was scheduled to depart Chicago's O'Hare Airport at 7:25 p.m. U.S. Airway's flight 189 to Charlotte was booked, but his chance of getting a seat off the standby list was good. As he flung his cabbie several twenty-dollar bills, he simultaneously tossed his black Andiamo carry bag over onto the Departures curb, followed by his faded brown leather duffle. Avoiding the curbside agent's offer to check the bags, Jeb instead hustled through the double doors with each in tow, on a steady trot for the ticket counter.

Moments later, his mind raced through the flurry of the afternoon's events as he sprinted to his gate. The call to Larry O'Grady from the cab had been hurried.

"Tolliver is plenty pissed. But you knew that would happen."

"Tolliver would miss his own mother's funeral if it interfered with the company's numbers," Jeb answered.

"That's assuming he ever had a mother."

"So give it to me straight. What have we got?"

"We got agreement on the new strategy, so at least we have the start. But it's provisional, and we'll still need to run it by the board sometime next week." Larry said. "You *will* be back by then, right?"

"No later than Monday night...guaranteed."

"You want to tell me who this guy was that you blow off Tolliver and fly down to Hooterville for?"

Jeb paused.

"Jeb, you there?"

"Larry, he was a good friend a very long time ago."

"Thought you told me once you lost all your ties to North Carolina."

"You ever remember the best time of when you were a kid?"

"What?"

"Best time. Best *memory* growing up."

"Well, it's not like I sit around thinking about it," Larry said.

"Neither do I. But can you remember it?"

"No…I mean, yeah, maybe. There are lots of memories…"

"Well, I can. I remember the place, the people, the events…as clearly as if it were yesterday."

"This guy was a part of that?"

"Some ways, the biggest part."

"Hey, we all get nostalgic from time to time."

"No, not that."

"So, a good friend that you want to say good-bye to. Nothing wrong with that."

There was no answer from Jeb's end.

"FYI, as far as Tolliver knows, this is a family member who kicked the bucket. That seemed a better explanation for the old bastard."

"Appreciate the air cover. Give you a call tomorrow. You got everyone rolling on this over the weekend?" Jeb asked.

"Covered. Say goodbye to your buddy. Just remember you got some people here *depending* on you for next week, pal."

"Depending on me," Jeb repeated the words. "Talk to you, Larry."

• • •

Larry O'Grady clicked his cell phone shut and turned to Margie. They sat in their Volvo sedan in the parking lot of the Harada Japanese Steak House, waiting for William and Lynn Grant, the couple that would be joining them that evening. Bill Grant was Larry's financial planner and part-time poker buddy. Margie was focused on the vanity mirror, adjusting her make up a second time.

"Known him for twenty years and can't figure this one out," Larry said.

"It's an old friend. What do you expect him to do?" Margie asked as she formed her mouth into an "o", and circled her lips with a muted red shade of lipstick.

"Margie, he hasn't even spoken to anyone from that little town since he was a teenager. Why in the hell is he going back to bury somebody?"

"Maybe Mr. Mason actually took the time to have a life back then, Larry. Is this straight?" She pointed to her lips.

"Wished he'd worked on a better time to reconnect."

"I thought I heard you say you got your deal worked out or whatever."

"I said we got Tolliver to agree on a new business model. But the board is going to have to see the rationale, the numbers, the works."

"I don't follow you."

"Let's put it this way. Brendan Tolliver is a master of distancing himself from new strategies until they're proven successful. No way he will present this to the board. That will be Jeb...or not at all."

"So, Jeb can do that when he's back...my lips, good?"

"Better be. Tolliver will go ballistic if he isn't back Monday, I can tell you that," Larry said. "Your lips look great."

Margie frowned. He hadn't even looked at her lips.

They watched the black Benz sedan enter the parking lot and pull slowly to the valet attendant, a freckle-faced boy who looked like a middle school basketball player. He hustled to open the passenger door and greet the Grants. William Grant last parked his own car in the regular lot at about the same time that Jeb left North Carolina, by Larry's reckoning. Larry, along with another hundred or so "select" clients, paid the valet charges. The O'Gradys left their conversation and Jeb behind, and their thoughts turned to Peking Duck and ginger sauce.

CHAPTER ELEVEN

Jeb plopped into his window seat at 7:23 p.m. Twenty-nine minutes later he watched the lights of Chicago fade away as U.S. Airways carried him home.

"I hate take offs, don't you?" The woman was fiftyish with the look of a librarian, complete with the thick spectacles and pulled back gray-sprinkled hair. She sat in the aisle seat, and Jeb was grateful for the empty one that separated them.

Jeb grinned back at her, but it was the non-committal smile that acknowledged but did not engage. He wanted the quiet that the hour and a half flight would offer. Air travel demanded diplomacy, but not too much of it.

"Are you from Chicago?" the librarian asked.

"Yes...sort of." He immediately regretted the response.

"And what brings you to Charlotte?" she asked. Jeb's sensors began to tingle. This might be a talker, the businessman's worst fear.

"Funeral, actually. Old friend." He wondered if he could gracefully escape this line of dialogue.

"Oh. I'm sorry. Those are never easy." She sounded sincere.

"No. Never easy."

"But it's nice that you are coming back, though. It's so easy not to, after all."

Jeb smiled. The librarian had a kind face.

• • •

Jeb ordered a third beer for each of them by the time the pilot announced they were passing over Knoxville. Jill—who turned out not to be a librarian, after all, but a nurse practitioner on the way home from an association meeting—was hesitant but agreed.

"My husband will kill me if I turn up at baggage claim drunk."

"Blame it on your fellow passengers," Jeb said.

"So tell me about Andy Gardner."

"Best buddy I ever had. When my dad relocated to Stacey I met Andy on my very first day. Ballpark. Went there to maybe find a pickup game. Didn't know anyone in the town. Figured baseball would be the best place to meet somebody. Showed up that day...middle of the summer...hoping."

"I grew up in North Carolina and can't say I've ever even heard of Stacey. So, it's small, right?"

"No, it's not quite up to the status of small. But it could be. I mean, if oil is discovered or something."

Jill laughed. "So you're the new kid in a village of a few thousand people. Must have been a little tough."

"Think we used to have a cantaloupe festival that sometimes swelled the population to close to ten thousand and yes, it was plenty tough."

"And Andy just turned up?"

"Not even ten years old yet. Skinny as a broom stick with sandy blonde hair and the most worn out New York Yankees hat I had ever seen. Had a big plug of chewing tobacco stuck in his jaw and a glove on the front of his bike. Just rode up to the field and sat there."

"And you?"

"I was standing on the mound and rehearsing my pitching delivery. Didn't even remember to bring a baseball. He sat there. Watched for a while. Then he rode onto the field. First thing he ever said to me was to ask if I was a pitcher of just pretending to be."

"And that's how you started to become friends?"

"Yeah...ended up playing baseball together for the rest of that summer. Kind of went from there."

"So, kindred spirits, so to speak?"

"Not like you might think. I was the calculating one. Andy was the impulsive one. I kind of found school a little boring."

"And this Andy?"

Jeb laughed. "He hardly ever found school at all." He paused. "You know, when I think back, the difference in the two of us was I aimed to be somebody someday. And Andy...Andy had decided he already was."

Jill smiled. "And...the boy who died?"

Jeb paused. Describing Zeke was more difficult.

"Zeke was younger than Andy and me. Two years. He was the little brother neither of us had...the third amigo who tagged along. Always wanting to be in the middle of everything, I guess."

"And you two allowed him to be that...the little brother, I mean?"

"Not sure if we adopted him or vice versa. Zeke was...I don't know...infectious."

"Infectious?"

"Did you ever meet someone that you just automatically liked? Someone who had no pretense. Who just loved living and made you love it, too?"

"Was Zeke that kind of person?"

"Once when we were playing a basketball game...I was in maybe fifth grade by then. Game against another elementary school. We had a fight break out in the stands. Can't remember what it was about, but you had kids, parents, teachers...all yelling and pushing. You know, hotheads and cursing. Kind of stuff you didn't see that much back then but all the time now. Some of the coaches finally got everything under control, but they were going to just stop the game. Send everybody home."

"Oh my..."

"Zeke was in maybe third grade. I'll never forget. He walked right in the middle of the stands. All these grown-ups still grumbling back and forth. He calls for everyone's attention. Whole gym grows quiet to watch this little kid who's standing there with his hands in the air."

Jill smiled and leaned closer.

Jeb continued, "He says, 'Ladies and gentlemen, I've made arrangements with the concession stand. The drinks and popcorn are on me for the conclusion of the evening. Now, let's return to the game please.' Then he walked right down the bleachers, pointed his hand in the direction of the gym door. Sort of like those old John Wayne movies where he signals the cavalry to follow him, you know? Damndest thing I ever saw."

"And what happened?"

"First, no one said anything at all. I mean this little squirt who just stands there like the president, then walks solemnly out the door. His arm raised and his head down. Then one of the parents giggled. Then another one. Then another one. Then it spreads to the players. The whole gym erupts. It was crazy."

Jill laughed and Jeb joined her. He watched a tired businessman, his paunch extending well beyond his seat belt, glance over from an adjoining row. The third beer had made them louder than he thought.

"And so you finished the game?"

"We finished the game. For the life of me, can't remember anything about it or who won. But we finished the game."

"He sounds like a very special person."

Jeb studied her face as she spoke. It felt strange to discuss a chapter of his life that was so distant and yet felt so much a part of who he was. No one had ever attempted to in someway frame the three-and-a-half years he'd spent in Stacey, North Carolina. Now a stranger, someone he would most likely never see again, was doing it for him.

"Did you…see him often over the years?" Jill asked.

"No, I'm sorry to say I didn't."

She looked down at her beer and grew quiet.

He answered the same question that was on both their minds. "And I can't really say why."

They gradually moved to other topics involving life and occupation, but Jeb stayed behind, lingering at a tiny basketball gym at Steadman Elementary when he was twelve years old. He studied the balding pate of the man in the seat in front of him, and even as he nodded at his seatmate's comments, he was back to a time he had almost forgotten. And two friends who he left there.

•   •   •

The attendant's request that passengers "return their seats and tray tables to the upright and locked position and dispose of any remaining cups or cans" wrenched Jeb back to the 737 that was now on final approach to Douglas International. He quickly downed the rest of his beer and turned his attention to the skyline of Charlotte, awash in the lights of skyscrapers that rose to the clouds—far different from the city that he remembered. In its place a teeming metropolis now stood.

In all the years of rising up the corporate ladder, necessity had never demanded a visit back to North Carolina. Granted, one or two medical conventions along the way presented an opportunity. And as vice president for first Maylor and now Tolliver, circumstances had sometimes conspired to demand his attention there, but never a physical visit; always a phone call, a memo, or a subordinate handled the situation.

The terminal rising up to meet them bore little similarity to the one that bade him farewell so many years before. That small brick outpost now served as cargo storage on a far corner of the five massive runways that handled the 400 plus daily flights through Charlotte Douglas International. Like the city it served, the past had been supplanted with state-of-the-art technology, glistening steel, and pulsating lights—the ebb and flow of people and commerce.

Jeb's mind drifted back to the day he said goodbye.

•   •   •

The other two families had come to the airport with the Masons on that chilly February morning in 1982. Zeke's father was working so his mother and Zeke had caught a ride with Andy and his parents. It was a Thursday and normally skipping school would have been a special occasion for the boys. But Jeb was leaving for good. And they all knew that.

Andy wore the same sheepish grin he always wore when adults were around and matters took on a more serious tone. So they talked about airplanes and the weather and what this year's baseball team might look like. And the parents contented themselves with the awkward conversation that always accompanies a protracted good bye. Until the portly attendant at the Piedmont Airlines counter announced boarding was about to begin.

Then Zeke began to tear up. But he hid it by walking to the large windows and pretending to study the cargo plane that had taxied to the gate across the way from Jeb's gate. And he would only talk if someone asked him a question directly. So no one did.

They promised to stay in touch. Both of the older boys were only a few years from getting a driver's license. There would be road trips. But Jeb was moving to another state and each of the boys knew, even then, that it was an empty pledge. They said it anyway because that's what you say when there's nothing else that can be said.

The parents hugged each other before they boarded and Mrs. Gardner gave Jeb a kiss. And then there was nothing left to do but to get on the plane and so Jeb shook Andy's hand and punched him once on the arm for good measure. Zeke stuck his hand out to shake but he was crying then and everyone could see it. But he kept his hand out anyway. So Jeb grasped it and then he hugged him.

And the last thing he said to Zeke Andrews was," It will be OK, Zeke."

• • •

The plane bumped lightly on the runway as it set down. Jeb studied his face in the reflection of the window, the bright lights of the city beyond.

"Took me thirty years, didn't it, Zeke?" Jeb whispered. "Thirty years."

The Hertz rental car, a shiny, new, maroon Camry was waiting at the "Preferred" counter, and after a few moments of explanation from a gentile counter agent, Jeb was headed east, skirting the corner of the Queen City. He marveled at how much change had taken place. The skyscrapers of Bank of America and Wells Fargo rose up as pronouncement of Charlotte's emergence as one of the major banking centers in the country. The older buildings he could dimly recall were now dwarfed in comparison.

Jeb headed south as the gray-haired Hertz agent had directed, soon coming to the exit for the belt line that looped underneath Charlotte to the south. His watch read 9:20. He realized he was still on Central Standard Time and corrected it, keeping one eye on the four busy lanes of traffic in front of him. Twenty minutes after ten on Friday evening, July fifteenth.

He settled in for the sixty-minute drive that lay ahead by switching on the radio. He scanned until the sounds of a golden oldies station blurted into focus. Ricky Nelson's musical salutation to Mary Lou demanded his help on harmony.

At 11:15, Jeb's Camry wheeled into the Dogwood Inn on Highway 73, just two miles west of Stacey. His feelings of nostalgia had given way to fatigue from the long day, and he decided to delay a drive downtown until morning.

As he pulled his bags from the car and lugged them along the long porch that led to room 217, he paused to gaze to the east, in the direction of the town. The lights of Stacey lit up the nighttime sky, and he wondered if, like its big sister to the west, Stacey had also undergone a metamorphosis. He assumed it must have. It would have otherwise taken a lot of street lamps to create a glow that impressive.

CHAPTER TWELVE

Just as Jeb was dropping his Andiamo on the pale green floral bedspread in room 217, Bill Price was making his nightly pilgrimage eight miles away. As he did every evening, Bill retired promptly at 9:30 p.m., leaving his wife of thirty-four years, Edna, curled on the living room couch, engrossed in her latest dime-store novel. Bill was fifty-seven years old, and for thirty-five years, he'd been a mechanic at Covington Chrysler Plymouth, the only local dealership in two counties. Tomorrow was Saturday but the shop stayed open from 8:00 a.m. to midnight, as a way to promote Covington's "putting the customer first philosophy." At least that was how J.T. Covington Jr. explained it when this enlightened quality initiative had commenced two-and-a-half years before. Bill considered it pretty much a pile of crock, but since J.T. Covington could find a thousand different ways to stick it to his patrons on price, also a necessity.

So Friday night was just like every other weeknight for Bill. Turn in early; get up early to open the garage at 7:00 a.m. And like every other evening, it seemed, somewhere between 11:00 p.m. and midnight, Bill's prostate gland provided a wake-up call. His doctor, when this physiological timepiece began its nightly routine some ten years before, had explained that this was simply part of the normal aging process. "Cut back on your fluid intake before bed, urinate just as you're retiring, etc., etc., etc.," he had advised. Bill listened quietly, nodded acknowledgement, and promptly forgot everything the doctor said. He could still lift damn near anything in the garage that the young kids could and outworked any two of them. The doctor could take his advice and his bill and find a similar place for both.

And on this night, Bill's sleepy-eyed stumble toward the bathroom was not unlike any other. Edna was still somewhere in the front of the house, poring over that romance novel with the long-haired Italian model on the cover. Bill suspected the man was a long time steroid user.

Lifting the commode lid, a generous concession to domestic bliss that Bill had first made after only three years of marriage, he proceeded with the nightly game plan, his eyes blearily focused on the rose garden watercolor painting on the wall over the toilet. For some reason, this night, the roses were dancing and vibrating in time with Bill's own cadence, from light to dark, deep pink to crimson to black. Bill's mind pondered this phenomenon for some seconds, but as his bladder emptied, his visual acuity increased. The panorama before him wasn't the picture but instead light and color reflecting off it.

Bill had finished his work there and was restoring order to his jockey shorts when he turned to gaze out the window behind him, the one that looked out across his backyard and the empty lot that separated his property from the school.

In the living room, Edna had just gotten to the juiciest part of her book, where the star-crossed central characters were to seal their love, when Bill's screams jolted her back to Stacey.

CHAPTER THIRTEEN

If anyone could be blamed or praised for the scanner that sprang to life in Thad Bingham's trailer at 11:18 p.m. that evening, it was Richmond County Commissioner Benjamin Healey. It was, after all, his brainchild—or so he claimed in his re-election campaigns since its introduction.

Eight years before, county fathers, concerned about the delays in fire and medical response time, had contracted an emergency technology company out of New Orleans. AlertTech, Inc. developed integrated communication systems where police, fire, and medical emergency calls could be funneled through one central dispatch to appropriate government or volunteer agencies. This derivative of the more elaborate 911 systems employed in major municipalities pulled small towns like Stacey into the twenty-first century

Benjamin Healey first contacted AlertTech three days after a car blaze on Highway 73 had quickly spread to a brushfire that claimed over thirty acres on one very hot and dry September afternoon. Though local residents were frustrated by the delay in local agency response, most also knew that twelve of the thirty acres were owned by one Benjamin Healey. Insurance settlements notwithstanding, Healey's plans for a trailer park were temporarily stalled. The roadside fire of 2003 ushered in a new era of citizen service and care.

The system was fairly simple. A citizen's call to 911 was immediately patched through to a dispatcher in the police department's offices on Dixon Boulevard. That dispatcher could immediately gather, code, and forward the distress call to the appropriate department in a matter of thirty to sixty seconds.

The phone call from Bill Price that night had set the entire process in motion only two minutes before the scanner, which sat on the coffee table beside Thad's new sofa, had screeched its announcement. The sofa was a housewarming gift from his parents for Thad and his wife of three months, Becky. That's where Thad lay curled with the remote, waiting for Becky, who was showering in preparation for the night's festivities.

Commissioner Healey's vision and the scanner changed those plans dramatically.

Thad frantically raced to outfit himself even as he stumbled out the front door in the general direction of his '97 Dodge Ram pickup. There was usually a mad rush for the volunteers to be the first on scene, and Thad did not intend to allow anyone else to stake that claim this evening. The dispatcher had said Dekalb and Fullner Avenue. That meant downtown and most probably a house fire somewhere in the vicinity of Steadman Elementary. This would be the biggest job Thad had been on in his four months of fire-fighting experience.

He was pulling up his suspenders as he stumbled out the front door, his heavy fireman's boots in hand. His coat and helmet were behind the seat of the pickup, and the heavy white socks he wore offered little protection against the graveled driveway, resulting in an odd dance of "oohhs" and "aahhs" as he neared his vehicle. That, combined with his partial attire and the boots he carried, might have made for quite a comical sight if anyone had been driving by at the time.

But the only audience this night was Becky, who stood dripping wet and draped in a bright yellow towel at the trailer door, as her husband and his Ram went squealing out of the driveway.

She did not look amused.

CHAPTER FOURTEEN

Thad lived only five miles from DeKalb and Fullner. He swung his truck onto DeKalb five blocks south of the intersection and gazed through the oaks that lined the street, craning to see the source of the orange brilliance that seemed to fill the sky. He knew exactly where DeKalb and Fullner met, as did every resident in Stacey. It was where Steadman Elementary stood, where Thad and almost every other adult in town had gone to school.

He prayed the mounting luminescence was the vacant lot behind, another brush fire brought on by the dry weather conditions of the last several weeks. By the time he was within two blocks, he knew his prayers wouldn't be answered.

He could feel the heat of the inferno even as he ran from his truck. Silhouetted in its glare were a dozen figures, dwarfed by the size of the blaze. They were standing at least a hundred feet in front, gathering like sheep bewildered by the arrival of a wolf. Thad stumbled to pull on his boots as he too gaped at the spectacle. Donning his coat and helmet, he ran to join the onlookers. A youngster, perhaps ten or eleven, was the first to notice him. Looking at Thad, then the blaze, then back to Thad, he asked, "Where's your fire truck?"

Thad wondered the same thing.

The designated driver was Farley Tuttle, who lived only a half of a block from the Stacey Volunteer Fire Department, west of the courthouse on Montgomery Street. Farley had been the driver for at least twenty years. Some said it was because he was the only fellow in the county who had, on three separate occasions, outrun the highway patrolmen who'd tried to stop him for license checks or unsafe vehicular movements, thus earning the nickname of "Farley Davidson." Others suspected it was because his uncle, Barney Tuttle, was a member of the city council. The third theory, and the one Thad assumed was accurate, was that Farley lived next door to the fire house.

As Thad, in full gear, considered the boy's question, other volunteers and townspeople were also arriving, most in pajamas and bathrobes. They stood there, in the brilliant light of the fire—the first witnesses to the tragedy as it unfolded.

Four fellow volunteers had joined them by the time the city's ten-ton Ford fire truck's siren could be heard, growing in volume as it careened down DeKalb. The sound of it seemed to break the trance of all concerned, and Thad and his colleagues raced to the hydrant at the northwest corner of the school's lot, yelling and motioning to Farley to pull the big rig alongside. Other firemen were also arriving, the tires of their vehicles screeching to hurried stops, running to their assigned positions.

At 11:32 p.m. that night, the first plumes of water began to bombard the monster that was devouring their beloved school.

CHAPTER FIFTEEN

Fire Chief Brett Hampton shuffled through the soggy debris, shaking his head at the carnage. He was a tall man, with a long, loping stride. The glasses he wore were smeared with ash. He glanced down at the sooty clump of his wrist watch and wiped away enough of the grime to read the time, 5:10 a.m. Only an hour from sunrise. He looked out at the heaping mass still smoking in front of him and watched the wrap-up activities of the two brigades that had finally wrestled the fire to the ground.

Some forty firemen sifted carefully through the remains of Steadman Elementary, drenching hot spots and tamping out the last of the embers. A few emergency personnel lingered on the perimeter, still studying the carnage. A heavy-set police officer, his radio blaring in a staccato of voices, was checking the crime tape that circled a large part of the parking lot beyond. The glare of blue and red lights that engulfed the area went on for another city block, casting a bizarre focus on the rotted core of Steadman.

The fire had completely destroyed almost half the school. The gymnasium and administrative offices, along with the classrooms that adjoined them, were reduced to a pile of smoldering rubble. Only the frantic efforts of the first volunteers had managed to create the fire wall between that area and the remaining classrooms. But even there, the smoke damage was extensive.

The fire trucks now stood on opposite sides of the main building, and the last of their powerful hoses rained down on the blackened hulk. Hampton's uniform suddenly felt very heavy. He looked for a dry area to sit down.

He looked up to see Randy Bivins, the Mt. Pleasant Fire Chief approaching. Bivins's face was black, and the goggles he had worn were now draped around his shoulders, creating the look of a raccoon in a photo negative. "You know we're going to have to get the state guys in on this, don't you? No damn way this thing was electric."

Hampton didn't answer. He bent down to sift through soggy ashes of what was once an office floor. The smell was even thicker there.

"Guessing not a gas leak either," Bivins continued. "Bellamy, son, if you're going to stand there with your finger up your butt, go ahead and spell Sam over there. He looks like he could use the rest," he barked in the general direction of one of his firemen.

Bivins's crew had been called in early, when it became obvious the Stacey department could not contain the blaze. Between volunteers and "regular army," the two crews had worked for over four hours to rein in the devastation. Even then, there had been serious consideration of calling in a third team.

"Hamp!" someone yelled from behind what was once the far wall of the gym. "Hamp!" The voice grew more urgent. "We got a car back here!"

The fireman stood atop the rubble some seventy feet away. That wall had already been ablaze when the first firemen had arrived and had collapsed before the second truck had come on the scene. Hampton recognized the man that was pulling bricks and debris away from the top of the pile. Willie Botts was the youngest of the volunteers and, by the chief's reckoning, the one most likely to be killed in the line of duty.

"Damn it, Willie. Crawl down off of there! You got hot spots all over this place!" Hampton yelled.

"It's a Toyota pickup, Hamp!" Willie stood up. "It's a damn truck down here."

"Get the hell off it, you dumb son of a bitch!" Hampton roared. "It's got a fuel tank that's probably about ready to blow!"

Botts was gazing intently into the crater he had carved in the cinder blocks and gunk.

"Oh shit." He slowly looked up toward Hampton and Bivins. "I think I know whose truck this is."

"*Body*!" The scream curled through from the other side of the building, and the air changed as each of the fireman suddenly stopped to look up. "We got a body here!"

Those that had a line of sight back to the main building could see Thad Bingham standing there. He was waving his hands and gesturing toward a dark mass that was curled into a darkened corner of what was once a wall.

He continued to scream until he turned away and bent over, and then began to wretch.

CHAPTER SIXTEEN

The Dogwood Inn's bed was hard. The air conditioner rasped like a blender on its last legs, and it seemed that every siren in this end of the county had decided to drive by during the night. Yet it was maybe the best sleep Jeb had enjoyed in years. The cell phone alarm sounded at 6:30 a.m., and he rolled easily in the general direction of the shower.

Thirty minutes later he tossed on his favorite light blue polo shirt and khaki shorts and began to give serious thought to breakfast. He glanced at the bathroom mirror and considered the necessity of shaving. Informality still reigned in Stacey, he guessed. The shave could wait.

He worked hard to keep himself in shape. At slightly over six feet, he maintained the same solid 180 pounds he had carried since college, regularly honed by workouts at the local health club and daily jogs on the shores of Lake Michigan, which was some four blocks from his condominium. Though his dark brown hair had begun to thin a bit on top, he could easily pass for his mid-thirties. He told himself that, at least, whenever he questioned why he had never remarried.

He checked his cell phone. No messages. That was good. The office knew he had personal matters to attend to, but that seldom made a difference. Larry O'Grady was running interference, and Tolliver had most likely already returned to his cave.

But no message from Andy Gardner, either. Jeb had left three the day before and had attempted a fourth before a recording came back that the Gardner mailbox was full.

No one here even knew he was in town.

He punched in Andy's number as he walked out the motel door toward the lobby and what he thought might be a restaurant of sorts that was adjoined. He thought he could detect the hint of bacon in the air. A cleaning lady, bent over her cart, was stocking a corner with what appeared to be mini-bottles of shampoo. He considered asking for some but thought the better of it. Maybe he had just overlooked it before. She glanced up as he passed and smiled. She was missing a tooth in front. Jeb held his phone to his ear, waiting through the rings.

"Yeah…hello?" the voice sounded slightly dazed.

"Andy Gardner?"

"You got me…what's up? What time is it?"

"You country boys must not get up too early, I guess."

"Not if we don't have to. Who is this?" Andy responded.

"You remember a fellow by the name of Jeb Mason?"

"Jeb…*Jeb*, is this really you?" Andy's voice suddenly came alive.

"Damn right it's me."

"Son of a gun. You got my message after all. Man, it is good to hear from you. I'm sure glad you called…where are you? Are you going to maybe come in for the funeral?"

"Already here."

"What? Where are you?"

"The beautiful Dogwood Inn on 73. Know where it's at?"

"There's only three hotels, Jeb, and one of 'em's in foreclosure… stay right there. I'll be out front in twenty minutes." The phone went dead.

Jeb looked at it and laughed. He suddenly felt twelve years old again, and could see himself sitting on his old red Schwinn parked at the corner of Grimley Field. Waiting for Andy to show up on his equally beat-up old blue Sears model, a dusty sack of baseball bats flung over his shoulder. He carried the same bag to every game, while managing to use only one bat for all the games he ever played. The smell of sandlot baseball and snow cones and sweaty cleats seemed to suddenly replace the aroma of bacon. He looked out over the mostly empty parking lot and the soybean fields beyond.

Stacey sat out there; the little town that had traveled with him over the years. The stately courthouse with the towering maple trees. The simple streets and sidewalks where people stopped to talk about their flower garden or the movie that was coming to the Roger's Theatre over the weekend. The old guy with the red-flecked beard who drove the ice cream truck and pretended not to hear the kids who yelled for him to stop until he'd traveled an extra half of a block, then laughed as if it was a practical joke that would never grow old.

The powder-blue BMW that swung into the parking lot minutes later screeched to a stop in front of the lobby. The man that clambered out was tall and slender, with a thick mop of sandy brown hair and an easy smile. It grew larger as he spotted Jeb.

• • •

The drive into Stacey was Andy's idea. It was a beautiful morning, the Bimmer had a sunroof, and Andy said you only ate at the Dogwood Inn if you were out of town and didn't know any better.

He was just shifting the coupe into fourth gear as they began to pass the large antebellum homes on the outskirts of town. Huge oak trees created a canopy over the two-lane highway, and Jeb looked out onto well groomed lawns and large Georgian houses that spoke of a bygone era. He drank in the aroma of deep orange day lilies and glistening dahlias, splashed against the backdrop of golden zinnias. Early morning and the little town was already alive with people walking along the sidewalks and working in their yards. A small farmer's stand stood just outside of the city limit sign, and the old fellow sitting out front was busy stacking jars of honey against one corner. His pickup was parked under the shade of a large magnolia tree, and a little boy sat on the tail gate, with a collie asleep at his feet. The boy waved as they passed.

"Has it changed much?" Jeb asked, soaking in the sights and sounds of his past.

"Well," Andy said, "we do have a Dogwood Inn now."

"That's not new. That place has been there forever."

"When you were here it was the Gladstone Motor Inn, and the Bledsoes ran it."

"Should I know that name?"

"Don't you remember Bobby Bledsoe? He was that kid that broke his foot in the Festival Day Sack Races when we were in sixth grade?"

Jeb looked at him.

"Bobby Bledsoe. Wore that big cast on the school bus the whole year. Got out of class early so he could board before everybody else. Got to skip the last math exam Old Lady Sullivan had…" Andy's voice trailed away.

"How in the hell do you remember that kind of stuff, Andy?"

"Well, there have been some changes, I guess." Andy ignored him and went on. "We finally got a mall going in, five miles on the other side of town. More people moving in and commuting to Charlotte. Good for the locals for the most part. Got the one car dealership we always had."

They turned onto Alexander Street and into the heart of downtown. The tiny storefronts looked exactly the same, it seemed to Jeb. The first empty parking space was right in front of the Stacey Café and only a block from the courthouse.

They walked into the smell of pancakes and sausage mixed with the clatter of dishes and the steady drone of conversation of the regulars. A lady with poorly-tinted blonde hair and a light pink dress at least one size too small seated them in a red vinyl covered booth in the corner. She smiled extra hard for Jeb as she handed him a menu that seemed a little sticky. Her name tag said "Gladys." She rubbed her hands on a coffee stained apron and pulled out her order pad.

"All right, Shoog…what are we going to have?" she asked. Her voice was deep, and Jeb could see the outline of the cigarette pack in the pocket of the apron.

Shoog wasn't quite sure since he'd just been handed the menu. Andy took the lead and ordered the Early Bird Special. The extra ten seconds gave Jeb the chance to choose the Western omelet and a cup of coffee.

Gladys slapped down two sets of silverware, and then disappeared with a closing wink for Shoog and Andy.

"Shoog?" Jeb asked.

"Short for sugar. She likes you." Andy's eyes twinkled as he spoke. "Maybe we'll get better service." Then he glanced around the restaurant before saying, "Damn, they must be giving it away today. Never seen it this busy."

The two old friends began to reacquaint themselves just as the first cup of coffee was poured.

Jeb learned that Andy had spent most of his life right there in Stacey. After high school, he'd gone the junior college route, attending Richmond County Community, and then transferring to Elon College over in Burlington. A degree in business had been the ticket to ultimately enter into commercial real estate in Atlanta. For eight years he developed shopping malls in Fulton and Gwinnet counties, making money and developing the beginning of an ulcer by the time he was twenty-nine. Somewhere along the line he met another ex-Tar Heel by the name of Brenda. She was an account executive at the bank around the corner from his apartment. She was cute and sexy and loved to laugh almost as much as Andy. And she was just as homesick. Three months after he had first found himself at her desk to negotiate a car loan, he asked her to marry him. That night, drunk on a bottle of cheap wine and love, they both drafted their resignation letters.

That had been ten plus years and three kids ago. They'd added a boat, a flea-bitten beagle by the name of Barney, and a large brick home on the north side of town. Brenda drove the Volvo SUV and spent much of her day chauffeuring one kid or the other to baseball, dance, or the local skating rink.

"We are the poster children for Middle America, Jeb."

Jeb could see he was very happy with the designation.

"That mall I mentioned...I have it on very good information that it was the best developed property in this end of the state."

"So, you're the local land baron, huh?" Jeb took another sip of the coffee. It tasted better than any cup he'd had in years. Gladys flittered by. He was certain she winked again.

"And what happened to you...after Melissa, I mean?"

"I was thirty-two years old," Jeb began. "Getting ready to make another move with the company. Maybe not as focused on the marriage as I should've been."

"So...you just went separate ways?"

"Melissa was even more career driven than I was." Jeb dabbed the last bit of a buttermilk biscuit into plastic container of blackberry jelly. "I haven't talked to her in over five years. She remarried. I heard from a mutual friend that she's a Senior VP now and running one of the global divisions of one of the big accounting firms."

"No kids, I guess."

"Thank God."

"And you're a big shot yourself. Big medical company, big salary, big position..."

"Big headaches."

Andy smiled and shook his head. "I knew you'd be a wheel someday, you know."

"Yeah, well you were wrong."

"It would mean a lot to Zeke, you coming back and all." Andy's expression grew darker. He absently tapped his stirring spoon against the table. For a few moments the din of the café seemed to grow quieter.

"Tell me about Zeke, Andy."

An older man, bent over with age and shuffling along with his eyes focused on the black and white checkerboard tiles of the floor, suddenly appeared at their table. He clapped Andy on the back and for a few moments the two chatted about the weather and the price of gasoline. Gladys showed up with the bill he had left at his table and the eye glasses that had sat beside them. Though Jeb hadn't caught his name, it appeared that the waitress had named this patron "Baby," a moniker he appeared to enjoy immensely.

Jeb took the opportunity to check his cell messages. Four received. He could guess the source. He glanced over to a far table of soot-covered firemen. They were huddled over their plates and scarfed down their food. One of them had a thick bandage on his left hand. They spoke in low voices when they spoke at all. The youngest of them, a slender kid who looked like he might barely be out of high school, gazed quietly out the window. He didn't seem to notice the pancakes that sat in front of him. Jeb watched a man from one of the other tables walk over and speak to them. He wrapped his arm around the shoulder of one, as if to console him.

Baby finally shuffled on to greet another table, and Gladys, coffee-pot in hand, went in a different direction.

Andy peered into the fresh cup in front of him and listlessly stirred the cream into it, watching the brown swirls.

"It didn't go so well for Zeke, Jeb," he began.

CHAPTER SEVENTEEN

"The kid we both knew…he changed a lot as he grew older." Andy bit his lip and stared blankly at the wall behind Jeb. He shook his head and his eyes returned to the coffee.

"It seemed like he found trouble at every corner…fell into alcohol, drugs, you name it."

"Damn…Zeke was a follower, sure."

"Yeah, well, he decided he would follow Jack Daniels, I guess. Never could keep a job after high school. I still remember when I came back to town after Atlanta. I was late-twenties. Had Brenda with me that very first weekend and we went out to a steakhouse over in Rockingham. There was a bar there where a lot of the locals spent their Saturdays. Halfway through our filets, we hear a ruckus over in the other side of the restaurant, where the bar was. Yelling, glasses breaking. I got over there in time to see two guys pounding on some drunk who was tucked between two of the bar stools. Wasn't until I could get closer that I recognized who it was."

"You mean?"

"Yep. Zeke Andrews."

"So what did you do?"

"Got my nose broken. Almost tossed in jail."

Jeb laughed. "So you helped him out, huh?"

"Well, if you can call stopping some of the punches with my head help, I guess you could say so." He rubbed his nose and frowned as he spoke. "Turned out Zeke started it all to begin with.

"Took me a while to sort it all out, but it became pretty obvious that Zeke had some real problems. Had seen the inside of the county jail at least a dozen times by then. All minor kinds of stuff, but every badge in the area knew Mr. Andrews."

"Zeke?"

"Yeah…Zeke. Believe it, Jeb. The guy's life went down the shitter. It was scary."

"What happened?"

"Who can say? Maybe it was his family situation. There was a failed marriage along the way. By the time he was thirty, it was like everyone in the county knew he was a good-for-nothing."

Jeb looked away and considered the slow stream of traffic that rolled by on Alexander Street. Life continued on. Even as the tragedy of Zeke Andrews's story unfolded across a breakfast booth inside the Stacey Café.

"Got him a couple of jobs. Last one was on one of my construction crews. Made it two weeks before the foreman found him curled up with a bottle on the back end of a road grader."

"So you're telling me nobody could help him."

"Lot of people tried, Jeb. Detox, AA, anything. He went through spells where I thought he'd straighten himself out." Andy's voice waivered. He found the space on the wall again, as if searching for the answers there. "He drank himself to death, I guess." For a moment his eyes glistened before he shook it away.

"So what? You telling me his liver…his heart…?" Jeb tried to grasp what he was hearing.

Andy looked at Jeb closely. "What do you mean?"

"I mean what killed him? Was he such an alcoholic that his body gave out on him?"

"I guess you wouldn't know."

"What in the hell are you talking about?"

Andy paused, and then stared down at the time-worn table as if the words might be written there. "I should have told you…should have said it in my message. It was just so crazy at the time. I wasn't thinking as clearly as I should have."

Jeb leaned back and braced himself.

"Zeke…Zeke killed himself, Jeb."

CHAPTER EIGHTEEN

The body of Ezekiel Sanford Andrews was found at approximately 10:00 a.m. on the morning of Wednesday, July thirteenth. Two local residents, Craig Phillips and Lawrence Bramble, ages thirty-three and twenty-four respectively, had stumbled on it while hiking along an overgrown ridge that overlooked the Yadkin River, which ran west of the town.

Both claimed to be in the area to scout locations for an upcoming lodge campout. Sheriff Roy Yates suspected they were checking deer stands and/or hunting out of season. Neither had weapons, however, when the first law enforcement vehicles arrived on the scene.

The two men were high on Darby Ridge when Bramble had felt the call of nature and had taken the opportunity to relieve himself, scaling one of the outcrops of rocks that overlook the river, hoping to greatly enhance his range. Phillips was prepared to support that with a cell phone photo he planned to use to capture the event.

Bramble's estimate of distance had been interrupted with the sighting of a body sprawled amid the rocks at river's edge, some one-hundred-and-fifty feet below. The body wore a bright red shirt, a stark contrast to the tangle of brush that ran along the water.

The first emergency call came into the county sheriff's office at 10:20 that morning. It was almost 11:00 before the first law enforcement vehicle arrived on the scene. The department's one SUV had been called only after a cruiser could not handle the gullied dirt road that led to the top of the ridge. Sheriff Roy Yates was a passenger in the SUV.

Emergency personnel from Richmond County Hospital, along with sheriff's deputies who had gone through wilderness rescue and recovery training, spent the better part of two hours trying to clamber down the treacherous cliff walls. Though underbrush and a few scattered scrub pines dotted the face of the ridge, the drop off was almost a completely vertical one. Eventually, ropes and rock climbing equipment were brought in from Gaston County, some hundred-plus miles away. Mountain rescue was not a part of traditional operations this far east.

The relatively remote location added to the difficulty in recovery. The one road was once a logging trail, and could only be accessed from the south. The body could not be easily reached by the river because of a series of rapids to the north and a small waterfall downstream.

Sheriff Yates was one of the men who rappelled down the side of the mountain to assess the situation. At sixty-four, he did so with some degree of trepidation, and several of the younger men on site advised against it. Yates insisted. He found the dead man lying face down on the rocks some ten feet from the water's edge. His arms splayed away from the trunk. One leg was contorted underneath. He bent low to get a closer look at the bloodied and distorted features of the man. Even with the lifeless eyes and the crushed facial bones, he knew Zeke Andrews. And he was not surprised.

Eventually fire and rescue personnel rigged up an apparatus that allowed them to hoist the broken body of Zeke Andrews to the top of the ridge. It was almost 7:00 p.m. that evening before the last emergency technician left the scene.

County Coroner Dr. Blake Carter was unable, under the circumstances, to examine the body at the death site. Following accepted medical guidelines, he did not examine the corpse until it arrived at the county morgue. The cause of death was determined to be blunt trauma. The physiological factors that ended Andrews's life included multiple compound fractures-to include both the neck and femur of the right leg, lacerations, and organ trauma. All were consistent with a fall from that height. Blood alcohol content indicated a relatively low level of .06.

It was almost 9:00 that evening before Andrews's relatives were notified of his death. By that time there was a growing consensus among law enforcement personnel and the Coroner's office that it would be judged a suicide. Though no one had seen or heard from Andrews in over three days, no missing persons report had been filed. A review of the arrest record and medical history indicated the victim had, on at least two occasions, attempted suicide in the past. The third time was the charm.

Andrews's former wife, a Mary Tully of nearby Mt. Pleasant, was notified at her workplace, a truck stop on Highway 73 named Big Pete's. Mary had remarried several years earlier. The only other relatives that could be reached included an uncle in Florence, South Carolina, and a cousin who now resided in Coral Springs, Florida. Neither had seen or heard from Zeke in over twenty years, nor did they ask for more information on the circumstances around his death. The uncle asked to be informed if there was a will involved in the settlement of the estate.

It was the next day before Andy Gardner was made aware of Zeke Andrews's death, and then only because a nurse at the hospital had heard about it during her break the evening before. One of the emergency room technicians knew Zeke from her bar-hopping days and had been regaling others in the canteen when the nurse, a friend of Brenda Gardner's, heard the name. She had often listened to stories of Zeke Andrews at the weekly Bunko game she sometimes hosted. She called Brenda the next day.

That afternoon's *Stacey Star* noted Ezekiel Andrews's demise in its daily obituary. The two paragraph announcement was tersely worded, with no mention of the cause of death.

CHAPTER NINETEEN

Gladys pulled up a chair and propped her head on her hands. She smiled seductively at Jeb.

"So Andy, you gonna tell me who your friend is?" she asked, never taking her eyes off of Jeb.

"Well...that depends, Gladys. You going to start stalking him if I do?"

"I just might, Honey. Shoog, what's your name?"

Jeb wondered if that shade of pale pink lipstick could be ordered only online or if local stores actually stocked it.

Andy glanced down at his watch. They had spent two hours at the café, and most of the restaurant was empty now. This meant Gladys could devote her full attention to their table. He tossed a few bills on the table and began to slide out of the booth. Gladys did not seem to notice.

"He's a very old friend, Gladys. And I promise to bring him back in here real soon."

Jeb followed Andy's lead. Gladys reached out and caressed his forearm as he did. "Well, I'll just be looking forward to that, Shoog, OK?" She winked as she spoke.

"I will do that. It was a nice to meet you." Jeb estimated only twenty-five steps and he would be at the door. Andy was moving quickly in that general direction.

"So...what is it?"

"Ma'am?"

"Your name, Sugar...what's your *name*?"

"Jeb...Mason." Was he stuttering?

"Well, Jeb Mason," Gladys's breasts seemed to swell as she spoke, "I'll be seeing you real soon then." She watched him cross the café and stride out the door.

Andy was leaning on the BMW, his arms folded across his chest as he crossed the sidewalk. He had a smug look on his face.

"Were you just going to leave me in there?" Jeb asked.

"Course not. I would have gone back in if she just threw you down right there on the table."

Jeb felt the sweat beading on his upper lip. "She like that with every customer?"

"Only the out-of-town boys. Jump in. We're going for a ride," Andy said as he opened the car door. "Might do you good to run by your old house. Up for a ride by sixteen Poplar Glen?"

"You kidding me? Figured they had torn it down by now."

"Hey, we thought we would convert it into a museum. You know, the home place of the famous Jeb Mason. Make a fortune."

"Man, you have seriously not changed. You know that, don't ya?"

• • •

It was a narrow side street, lined on either side by towering maple trees. A young woman pushed a light green baby carriage on the sidewalk, a long-haired golden retriever loped along behind, stopping to sniff and trotting to catch up as they went. Somewhere up ahead, a lawn mower growled to life behind one of the small frame houses, and through the open sunroof Jeb could smell freshly cut grass, all mixed with the sounds of summertime. Andy slowed the car to a slow roll and a monarch butterfly fluttered alongside for a time, and then broke away for a nearby perennial bed. An old man sat on one of the front porches, watching every car closely as it passed. He raised his hand and waved. Jeb smiled and returned the favor. By his reckoning, more people had waved to him in one morning than they had in the last two years.

The BMW wheeled alongside the curb in front of a small, pale gray house. The front yard was bordered by a faded wrought-iron fence with a gate that looked to be missing some hinges. It sloped severely to the left. Boxwood hedges, neatly manicured, rimmed the front porch. One weeping willow seemed to shadow much of the small front yard. A child's tricycle, rusted and overturned, lay against the trunk. The red metal chair beside it had a well-worn pillow in the seat, and a spit can sat nearby, a cool respite from the hot summer sun.

"Well…" Andy gestured toward the house, "has it changed much?"

"No." Jeb drank in the sight of it as he opened the car door. "Can't say it has." And for a brief moment he could almost see himself bounding out the front door and mounting his bike. Through the gate and careening down the sidewalk, through the lawn sprinkler down the street he'd ride, headed to pick up his buddies. He glanced down Poplar Glen. A spray of water pattered against the concrete five houses away.

"Want to go in?" Andy asked.

Jeb roused himself from his daydream. "Just how are we going to go in?"

"'Cause I sold this house twice. Hey, I'm not just a developer. I also own a residential real estate office."

Jeb looked back at Andy as he crossed the sidewalk and stood alongside. "So…are you in on everything in this town?"

"Only the ones that will make me an honest buck. Current owner is Clarence Parker, age eighty-one. Used to be in the lumber business over in Bessemer City. Wanted to come back to be close to his grandkids… and his great-grandkids."

"Well, I hope you gave Clarence a good deal." Jeb grabbed the gate and pulled it. "This darn thing has been broken for thirty years, at least."

Andy yanked it back and forth a few times then smiled. "This gives the house character, old buddy. Means it's been lived in. Come on. We'll knock on the door."

"That's OK, Andy. Maybe better to leave it in my past."

"Come on." Andy opened the gate and stepped onto the front yard. "You got an oak tree you gotta see."

"This is called trespassing in Chicago, Andy. And don't tell me the tree is still back there."

"Clarence said his great-grandkids would love it," Andy said as he made his way around the narrow side row of hedges. Standing there, in the middle of a well-worn dirt backyard, rose a mammoth old tree, its branches gnarled as they curled toward the sky. High up, wedged between its tangled fingers, was the remnant of a wooden platform and what once were walls. Andy smiled as he looked up. "He freaked when I told him I could vouch for the construction, since I helped build it."

"My God." Jeb smiled. "That was the summer they re-sowed Grimley Field."

"And Zeke got us banned from the city park pool."

"It was...a good idea." Jeb whistled. "We're lucky we didn't get killed, you know."

"Zeke almost did, as I recall." Andy propped one foot against the tree and gazed up. "Man, that's three stories at least."

"My dad said he never did get his hammer back."

"My pa said the same thing about his saw and the same for about a half-pound of nails," Andy added.

Jeb picked at a rusty nail that protruded from the trunk. "You do remember where we got the planks, right?"

"Remember? For years, old Ollie Bridger hated me. Not sure if he cares much for me now."

"Ever wonder how he ended up vertical on that rope ladder?" Jeb asked.

"Didn't have to," Andy said. "It was Zeke."

"Yeah," Jeb answered. "It was Zeke."

CHAPTER TWENTY

Four city blocks away the discovery of Bump Patterson's body had triggered a very different response than that of Zeke Andrews. Though the identification was nearly certain, the verification would not be official until midday at best.

Thad Bingham's grisly find drastically changed the scope of the fire investigation. A body, particularly under the circumstances of a questionable fire, set off a chain of events.

Fire Chief Brett Hampton's first phone call had been to Police Chief Benny Greer. The second was to Sheriff Roy Yates. Though Steadman was in the city limits of Stacey and rightfully under Greer's jurisdiction, Hampton and Yates were old friends and still attended monthly veterans' meetings at the town armory. It was Yates who immediately placed the call to State Bureau of Investigation headquarters in Raleigh. Agents were being dispatched by the time Jeb and Andy had bid Gladys and the Stacey Café adieu.

News of the tragedy swirled through the town, and police and sheriff's deputies had successfully roped off the burned areas of the elementary school with yellow crime-scene tape before dawn at the Police Chief's insistence. The move proved prescient, since most everyone had a reason to see the fire's aftermath for themselves.

Dr. Blake Carter was roused from bed at 5:15 that morning and was on the scene by 6:00. There, he was directed to Patterson's body, still curled amid the gray, soggy debris of what were once the administrative offices. Carter cursed to himself as he stepped through the mushy gunk, wishing he'd thought to don a pair of his old hunting boots rather than his relatively new Bass Weejuns. Damn fools should have told him it was a fire investigation. The shoes were already hopelessly ruined.

The stench of the place assailed him, and Carter yearned for the comfort of his own bed and his wife, Angela. Running for county coroner had been his father's idea. Roland Carter, a prominent defense attorney in Stacey, had encouraged his thirty-three-year-old son to take this position as a springboard for a run at city council a few years later. The Carter family was one of the most eminent in Stacey and boasted strong political ties in Raleigh and even Washington. Blake, the second of three sons, was predestined to be a politician. The medical degree, in his father's eyes at least, was considered to be of secondary importance.

But at the moment, Blake Carter privately wished he'd never consented to his dad's wishes. Saturday was his day off, and the week had already been a nightmare with the body over on the river. Political office wasn't worth this level of hell.

A cluster of firemen ahead were motioning him forward. He could smell the taint of burned flesh—of death.

The preliminary examination at the scene established only a probable cause of death. The body was badly burned, but it was clearly a black male, probably older, approximately one hundred fifty pounds. There were no signs of severe trauma, with the exception of a large contusion on the back of the skull. The obligatory photographs were taken by one of the policemen on-site. A number of additional photographs were taken by Carter. At the direction of Chief Greer, the body could not be moved until State Bureau of Investigation agents from Raleigh arrived later that morning. Greer had not been in the best of moods after being notified that the SBI had been alerted without his approval.

Almost immediately, Carter began to wonder why the victim had been trapped in the inferno. He had seen fire victims before. In his first six months as coroner, a family of four had succumbed in a trailer fire in the southern part of the county. The husband and wife were found huddled in a hallway, clutched together, their two small children tucked in between them. The image still haunted him.

This was a different scene. The body wasn't curled into some far corner. It was sprawled in what appeared to be a relatively large room. One arm was thrust awkwardly overhead. The face of the dead man was locked into what appeared to be a grimace, but the damage inflicted by the flames made even that difficult to determine. A significant amount of the body's tissue had been burned away. He instructed one of the firemen to make arrangements for an ambulance to transport the body once SBI agents had OK'd its removal.

The firemen rustling through the carnage nearby looked up as Carter straightened, concluding his preliminary examination. One of them, the same sandy-haired young man that had first directed him toward the body, approached him now.

"We think it's Bump Patterson, Doc. Did ya already know that?" he asked. Carter realized the fireman was obviously badly shaken, but the name meant nothing to him.

"Bump...Bump's the janitor. We all knew him," Thad Bingham began to explain. "Man...he's been here forever..."

"Did he live here?" Carter asked.

"What? No, I don't think so, anyway...why?"

Carter looked back at the body.

"Don't know. Just seems strange for him to be here at midnight on a Friday, I guess."

"Wrong place to be," Bingham muttered. He shook his head and cast his eyes down. "You're going to have to get some new shoes, Doc."

CHAPTER TWENTY-ONE

"Andy, there is no argument here. I'm going to help out with this," Jeb insisted.

"Jeb, it's not your responsibility." Andy adjusted the rearview mirror and whipped the BMW across a lane of traffic.

"The hell it's not, man. He was just as much my friend as yours."

"You haven't seen Zeke in thirty years. Believe me, I got this covered."

"I know you do. And it's something I need to do, too."

"OK, we'll figure it out when we get to the funeral home," Andy said.

"Look, it was always the three of us, right?"

"Still doesn't mean...now what?" Andy said, as he slammed the car to a stop. Cars were honking up ahead. A long line of automobiles stretched the length of the block and beyond.

"You mean even Stacey has traffic jams now?" Jeb unhooked his seat belt and stood up in his seat.

"Only if there's a run on the bank, and I haven't heard of one." Andy answered. He did a quick U-turn and headed back down Dekalb.

They crossed over two side blocks and approached the downtown from a different angle. A block away a similar line formed.

"What in the hell is going on?" Andy pulled the car to the curb. "Want to take a walk?"

A block away from Steadman they began to encounter the steady stream of foot-traffic that was meandering to and from the parking lot across the street from the school. They approached the yellow crime-scene tape and joined the throng that had gathered there, everyone gawking at the hulking mass that had once been Steadman Elementary.

There were whispers that a body that had been carried out earlier. Beyond the tape, standing amidst the rubble, were a number of police and firemen, milling through the refuse. Beyond them were four or five official-looking men in suits. One of them was writing on a clipboard and speaking into a small tape recorder. They surrounded an area of the debris that had been cordoned off from the rest. A beefy policeman barked an order to the uniformed officers, and they immediately dispersed to different corners of the building.

Andy gave a short whistle and the heavy-set man glanced up. He called a younger officer over. To Jeb's surprise, the officer walked over to the tape.

"Chief says you can come in if you want." He raised the tape for them to walk in. The people around them murmured in surprise, and Jeb wondered again just how much influence his old friend enjoyed in this town.

Andy grabbed Jeb by the wrist. "Come on," he said.

The big man watched their approach. He was barrel-chested and at least 250 pounds, with a red face and what seemed to be a permanent scowl. He had deep-set black eyes that looked through you. Jeb wondered if he was capable of smiling.

Andy shook hands and introduced him to Police Chief Benny Greer. Jeb watched his own hand disappear in the meaty paw of a right hand.

"Why you here in Stacey?" Greer's voice rumbled. He watched Jeb closely.

"Funeral," Jeb answered. Greer's question had seemed less of a friendly "get to know you" and more the opening of an interrogation.

"That Andrews boy?" he asked.

"We went to school with Zeke," Andy answered for him.

"You from around here?" Greer kept his gaze on Jeb.

"No," Jeb answered. He decided he didn't care much for Chief Benny Greer. He didn't intend to embellish his answer.

"What happened here, Benny?" Andy asked. He was eager to end the line of questions.

"Can't say," Greer said, and Jeb wondered if he couldn't or *wouldn't*. He noticed that Andy had called him by his first name. "Hampton says the fire marshal won't have his investigation completed for a couple of days."

"What do you think?" Andy asked.

"Pretty damn clear," Greer grunted. "You got an old black fool that got hisself liquored up and sneaks off to the school to sleep one off. Probably nods off with a cigarette in his hand..." He gestured at the debris around them. "Poof...we got a million dollars of damage."

Jeb decided his first impression was wrong. This guy wasn't probably an asshole. He was a card-carrying one.

"Who are we talking about?" Andy asked.

"Why, that janitor. What's his name?" Greer looked over to the same young officer that had ushered them through the crime-scene tape. "What's the guy's name they carried out of here?" he asked.

"It's Bump Patterson, Chief," the young man replied.

Andy gasped. "Bump Patterson? Is he OK?"

"Sure, if you call well-done rotisserie OK."

"Bump is dead?" Andy asked.

"As Julius Caesar," Greer answered. "Damn fool." He repeated himself, as if no one had heard his first description of the deceased. He rubbed his hand over those fat jowls and nodded toward the knot of men some fifty feet away. "They got SBI, ATF...shit, they got half of Raleigh down here."

"Bump Patterson..." Andy mumbled the words, shaking his head.

"Damn, they got a little skirt down here, even. A fucking female of all things." He spat the words. "Son of a bitch Yates called them in. Never mind it was my jurisdiction. The little bastard."

Jeb wondered if this guy hated everyone or just those he had met personally.

"Principal Lindsey says it will be weeks before they can decide about what to do about the school. Hell, you'll end up making money out of this deal, Gardner."

"They'll bid the work like always, Benny," Andy answered quietly.

"Bullshit." Greer answered. He leaned over and spat tobacco juice onto the black sludge at his feet, then looked back up at Jeb.

They watched a white van pull up in front of the school. Big red letters on the side read "State Fire Investigation Unit." A sheriff's deputy hustled to pull the tape down and point the driver to the edge of the burn site.

Greer trudged away.

CHAPTER TWENTY-TWO

"Good to know that absolute SOBs are not just limited to the larger metropolitan areas," Jeb said as the BMW pulled out of town. "Is that guy the biggest jerk in the state or just the county?"

"Pretty good chance in the entire Southeast region." Andy smiled. He pressed the gas pedal and the car roared down the street, moving quickly away from the depressing hulk of Steadman Elementary.

"So how is that you have the honor of a special invitation from Mr. Warmth?" Jeb asked.

"No honor. Greer's brother-in-law works for me, and Greer sponges off of him all the time. Indirectly, I'm responsible for half his income."

"Not sure if that's a good thing or bad thing," Jeb said.

"Probably neither. Greer is a blowhard and a hard case when it comes to the local toughs. But he's not that bad. The key is not to spend any time with him. That makes his self absorbed narcissism and outright dislike for most of mankind almost quaint."

Jeb looked at his old friend and laughed out loud.

They pulled into the Flannery Funeral Home parking lot fifteen minutes later. It was a third generation establishment and the only facility of its type in the southern end of the county. Though it wasn't generally advertised, it was the most profitable business in the area, a fact that the proprietors did not care to acknowledge and that the patrons were not in a position to inquire about.

Harold Flannery, age forty-six, bore his responsibilities well. Bald and with the dignified paunch of the well heeled, he had learned at his father's side the subtleties of the business many years before. He could, on command, put a glisten of tears in his eyes or drop his voice to a barely perceptible whisper, when necessary. And he could do it while affecting the demeanor of a professional barely able to fulfill his duties in the midst of his own personal bereavement at his clients' loss. He was good at his chosen field, and he considered his sizable income fair remuneration for the invaluable service he provided to his community.

Of all the sundry duties associated with being a funeral home director, he enjoyed his "pre-service arrangements meetings" most. It was there that he managed to double and sometimes triple his revenue stream. Grieving relatives were more susceptible to his sales spiel than any other client group. Providing them with the choice of the top-line, steel-reinforced casket versus the more economical "middle of the road" version could almost always be made more persuasive if one managed to equate the former with a greater love for the dearly departed. After all, "Do you really want dear old Momma to be forever interred in a home that might leak in a few years? I should think not!"

That's why that afternoon's meeting originally hadn't been very appealing for Harold Flannery. Ezekiel Andrews apparently had no family to speak of. Dirt-poor and divorced. If an old friend hadn't stepped forward, this would probably have resulted in a pauper's funeral, paid for by the county, with virtually no profit for the funeral home. Only the barest of reimbursement schedules. Harold's stomach turned at that possibility. Thank God Andy Gardner had agreed to pay the tab. Everybody knew Gardner had money.

Jeb and Andy were ushered into Flannery's offices once the pleasantries were exchanged and Mason's attendance explained. Harold's interest was piqued when Jeb offered that he planned to assist in paying funeral expenses. Though Gardner seemed resistant, it was clear to the funeral director that there were old ties there. He began to lay out the various options with a relish.

They were well into a candid discussion on the Evening's Rest Deluxe package when they were interrupted by a knock on Flannery's office door. The portly director turned an aggravated glance in that direction.

It swung open slowly to reveal a gaunt, brown-haired lady, dressed in a plain white cotton dress with a large black belt and ordinary, soft tan sandals. Her hair was pulled back into a short ponytail. There was a hint of beauty in her face, but time and worry had tightened it, so that the lines were hard. Jeb guessed she was no older than her mid-thirties, but her eyes seemed tired—almost mournful. The hint of make-up didn't hide the crow's feet. A worn brown pocketbook was tucked under her left arm. She clutched the hand of a young boy with her right. She stood there in the doorway for a few moments, looking at each of the men, unsure of whom to address.

But Jeb barely saw her there. His gaze was fixed on the boy who stood half-hidden behind her. He was slightly built with long brown bangs and big almond eyes that blinked sheepishly as he looked at each of the men. The freckles that adorned each cheek were so pronounced that they almost seemed painted on.

He had the same pug nose. The same way of standing.

Jeb was looking back in time.

He was looking at Zeke.

CHAPTER TWENTY-THREE

Much of fire investigation focused on answering very basic questions. It began with identifying the point of origin and advanced quickly to then determining what caused the blaze. The first piece requires an understanding of burn patterns. In general, damage will be the most severe where the fire begins. Most then tend to move laterally and up as they develop, creating what arson experts refer to as the traditional "V pattern." Though the same is true for accidental fires, incendiary events, those set intentionally, can offer many clues at their base, especially in the absence of other potential catalysts.

A working hypothesis developed quickly on the charred grounds of Steadman Elementary. It began with a structural engineer first clearing Police Chief Bennie Greer and Fire Chief Brett Hampton and their men from the area. Once deemed safe enough for the Fire Investigation Team, the Chief Investigator and three other experts descended on the blackened building to begin their work. And finding the starting point, as one of the investigators suggested, "was about as tough as finding your toes."

"Got multiple start points," the Chief Investigator said to the small group gathered around him. He was a round-faced, middle-aged man with a thick pair of glasses that made him look like a hoot owl. "My guess is your arsonist tossed the accelerant here." He waved to the place that Bump Patterson's body was found. "Then here, then over here."

SBI Agents Shauna Spencer and Mac Boller followed his explanation closely. Fire Chief Brett Hampton stood alongside.

"Got an amateur here, Hampton," the owl said. "Stupid son of a bitch too."

"Why do you say that?" Boller asked and the owl looked up at the agent, as if he noticed him for the first time.

"Obvious, too many spark points," he answered, as if it were so obvious that someone on the street would know it. "Right there." He pointed.

"Spark points?" Boller asked.

"You know, the fire started pretty much everywhere in this room. My guess is he used gasoline. It spread quickly, maybe too quickly."

"How long to verify that?" Shauna Spencer asked.

The owl considered the pretty brunette and smiled.

"We're going to take a close look at all of this the rest of the afternoon, Agent Spencer." His accent was so thick that Spencer sounded more like "Spencah," Shauna thought. "Gather the materials. Test them. But we are talking a petroleum-based hydrocarbon. Bet money on it."

"The deceased…his name was Patterson, right?" Boller looked toward Fire Chief Hampton and Hampton nodded. "What do you think the chances are he could have accidentally set this thing?"

"Like I said, got some testing to do but if you're asking me if ah think that man came in here and just accidentally showered himself in gas and then set himself on fire, well…" the owl said. He sized up Boller as he spoke and the brief picture of a bowling ball with legs passed his mind. "Tell you this, though, whoever set this damn thing don't know much about covering their tracks."

"Meaning?" It was the pretty one asking and the owl liked to answer her questions.

"Ah believe they picked up what was handy and just dumped it on the body. In that room. Throughout the building. Tossed a match out there." The owl assumed his most authoritative voice.

"Hell of a way to die," Hampton said. He ran a hand through his wiry gray hair and shook his head. "Bump deserved better than this."

"Know this sounds little strange but going to ask you anyway," Boller said. "You get people who are depressed…"

"Up to you boys…well, you folks." The owl cast an appreciative glance toward Shauna again. "But like I said, multiple locations that the accelerant was used. Kind of hard to imagine, ain't it?"

Boller looked over to the circle of local police officials that hovered some thirty feet away. They watched the "state boys" carefully, like hyenas forced away from a fresh kill by stronger predators.

"Want to complete a Vapor Trace Analyzer," the owl continued. "Test the hydrocarbon residues; give us pretty good idea of what we're talking about. Do some more work in the lab, have an answer for you pretty soon."

"I ain't buying a suicide either," Boller said. "But it looks like they've had a rash of that around here lately."

"What are you talking about, Mac?" Shauna asked.

"One of the officers told me they had a jumper here couple days ago. Came over the wire," Boller said. He looked over at the small group of onlookers that stood outside the crime scene's boundaries. A little girl sat on top of her father's shoulders. She was munching on a strawberry snow cone and some of the syrup had begun to leak down the sides. She sat there as she might if they were waiting for a parade to pass by.

"Seems to me this town has had its share of bad luck over the last week," Boller said.

CHAPTER TWENTY-FOUR

"Medication's going to knock her out for a while." Dr. Lorenzo Maynard glanced back a last time at Ilene Patterson. Her eyes were closed. A pile of Kleenex lay beside her in the bed. Her sister Jules sat beside her; her eyes were closed, too, and her head rested against the back of a high-back chair someone had brought in from the living room. Her mouth was pursed and she dabbed at her eyes with a pale lavender handkerchief. Dr. Maynard quietly shut the bedroom door behind him.

The phone call to Bump Patterson's residence had come at 5:05 a.m. that morning. Ilene had fallen asleep before Bump returned from the school the night before. The call had at first bewildered her. Her husband was at home she insisted.

Then the terror came.

The police officer had been vague. There was an incident at the school. There had been a car dispatched to pick her up. And then everything swirled out of control.

Her husband was gone. She knew that now. The trip to the police station had been a frightening, overwhelming event that resulted in a number of official-looking people simultaneously comforting and interrogating her on Bump and his comings and goings. By midday, her blood pressure soaring, her nephew, a young officer on the force named Bobby Patterson, had driven her home. Dr. Maynard was an old friend. He joined all the others that had converged on the small frame home on Sumter Avenue.

Outside the house, two television vans, dispatched from Charlotte to cover the Steadman fire and its aftermath, were conducting "on air" reports with the Patterson house as a backdrop. Several bereaved family members had been interviewed as they entered the house, as had a number of local citizens. The "human interest" aspect of a well-known local tragically dying in a suspicious fire was relatively sensational news.

In the last few hours, there had been unsubstantiated rumors from sources in local law enforcement that questions were being asked about Patterson's death, and more than a few whispers of murder. The emerging story had been pushed to the lead item on the 6 o'clock news for at least two of the four Charlotte stations, a rarity for a small town in a mid-major market.

News reporter Blaine McQuinn waited for his cue from the truck, then read his intro with relish. He was a slightly built man with the hint of a receding hairline and an easy smile for the camera. He wore his best navy blazer, which he had slipped over his cobalt blue shirt only seconds before. The Patterson home, awash in camera lights, stood prominently behind. The story angle, at one point a salute to a local "character," had been re-written by McQuinn and his camera man, Steve Coombs, in the last forty-five minutes. The Stacey Police Department was comprised of only eighteen people. News traveled fast, and the Patterson case had attracted a lot of attention. State officials were on hand, and the whole thing had begun to make Blaine McQuinn think he might have just stumbled on something big. He patted his shirt collar and wondered if not donning the tie was a mistake.

The forty-five-second lead was followed by a taped segment that captured the final stages of the fire, the removal of Patterson's body, and a few brief comments from the local citizenry, including Mayor Preston Wehunt. McQuinn's voice-over had been taped several hours before. At the conclusion of the video, the camera went back to McQuinn.

"Though authorities aren't saying much about the investigation, there are preliminary reports that both the origin of the fire and the circumstances surrounding Arthur 'Bump' Patterson's death are being called into question. We've learned that officials believe the fire may have been intended as a device to hide Patterson's murder, or to, in some way, conceal the nature of his death. We talked to Fire Chief Brett Hampton only a few moments ago. He would not speak to the specifics but did confirm the investigation is ongoing.

"We've also learned that this is not the first time that Steadman has experienced crime problems. Twice over the last six weeks, there have been acts of isolated vandalism. But certainly, Bob, nothing to compare with the events here last evening."

With that cue, the broadcast shifted back to anchorman Bob Nicholson, who asked the perfunctory follow-up question.

"Is there any indication, Blaine, that an arrest or arrests are imminent?"

"Bob, at this point, officials aren't saying. But there is clearly a lot of attention being focused on the circumstances around the fire. As we get further updates, we'll be reporting them."

The station cut away and McQuinn tossed the mike toward Coombs.

"You gonna buy me a beer on the way out? Saw an old steakhouse on the edge of town," Coombs said.

"Got my car," McQuinn answered. "Meet you back in Charlotte. Got one more person to talk to."

Coombs shrugged and headed in the direction of the station van. McQuinn wondered if that beer might be a good idea before his next conversation.

CHAPTER TWENTY-FIVE

"So," Jeb said. "You think it's a good idea. Me going with Mary Tully over to Zeke's trailer and all?" He looked over to Andy as they pulled out of the Flannery funeral home parking lot.

"My guess is the county might assign someone as an administrator for Zeke's estate." Andy slowed the car, checked the on-coming traffic, and then whipped the BMW onto the highway. "And the whole 'estate' you can probably drop into one cardboard box. Might be something there you can find for the boy."

"She was going to try and pay for his funeral..." Jeb said, "Says something about her."

"Don't think Mary has much to pay with but yeah, says a lot about her."

"Funny, almost felt like I knew her..."

"Got news for you, old buddy. Can guarantee you Mary has heard your name a thousand times. Zeke always talked about you."

Jeb stared at the road ahead. Let the words sink in.

"Tell me about Mary Tully."

"Not sure what I can tell." Andy shrugged. "Hadn't seen her in a while. Last time might have been when Zeke was in the hospital a few years back. Few times she showed up at a construction site to pick up a paycheck or something...before, I mean."

"Did she still see him?"

"Doubt it. I know they split up maybe four or five years ago. I heard she remarried but I'm not sure."

"And the boy?"

"His name is Joe. Zeke never brought him around. I'm sure I haven't seen him in years…but since the divorce and all, wouldn't expect to."

"Damn, Andy. Did you look at him?"

"How could you help it? He's a dead ringer for his old man."

"Looked to me like she has lived a pretty tough life. So…the deal with Zeke?"

"I think Mary was the best thing that didn't happen for Zeke," Andy answered.

"What does that mean?"

"It means that Mary tried. She really tried to help the dumb son of a bitch. I think she kept going even when everyone else had long since given up."

"How did they meet?" Jeb asked.

"Couldn't say. I just know Zeke came by my office one day after I had gotten back to town. He was in one of his rare moments of sobriety at the time. Said he'd met a little honey that he aimed to marry some-day…must have been twelve to thirteen years ago, maybe longer."

"She, she knew about Zeke though?"

"Sure she knew. Everybody in a five-county area knew by then. But I don't think it made any difference to her. They were in love."

"And it worked for a while?"

"Yeah…" Andy smiled at the memory. "There was a short while there when it almost looked like he had turned the corner."

"Then?"

"Reality came a-knocking…and it darn near knocked Zeke out."

"How about Joe?" Jeb asked.

"Kind of eerie. The resemblance, I mean."

"Like walking into a time warp, Andy. Same eyes, same expression. Hell, he even stands like Zeke." Jeb paused. "Is he…OK?"

"Well, if you mean intelligence-wise, Mary told me once he was darn near a genius. Said he had one of the highest scholastic end-of-school scores ever seen for first grade. Yeah, he's plenty smart."

"How about everything else?" Jeb asked.

"Guessing he's got some baggage, if that's what you mean." Andy's expression grew darker. "I mean he watched his old man stumble through a hundred different jobs in an alcoholic fog. Has to have left some scars."

Jeb considered the quiet little boy he'd met at Flannery's. He seemed so sad there, lurking behind his mother.

"Think she'll bring him to the funeral?" Jeb wondered aloud.

"Absolutely. No question about that. Mary always stayed loyal to Zeke, even when he no longer cared. And she did a damn good job of shielding the boy. From what I heard, there were never any knockdown drag-outs that the kid was involved with."

Both men fell silent for a time.

"You know, the one story I'll always remember about that boy... 'bout him and Zeke?" Andy asked.

Jeb turned and looked at his friend. Andy's lip trembled slightly.

"One of my friends...had a son who played on a baseball team that little Joe played on. Said Zeke would show up for his games sometimes in a taxi cab or just walk up. Had his driver's license revoked couple of times by then so he couldn't drive anymore. Always smelling of liquor." Andy paused, collected himself. "Said he'd be there for just about every game...but he would stand off by himself. By the right-field fence. So he wouldn't embarrass Joe, I guess. But he wanted that boy to know he was there..." Andy's voice choked. "Ain't that something?"

Jeb could not answer. He turned and watched the fields zipping by.

Andy's voice had grown coarse. He said, "I think Joe was the one thing Zeke really valued...the one thing. I remember him telling me once that his whole life wasn't worth a cup of coffee and a sweet roll 'cept for Joe...Zeke loved his boy."

CHAPTER TWENTY-SIX

County Coroner Blake Carter adjusted his glasses and finished his final notes. He glanced out of the wire-covered glass window onto the well-manicured grounds of Richmond County General Hospital. A police cruiser, an officer standing outside of it, sat in the half-empty parking lot.

Carter rubbed his eyes and wished he'd remembered to replace the bottle of scotch he had finished off the week before. He involuntarily checked the bottom drawer of the metal desk anyway. Maybe there was a bottle he had forgotten.

He expected the two SBI agents would be stopping back by soon. They had requested the autopsy be made "priority." There had been more than a hint that they wanted to transport the body to Raleigh.

Carter was adamantly opposed to that proposal. He offered two compelling reasons why the post-mortem should be conducted in Richmond County. The first was local residents' genuine affection for Bump and their need to pay homage to him in the near term, an outcome that would be significantly delayed if the body were transferred to the state capital. The second was the Patterson family's resistance. It was clear Mrs. Patterson didn't want any kind of "operation" on her husband's body. Even the possibility of homicide did not move her from that position. She wanted Bump home. If, as a local police detective had suggested to her, her husband had been assaulted in some way prior to his death, "cutting on him wouldn't change it."

More important to Blake Carter was the potential of some much needed notoriety if this matter turned out to be of interest across the state. He wanted that attention to come to this office, not the state capital. He made a mental note to give his father a call later that evening. The old man would love this.

His examination had been decidedly unspectacular. Patterson was relatively fit for an older black male. No signs of the hypertension which typically afflicted the race. The heart looked strong. Very low body fat. Internal organs healthy. Muscularity pronounced for a man nearing seventy. Patterson was obviously someone who had worked hard his entire life. The overall physical condition reflected as much.

Carter had decided he was the only person in town who didn't know Arthur Patterson. He had spent his adolescence at Bishop's Academy in Charlotte, followed by prep school in Virginia. Undergraduate work at nearby Davidson College. Med school at Duke and an Internal Medicine Fellowship at Emory. Roland Carter's second-born was a life-long guest in Stacey.

Apparently every product of the public school system knew his autopsy subject, however. In the hours since his return to the hospital, the switchboard had lit up with calls of inquiry. There were sticky notes spread across his desk from Mayor Wehunt and Sheriff Yates. Carter always found it intriguing how the general public responded to his part-time role as County Coroner. It was as if his official proclamation was required before anyone was able to accept death's dark notice.

And it was clear that very few were ready to, in this case. This uneducated little man seemed to have more friends and family than anyone Carter knew.

Carter's first impressions around the blunt trauma injury to Patterson's skull were confirmed by the autopsy findings. There was not one but two major contusions to the base of the skull. One created a hairline fracture, suggesting a substantial weapon had been used, since there was heavy hemorrhaging over a three to four-inch area. Both were concussive blows, and one had effectively created a circular fracture of the skull. It was potentially a lethal blow. The severity of the injuries seemed to preclude a fall or what might be a typical accident. Carter felt certain that the circumstances around Arthur "Bump" Patterson's death were now highly questionable.

He picked up the telephone and placed a call to the cell phone number Agent Shauna Spencer had given him. He looked forward to the conversation. She was surprisingly attractive, with light brown hair and big blue eyes. No, not light brown. Dirty blonde, maybe. Her blazer and tan skirt were professional to a tee, Carter thought, but it didn't manage to mask a shapely and athletic body. He imagined her in a form fitting tennis skirt at the country club, sipping drinks on the balcony.

Agent Spencer answered his call on the second ring. Her voice sounded even better on the phone, he thought.

"I think we may have something on the Patterson case," Carter began, trying his best to affect an official tone.

"Yes," she answered.

"You do understand, first of all, that the position of the body has no real bearing on whether the victim was alive. It's the dehydration brought about by the heat that..."

"Very familiar with the pugilistic position, Dr. Carter. What can you tell me?" Spencer interrupted.

"Well, it, uh...appears highly probable that Patterson was hit at least twice with some type of blunt instrument before his death. Significant contusions. Can't say the scope of damage to the brain, but the resulting hematoma is obvious," he opined.

No response from Spencer.

He continued, "I would say that those blows were of sufficient force to render him unconscious. At least one was potentially life threatening. Whoever hit him did so from behind. The injuries were both to the base of the skull, but the clotted blood is clearly defined. My guess is that both blows were premortem, within minutes of his death."

"Any evidence of defensive wounds...hands, arms?"

"No, Agent Spencer. I believe he never saw the blows coming."

"What type of blunt instrument?" Spencer asked. Her voice lacked the enthusiasm that Carter had hoped to hear.

"What...well, it's difficult to say. Could be almost anything, I guess. As I said, the bruising is confined. Blood didn't have the time to spread." Carter felt unprepared for the question.

"Are you saying a coup injury alone, or was there an indication of a contrecoup as well?"

Carter paused. The average police officer had as much understanding of the impact of a blunt force trauma to the head as they did the mating habits of the African Blue Swallow.

"Not really prepared to say...er...definitively. I'll need to..."

"I'm wondering how substantial the weapon would need to be to cause an injury of that magnitude, Doctor," Spencer continued.

Carter was not pleased. She referred to him in the professional sense. The image of the informal chat on the veranda began to fade.

"It would...have to be pretty substantial. Either a metal object or something pretty hard. A brick, a telephone, anything, really."

"Did you find any fragments in the scalp or in the hair that would offer additional clues?"

"Well...I really didn't look for..." Carter hadn't anticipated that anyone would really want to know details with that degree of specificity.

"Dr. Carter, we're going to ask that you suspend your autopsy at this point. Based on what you've shared, we're going to want to complete the examination with our forensic pathologists in Raleigh." Spencer's voice was authoritative.

"*Complete*...but...Agent Spencer, I've already..."

"Dr. Carter, we have probable evidence that this is now a homicide investigation. It's critical that we maintain the integrity of the evidence. I'm sure you understand."

"Yes...of...course." Carter had hoped for a different response.

"Need to have one of our people take over now, Doctor. Stay by your phone. Someone will be contacting you in the next fifteen minutes to arrange details around transferring the body."

"I'll be happy to..."

"Dr. Carter, you've been a tremendous help. Thank you."

"Certainly...certainly," Carter began.

"Just one more thing, Dr. Carter. You did find definite evidence of smoke inhalation in the trachea. That's what you're telling me, right?"

"Yes ma'am. That's what I'm telling you."

"And carbon monoxide intoxication, clearly evident?" Spencer asked.

"The muscles, the blood...all brighter than Santa's best Sunday suit."

"No question?"

"No question, Agent Spencer. Mr. Patterson was burned alive."

The phone line went dead. Blake Carter looked at the receiver for a few moments, and then returned it to the cradle.

CHAPTER TWENTY-SEVEN

Jeb hoisted the Miller Lite can and gulped down several long cool swallows. He was seated in a faded Adirondack chair on Andy's back deck, looking out over a small fishing pond and the last fading streams of sunlight that peeked over the pine trees beyond. A crimson glow reflected off the few clouds that remained on the horizon. The summer's heat had finally begun to subside, and the pond frogs had started their evening soliloquy. The blue-green water glistened in the shadows.

A well-worn path led down through Tonka Toys and Big Wheels to the beginning of a simple wooden deck that led out over the water. A lounge chair sat at the end of the pier.

"Why am I not surprised you live near a lake?" Jeb asked.

Andy sat beside him in another Adirondack. He sipped a glass of scotch and jostled the ice as he spoke. "Mrs. Peeler's class?"

Jeb turned to him. "You damn well fixed our wagon that day, you know."

Andy grinned. "*You* screwed up the doctor's note, not me."

"You showed it to everybody in the sixth grade before we turned it in," Jeb answered. "And you hid the bait underneath Mrs. Queen's classroom."

"I'll assume some culpability." Andy took another sip of the scotch. The frogs' chorus had grown louder. "You know who found us out, don't you?"

Jeb turned, waiting for the answer.

"That was Bump Patterson."

"My God...I guess I didn't put it together." Jeb grew quiet. They watched a starling dart across the deep crimson sky, hurrying to nest in the last moments of daylight. "I remember him now."

"Let me tell you something about Bump Patterson," Andy said and he sat up in the chair, watching the starling land in the trees to the right of the pond. "Back in the sixties, they had a gas line break at the school. Back when it was a one through twelve deal. You know, all grades. No high school or middle school."

He took a long deep swallow of the scotch and let the burn settle into an easy glow. "Story goes that Bump carried out about half of the first and second grade that day. They had teachers that were just freaking out. My daddy said they cordoned off the area. Sirens everywhere. Somebody finally figured to do a class-by-class count. Took them maybe a half-hour to realize they were one short in Mrs. Cline's first grade class."

"One short?"

"Left some kid...or lost some kid. Firemen on hand by that time. Wouldn't allow people back in the building."

"So what happened?" Jeb asked.

"Bump goes back in. On his own. Know where he found the kid?" Jeb shook his head.

"Hidden in the crafts' closet. Scared shitless and crying. My old man always talked about that day." Andy stood and walked to the deck railing.

"You got to understand. This was the 1960s. Different world... you're not going to find a better man in this town, I'll tell you that."

"What does your buddy the chief say about all this?" Jeb asked.

"He's not my buddy," Andy said. "And my guess is he doesn't give a hoot about Bump Patterson."

"All over the news," Jeb said. "I'm guessing he better start giving a hoot. They're saying this might be a murder."

"What kind of sick son of a bitch would want to hurt Bump Patterson?" Andy asked.

"All right, you two. I've got three kids who are preparing to say goodnight." Brenda Gardner appeared at the sliding deck door. She wore a yellow blouse and jeans and her eyes sparkled as she spoke. There were three pajama-clad kids at her side. The youngest was dragging a faded blanket and had a pacifier sticking out of one side of his mouth.

"Think you can interrupt your trip down memory lane long enough to wish them sweet dreams?"

Barry, Audra, and Mitch dutifully lined up to kiss their father good-night. Each then hugged Jeb in turn. Mitch climbed into his father's lap and immediately curled into a ball as his father plunged his head into his belly and made sounds like he was blowing a tuba. Mitch giggled and squirmed in response and the pacifier went rolling across the deck.

Four-year-old Audra climbed into Jeb's lap and studied their visitor closely. "Where do you live, again?" she asked.

"I live in Chicago," Jeb answered, marveling at this little creature who could so easily make herself at home in his arms.

She considered his answer carefully, as if mentally measuring the distance to Illinois from this house on the lake.

"You know what my mama says?" she asked.

"Now wait a minute, Miss Prissy," Brenda interrupted. "It is just about time for you and your brothers to go beddie-bye."

"She says you and my daddy used to be bestest friends." She studied him with her big blue eyes. "*Were* you bestest friends?"

"Yes we were." Jeb grinned and glanced over to Brenda. "Your mama was right."

"That's good," she said, and she reached up and kissed Jeb on the cheek. "Mama says everybody needs one."

With that she clambered off of Jeb's lap and padded back through the screen door.

CHAPTER TWENTY-EIGHT

Jeb glanced down at his watch. Almost 1:00 a.m. Three-and-a-half hours and a few drinks too many. He looked up at the canopy of stars overhead and wondered how many years it had been since he had seen a night so brilliant.

"Jeb, why *did* you come back?" Andy's question hung in the darkness. "I mean...why now?"

Enough alcohol had been poured that now, in the darkness of the night, it could be asked.

"I mean, it's good, you know..." Andy continued. He was already wishing he hadn't.

"No...you're right. It's not like I did a very good job of staying in touch over the years, huh?"

"We were kids, Jeb. Our whole life was in front of us. Nobody blames you for that...The phone lines work both ways. We all grew up. We just went our separate ways."

They sat there, drinking in the sounds of the frogs and the crickets. Jeb looked down at the pond below. The waters were black. In the gloom, they appeared almost translucent.

"Andy, what do you think went wrong...with Zeke I mean?" Jeb's question cut through the darkness.

"Damn. Who can say, really?" Andy answered.

They fell silent again. A whisper of a breeze swept across the deck, and Jeb remembered again what it was like to actually smell the season, not just view it from a car or from an airplane or from a conference-room window.

"Andy," Jeb looked out, across the trees and into the past. "That last six months...before I moved away. We didn't see much of Zeke. You remember?"

"I think he...I don't know. Things changed," Andy said.

The pond frogs' steady drone took the place of their conversation for a time. The two middle-aged men gazed out over the rolling hills and into a summer's night many years before.

"You ever wonder," Jeb said at last, "...if it had something to do with that night?"

Somewhere in the distance a nighthawk gave a shrill cry. A first gust of wind whipped over the deck. It came from the west and carried the faint hint of rain.

Andy leaned back in his chair, and the wood creaked as his weight shifted. He slowly rocked the ice cubes in his glass and they listened as the nighthawk's call died away. "Think I'll get another drink," he said finally.

CHAPTER TWENTY-NINE

The heat wave of 1981 was considered the most severe in twenty years, and by early July lawns had begun to brown and gardens to die. Much of Stacey and the surrounding county could feel the effects all too well. Those who were fortunate enough to have air conditioning stayed inside. Those who didn't complained about those who did. The night of July seventh would prove to be no different.

The weekend's campout had been planned for weeks. Zeke's mom had been a bit of problem, but they told her they would be sleeping in the tree house. And most parents never bothered to check after nine in the evening. The boys waited until eleven to leave for the river.

Their camp was two miles north of town, hidden in a small stand of pines that butted up against the pastures of one of the cattle farms. Normally it would have been easier to make camp on the river, at the sand bar where most of the kids swam every day that summer. But on this night they wanted to be closer to town. And well hidden.

It was hard to say who started the Rite. Rumor had it that it was Bailey Jordan way back in the sixties but Bailey had left town in his eighteenth year. He never came back from Viet Nam.

In the early days the Rite had involved a plunge off of the Southway railroad trestle into the Yadkin River. But over the years the mystery and notoriety of the Rite had changed. Most of the boys "of age" had forgotten about it. But not Jeb, and not Andy. And that meant not Zeke.

It was Jeb who had suggested the Thompson house for the younger boy. If he died leaping off a cliff or trying to swim a river or something, his mom would kill all of them. Any kid with the balls to soap the old man's house would be famous. For a while, anyway.

Franklin L. Thompson was an admired and feared local citizen. He was a Superior Court Judge and, for many years before that, a local trial lawyer. He was an impressive man physically—well over six feet tall with a ruddy pock-marked face and a shock of thick white hair that more often than not fell over a pair of gray, penetrating eyes that intimidated the wayward and law-abiding citizens alike. There were those that whispered Judge Thompson had sent a half dozen to death row and once sentenced a recalcitrant juror to a month in jail. Even the most reckless of teenagers were careful not to burn rubber on the quiet street in front of the Judge's house. In this end of the county, he wasn't just the law. He was the jury too.

There were rumors he would retire soon. His gait had grown stiff over the last years. His enemies prayed for it. His few friends might have, too.

Soaping the Thompson house would make them famous, Jeb reasoned, and Andy agreed. They knew no one would be home. It didn't matter. This would make the trestle jump seem like a stroll in the park. When it came out what they had pulled off every adolescent in Stacey would know about it. They would be talked about for at least a year.

And so they found themselves on this night hiking from base camp across the rolling pasture land of the cattle farm and into the band of trees that lay at the back of the Thompson property. Zeke carried the knapsack that included two bars of soap and a small can of spray paint to sign his work. Jeb and Andy would stand guard. No one would ever see them. They would hike back home early the next morning and wait for the story to begin to spread.

If they didn't go to prison, they would become cult figures.

Even now, all these years later, it was hard to say what went so horribly wrong.

• • •

"I remember the storm, Jeb. More than anything, I remember the storm," Andy said. "Don't think I can ever forget the panic when we were running away."

"Neither can I. But just what do you remember about everything else?" Jeb leaned up against the railing of the Gardner back deck and studied his friend in the darkness. "I mean, are there things now that… come back to you?"

Andy shook his head and said, "The hike in went fine. Remember standing out there in the middle of those woods doing a "reconnaissance" because you always made double-sure on all our…adventures." He laughed and said, "You were an administrator even then, you know that?"

"Yeah, well we should have turned back. When we heard that music, we should have turned back," Jeb said. He looked out over the blackened trees, beyond the pond, thinking back to that night.

"Man. I still think about that music sometimes," Andy said. His voice was low, as if speaking about it aloud made it suddenly more real.

"What do you remember? I mean, about Zeke at the window?" Jeb asked.

Andy paused, trying to step back to the events of the summer night so long ago. "I don't know. Remember…Zeke standing there," Andy began. "And then, something happened."

Jeb searched for his friend's face in the darkness. "What was it that happened, Andy?"

"There was someone there. Someone watching."

"*Was* there? Or were we just imagining there was someone there?"

"I know there was someone, something…at the second-floor window," Andy insisted. "Can't forget that. Never can forget that."

"Andy, can I ask you something?"

The other man shifted and leaned closer.

"You ever…dream about what happened to us that night?"

Andy sighed, then said, "Sometimes…yeah, sometimes I still do. But not so much anymore."

"So…what was Zeke doing? At the end…what was he doing?" Jeb asked.

"What do you mean?"

"Zeke was soaping the bay window on the ground floor. Why did he suddenly stop?"

"Maybe he heard something. Maybe we yelled to him."

"Don't think he heard anything, Andy. And I know we didn't yell to him."

"So what then?"

"I think he saw something," Jeb said. "I think he saw something he was never able to forget."

"We know what he saw, Jeb," Andy whispered. "He saw Judge Thompson die."

CHAPTER THIRTY

A half hour later, Jeb pulled the Camry out of the Gardner driveway and headed back in the direction of the Dogwood Inn. There were no cars at this time of night, and the thought passed his mind of driving back through town.

His cell phone buzzed in his pocket and he checked the messages. Nine new ones. He hit the speaker option and began to clear them. Chicago was never too far away.

The dirt road was a half-mile from the Gardner house and across the highway. It separated two large soybean fields and led away from the main road into a pine forest. There were more fields beyond but they couldn't be seen from the highway.

The car sat parked in the darkness of the trees. From that vantage point the occupant had a clear view of the house. It was only after the Camry passed that it pulled silently back onto the highway and followed.

• • •

Jeb slowed when he hit the city limits of Stacey. The town was quiet, the streetlights bathing the darkened storefronts in a pale glow. Only a few cars were parked on the street. He slowed the Camry at a stoplight, pondering the drastic contrast of this sleepy village and the trendy downtown Chicago bistro that forty eight hours ago he had been holding court in.

A world away.

A few blocks later, he turned down Poplar Glenn, stopping at his old house for a few seconds to study its simple lines. One single light still was on, but it was tucked away somewhere in the back.

He found himself wondering if his bedroom still looked the same.

Then he accelerated and continued on, turning at the stop sign and along another tree-lined residential street. He slowed as he struggled to make out the house numbers. But then, he didn't need to read the number to know when he found it.

It sat on the left hand side and the lawn was slightly overgrown; a white frame house with what might be black shutters but in the dim light was difficult to say. For some reason, he guessed it was empty.

It was Zeke's house.

Jeb parked the car and got out. He leaned up against the Camry and stood there in the darkness.

"Jeb said it was OK."

That was the last thing Zeke said to them that night.

The far-off sound of a train whistle floated through the trees and Jeb turned to consider it. The tracks were on the western side of town, near the river.

Not far from the Thompson house.

CHAPTER THIRTY-ONE

Eight miles away, SBI agent Shauna Spencer shuffled through her notes a final time. Her eyes were tired and she seriously wondered if she should consider glasses.

The call from the coroner, Carter, had put a chain of events into play that continued to run through her head. A vehicle had been sent from Raleigh to pick up the Patterson body, and she suspected forensics would be starting their examination in the morning. She had been told they could anticipate a more complete "preliminary" by Monday evening.

The circumstances surrounding the death seemed odd, she thought. The evidence suggested the old man's demise might have been coincidental, that he might have stumbled onto an individual or individuals who had already broken into the school. There was no indication that any of the locks had been jimmied or broken. The same for the windows. All were secure. Only one entry was unlocked, the rear door to the gymnasium, the access Patterson had most likely used.

Her interview with the Patterson widow had been less than conclusive. She was heavily sedated and still in shock, but able to confirm that her husband had left their home the previous evening shortly before 11:00 p.m. There was a family reunion his sister, a Mary Ruth Seely, was hosting the next day. A grill was needed, and she asked her brother to provide one. According to Mrs. Patterson, her husband occasionally borrowed school property for special occasions. Her colleague Mac Boller was to meet with Mrs. Seeley early the next morning.

Spencer sketched her notes randomly at first, trying to collect her thoughts. There was an evidentiary trail they would need to establish, but it wasn't too early to begin to consider possible motives for the homicide.

The first was robbery. The old man carried a wallet and fourteen dollars in cash, along with a few credit cards. It remained with the body. His truck was found parked behind the gymnasium wall after the fire was contained. There was nothing missing from the vehicle to the best of their knowledge.

The second possibility was domestic. Family tensions had been known to spill over to more serious cases of assault and even murder. Most victims knew their assailants, and a high percentage of those were in some way related. More often than not these were crimes of passion, and there was little evidence of premeditation. Something had happened inside that school on Friday night. It had happened quickly and violently. And the attempt to in some way cover it with the arson had failed miserably. It would require further assessment.

The third possibility was a hate crime. Racism was not non-existent in this part of the world. The victim was black. The victim did not enjoy great wealth. The victim was elderly and vulnerable. The location of the crime and the time of night lent itself to that type of crime. And more often than not, the perpetrators were young. A school was not the most unlikely of locations.

There was another possibility. Collusion. A planned robbery and conspirators turn on one another. Patterson enjoyed access. His partner or partners may have decided to divide their share of the spoils differently. Assessing what was missing would be challenging and the cover of fire further complicated the situation.

She considered each of the scenarios and began to build branches on her notepad that borrowed from each. There was another option, one that continued to bother her. Was it possible the old man simply ran into someone who was already there? If so, what might be so valuable that they would be compelled to kill him and then set fire to the school?

Agent Spencer pulled out two typed copies of information that the Steadman principal, Malcolm Lindsey, had provided to her partner earlier that afternoon. The first summarized the parts of the building that had been destroyed and the materials in each room. The damage was so severe that it would take several days to inventory what might be missing. But some evidence of theft was important and significantly changed the complexity of the investigation. It might explain why the fire had been started in the first place.

A separate sheet listed the inventory of the materials contained in the administrative storage room, the point that investigators believed the fire began. She stood up from the tiny desk at the corner of the room and carried it to one of the beds, laying it across the flower-print bed spread. It seemed wholly unspectacular. Utility bills, architectural blue prints for the new art room, dated teacher personnel files, student records, miscellaneous cleaning materials, some limited athletic equipment, and what appeared to be a lot of junk. There was nothing there that suggested significant value on the street.

She yawned and walked to the mirror. She was dressed in a floppy gray sweatshirt and black cotton sweatpants and was barefoot. She considered the bright blue and white Nikes. It was already early morning. Too late for a jog, she told herself.

At thirty-three years of age, she still considered herself something of an athlete, but the playing field had certainly changed.

She was the first born of Dr. and Mrs. Jerome Spencer, long-time general practitioner in Birmingham, Alabama. A tomboy at heart, she grew up in the prestigious Mountain Brook area, and excelled in academics and sports as a child. She was the valedictorian of her graduating class at Bartholomew High School, and she went from there to Auburn University on a partial academic scholarship, where she majored in Criminology, followed by graduate work at North Carolina State in Organizational Behavior.

She joined the Raleigh police department four days after completing her masters', and at twenty-three became a street cop. At age twenty-seven she was a detective. At twenty-nine she was recruited by the SBI, becoming one of a dozen female investigators. Four years later she was considered one of its rising stars and had played significant roles in solving several major homicides. SBI Director Clinton McHugh knew who she was. A lot of people knew who she was.

There was a reason she had been paired with Boller. One was young and eager. The other was jaded and hard. But they made a perfect team. She did not care for the label she occasionally heard whispered in the hallways—"Beauty and the Beast" was demeaning to both.

Beauty glanced at her cell. Mac was asleep in the room next door. The motel walls were thin, and she had heard him switch off the baseball game an-hour-and-a-half earlier. A west coast game for the Braves was particularly troublesome for Agent Boller. A last-call to Dottie and light's out by midnight.

She considered the Nikes a second time. Twenty laps around the Dogwood Inn parking lot, even this time of night, were not out of the question. And Mac Boller, who went "postal" when he heard about her late night exercise bouts, would never know. She thought she could just make out the low rumble of his snoring. Shauna slipped out of the sweatpants and pulled on a pair of red running shorts.

The air outside her room had begun to cool. Jogging down the stairs to the ground floor she was surprised to pass someone coming up from the opposite direction. He was attractive and fortyish, with tan shorts and a powder blue polo shirt. He looked like an athlete, she thought to herself. Their eyes met as he went by. They both smiled, but she instinctively felt for her handgun, which remained safely tucked in her fanny pack.

After all, Stacey had proven to be not quite as safe as a typical visitor might imagine.

CHAPTER THIRTY-TWO

The sun was just beginning to rise as Sheriff Roy Yates pulled his cruiser up to the police tape that surrounded the Steadman fire scene. He slowly crawled out and grunted as he straightened to look out over the ravaged building. It was quiet now. A lone police cruiser sat on the other side of the parking lot—one of Greer's men.

Finally, time to think.

He carried the Quickie Mart coffee he had picked up ten minutes before. The cup felt good in the early morning chill, and he watched the steam rise up as he gulped its contents. Sleep had not come easily last night.

This was his thirty-first year in law enforcement. At age sixty-four, he was wiry and as tough as a knotted old rope, with a salt-and-pepper buzz cut that made him look more like the Marine he once was than the middle-aged, small-time cop he'd become. He wore the years on skin callused by too many days in the sun. And on this day, each line in his wrinkled brow had grown deeper. He rubbed his jaw and looked across the debris, pausing when he came to where Bump's body was found.

His watch said 6:15. By his reckoning they would have been on the lake by now. Bump would be finishing off his second sandwich and starting to dig into the cooler for a beer. Yates would be working to get his trolling motor to keep running and complaining about the late start they'd gotten because Bump overslept again. By rights, that's what they should be doing right about now.

But instead, he was standing in the middle of a pile of damn ashes. And his friend's body was somewhere on an autopsy table in Raleigh being dissected like a lab animal.

"Merciful God, Bump," he whispered as he nudged a blackened clump of swollen debris with his boot, surveying the corpse of the school as he did. "What the hell happened to you?"

He'd stayed at the Patterson house until eleven the evening before. Had spent a few moments with Ilene before the medication knocked her out again. Had spoken to the family and offered the same condolences that were expected at times like this. Had repressed his anger until he got back to his small two bedroom house. The bourbon hadn't tempered the rage.

He trudged through the smoldering heap, almost grudgingly making himself walk closer to the partitioned area where Bump Patterson's body was found. His mind flashed back to the knot of firemen who had circled him and the blank look on their faces. To the simple cross and necklace that lay twisted around the victim's neck and the smell of human flesh that drifted up to assault them. And finally to the sinking realization that he was looking down at the terribly deformed body of his friend. It was seared there, an image he would live with the rest of his life.

But it was different now. In the fresh light of day, decay had already begun to replace the wound. The bleeding was done. Now the corpse of Steadman Elementary had begun to rot too.

Some ten feet away, what was once a metal file lay on its side, still intact but melted and misshapen by the intense heat. Yates knelt down and ran his hand over the black layer of sludge that covered it. He felt the ridge of what was once the placard holder. It was similar to the file cabinets in the sheriff's office. They used it for alphabetical filing systems, but there was no label here. Or the heat had removed it. In the soot, he saw what was left of another. It read "Student."

Yates stood and looked back toward the street. A second police cruiser drove by slowly. A uniformed officer acknowledged Yates with a slight wave, but in the distance the sheriff couldn't make out the driver. It continued on around the school until it pulled alongside the other cruiser.

Roy Yates counted nineteen file cabinets, each in a similar condition to the one he had just examined. He reached down and pulled on the drawer of a second cabinet. It was locked.

He made a mental note to drop by Malcolm Lindsey's house. The principal should have a key if anyone did. Of course, the family would probably be in bed this time of day. He decided to stop by Hardees on the way. A couple of steak biscuits with the Sunday paper would be just what the doctor ordered.

CHAPTER THIRTY-THREE

Officer Bobby Patterson guessed that Yates didn't recognize him. If he had, he would have hailed him. Patterson had been with him at his Aunt Ilene's until his shift call the evening before. He wanted to talk with Sheriff Yates, but Sam Justice was sitting in the cruiser across the way, so that wouldn't be smart. Everyone knew what Police Chief Greer thought about the sheriff, and consorting with the enemy was not a smart career move. Not when Benny Greer was involved.

Officer Justice was asleep with the car running. His head drooped against his chest. The window was partially rolled down. Justice never allowed something like his duty get in the way of a good night's sleep.

Patterson clicked off the engine of his car and entered the time of his drive-by into his log book. Chief Greer had requested they document any activity around the school and the exact time of surveillance. The chief was tightly wound about this one. The appearance of the SBI had unsettled him even more. He knew a lot of people were watching, and his reappointment by the city council might hinge on this case.

Five minutes later, Bobby Patterson pulled back out again. He quietly surveyed the area where his uncle's body had been found the day before. Sheriff Yates wasn't looking as he drove by this time. He was kneeling, apparently lost in thought.

Patterson wondered if perhaps he was praying.

CHAPTER THIRTY-FOUR

Jeb Mason stuffed another pillow against his head and considered the wisdom of trying some other method to block the stream of sunlight that still managed to pour between the blinds of the large window of his room. He could hear the steady roll of the cleaning lady's cart as it rumbled by on the porch outside.

He checked his watch. Almost eight. So much for actually sleeping in for a change. He quietly padded to the window and pulled back the curtain. Sunlight bathed the room.

There was an exercise area just outside the lobby with machinery that looked just this side of 1960. A worn treadmill and a few dumbbells. He guessed the world's fitness gurus did not include the Stacey Dogwood Inn on its Top Ten list.

He pulled on a faded red tank top and tan gym shorts and headed out the door. The streets of Stacey would be a beautiful alternative to the shores of Lake Michigan for an early morning jog.

Ten minutes later he pulled the car underneath a mammoth red maple beside the courthouse. He waved to a couple of old men who had already taken up positions on one of the benches, and were clearly intrigued by the sight of a stranger arriving in the middle of their checker game. He breathed in the warm summer air and broke into a steady trot in the direction of Poplar Glen.

When he slowed to a walk fifty minutes later, the humidity lathered him in sweat and sixteen Poplar Glen seemed a perfect resting point. At least with the lake he knew where he was. The side streets of Stacey seemed a little more confusing that what he remembered.

He watched the old man trudge slowly down the front porch steps
and make his way in the direction of the newspaper that lay at the gate.
He was bow-legged and wore a rumpled brown suit. Clarence Parker
looked to be dressed early for church.

Jeb scooped up the paper and handed it to the old man. Mr. Parker
seemed pleased to have saved the last ten steps of the walk.

"It might have taken me 'til lunch to get back up those steps, huh?
Thank you, son." Parker smiled. "You're not that feller who bought
down the street are you?" He looked intently at Jeb, trying to recognize
him.

"No sir...I'm just visiting." Jeb grinned in return.

"Uh huh, uh huh," Parker said, as if that made perfect sense to him.
"Where you from?"

"Chicago, sir."

"Chicaga? Chicaga!" Parker exclaimed and Jeb wondered if he had
announced he was from the moon it could have impressed Mr. Parker
more.

"Yes sir...but I used to live here in Stacey." Jeb felt the need to
impress upon the old man that he was not a complete alien.

"Chicaga!" Clarence considered the plausibility of someone from
that far away delivering his paper.

"I used to live here, Mr. Parker," Jeb continued. "I mean right here
in this house."

Clarence's mouth dropped open in astonishment. This day carried
one stunning development after another. He looked back at the house.
"Well, it's a good house, a good house, huh?"

"Yes sir, we..."

"Did you have any trouble with the kitchen sink then? Did it leak
on you?" Clarence asked, his brow beginning to furrow.

"Well...to tell you the truth..."

"Can't understand that..." Clarence continued. "Had the fellow put
new washers in. Still leaks though, huh?" He studied the kitchen window carefully, as if he expected water to suddenly spring through the
pane. "Did you put new washers in too?"

"Well, see I was only twelve and..."

"Good house, but that dad-gum sink beats me," Clarence went on.
"I'm thinking about just pulling the whole thing out, huh? Just pulling it out."

"Yes sir. Yes sir." Jeb began to fade back toward the street. A good ten minutes and he would be back to the courthouse.

"Come back to see us sometime, son." Clarence smiled. "Just me and my wife. Have you met Hattie?"

"No sir. Look forward to doing that sometime."

"Tell me your name again, son." Clarence followed him.

"It's Mason, sir."

"That's right. That's right." Clarence confirmed. "And you used to live here, huh?" He turned back to the house. "I'll tell that other feller I saw you."

"Mr. Parker? What other fellow was that?" He guessed Clarence might be a little addled.

"That feller who was asking about the Masons still living here."

Jeb stifled a smile. Chances were good they didn't let Clarence out very often.

"Wanted to know if we knew any Masons...that's why I can remember him." Clarence continued. "On account that we used to know some Masons down in Gainesville. You're not related to Nate Mason, are you? Nate ran a cement company down in Gainesville, huh?"

"No sir." Jeb said.

"Well, I didn't think so. That's the only Masons I ever know'd. Nate was a pretty good carpenter too." He looked dutifully at the house. "Betcha he could have fixed that sink."

"Who was this fellow, Mr. Parker?"

"Huh...couldn't say. Didn't know him. Wanted to know about the Masons. Not Nate though."

"When was that, Mr. Parker?"

"Well just the other day I reckon, huh?"

Jeb started to jog away. He stopped. Walked back toward Clarence. "Mr. Parker, did he ask anything else?"

"No...no." Clarence said as he trudged back up the front porch steps, carefully gripping the railing with his free hand. "Weren't Nate they was a looking for, anyway."

Jeb watched him make it to the porch and pause to get his breath.

"Come back and see us, Mason," he yelled, waving the newspaper in his hand. Jeb waved in return and started back down the sidewalk.

"Hey, Mason," Clarence called after him. "You know anybody that can fix sinks, you have him give me a call, huh?"

CHAPTER THIRTY-FIVE

"You apologize to Sally for me now. Don't want her mad at me 'bout dropping by like this." Yates sipped from his coffee cup as he spoke. The gentle sound of a radio drifted across the screen porch from inside the house.

So, tell me again, Sheriff Yates, why I'm sitting here in my bathrobe and slippers and talking to you a good three hours before church?" Malcolm Lindsey pushed his coffee cup aside, leaned back into his deep red sofa, and groaned. "Darn, Roy, done told everybody and his brother about what we might have had in the school."

The Steadman Elementary principal looked more like a monk than an educator. He was short and puffy around the eyes. His fine hair had thinned to the point that he was mostly bald but he made certain the few strands that remained were well tended. He usually laughed easily but Roy Yates could see the last twenty four hours had worn on him.

"One of my deputies said he saw you on the news last night. Said you looked like a congressman."

"Bullshit and you know it."

Yates shrugged and wiped the remaining crumbs of the last sausage biscuit from his mouth and leaned back in the white rocker. The two had a beautiful view of rolling pasture land from the screened porch. They watched a single gray mare amble over to the fence and begin to nose around the feeding trough, hoping to find a few remnants from the evening before. Her tail swished at the summer flies that were already buzzing around her.

"How many you got now, Malcolm?"

"Nine, but I'm going to get rid of that stud over there." He pointed to a large, auburn male that was nipping at the ear of one of the mares across the field. She kicked and quickly scooted away from her tormentor.

"He's just damn mean. Kicked the hell out of Goldie the other day. And he's going to kill my dog if he ever manages to get too close."

"They been out to see you yet? Those SBI boys?" Yates asked.

"No, but I got a call from a female agent. Sent her over a list of the inventory we think we had on hand. Said she wanted to talk to me. Going to meet her over at the school this afternoon." Lindsey wrapped the unused portion of his biscuit up. He could save it for when he had a little more of an appetite.

"They say much?"

"Only what you already said. Patterson was murdered. Fire was set. That's enough for me," Lindsey said. He watched the mare wander back toward the other horses. "Haven't you talked to them?"

"Not much. State boys don't generally make accommodating local law enforcement a priority," Yates said. He swigged another gulp of coffee. "Mind giving me a copy of that list?"

Lindsey stood and walked over to a mahogany desk in the corner, picked up a manila file that lay on top. He handed several papers to Roy Yates as he sat back down.

"What do you think, Malcolm?"

"Hell, Roy. I don't know. Why in the hell does anyone kill the damn janitor for God's sake?" Lindsey answered. "Then they burn down the fucking school on top of it." He shook his head and looked away.

"You have anything in there that might be of value?" Yates asked.

"Course we do…computers, printers, copiers…guessing all of it has value on the street."

"This says 'new iPads.' Ain't they pretty pricey?" Yates handed the first page back to Lindsey as he spoke.

The principal squinted to read the small print. Yates grinned and handed him a well worn pair of glasses that sat on the end table beside his chair.

"Damn, Malcolm. You're worse off than I am…"

Lindsey frowned and accepted them, still struggling to make out the list.

"Five iPads." He said finally. "And they are not cheap, Roy."

"Alarm system?"

"Roy, you know the situation on that. We've talked about it. You were there when I presented it to the board."

"Every painful line of it, forty-five minutes and sixty-one pages as I recall."

"Rest my case. Hell, I can't get new erasers. You don't just plug something like that up. Not in Stacey, anyway."

"Well, they were after something," Yates said.

"I hear Bump was a friend of yours," Lindsey said.

"Yup. A good friend."

They watched the stallion sidle closer to the mare, moving her away from the trough with a slap of his head.

"So...what do you think happened?" Lindsey asked.

"Can't say. Know for a damn fact Bump Patterson wasn't there for mischief. I'm guessing he walked into a bad deal."

"A robbery." Lindsey let the statement linger there.

"You got any other ideas?" Yates asked.

"No...but who do we know that's so damn mean that they kill an old man...just because he comes up on them in the night?"

"Somebody that's a pretty bad son of a bitch, I guess," Yates answered.

"Nobody in this town is like that, Roy."

Yates considered that carefully. "Can I tell you, Malcolm, you don't know what somebody's capable of."

"Yeah, but Roy..."

"And one thing's certain," Yates continued. He stood and walked to the window, tapping his finger against the pane as he stared out at the pastureland. "Ilene Patterson no longer has a husband and you no longer have a school."

CHAPTER THIRTY-SIX

Jeb pulled the Camry onto the dusty gravel driveway. Overhead, a faded canvas banner once read "Logan's Trailer Park," but part of the sign had torn away, so it looked more like "Logan's Trail P." The cables that held it in place were each tied to a tall loblolly pine that sat on either side of the road. Someone had nailed a "Fishing Worms for Sale" sign onto the tree to the left. The telephone number was no longer legible.

The trailers were dated and most were battered from years of use. They came in every size and shape. More than a few appeared abandoned. Here or there was an occasional pickup truck or large cable dish, a lawn chair, a clothesline with a smattering of diapers and bed sheets.

Jeb followed the potholed road until he came to a sign that pointed to the left. From what he could tell, the fork to the right was a washed out gully. Cone Trail had less gravel than the main road, and he wondered if the wrong side of the tracks actually had a wrong side of the tracks. A half-mile down, he came upon a dilapidated brown camper on the right. A sofa chair sat out front. Beside the sofa sat Mary Tully's Impala.

Zeke Andrews's final place of residence.

They'd arranged to meet to collect any of Zeke's things that might be meaningful to Joe, or perhaps that Mary could resell.

She sat in the car, idly thumbing through a National Enquirer, when he pulled alongside. She was alone this time.

"Didn't feel much like going in by myself." Mary nodded toward the trailer.

She was dressed in jeans and a faded orange sweatshirt. She looked younger, Jeb thought.

"You have a key?" Jeb asked. But she was already pulling one out of her pocket.

"Police been here," she said as they made their way to the front door. "Sheriff Yates told me they had to on account of it being suicide and all." She pushed the door open slowly.

A musky smell assailed them, and they struggled to see in the darkness. Mary waded through several piles of clothes to a small lamp. She switched on the light.

"Still got electricity," Mary said. "Didn't expect that."

It was a barren living area. A stove, a mini-fridge, a small patched couch. Cans and plates were stacked in different places around the room. There was an open door in the corner, and Jeb could see a toilet and a cracked mirror over a stained sink beyond. Someone had draped the windows with old bed spreads, as if trying to drive out the light.

They wandered through the mess, opening drawers, checking cabinets. The trailer was only one small room. Zeke's home was as barren as the life he lived.

Mary did not speak.

"Anything you want to look for?" Jeb asked as he picked up an empty beer can and tossed it toward a trash can that already overflowed.

"No. Gave Sheriff Yates a list of Zeke's possessions. He said they'd want that. Guessin' maybe some stuff could be sold or somethin'." She pushed a pile of old magazines stacked against one of the battered end tables with her foot.

"Was he in debt?"

Mary laughed. "Yeah, you might say that. Every high dollar lender in the county owned a piece of him." She scanned the room with a grim stare.

"Don't think they'll find much here," Jeb said quietly, following her gaze. "What's this?"

He pulled up what might have passed for a gray canvas apron and held it out for Mary to inspect. "*Northbrook Retail and Stale House*" was printed across its front.

"Think Zeke worked there for a bit, maybe up to a week or two ago. They sell day-old bread from the local bakeries. He loaded trucks or something."

"Know what happened to him?"

"No…but guessing they probably fired him or something."

Jeb tossed the apron into a mound of clothes piled behind the couch.

"I got him a nice suitcase a few years back, when he took a job down in Fayetteville. But he probably lost it long time ago." She shook her head as she considered the refuse bin Zeke called home.

The corner of a metal box peeked out from under a stack of yellowed newspapers. Jeb pulled it out to take a closer look.

"Used to keep a gun in that. Saturday Night Special he got off a guy who worked the door at a strip club over in Raleigh," Mary offered. She fingered the metal fastener where a lock had once been. "He was good 'bout keeping it locked up though. Always worried me he might use it on himself or somebody else when he got liquored up."

"Did you…see him very often?" Jeb asked.

"Tried to check on him every couple weeks," she answered as she pulled a blue flannel shirt out of one of the piles. She held it up to the light and then sniffed it.

"I see."

"Mr. Mason, Zeke was usually dead drunk anyways. Many's the time I came and went without him even knowing."

"Guess it was pretty bad, huh?"

"Pretty bad." She stuffed the shirt under her arm. "Sides, Billy didn't like it…me coming over here, I mean."

"Billy?"

"That's my old man."

"Yeah…forgot you remarried."

"Billy, he's good about some stuff. But didn't put much stock in me or Joe coming 'round here."

Jeb walked to the window. Pulled back the bedspread that served as the curtain and looked out over the rubble of a washed-out field behind the trailer.

"But he's a good man. Mean he don't hit me or Joe or nothin'. Drives a truck, so's he's gone a lot."

"Think they can sell this thing? The trailer I mean…could they get anything for it?" Jeb asked.

"Not likely," she said. "Cost more to haul it off than it's worth." She studied Jeb closely.

"You know…he talked 'bout you," she said.

"What?"

"He talked 'bout you…when he was…you know, doing all right. He talked 'bout you."

Jeb turned away.

"Always talked about Jeb. Jeb this and Jeb that." She smiled at the memory. "You and Mr. Gardner…Andy, I mean."

"Zeke was a…" He struggled for the words.

"Wish I'd a known him. Back *before*, I mean," Mary Tully continued.

"Before?"

"I don't know. Just before all the trouble came down on him, I guess." She straightened three empty Miller cans that sat on a side table, aligning them as she might a formal dining table.

"There was a lot of good in Zeke. You know that, right?" Jeb said, his voice husky.

"And he tried. Mr. Gardner…he tried, I mean…to help him." Her voice trembled suddenly. She straightened and turned toward the door. "Well, got to get back to work anyways. Sunday afternoon is kind of busy at the restaurant."

Jeb followed her out the clutter. They closed the door to Zeke Andrews's life, locked it behind them, and walked back to the cars.

"I want you to know, Mr. Mason. I appreciate what you and Mr. Gardner are doing for my Zeke." Her eyes glistened as she spoke. "He told me once. When he was crying and hurting one night. Said that you and Mr. Gardner were the best friends he ever had." She wiped at her eyes and began to turn away.

"Everybody…needs a best friend." Jeb said as he closed the car door behind her. "Thank you…for coming over here."

She smiled back at him.

He watched the Impala bounce back down Cone Trail and felt the grief well up in him. He looked back at the trailer.

"Shouldn't have ended like this, Zeke," he whispered to the stillness that suddenly surrounded him.

In the thicket of trees that lay on the other side of the road, a solitary figure watched the Camry pull away a few minutes later.

Only when it was out of sight did the figure begin to slide quietly toward the trailer.

CHAPTER THIRTY-SEVEN

Blaine McQuinn's Mustang wheeled into the Police Station parking lot on Montgomery Street. The Stacey Police Department was a three story red brick that dated back to the early 1800s. There were those that suggested the bricks went back to the 1700s, but it was difficult to prove. Its tenants could not vouch for the building materials, but were convinced the plumbing was at least that old. It sat beside the Stacey Fire Station and the firemen often strolled next door to take advantage of the canteen on the first floor.

McQuinn had an "appointment," such as it was, with Police Chief Benny Greer. It was a meeting he did not necessarily look forward to. He'd dealt with him before.

By his estimate, Greer had been Chief for at least fifteen years, and a city cop for at least ten years before that. He was a barrel with two arms and two legs who rolled easily over the local citizens in much the same manner. McQuinn knew he kept a fresh bottle of Jim Beam in his front-desk drawer. Had seen him pull a few long drags when he'd had occasion to visit the department in the past. Greer couldn't care less if people knew. He was the Police Chief.

There were rumors about Benny Greer—vague references to an incorrigible delinquency, spent as a boozer and a thug. But at some point he'd channeled those aggressive tendencies in a more positive vein, attending a police academy in his mid-twenties and soon thereafter returning to Stacey to join the force. His appointment as Police Chief came after the death of Chief Rollie Callahan. By that time Greer had built enough alliances with the political powers in Stacey to insure his selection. Local boy makes good.

McQuinn glanced down at his pocket notebook as he hustled through the front door of the department. He didn't want to be late for an appointment with Chief Greer. Truth be told, if this wasn't such a hot story, he would prefer not to be here at all. Benny Greer, in his opinion, was clearly the biggest prick in the eight-county area he covered for Channel Three.

He remembered, with almost painful clarity, the last local media visit to Stacey, some eighteen months before. The pull then was the allegations of police brutality that surfaced against two city jailers. The story had broken in the *Charlotte Observer* after a complaint was filed by two teenagers from South Carolina who were arrested for drunk driving. They were tossed into the cooler late one Saturday night, and when they were released midday on Sunday, they returned to their home state with stories of being beaten up. They had the bruises to match their story.

The piece eventually died out. One of the jailers resigned, and the other was placed on some type of administrative leave. No charges were ever formally filed.

But McQuinn vividly recalled being among the first reporters on the Monday after the story broke. Three of them were standing at the sergeant's station, demanding time with the Chief, when a bellow came from down the hall. The place fell silent and everyone turned to see Benny Greer charging down the corridor, his face a mask of blood-curdling rage. He carried a billy club in his right hand.

He screamed invectives as he approached and McQuinn remembered he flashed back to television documentaries where a great Silver Back gorilla roared and charged interlopers. On that morning, Benny Greer was the Silver Back. The three reporters, stunned by the fury of the moment, had stumbled back through the lobby and out the front door. They escaped with their skulls intact and at least one television crew had captured the moment for all posterity. It did not rank as a highlight in McQuinn's journalistic career.

The young lady who ushered him into Greer's office seemed normal enough, he thought to himself, as she invited him to sit in one of the two chairs across from a large oak desk. Behind it sat a deep-red leather chair. Adorning the walls were a variety of local, civic-oriented awards and one needlepoint plaque that read, "Our Sisters of Charity." Deep-cherry wood shelves lined the pale blue walls to the right of the desk. They clearly weren't standard department fare,

McQuinn noted. Powerful furniture that conveyed a sense of great importance. The shelves, with the exception of a few legal books, a Department of Corrections manual, and a ringed binder labeled "City Council," remained empty. Greer's desktop had nothing but a heavy glass paperweight with NASCAR written across its base. McQuinn could see his reflection in the gloss. A folded newspaper lay beside it.

He heard the booming voice from down the hall before Greer filled the doorway. McQuinn drew up all of his one hundred and fifty pounds and prepared for whatever was to come. His fingers tightened around his notebook.

He wondered if the Chief even had the slightest recollection of their earlier meeting. He suspected not. Benny Greer seemed like the type who remembered only those he deemed important. In a town like Stacey that would be very few.

But he would not be bullied. Not this time. This was a serious investigation. He had a job to do. The heavy footsteps were coming closer.

Greer burst into the room with the energy and demeanor of a rhino. He covered the few steps to the desk with several purposeful strides without glancing at his visitor. Tossing down a manila binder, he thumbed through several sticky notes he carried with him as he stood over his desk.

McQuinn took his seat. He wasn't a servant waiting for the master. He crossed his legs and calmly looked down at his watch. He guessed the Chief no more cared about the notes than he did the morning's commodities report. This was for his benefit. Even yesterday's messages were more important than the little weasel in the corner.

McQuinn pulled out his cell phone and punched in a series of numbers in rapid order.

"Marilyn? Blaine...heard anything yet from Raleigh?" He paused, listening. "OK...so what's he saying about it?"

McQuinn could feel it when Benny Greer looked up. He didn't look at him but he knew. The sticky notes had apparently lost their appeal. "Tell him National called...they're saying..."

"What in the hell are you doing?" Greer's low growl of a voice reverberated across the room. McQuinn looked up. The Chief was glaring at him. He looked bigger than last time, McQuinn thought.

"Marilyn...hold for a second." He put the phone aside. "Is there a problem, Chief?"

"Son, you plan to interview me, you better get your ass back to Stacey and stay outta Raleigh. I ain't got time to pussyfoot around with no Gawddamn reporter." Greer's temples bulged as he spat the words.

McQuinn felt the first taste of panic in the back of his throat, but he pushed it back. Not this time.

"Chief, our interview was scheduled for 3:00. It's now almost 4:30. If you want to talk to me, I'll be happy to do so. But I'm not going to sit here while you check your mail." McQuinn felt his heart begin to pound.

Where the hell did this come from?

The effect was just as startling for Greer. The scrawny, bespeck-led figure seated in front of him looked back with an almost placid expression.

"Boy, lemme tell you somethin'. You're in my office, in my town... if I say so, you'll spend your whole fuckin' day sitting here waitin'..." Greer spewed the words. He bent over the desk, roaring down at the reporter.

McQuinn felt his insides swirl and his throat go dry. "Not this time" he repeated to himself.

McQuinn stood up. He put the phone to his mouth.

"Marilyn...I'm still here..." He muttered the words.

Greer roared. He bounded from behind the desk. McQuinn braced for impact. From behind, voices shouted. Sounds of scuffling. Others had burst through the open doorway behind. Someone grabbed McQuinn. His cell phone went sailing, clattering across the floor.

A uniformed officer was suddenly dragging him away. Two others were trying to impede Greer, who wore a crimson mask of rage at the temerity of the reporter. The mayhem had spilled into the hallway, but McQuinn was only marginally aware of others converging on the scene. Someone upset his glasses with a forearm and he felt himself being carried by several people at once. He slammed into the wall as two officers pressed against him. A knot of uniforms were trying to slow Greer, who still hurled curses in the direction of the reporter. McQuinn struggled to catch his breath as others hustled the reporter down the hallway.

In the parking lot, someone handed him his glasses. They shoved the cell phone into his front pocket at the same time. The reporter trotted across the lot to the Mustang. He could still hear muffled yells from the police station. He groped clumsily for the keys. The engine sprang to life, and he careened out of the lot. The tires squealed as he gassed it.

"Damn," he muttered to no one in particular. He grabbed his cell phone. Wanted to report the story to his producer. Laughed when he realized the taped weather forecast was still playing from his call minutes earlier. "Marilyn," the recorded voice on the other end, said that the chance of late evening thunderstorms was increasing over the piedmont area. Temperatures in the low nineties.

CHAPTER THIRTY-EIGHT

Jeb's drive into Stacey was a short one. The east side of town was a maze of strip malls, worn one-story retail stores, and a few pawn shops littered between parking lots and ramshackle shacks. He smiled as he passed a hand painted sign that pointed to "Uncle Ezra's BBQ and General Merchandise." He guessed the building might have been new at the turn of the twentieth century, about the time that Uncle Ezra's barbecue was edible.

The two story brick outpost one block beyond was white washed and as faded as much of its surroundings. A gravel parking lot fronted it and a line of delivery trucks sat alongside. Each had the same name pasted on its side as the logo painted across the front of the building.

Northbrook Stale House and Retail

Jeb slowed the car as he passed. One block later he wheeled into a gas station and turned around.

• • •

"You looking to pick up a check for him, can't help ya." The man was lean and pale, with a pair of glasses that made his eyes bug out like a lizard about to snap up an errant fly. He wore a white shirt and pants, white shoes and a white hard hat. The only part of him that wasn't white was the plastic pocket protector and the series of pencils that protruded from it. The man stood behind what might pass for a preacher's podium in the very center of a cavernous room, surrounded by towering stacks of metal trays, each brimming with buns and various sizes and shapes of loaves of bread. The room buzzed with activity as the stacks moved to loading docks and far corners of the building in preparation for loading onto trucks that filled the bays.

The man in white seemed the most likely to ask about Zeke Andrews. His response was terse and he barely looked up from the sheet he appeared to be using to in some way direct the blur of activity.

"Going to have to wait and talk to the lady in personnel. Open up on Monday. 8 am. Can't help you with no check."

"No sir. Not interested in a paycheck. I was a friend of Zeke Andrews. Just back in town for his funeral. Just wanted to talk to somebody that worked with him."

"Can't help you there either. That Andrews fella only worked here month or two. Like I said, not my department."

"Anybody around here that worked with Zeke?"

The man looked up and studied Jeb.

"You don't look like no friend of Andrews. You a bill collector or somethin'?"

"No. Just a friend...from a long time ago."

"Not much of a worker." The man sniffed and returned to his checklist.

"Look, I would really appreciate it if you could point out someone who worked with Zeke. Think you could do that for me?" Jeb laid his hand across the spreadsheet and growled. "Whether he was a good worker or not. He was my friend. You get that, don't you?"

The man placed his pencil down. When he looked up a second time Jeb's countenance had changed. He didn't smile.

"Hey look, I got a job to do, Mister..."

"Understand that. Who here worked with Zeke Andrews?"

The man looked around, an exasperated expression on his face. He said, "Mebbe old Ben out in the farmer's pick up could help. I don't know. Think he talked to him more than most."

"Farmer's pick up?"

"Stale house. Old bread the hog farmers and such get by the barrel. I think they had Andrews out there."

"Appreciate it." Jeb's smile returned. The man went back to his checklist.

Old Ben was a bear of a man with whiskers the color of a wheat field and eye brows that matched. He smiled easily.

"Terrible deal…what happened to Zeke. Terrible deal," Ben said as he loaded one of the barrels onto a pair of hand trucks and rolled it toward the bay where a dilapidated Chevy truck awaited. "Liked Zeke."

"He say much…I mean, were you surprised to hear about his death?"

"Damn right I was. Damn right." Ben grunted as he shifted the barrel and began to pull the smashed loaves onto the flat bed of the truck. "Still don't make no sense to me."

"Why's that?"

"Dunno. Old boy only worked here coupla months but seemed to me he was in a good mood most of the time."

"Show up for the job? I mean, was he dependable?"

Ben grinned and said, "Look, Zeke was not what you would call the model employee but he wasn't a bad guy. Did his job."

"Was he drinking a lot?"

"Nothin' wrong with drinkin'."

Jeb let the response hang there until Ben said, "Zeke liked the bottle. Guess you know that if you're a friend of his though."

"Hadn't seen him since we were kids." Jeb picked up one of the loaves that had fallen off to the side and tossed it into the back of the truck.

"You come back just for Zeke's funeral?" Ben stopped and wiped his forehead with a pale blue handkerchief he kept tucked in his front pocket.

Jeb nodded.

"Tell you what I think. I think Zeke had his share of problems. Not a lot of bright spots 'cept maybe for two things. The first was his boy. Used to talk about that son of his all the time. Second was whiskey." Ben stuffed the handkerchief back into his pocket and continued. "But even alcohol wasn't close to that boy."

"What got him fired?"

"Huh?"

"What got him fired from this job?"

"Didn't get fired. Went up to supervisor 'bout a week and half a go and up and quit. What I heard."

"You mean he didn't lose his job. You saying he left voluntarily?"

"Came back from break and told me. Said he had something else planned. Surprised the shit out of me too."

"Was he acting differently? Seem depressed to you?"

"Hell no. Some ways, he seemed high strung maybe but definitely not depressed."

"High strung?"

"I dunno. He was weird that last week for some reason."

"But not necessarily sad."

"No, he wasn't sad." Ben returned to the hand trucks and rolled back to the next barrel, pushing the blade underneath and tilting it so the weight shifted back toward him. He grunted under the strain and said, "Scared was more like it."

"Scared?"

"Nervous. Jumpy. He came in the day before he quit and asked me if I had noticed a car or something in the parking lot. Like I said, weird."

"Was that typical? Normal for him, I mean?"

"Nope. Zeke didn't run hot. Hell, never saw him get too bent out of shape on anything. But he was like a cat in a box of snakes. Wrung out."

"Got any theories on what was on his mind?"

"Guessed he was worried 'bout getting busted. Kind of thought he was on the look-out for the law."

"The law?"

"Like I said, something sure as hell was on his mind."

Jeb gazed out at the parking lot and watched another truck round the corner and pull to a stop. The next hog farmer was in line.

"What's going to happen to that boy of his?" Ben asked.

"Couldn't say."

They watched the driver of the second truck slip out of the cab and lower the tailgate. He propped up against it and folded his arms, waiting for his turn at the trough.

CHAPTER THIRTY NINE

The storm front descending on Stacey was the result of warm, humid air rising from the ground in the hills of western North Carolina in the form of updrafts. As that air cooled to its dew point, it began condensing to form massive clouds, ice crystals, and eventually rain. The presence of unstable upper air gave the burgeoning storm greater strength, creating pockets of cold air that moved along with the upper atmosphere's winds. At that point, the continued updrafts of warm, humid air that fueled the monster collided with the falling precipitation and air being dragged down by the downdrafts. The combination insured the storm would be a violent one.

It gathered itself in a series of ominous black thunderheads that swept into town at 9:15 that evening, just as Jeb wheeled the rental into the empty parking space beside the courthouse.

He considered the towering giants as he climbed out of the car, remembering with great clarity the savage nature of the storms in the southeast. He watched the first crack of lightning lash the sky. Time for a last walk before the rain came. A last stroll along the storefronts.

After leaving Old Ben and the Northbrook stale house, Jeb had spent the rest of the day rediscovering a small town on a lazy Sunday afternoon. The highlight might have been the visit to Stacey Community Pharmacy for a hamburger and fries, an event no one in Chicago would believe. The last time he had sat at a counter with a milkshake and a burger was when he parked his bicycle outside. There were few cars. Even fewer people. Andy's invitation to dinner had been gracefully declined. He wanted some time alone. He even ignored the occasional buzz of the cell phone. For at least one last time, he would experience Stacey.

Maybe just this once, the world could wait.

At ten that night, he pulled the Camry back onto the now empty city streets to make the final trek back to the motel.

He didn't notice the other car at first. A mile out of town, when the highway straightened and the fields opened on either side, it suddenly appeared in his rearview mirror. It followed closely on his bumper, and Jeb glanced at up at it.

"Moron," he said quietly.

The car shifted and swept around him. It was an older vehicle with flaking yellow paint. A solitary occupant.

Jeb began to adjust the car radio. He was only minutes from the motel, but there was time for a last song before he turned in for the night. The humid night air blew in through the open driver's window.

The car in front suddenly slowed, and he found himself pulling off the gas pedal.

"Give me a fucking break..." he whispered under his breath. "Jackass!" he yelled as he gunned the Camry to pass the car.

In the distance, just cresting a hill, he could see the headlights of a large eighteen wheeler. But he had plenty of time and glanced in his rearview mirror before easing back over into the right lane. The other car wasn't there.

Then suddenly, there it was beside him. It had sped up to match his car's speed. There was no room to get around.

"What the hell..." Jeb muttered and floored the gas pedal. The Camry surged forward. The big rig loomed larger.

But the other automobile did not back off. The two cars screamed down the highway, two pairs of headlights cutting through the darkness.

He was not going to make it around.

Panic suddenly swept over him. He yanked his foot off the gas and began to brake. His only option was to fall behind the other car. But then the other driver was slowing their vehicle as well.

He could hear the blaring foghorn of the transfer truck as it rumbled closer.

There was no time now.

Jeb braced for impact even as he desperately whipped the steering wheel to the left. The protests of the car's tires ripped through the night, mixing with the scream of the truck's horn.

Then the car began to slide.

• • •

His fingers were still locked onto the wheel when he managed to realize where he was...and that he was still alive. He waited for the dust storm surrounding the Camry to subside before he could recognize the soybean field he was sitting in. The road was a hundred yards away and to his right. He thought he could still make out the final wail of the truck as it rumbled on in the distance.

"Damn...damn." He looked out and watched the spray of dust and rocks begin to fall away.

He tried re-cranking the car. It roared back to life.

The Camry began to slowly limp back toward the highway.

Five minutes later he pulled into the Dogwood Inn parking lot and slowly surveyed the damage, walking around the car and examining it closely. It seemed none the worse for wear, but part of the bumper was dented and there were a series of long scrapes on the left hand side.

"Stupid son of a bitch," he said to himself. "This will probably cost me a couple hundred bucks."

He knelt down and looked under the car. He could smell the engine hissing. Something was leaking onto the pavement.

"I would like to get my hands on..." He stood as the first hot drops of rain began to plop against the asphalt. The storm had finally arrived.

• • •

Jeb considered the stack of files on the table as he lay down on the bed. There was work to be done, but tomorrow's flight would give him a few hours of prep time. He used the remote to switch on the television. As the storm bellowed outside, he settled on a *Columbo* rerun. He watched the plumes of rain through the half-drawn curtain, settling into the comfort of the bed. The air conditioner in the corner rattled away, its noise drowned by the storm.

He needed to check voicemail soon, he reminded himself.

He began to doze just as Lt. Columbo began to draw the murderer into his web. And then, to dream.

In his dream, the three of them were running through a long black night, over fields swept by the intense pounding of a violent storm. Somewhere behind they could hear Zeke's screams. But they did not stop. He could hear the clang of something advancing toward them in the darkness. Pushing closer.

Jeb awoke in a frantic rush. Bathed in sweat, his heart pounding, he bolted upright, unsure at first of where he was. The storm overhead still raged. He gathered himself. "Just a dream...just a dream," he muttered to no one.

He glanced toward the window.

A figure stood there, its outline illuminated by the brilliance of the storm behind. He heard the same dull clang and recognized it was the chain lock.

Someone was trying to open the door to his room.

CHAPTER-FORTY

At that very same moment, the headlights of SBI Agents Spencer and Boller's brown Crown Victoria swept across the front of the motel as they pulled into the parking lot. Mac was anxious to get back. His oldest daughter was coming home from summer school at the University of Tennessee. She was a Resident Advisor for one of the women's dormitories and would only be home for a week before returning to Knoxville. Mac was already pissed that it looked like he might end up spending another night in the backwoods, anyway. He wanted to call Dottie and make sure Steph was home safe and sound. Seven-hour commutes for nineteen-year-olds worried him.

Boller saw the man first. Noticed the startled reaction to car lights. The sudden movement away from the door. "Check the second floor," he gestured toward the balcony.

Spencer saw him. She gassed the car. It shot across the empty lot toward the building. The man was running now. His head bent down against the blinding rain toward the stairs on the far corner.

The Crown Vic squealed to a stop. Spencer and Boller threw the car doors open. Spencer was running to the left corner of the building. Boller was heading toward the stairs just in front of them. The angle of the building gave neither a clear view of the man, but both agents surmised he would either be heading down the stairs at the far corner, or perhaps doubling back. They moved to flank him.

Spencer felt for her nine-millimeter just underneath the tan blazer. She yanked it out as she skidded to a stop at the base of the steps. A crash of thunder overhead drowned the night, and the rain pelted her as she assumed a ready stance with her pistol drawn. She cautiously swept the area, grimacing as the sheets of rain obscured her vision.

A flash of lightning and she automatically flinched, jerking the weapon around as she did so. Then from up above, heavy footsteps pounding down the stairs. She screamed, *"Hold it! Police!"*

The black figure that was careening down the stairs suddenly slammed to a stop, unsure.

"Don't you move. Don't you move," Agent Spencer repeated, her voice a coarse bark. Adrenaline rushed through her.

"Show me your hands!"

The figure didn't move.

"Show me your damn hands!" she ordered. Her hands trembled slightly, but the gun was pointed squarely at the chest of the man.

"D-don't shoot...don't shoot." The man was raising his hands slowly.

"Step forward. Get on the ground. Keep your hands up!" she ordered. Her training was taking over.

The man willingly obliged. He stretched out face first on the wet pavement, his hands spread out.

Agent Boller yelled from above. He was coming down the stairs, his pistol also drawn. Shauna Spencer kept her gun aimed at the man.

"I've got him! I've got him!" she yelled. Boller rounded the corner cautiously, his weapon pointed on the prone figure. His steely gaze gave way to a grin.

Agent Spencer stepped forward now. She cuffed the man, and then patted him down. He was cursing, but remained still. Boller swept the area a second time.

"Wanna tell me what you were up to, sir?" Spencer stood. He was clean.

The man rolled to his side. He looked up as the agents holstered their guns. His face was drenched, as were his khaki shorts. Bits of gravel were splattered over the side of his face. Spencer thought the face seemed familiar.

"Yeah, I'll tell you what I was doing...I was trying to catch some asshole who was trying to break into my room," Jeb Mason spat the words, "before you two idiots got in my way!"

CHAPTER FORTY-ONE

Roy Yates took off his reading glasses and rubbed his bloodshot eyes. He poured himself a third cup of coffee and tossed the cardboard box onto the table. It was going to be a long night. He'd thought about taking his girlfriend Lou to the movies, but reconsidered at the last moment. She was a clerk of court and would need to be at work early tomorrow. And if he saw one more mafia movie he figured he'd be sick. Besides, it wasn't a good night. She was leaving for the Ladies Club meeting in Raleigh on Monday afternoon along with half the women in Stacey, it seemed. Designated drivers needed plenty of sleep.

Dating was, at best, a pleasurable ordeal. He had managed to finally re-enter that portion of society after considerable coaxing from friends. When Linda passed away six years earlier, so too did a big part of Roy Yates. The last year of her life had been a blur of hospitals and clinics, strange sounding specialists' titles and constant medical tests.

On that dreary October day he lost her, there were no doctors at her side. No other family. Just Roy. Holding on until the last moment.

Lou was an old friend. He'd known her since they were both kids, and she helped fill the emptiness. But even after eight months of dating, Yates found the whole thing pretty damn uncomfortable. There was something about the formality of it all that he did not quite get. The notion of courting was not natural—not in his book.

It was on nights like this that Linda's absence was the most unbearable. When the storms passed through town on hot summer winds, rattling the buildings with their fury. Or when the storms of life, the ones that ripped old friends like Bump away, whirled through with the same rage. Yates wondered at how seldom they both seemed to arrive together, as they had this time.

He glanced over at the aging Kenmore refrigerator, listened to the quiet purring of the electric motor. The small magnetic sticker near the top read "I Love You" in the shape of a heart. They bought it on a trip to Myrtle Beach when they were newlyweds, thirty-one years ago. The magnet still held its attraction, though he wondered if at some point, it might just fall to the floor. He fingered its outline and prayed that it wouldn't. He allowed himself to linger there a few seconds.

Stacey was a small town, pretty much a rest area for people headed across the state. That was true enough. But it had its share of big city problems too. Not the drugs and gangs that so infiltrated the large metropolitan areas, but more than its quota of meanness. There were at least two crack houses that had been in operation at some point in the county over the last several years. Transplants that preferred the more rural setting to the hustle and bustle of Charlotte, and the prying eyes of local law enforcement there.

Theft was on the rise, too. The four major department stores in Stacey had all reported break-ins over the last eighteen months, an unparalleled wave of crime for that city. Though this fell under Chief Greer's jurisdiction, it affected Yates all the same. Besides, Greer couldn't find his gun in an empty room, the way Roy Yates figured it. The sheriff had known Benny Greer since he was a boy. Had watched the hulking adolescent grow from a loud, bullying teenager to a louder, abrasive adult. Four years in the military had only honed those instincts. When he came back to Stacey and applied to become a police officer to then Chief Callahan, Yates shuddered. Nothing in the years since had dampened his opinion.

Roy Yates picked up the arson investigation file he had begun on Steadman. Inside was a separate manila file that outlined the circumstances surrounding Bump's death. Both were sparse and had been built by piecing together separate conversations with the firemen on the scene, investigation officers, Malcolm Lindsey, Dr. Carter, Bump's family, and a very short meeting with the two SBI agents.

Technically, neither of the agents was under any obligation to talk to the county sheriff, and whatever dialogue had taken place so far had been primarily with Greer's office. Yates knew that Benny Greer would rather place a collect call to a terrorist cell in the Middle East than reach out to the sheriff for help. So for now, Yates would conduct his own private investigation.

Though something of a patchwork operation, Yates's records were concise and objective. He'd developed the habit years ago of jotting down copious notes from his interviews with the principals involved at the crime scene, along with his own observations. He kept a wire-rimmed pocket notebook for each. He believed it was critical to keep separate his interviews and his personal assessments. One could color the other.

Now he was meticulously pulling the pages from each and placing them in the appropriate file. It was a laborious process, but one that he loved. It was disciplined. It helped to create a sense of order to situations that were often chaotic and confused. Yates deductive approach also helped him to assimilate things, to build in his own mind a balance between fact and opinion. Eventually, he thought, when he'd built enough facts, he'd start to consider the one point that bothered him most.

Motive.

He read back through his records of his tortuous conversation with Ilene Patterson. Though he'd not been so crass as to make notes as he tried to console the family, he'd made sure to write everything down afterwards. The nature of the call that pulled Bump from the TV over to Steadman, the estimated time, past problems with break-ins; whether, even Bump ever carried a weapon. Though he couldn't bring himself to broach the subject with Ilene, he did pull Bobby Patterson aside and asked him whether Bump had any known enemies or perhaps consorted with people who did. Even asked him about possible drug trafficking. Bobby's pained expression and look of disappointment in Yates felt like a blade. Roy Yates knew all too well that whatever circumstances led to Bump Patterson's murder, they were not of his doing.

He flipped the papers, turning to his notes earlier that day of his conversation with Principal Lindsey. His eyes scanned the list of materials and supplies from the Steadman administrative offices. For a long while he studied them.

At around 11:00 p.m., Yates closed his file. He considered the cup of cold coffee he had long since forgotten. Outside, the remnants of the storm still rumbled in the distance. He glanced out the window of his tidy one story frame home and watched the last flashes of lightning on the horizon.

The coffee begged to be warmed. He obliged, entering his kitchen with the cup in hand, but reminded himself to turn off the pot. No need for more fires in Stacey, he thought.

When he returned, he stood at the small roll-top desk he used as an office at home. The bills and various miscellaneous mail stuffed into the slots of the faded oak were a constant annoyance to Yates. County sheriffs were not highly paid, after all.

He pushed the Patterson file aside and breathed a long sigh. For the first time, he looked at the second file he'd carried home that evening. The second death in his county in the last five days. The taped tab at the top read "Zeke Andrews."

Yates laid the Andrews file beside Patterson's. For several long moments he stood there.

He placed his cup aside, forgetting for a second time about the coffee.

CHAPTER FORTY-TWO

Mac Boller had a hard time stifling a chuckle as he helped Jeb Mason to his feet. He'd spent too many years in police work not to recognize that the rain-drenched man in front of him was probably not the same one they'd seen running across the second floor catwalk. This guy was muscular, leaner. He looked more like a salesman on the way to the concession machine. Well-trimmed head of hair, nice watch—looked like a Tag Heuer. No shoes. No shirt. Unless the perp had managed to shuck his clothes over a fifteen-second time frame, this wasn't the guy.

His partner was doing her best to apologize to the man, brushing the gravel and grime off as she uncuffed him. Boller thought the conversation, abrupt at first, had taken a decided turn for the better when the guy had gotten a better look at Shauna. There were worse fates than being detained by his attractive junior partner, after all.

Jeb's anger had indeed undergone a bit of a transformation, though he was still pissed at the notion of being arrested outside his own motel room. He vaguely remembered the girl who had just threatened to shoot him. She was the pretty jogger he'd seen on the steps the night before. He was sure of it. Her demeanor was markedly different now, though. All business. Contrite, perhaps, but all business, Jeb thought.

"We saw a male running across the second floor walkway, Mr. Mason," she explained. A quick check of Jeb's identification and cross-check with the front desk had confirmed Mason was a registered guest.

Boller excused himself to double check the back of the building. The chance of apprehending anyone, some ten minutes after the incident, was virtually impossible. Whoever it was had plenty of time to slip into the rainy darkness. But a check of the parking lot wouldn't be a bad idea, either.

"We had a pretty good idea the guy was up to no good," Shauna Spencer continued.

Jeb considered her as she spoke. Early-to-mid-thirties, around five foot five or five foot six, well built, athletic with short, brown hair. Pretty eyes, he thought to himself. Stacey's police force was much more impressive than he remembered.

"What exactly did you see, Mr. Mason?"

The two still stood in the exact spot where Agent Spencer had ordered Jeb to the ground. The pelting rain had reduced both to the point that they resembled drowning victims. Neither moved toward the shelter of the overhang a few scant feet away.

"I think I saw someone trying to get into my room. I was asleep on the bed. Heard something. That's all." Jeb's voice was louder, he thought, than normal. He could taste the rain and it mixed with his sweat and adrenaline as he spoke.

"Where's your room?" She watched his reaction. Registered guest or not, there was still every possibility that something other than a burglary had gone down, and that this guy was involved in some way. Small motels were notorious for drug trafficking. Neutral ground. Safe meeting place.

He gestured in the general direction, glancing above. "Room 217… up there."

"Why don't we take a look?" she offered. Standing aside, she allowed Jeb to lead the way back up the stairs. Since it seemed more like a command than a request, and since she still had that a big gun underneath her tan blazer, Jeb considered it a good time to show her his room.

Shauna watched as he climbed the stairs. She recognized him. Blue-polo-guy from before. Nice smile, clean shaven. No wedding ring. Professional maybe. Tad more affluent of a look than normal Dogwood Inn customers. She watched him bound up the stairs. He works out, she thought to herself. His tanned legs were muscular.

CHAPTER FORTY-THREE

Room 217 was some forty rooms down the walkway, approximately one hundred seventy-five to two hundred feet from the stairwell. A long distance for a solitary runner, she thought. The perp hadn't taken the first stairwell he'd come to, but instead continued around to the back of the building, where he either had taken the next set of stairs that exited to the back parking lot or perhaps even entered into another sleeping room.

"Damn...," Jeb muttered as he reached the door. "My keys are still inside." He looked through the glass window. Another flash of lightning illuminated the room.

Standing beside him, Shauna Spencer scanned the room in those few seconds. Blue shirt tossed across a chair. Suit bag stored in one corner. The bathroom counter in the back of the room littered with various toiletries. A white towel tossed across the faucet. She could see a dark blue sports coat hung in a corner in the far right of the room, along with other shirts and slacks. Typical businessman's room, she thought to herself. The television's glare blanketed the room in a pulsating stream of color.

"You say you were asleep?" Shauna continued to peer inside.

"Yeah...just dozing, really." Jeb continued to feel for his keys in his khaki shorts, even though they lay in full view on the table beside his bed, as if in some way a second set might suddenly materialize.

"How long had you been in the room?" Shauna's tone remained official, which was somewhat irritating to Jeb. She might be cute, but empathy didn't appear to be her strong suit.

"Maybe an hour. I'm not sure." Jeb wondered what the questioning was all about. The guy had gotten away, anyway.

He looked over at Spencer and watched her intently gazing into the room. Her hair was matted to her head. Rain dripped from her chin. She didn't answer.

"What kind of policeman are you?" he asked.

She seemed not to notice his question, but then without looking toward him, reached inside her blazer and pulled a brown leather wallet. She snapped it open. "I'm not a policewoman, Mr. Mason. I'm a State Bureau of Investigation agent." She turned her blue eyes on him now.

"You guys generally work Dogwood Inns?" Jeb focused on her name. Shauna Spencer. The photo didn't do her justice.

"No sir. We don't."

For the first time, Jeb smiled. Shauna smiled back. It was a pretty good bet this guy wasn't involved in funny business. The room was clearly a businessman's. One who had the misfortune of running into a pretty bold burglar, she thought. "See anybody around, in the parking lot or lobby, when you came in, Mr. Mason?"

"No, and my name's Jeb," he answered. Maybe she wasn't so stiff after all.

"Carrying anything that might attract a thief's attention?" She turned back toward the room. A sheet of rain splattered against them. They both shivered. The adrenaline had started to wane.

"Not unless they're really into Bass Weejuns or Drakkor after-shave," he answered. What the hell was an SBI agent doing here at the Dogwood Inn? And who was the chubby older guy? Where had he disappeared to?

She suspected Jeb Mason was nothing more than unwitting victim. But something still bothered her. "You say you were asleep. Something woke you up?" She looked at the bedspread, still in place across the bed.

"Yeah...I was just napping."

"What was it that woke you up?" Her tone suggested she'd converted back over to official "agentese" Jeb thought.

"Dunno...just woke up." He tried to remember the swirl of events. Couldn't exactly.

"Think back. I mean when you heard somebody at your door. Did you get up and pull the curtains open?" Shauna looked at him closely.

"No, just looked up. I could see a silhouette of somebody opening the door."

"You mean they were actually coming in?"

"Yeah...they were." Jeb's memory was suddenly vivid. "It was the chain lock. The door hit the chain lock. That's what woke me up. I heard the door hit it...then there was a flash of light in the room. Car lights, maybe."

"That was our car's lights," Shauna responded. "We saw someone at this door. When our headlights swept across the second floor, it spooked 'em. They started to run."

"I just remember yelling. Jumping up from the bed, running toward the door."

"Can I ask you, Mr. Mason? What were you planning to do?" Shauna asked.

Jeb smiled again. He hadn't really considered the potentially dramatic outcome of a face-to-face meeting with the intruder. At the time, it seemed like the appropriate course of action.

"This guy might have been armed. Might want to rethink the Jean Claude Van Damme stuff next time, Jeb." Her tone was not quite chiding, but close, he thought. But it did seem like pretty good advice after all.

Shauna considered Mason's muscular torso. Not much of a match for a bullet, she thought. Privately though, there was a certain admiration for the guy. He didn't seem the type to hide underneath the bed. You try to break into his room, you better be ready for a fight. Looked like he could handle himself.

Shauna's reproach accepted, Jeb asked, "So what do you think this guy was after?"

Agent Spencer shook her head. Something wasn't right. She contemplated whether to say anything. She looked at him closely. "It's a little funny, Mr. Mason." She lapsed into the formal tones again. "Most motel thieves are small time operators. Come in when the victims are out or else when they're in the shower. Maybe even when they're asleep, under the cover of darkness. But very seldom a direct confrontation."

"Yeah...so?" Jeb wasn't sure where she was going with this.

"This guy...was pretty bold. You can clearly see into the room, even from here. No jewelry or valuables visible." Shauna's tone was serious now. They both considered the sparsely decorated room.

"He could see you lying on the bed, apparently asleep," she went on. "If you woke up, there was a good chance you'd see him."

"What are you thinking, Ms. Spencer?" Jeb's interest had begun to build.

"Not sure. Guess I'm wondering whether this guy was here to rob you at all."

Shauna's words echoed in the rain. They watched the room grow bright and then darken in the distant glow of the storm.

CHAPTER FORTY-FOUR

Monday, July eighteenth began as a sweltering furnace. The humidity created by the previous evening's storms promised a sticky, shirt-stuck-to-your-chest type of day.

Jeb rose early. His night, when at last it settled down, had been a short one. He slipped into his jogging attire and made a beeline for the Camry. He noticed the brown Crown Victoria parked down the row and gave some thought to Shauna Spencer and the fireworks the night before. As he cranked his rental, he took the time to glance around the parking lot.

Crime has come to Mayberry, he thought to himself.

He jogged the same course again, passing by Clarence's, but this time there was no sign of Mr. Parker. On the way back to the motel, he checked in with Bonnie.

The real world was moving along briskly, it seemed.

"Want me to go ahead and book your flight tonight?" Bonnie asked. He could hear the steady drum of office activity in the background.

"No...I'll take care of it myself," Jeb answered. He missed the hands-free capability of his own car as he struggled to balance the cell between his chin and shoulder.

"OK...do you actually know *how* to book your own flights, Jeb?"

"Yes, Miss Smart-Ass, I do." He guessed it couldn't be that difficult.

"Hmmm...OK then." Bonnie laughed. "And you had better call Larry O'Grady. You know how he gets."

"I'll call him, I'll call him."

"Jeb?..." Bonnie paused. "I'm sorry about your friend."

"Thanks. You'll probably see me tomorrow."

"Do yourself a favor, Jeb Mason," Bonnie answered. "Spend enough time to make the trip worth it."

"You know how tough it is to take time away."

"Yes…and the world will come to an end if you don't come back immediately," Bonnie interrupted. "You went back for a reason, Jeb."

Jeb clicked the phone shut. Bonnie was a lot smarter than the whole bunch of them, he thought to himself.

• • •

The Dogwood Inn exercise room met his low expectations, but Jeb managed to complete some semblance of a workout and returned to his room feeling reinvigorated. He again glanced over to where the Crown Victoria had been parked as he walked back to his room. The space was empty.

The hot shower felt good. For a time he stood there letting the water pound against him, drinking in its warmth. There were still tiny fragments of gravel in his forearm from the previous evening's festivities, and he smiled at the image of the confrontation with Agent Spencer and her partner.

As he finished shaving, he found himself studying his reflection in the fogged mirror. Early forties, a success by most people's standards, in good health, with a number of friends back in Chicago. Life was good.

His divorce from Melissa seemed like an eternity ago. They were too much alike at the time. Two young professionals on the rise who actually believed they could blend two fast-paced lifestyles into one successful marriage. But he'd lost track of her in the last several years, though a mutual friend in New York called a few months back to say she'd married a real estate mogul in the Hamptons. She probably finally had that penthouse address in Manhattan they used to talk about on the rainy Sunday mornings they spent in bed. It hadn't been a bad marriage. The parting had been amicable. But there were times when he thought of her, even now.

His relationships in the years since had never hinted at a long-term commitment. The last breakup, with a Northwestern University mathematics professor, had ended two months before, at a tearful candlelight dinner during the second bottle of cabernet. The life of a confirmed bachelor was not without heartache.

He straightened his dark red tie and gave a second glance in the mirror. Yeah, life was good, he told himself. He had turned the page on this sleepy little mill town long ago. He seldom made it a habit to thumb through old chapters.

CHAPTER FORTY-FIVE

Jeb was perusing the *Stacey Star*'s account of the Steadman Elementary fire investigation when Andy's BMW screeched to a stop in front of the lobby. Jeb nodded to Earle, the front desk manager, whose mid-morning snooze had been interrupted by the Bimmer's arrival as he bounded out the door.

"Old boy, let's get this thing over with." Andy's tone was light, but emphatic.

"You still want to run out by the Tully's house?" Jeb asked as Andy wound through the gears, the BMW stretching its legs on the open highway.

"Got to. Promised Harold Flannery I would have Mary sign the rights to burial mumbo jumbo forms. And we gotta do it before we get to the cemetery."

"Damn...they were divorced," Jeb countered. "What's her signature count for?"

"Dunno...Flannery just said he needed the forms before the hearse left the funeral home, which means 12:45. Harold Flannery is a lot of things, but he ain't never late. Trust me."

"And Mary can't just give him the signed forms at the cemetery?"

"Nope. Harold's a stickler for protocol, Jeb. The guy probably has to fill out a dozen forms in triplicate before he takes a crap."

"We got to run by the police station before I leave this evening," Jeb said as they sped past one of the endless fields of soybeans.

"What's that?" Andy turned down the radio for a second.

"Had a little excitement last night..." Jeb began. He relayed the story of the attempted break-in.

"Holy shit, Jeb. I've never heard of anything like that out there!" Andy exclaimed afterwards. "So did those agents...did they get a look at him?"

"Not good enough. Brief glimpse. Headlights caught him for a second. Then he was off."

"Let me tell you something. Even in small towns shit happens, old buddy. Couple nights ago we had our burglar alarm go off when we were out to dinner. Got a call from our alarm company. When we were kids, this kind of stuff..." Andy shook his head in disgust.

"Get you a license to pack heat, man. Concealed weapons, that's the big thing in Chicago."

"Maybe we need to get you on that plane after all," Andy said. "Since you got to town, we've had one murder, one arson, and one attempted break-in. Maybe you're just bad luck."

"Maybe it's just safer in Chicago." Jeb chuckled and considered the sweeping fields of green as they flew by. He looked back at his friend and said, "Tell me something. What's going to happen to Zeke's son... will he be OK?"

"Hard to say. His mama loves him. Mary told me once that she wanted him to keep Zeke's last name. Guess that means her new husband never adopted him."

"Grow up never knowing his old man. Except maybe for the shit."

"He has a home, Jeb. He has a home."

"And he'll hear for the rest of his life how his dad was a drunk and a good-for-nothing."

"Small town, Jeb. Not many secrets."

The two men fell silent. The sounds of the highway and the low whine of the engine filled the void.

CHAPTER FORTY-SIX

Mayor Preston Wehunt tapped his pencil against the side of the faded green radiator in the corner of the Stacey Barbershop and listened to the debate that raged between Hank Lawson and Scooter Carp, two battle-hardened veterans of similar disputes for the past fifty years.

The shop was situated at the base of a narrow stairwell in a side alley off of Dekalb Street, with one broad window that opened onto the damp concrete wall that bordered the steps' decline. It was a gopher's hole of an establishment that had served the grooming needs of almost every male Stacey resident since 1956. On this Monday morning, the shop was alive with activity with all three barber chairs occupied and each of the nine waiting spots filled.

Wehunt had pulled a box used for some of the cleaning supplies into a corner so he could partake of the conversation but not take up a waiting chair. Hank and Scooter were funny about that when business was good. Everybody in town knew front row tickets would be in order today. The sound of clippers and conversation mixed easily with the sweet smell of hair tonic and aftershave. And old Hank was in rare form.

"Mark my words. They going to find out was gangs. Heard one of the firemen said there was a gang sign on one of the walls." Hank spoke to the room at large, occasionally glancing down at the well-carved head of the man in his chair as he addressed his audience.

"That's bullshit." Scooter studied the side burns of twelve-year-old Chris Miller as he spoke, carefully measuring the length with a well-placed thumb and comb. Chris' father, engrossed in a *National Geographic* that looked to be early '70s vintage, glanced up and grinned, then returned to the article on Solutrian tools of early Homo sapiens in middle Europe.

"Bullshit? Bullshit? You telling me gangs are not moving this way?" Hank paused, the straight razor suspended in mid-air over his patron's face, half of which was still covered by a thick dollop of hot shaving cream.

"I'm saying those gangs got better places to be than Steadman Elementary, is all I'm saying." The side burns met the comb test perfectly. Scooter glanced up at one of the men waiting and said, "Clinton, your Alice going to the Ladies' Club meeting?"

"Let me tell you something. We sit around and let them gangs come to town, we got a problem." Hank ignored the side parry from his long time partner. "Pretty soon we going to have 'em roving the streets. Wait and see."

There was a general grumble of what might've been consent from the waiting customers, though only a few looked up from their magazine of choice as they did.

"Brett Hampton said they just poured gasoline over Bump Andrews's head and set him afire. That's what he said," Hank's customer said. He glanced up to check the proximity of the straight razor as he spoke.

"There you go. Damn fire chief says they burned him alive," Hank added. "Now you tell me, what does that say?"

"Don't say nothing about no gangs." Scooter slapped a generous portion of hair tonic over Chris Miller's head. The boy tweaked his nose and smirked as the halo of the smell engulfed him.

"Course it does. Old Bump just walked in on 'em."

"So why didn't they just shoot him? Or stab him? Thought all of 'em carried guns or knives..." Scooter carefully brushed the few remaining hairs from the bib that covered the boy before signaling Chris's dad to take his place.

"My point is, they didn't know what they were doing. Hamp said the way they went 'bout it was stupid. Professional would know better. They panicked. Just thought of the meanest thing they could think of. If they had stabbed him or something, been easy to figure out. Am I right, Malcolm?"

Principal Malcolm Lindsey sat in the chair farthest to the right and directly in front of Hank, who had cut his hair since its first trim fifty-plus years before.

"Hank, I don't know about gangs. Doesn't seem to make much sense to me, either." He shifted in his chair, picked the wrinkled copy of the *Stacy Star* that lay propped against the chair beside him, tucked behind a yellowed *Sports Illustrated*.

Roy Yates sat in the third barber's chair, his tight buzz cut made even tighter after the electric razor of Petey Lawson, Hank's oldest, had been run over his head several times. Same routine every other week for what seemed like forever. Petey spun the chair around so the sheriff could inspect his handiwork, as if this week's cut in some way did not resemble the one thousand that preceded it. Yates nodded and began to climb out of the chair.

"Might be a gang but I'm guessing a simple robbery that went bad. Old Bump just walked in on 'em," Yates said. "Bastard decided to kill him."

"So," Preston Wehunt shifted his weight on the box. His left leg was beginning to numb. "What kind of leads have you got, Roy?"

"Nary a one. Nary a one." Yates brushed his tan uniform off, studying his lean form in the mirror and handing Petey a ten dollar bill, thirty percent of which was tip.

"How can that be, Sheriff?" Wehunt asked. His constituency was watching, and it was important that his was the voice of the citizenship.

"Not just as easy as dusting for prints and going out and grabbing somebody, Preston. Let's let the investigation take its course. We'll get 'em. Got to be a little patient, though."

"How much will it take to build the school back?" the man in Hank's chair asked. He rubbed the slick sides of his freshly shaved jaw. "How long to do it?" He looked back toward Principal Lindsey, who was now reading the lead article in the *Star* a second time.

"Can't say. Got some people coming down from Raleigh and a few contractors down Charlotte way. Let's put it this way, we could buy a lot of books, pay a lot of teachers, for what it will cost this county," Lindsey replied.

"Benny Greer says it was more than likely Bump who started it. Maybe a cigarette or something." It was an older man speaking. His hand rested on a cane that he used to occasionally tap on the floor.

"Benny Greer..." Roy Yates paused, collected himself. "Chief Greer is *mistaken*. Bump Patterson hadn't taken a puff on even a cigar in over ten years. Know that for a fact." Standing close to him, Petey Lawson could see the veins in Yates's temples bulging. The room grew quieter.

"Malcolm, like to be there when those folks from Raleigh come down to talk to you 'bout the school. Think that would work?" Preston Wehunt said.

Malcolm Lindsey nodded. "The *Star* says, 'State officials indicate the likelihood of arson is very high,' and 'Patterson's body will undergo a full autopsy with complete findings to be announced over the next several weeks.'" He slowly folded the paper, placing it back behind the *Sports Illustrated* a second time. "Never thought this little town would see something like this."

"You think Patterson had something to do with it, Malcolm? He worked for you all these years," one of the men said. A few heads turned to Yates as the question lingered in the air.

Lindsey glanced toward the sheriff before he said, "No, I'd buy gangs before I bought that."

Wehunt stood up and stretched his legs. His pipe clattered out of his pocket and bounced on the red and black tiles, landing on the fringe of auburn hair that remained from young Chris Miller's visit to Scooter's chair. He bent down and returned it to his pocket.

"Time I get back to business," Wehunt announced. His hardware store was a half-block away. He looked back over to Roy Yates. "Imagine quite a few people will be going to old Bump's funeral, Sheriff."

Roy Yates nodded. "'Spect so. I'll walk out with you, Mayor. Got me another funeral to take care of right now. Petey here's got me all spruced up."

CHAPTER FORTY-SEVEN

Billy and Mary Tully lived three-and-a-half miles past Big Pete's. A one-hundred-foot metal sign of a cowboy with an oscillating hand announced the truck stop long before travelers passed it, and the grand parking lot was already full of drivers pulling in for their midday meal.

The Tully house had a ranch style, with a sun-bleached fence that separated it from a soybean field on one side and a renovated car repair shop on the other. A rusted-out Mustang sat on blocks out front, as did the front-end of the shell of what was once an old Ford pickup. The grass was overgrown and several cement blocks served as steps to the front door.

Mary Tully answered the door in her bathrobe with curlers still in her hair. She quickly welcomed them, even as she hurried back into the house.

"Had to work the breakfast shift at Pete's," she called over her shoulder. "One of our girls had a big hangover from the weekend so we were short-handed...give me a minute!"

Andy pulled out the Flannery papers. He walked over to a small dining table and began to carefully lay them out. Jeb's eyes wandered around the house. It was neater than he would have guessed from looking at the outside. A cozy fireplace in the corner of the room with bookshelves on either side. A pale yellow sofa with a coffee table in front.

He saw Joe sitting in front of a small television on the other side of the room. The boy was slowly thumbing through a book, pausing at certain points and allowing his fingers to caress the page. Jeb couldn't tell if he was reading or simply looking at the pages, but it was clear his attention was undivided.

Jeb walked closer. The boy looked up. He didn't smile but a spark of recognition seemed to stir in his dark, brooding eyes.

"Hello there, Joe," Jeb offered. "I met you yesterday. My name's Jeb Mason...I was a good friend of your father's."

The boy didn't answer, and only looked back at Jeb blankly.

"What are you looking at there?" Jeb asked.

The boy looked down at the book in his hands, then back to Jeb. "It's a baseball encyclopedia...my Daddy gave it to me," he answered in a tone that was scarcely above a whisper. He held it up for Jeb's inspection.

"Well now...not sure I've seen one of these for a while." Jeb knelt down to take a closer look. It was a Major League Encyclopedia. "You a baseball player?"

"Sometimes..." the boy looked down again. "I'm not that good," he said quietly.

"Oh, I bet you're pretty good. How old are you?"

"Nine," he answered. "My birthday was February fourth."

"Well, you're the right age to start..."

Mary burst back into the room, pen in hand. "Joe, you ready to go?" she asked, and the boy nodded. "We got your daddy's funeral to go to, Honey." She walked briskly to the table where Andy had the papers prepared for her signature. Her tone was so factual that Jeb felt himself shiver. Brush your teeth, put on a clean shirt, clean your room, go to your daddy's funeral.

"Joe and I were just talking baseball, Mrs. Tully," Jeb offered.

"Call me Mary. Everybody else does." She smiled as she started scribbling her signature. She and Andy hunched over the kitchen table and attempted to decipher the Harold Flannery Bill of Rights.

Jeb turned his attention back to Joe. The boy glanced at him, and then pointed to a photograph in the book. "Know who that is?" he asked.

"Sure do...that's Mickey Mantle, number seven for the New York Yankees!"

"My daddy said he was the greatest baseball player in the world," Joe offered, his big brown eyes wide with excitement.

"Well, we all thought so, anyway..." Jeb grinned. "You know, you're a very bright young man, Joe."

"My daddy was a baseball player...did ya know that?"

"Well, I seem to recall your daddy playing some baseball. Joe, we were friends when we were little...when we were boys. I bet you didn't know that did you?"

The boy considered him carefully. He didn't answer, only returned to the book and began to slowly turn the pages. Across the room Andy and Mary were now into the third page of the Flannery Files. Progress seemed laborious.

"You wanna see my toys?" Joe asked. He seemed to regard Jeb with a curious look.

"Why sure, Joe. Lead the way!" Jeb smiled easily.

The adults didn't take notice as they slipped down a carpeted hall-way to a small bedroom, decorated with bright blue wallpaper that con-sisted of cowboys and Indians engaged in some wild exchange among desert mountains and rolling hills. A faded picture of Mark McGuire was taped to the door. Matchbox trucks were scattered across a small bureau, and a toy box extended from the window to a small dresser in the far left corner. It lay open. An assortment of balls, plastic guns, and stuffed animals crowded over the top.

"Look at this." Joe tugged a G.I. Joe from the box. "Know what his name is?" he asked.

"Hmmm..." Jeb paused. "Joe?"

"Nope...Freddy. I named him after a rabbit I used to have. He's dead now."

"I see." Jeb smiled. "It's a good name."

"Wanna play?" Joe seemed to smile for the first time.

"Yeah, sure. What do we play?"

"Dunno. What do you usually play?"

"Well...let's see." Jeb tried to remember the last time he'd played anything. "Just about anything I guess. What do *you* usually play?"

"Well..." the boy scanned the room. "Can you play Monopoly? It's easy." Jeb felt a slight concession was being made for him.

Joe's interpretation of the board game's rules varied somewhat from Milton Bradley's, but they had successfully set up the game when Andy's call from the den interrupted them. The signatures were com-plete. It was time to head out.

"Wanna see my car pictures?" Joe asked, reluctant to let his new playmate slip away easily.

"Yeah, buddy, but I gotta go."

"It's OK." Joe jumped up and pulled a step chair from underneath his bed. He carried it to the closet, put his baseball encyclopedia on top, and then climbed on it. Stretching as far as he could, he reached into a far corner of the upper shelf and uncovered a small cigar box. He handled it with great care as he carried it to the bed.

"Look at this."

Inside were clipped magazine photos of dozens of sport and exotic automobiles, each carefully snipped so that the edges were straight. Jeb whistled in appreciation.

"These are cool pictures, Joe. Where'd you get 'em?" Jeb thumbed through them, treating each with appropriate deference.

"Me and Daddy used to cut them out. It's what we'd do on boy weekends."

Jeb assumed that meant the time that Zeke enjoyed visitation with his son, if in fact the court had ever granted him that. The probability was greater that the time with Joe had been approved by Mary, rather than by any judge.

There were glossy photos of Porches, Mercedes, Ferraris, and an occasional Corvette. Joe pointed to a jet-black 'vette. He grinned broadly. "Daddy was gonna buy this one," he whispered.

"Was he now?"

"Yes." The boy looked up. "But don't nobody know 'bout it."

"Was it a secret?" Jeb asked.

"Yeah…it was a secret. Just me and Daddy knew 'bout it."

Jeb could find no words to offer in response. He dutifully studied each picture, and then handed them back to Joe, who replaced them with great care. Underneath the photos was a small plastic container of glue. The bottom of the box was carpeted with snippets of words and letters that looked like they also had been clipped from a magazine or a newspaper.

Jeb picked up one of the pieces of paper. It read "window." He pushed through the pile. Just random words and letters. Crumpled in a corner was a piece of paper with more words glued onto it.

"What's this, Joe?" Jeb looked at the boy, who was still immersed in the cars.

"Daddy's ticket," the boy answered.

"His ticket? What do you mean, Joe?" Jeb asked.

"His Towel Seed ticket," he answered plainly, "…for the new car. Daddy was going to be rich."

CHAPTER FORTY-EIGHT

Jeb looked again at the pile of clipped pieces. Joe had turned his attention to the rolled up copy of the *Stacey Star* that Jeb had carried with him, and he began to lay some of the cutout photographs onto the newspaper as he spread it out over his bed. The boy seemed lost in his gallery of automobiles.

Jeb thumbed through the various snippets. Just miscellaneous words or paragraphs with no rhyme or order. In one corner was a crumpled page that had been torn from a *Car and Driver* magazine. It was an article on a Porsche 911 with a photo from a recent test drive. But huge chunks had been clipped away.

It seemed an odd pastime. Jeb wondered if depression and alcoholism had taken such a heavy toll on his old friend that mindless games like this had served as a source of relief from the pain. It made no sense.

He looked back at the boy, who now sat Indian-style with the newspaper spread out in front of him. He held a magic marker and was studying the pages closely.

"Joe…what are you looking for?"

"Right words…" he murmured, but he didn't look up.

"The right words?"

Joe nodded. "I'm a good reader. I could find them before Daddy a lot of times."

"What do you mean, the right words?"

"The right words. Daddy couldn't see so good." The boy paused and began to circle a part of the text. "And I'm a good reader."

"Joe, would you mind if I took your daddy's ticket stuff with me? I would like to maybe borrow it for just a little while. Would that be OK?"

The boy considered him closely. He put the photographs down and walked back to the closet, clambering back onto the chair. He pulled a brown envelope out from underneath several quilts that were folded on the top shelf. He handed it to Jeb.

"S'posed to carry the ticket in this," he said.

Jeb's face wrinkled in puzzlement.

"Why's that, Joe?" The envelope seemed heavier than he would expect.

"Nobody's s'posed to know 'bout the ticket," he answered.

"Jeb, gotta ride, man. You guys having a party or what?" Andy popped his head around the corner.

"Huh, no. Ready to go, ready to go," Jeb answered.

He dumped the bottom of the box's contents into the envelope and then turned to the boy, who was meticulously refolding the newspaper.

"Thanks, Joe. I'll see you in a coupla hours, OK?"

"OK." Joe smiled in return. His brown eyes were so hauntingly similar to Zeke that Joe found himself wanting to stay, to talk to him longer.

Andy watched his friend carefully fold a brown envelope and place it in his blue blazer's inside pocket. He glanced at his watch. They needed to be at the cemetery at least thirty minutes before the actual ceremony began. He gave Joe Andrews a hug.

"I'll see you in the car, Jeb." Andy turned and headed back down the hallway.

"Thanks, Joe." Jeb bent down and kissed the boy on the head. "I'll see you a little later, OK?"

"OK." He looked at him carefully. His eyes seemed so much older than nine, Jeb thought.

"You were my daddy's friend?" Joe asked quietly.

"Yes, Joe. I was your daddy's friend."

The boy dropped his head and then wiped his eyes. But his sobs were silent ones.

Jeb suddenly felt the anguish welling up in him. "I didn't know your daddy as a man, Joe. I knew him when we were kids, about your age. He was...he was the best friend anybody could ever have."

Jeb knelt beside the boy and wrapped an arm over his shoulder. The boy looked away, trying hard to hide his tears.

He pulled away and walked quietly to the dresser beside his bed. He grasped a stained, brown baseball from its wooden stand and pushed it into Jeb's hand. In faded letters, written on the side, it read "District All-Stars Championship Game." The date had been smudged away.

"Daddy got it for the championship game," Joe said and he caressed the ball proudly. He carried it reverently back to the dresser and gently returned it to its stand, making sure that the inscription could still be seen.

CHAPTER FORTY-NINE

Roy Yates parked his cruiser at the entrance of Rose Hill Cemetery before the first cars began to arrive at the Andrews funeral. The large stone entrance was bordered by towering red maples which stood as solemn sentries for Stacey's oldest graveyard.

The sheriff watched the blue BMW as it wound its way up the narrow asphalt lane. He knew Andy Gardner's car, but the man that sat beside him was not familiar. He unconsciously fingered one of the small spiral notebooks in his front pocket. Habits were hard to break.

He thought back briefly to his conversation with Gardner when he'd showed up at Yates's office the day after the body's recovery. At the time he had hoped a childhood friend might be able to shed some insight into the psyche of a man who chose such an odd spot to end his life. Even a hopeless drunk still retained some logic, he told himself. The notebook was there. A reasonable explanation was not.

The few cars that drifted in later continued on to a far corner of the cemetery. A few minutes before the hour Yates moved his car closer to the burial site. There would be few traffic challenges on this day.

Gardner and the second man were talking to Harold Flannery some fifty feet from where the casket now rested underneath a large green tent with "Flannery Funeral Home" printed boldly across the top. Yates always thought Harold would have been better suited to working the big top at the circus. Only Barnum and Bailey did a better job of advertising their "show of shows." Over to the side, the Lebo boys stood, propped against their shovels. Arnold, the older Lebo brother, was sixty-two. Little Al, all 280 pounds of him, spat tobacco juice onto the grass and nodded quietly at Yates.

It was hot work here in late July. The sheriff was glad he had left his dress uniform at home.

Thirteen visitors ultimately gathered around the visiting preacher, a Lutheran from over in Concord. The graveside eulogy was short. A song was sung. And they quietly drifted away, leaving the Lebos to their afternoon chores.

"Andy, it's good to see you." Yates shook hands with Gardner as the few remaining guests milled around the cars.

Gardner smiled and introduced Jeb Mason.

"Mighty hot day for this kind of stuff, boys." Yates glanced back at the Lebos. Little Al had already begun to fling shovels of dirt onto the casket, his thick arms bulging as they worked. "So, Mr. Mason...you knew Andrews too?"

"It's Jeb...and yeah, a long, long time ago." Jeb found this local official to be a little more amicable than the police chief.

"I'm reckoning you footed the bill for this, Andy. No way Harold Flannery would plant Zeke Andrews if someone wasn't good for it," Yates said.

"Well Roy...turns out we both did." Andy gestured toward his friend. "It was either that or kill Jeb."

Yates considered the newcomer in a different light. "Must been an awful good friend."

Jeb nodded as he watched the Lebos seal Zeke's final resting place.

"You know...it still bugs me a little bit, boys." The sheriff pulled a worn handkerchief and wiped his brow.

"How's that, Roy?" Andy asked.

"Like I told you before, Andy. Your old friend was nothing but a drunk." He looked at Jeb as he said it. "No offense, Mr. Mason, but that's what he was. We're guessing he'd tried to off himself at least twice before. No question 'bout that." He paused.

"And..." Jeb waited.

"Helluva thing in my book anyway." Yates patted the omnipresent spiral notebook as he spoke. "Why in the world do you go all the way out to Darby Ridge, climb a half-hour to the top...just to fling yourself off?"

"I'm not following you, Sheriff," Jeb said.

"Well, son…you'd be just as dead if you drove over to Langston Bridge and took a swan dive off of there. It's couple of hundred feet up. And you wouldn't be near as sweaty on the way down," Yates answered.

"Jeb," Andy said, "the sheriff said it was *likely* a suicide because of his history, and he had no other reason to be up there in the middle of the night…but you can't…"

"Your friend was depressed. He was sick. Mrs. Tully told me his liver was ate up. Diabetic. Wouldn't take his medication. 'Cept for the liquor. Just made it worse," Yates said.

"Wait a minute. Are you telling me no one knows for sure…" Jeb found his temperature rising as he spoke.

"No way you *can be*, Mr. Mason." Yates tone became more formal. "Fact is, there was no note, no nothing. Only thing we have is a dead man at the foot of a ravine…five miles from anywhere. Chronic alcoholic with a history of suicide attempts."

"But I thought it had been, er…announced as a suicide, right?" Jeb said.

"Jeb," Andy began, "no one can say for sure, but it's pretty obvious. Either a drunken accident or an intentional suicide."

"Don't make much difference, I'm guessing," Yates said. "No insurance, nothing left behind."

"Jeb, wasn't going to go into it with you. The deal is that Zeke died because of his own actions. We're never going to know for sure," Andy said.

"Guessing we're going to have another storm coming in tonight." Yates looked up at the western sky. "Going to leave it with you, gentlemen." He clapped Andy Gardner on the back and began to walk back to the cruiser.

While Andy cranked the car, Jeb decided to walk over a final time to Zeke's graveside where he stood watching the last shovels of dirt complete the job. He scanned the hillside quietly.

When Andy looked back a few minutes later, Jeb was standing at another grave some one hundred feet away. It was more shaded than the rest with a large marble headstone that prominently announced to the world the life it gave tribute to. Even from that distance, Andy could read the name easily.

Thompson

He looked back to the horizon. The sheriff was right. The first hint of a thunderhead had begun to build there.

CHAPTER FIFTY

"Look, Wehunt, this is still my town. Responsibility for this is mine, not Roy Yates, not the SBI, not fire investigation people, not anybodies but mine..." Benny Greer sat propped behind his desk, his hands folded behind his head.

Preston Wehunt stood looking out the window. A single television van sat in the far corner of the parking lot but with no hint of the driver. Wehunt sighed and shook his head. "Look, Benny. Listen to me. No one is saying this is not your investigation. No one is saying you aren't in charge of all of this. But you need to listen to what the evidence is telling you. And you have to stop maligning the character of the deceased."

"'Maligning the character of the deceased'? What in the hell does that mean?" Greer growled.

"It means that everybody is saying there was an accelerant used. That there was a murder committed." Wehunt turned back to Greer and watched him roll his eyes and glance down at the file on his desk. "Why are you so damn convinced Patterson started the fire anyway?"

"'Cause it don't make no sense for somebody to break into that little one-horse school to begin with...much less burn it down and murder the damn janitor!" Greer shifted his weight and the chair squeaked in protest. "Nonsense."

"Benny, you listen to me." Wehunt sat down in the chair underneath the window. "You screw this up, my chances for re-election go out the window. That means *your* chances for reappointment go with it, you understand that, don't you?"

Benny Greer grinned, a wide, yellow-toothed smile that seemed to grow larger as Preston Wehunt stared at him.

"Tell me, Preston. You think that hardware store of yours is going to fall apart if you don't have that mayor's job of yours?"

"Least I got a full-time job, Benny. What you going to do if the chief's job goes away?" Wehunt asked.

"Don't you worry 'bout me, Mayor Wehunt. Long past worrying about hanging onto this city job," Greer said, and Wehunt believed him. "Long past."

"Benny. Listen to me. We got the news people in town. We got State Bureau of Investigation people in town. We got a lot of eyes on us right now. We come out looking like idiots, everybody loses. All I'm saying."

"You just let me handle the situation, Mr. Mayor. And keep that idiot Yates out of my hair." Greer's black eyes grew even darker.

"Most people seem to think pretty highly of Sheriff Yates, Benny."

"Yates is what got us into this mess. Kept his nose out of this fire thing, we wouldn't have had all of this to begin with."

"A school burned down, Chief. A state employee died. State investigators going to be here, whether you called them or Yates called them. You know that."

"Son of a bitch stepped over onto my backyard. City limits. He knows that."

"Benny, listen to me. Don't you screw this up."

Greer leaned forward and the tone of his voice dropped to almost a whisper. "I'll handle this my way, Mayor Wehunt. My way."

There was a short knock on the door. Fire Chief Brett Hampton stuck his head inside. "Benny, you got time to talk? That investigator called back...hey, Preston, you two in a meeting?"

"Come on in, Hamp." Wehunt stood. "Chief Greer and I were just wrapping up. So, get what you were waiting for?"

"Enough to know we got an arson investigation," Brett Hampton said. "Enough to say some damn fool didn't know any other way out than to kill an innocent man."

CHAPTER FIFTY-ONE

"Way you remember it?" Andy nodded toward the Yadkin River and took another swig from the beer bottle.

"Yeah, guess it is." Jeb sat on flat slab of granite a few feet away. They were both perched on a low bluff that overlooked the water. The BMW was parked in the grassy turn-off just beyond the Wilson Mills Bridge and the walk to this quiet bend had taken only minutes. They were less than five miles from the cemetery. But it was the longest five miles Jeb had traveled in his life.

"Funny...world goes sliding by. We grow up. We grow old. This damned old river just keeps on going. Just like when we were kids. Never changes." Andy looked out over the brown waters and smiled. A broken tree limb floated by as he spoke, its branches protruding out of the current like a mangled arm from the body of a great serpent.

"This river...amazing how often I've thought of it over the years." Jeb pulled a beer from the small cooler that sat between them and popped the cap. "Not sure I can think of this little town without picturing the river."

"Lucky we didn't drown down here, ya know? Some of the shit we pulled."

"This town...it was really..." Jeb paused. "You, Zeke..."

"Good times." Andy hoisted his bottle. "To Zeke."

"To Zeke. May he rest in peace."

They let the gentle flow of the water speak for both of them for a time, studying its mesmerizing wave as they once did when there was a third standing alongside. It whispered to them in the quiet just as it had before.

"Wish I could have done something, Andy. Wish I would have known."

"Look, Jeb. Something I want to tell you. Before you get back on that plane and go back to your world."

Jeb drained his beer, tossed the empty back into the cooler and turned toward Andy.

"You coming back. Would have meant everything to Zeke. You need to know that."

Jeb shrugged.

"No, want you to listen to me now. When we were kids, you were a lot more than a friend. You were the one that we listened to. Nobody more than Zeke. You know that, right?"

"Look, Andy…"

"What I'm trying to say is I know you well enough to know that you're going to beat yourself up over Zeke. Even though you haven't even seen him since we were kids. I knew you then. I can read you now. You couldn't have saved Zeke, Jeb. Nobody could."

"Could have tried." Jeb turned back to the river and tossed a small pebble out into the water.

"And I know you would have tried. Just like everybody else did. But you need to understand. Zeke was lost. Lost to everybody. Nobody was going to change that."

"You really believe that?"

"No, I *know* that. He was my friend too, ya know. But when I tried to reach out and find you…wasn't to lay some guilt trip on you, man. It was to let you know our old friend was gone. You coming back here… after all these years and all, it was the best gift you could have given to Zeke."

"You said he was lost. That kid that used to tag around behind the two of us, just can't figure out how he could have lost his way so badly."

"That's something none of us will ever understand. Hell, I've asked myself that same question a thousand times. But that's my point. We are not ever going to know."

"Yeah, but Andy…"

"No! That's my point. You could fix everything when we were twelve years old but you can't now, Jeb. For your sake, I want you to leave this here." Andy pointed out over the river. "Needs to stay right where so much of our lives were spent when we were kids. We have the memories...of three best friends. We bury any of the 'what if's' out there in the middle of the Yadkin. We go on."

Jeb paused and looked out over the water and then said, "You're still a knucklehead, you know that, don't you?"

"Yup." Andy reached in and pulled another beer from the ice and handed it to Jeb. "So, for one last time, two old friends will drink a beer and remember..."

• • •

"So, back in a couple hours to pick you up, all right?" Andy said as he pulled the Bimmer into the Dogwood Inn parking lot.

"Give me a chance to return a few calls. Thanks, man," Jeb said.

"Think we'll have time for a drink or two at the bar once we get to the airport?"

"After these last few days, believe I could use one." Jeb smiled. He looked into the front lobby window and spotted Earle, comfortably situated behind his newspaper. "Let's ride by Grimley Field on the way out. Think we could do that?"

"Sure we could. Hey, maybe we go out and toss the ball around. For old time's sake, how 'bout that?"

"Wish I had time. Man, we had some good times, didn't we?"

"Damn right we did. You thinking 'bout the game, aren't you?"

"Huh, what game?"

"You know what game. The All-Star Game with Asheboro. That's what game."

"Oh, remember it sometimes, I guess."

"Damn, Jeb. It was the best game of your friggin' life, and you know it. You were the winning pitcher and knocked in the winning run in the sixth. Don't go all humble on me now, man."

"All right, it was the best game of my friggin' life. I admit it."

"You damn well better. Coach gave you the game ball and everything. For about a week, you were the big cat around this little town."

"I peaked early, Andy."

"Well, at least you peaked. Now, let me run home, grab a shower. Back in a few."

Jeb watched the BMW spin out of the parking lot even as his mind wandered back to the giddy aftermath of *the game;* the roaring parents, the exuberant coaches, all crowded around him. The bottom half of the sixth inning and the double into right field. And Andy was right, for a brief time, he *was* the king. But when the crowd left, the only fan that remained was the biggest fan, Zeke Andrews, who stayed behind to carry home his hero's weapons and spoils of war, regaling him with a pitch-by- pitch account along the way. And Jeb Mason knew, even then, that he would never have a bigger admirer.

He always figured that's why he gave Zeke the game ball. Maybe because he could never cherish it as much as Zeke.

Maybe almost as much as Joe Andrews cherished it now.

•   •   •

"Late checkout" seemed to be an uncommon term for the Stacey Dogwood Inn, but Jeb had managed to negotiate one that allowed him to keep his bags there until mid-afternoon.

Andy had pulled a few strings to arrange for the rental to be dropped off locally rather than back at the airport. Less hassle, particularly since there would be a repair bill to discuss. And a few more hours with an old friend was suitable compensation.

The 7:30 flight would put him back in Chicago in plenty of time. Bonnie had him on a conference call with Tolliver at 8:00 tomorrow. Reality was coming a lot closer. He had skipped filing the police report. No need to elevate the Stacey crime level if he didn't have to.

As he climbed the stairs to room 217, he found himself quickly scanning the cars in the lot. When he saw the brown Crown Victoria parked in the corner, his mind flashed across the image of Shauna Spencer in her jogging attire. For a wild moment he considered ringing her room.

"Hello, Ms. Spencer? You probably don't remember me. I'm the guy you handcuffed the other night. Yeah…that's right. The idiot you met in the parking lot." Jeb smiled at the daydream.

At least it was a pleasurable image.

•   •   •

He invested the next hour clearing messages and beginning to immerse himself into his real life when the buzz of his cell interrupted him. The screen showed "unknown caller" so he didn't answer. He tossed the phone onto the rolled up newspaper he'd carried all day. Its edges had grown ragged from the humidity.

As he spread it out on the bedspread, he thought back to young Joe, who had also done the same, but with a Magic Marker in hand. He looked for a section index on the front page. Might be a good time to check the Cub's box scores. Tony Delvechio would be prepared for the debriefing tomorrow morning.

His gaze fell on the headline article. It looked like the Steadman fire eclipsed everything else, and there were front page photographs of the burned-out carnage. Jeb recognized the burly figure of the Police Chief in the most prominent one.

But his attention wasn't drawn to the print—instead, to the heavy black circles that had been drawn on one of the photos. Each circled one of four windows of the portion of the school that still was intact.

Odd, he thought to himself, even as he turned the pages to find an advertisement on page three for a vinyl siding company. The remodeled house that was its centerpiece had every window circled. On page six, there was a photo of a government building under renovation. Again, each window was circled.

He glanced over to the brown envelope that still protruded from his sport jacket, which now lay flung across a chair in the corner. He poured the contents onto the bedspread, for a time forgetting about the Cubs and Tony Delvechio.

A single padlock tumbled onto the bed. Along with what must be several hundred shreds of paper of various sizes, two clear tape dispensers, and several more markers.

Words. Carefully cutout. Some taped together.

"What in the hell…"

Jeb began to spread them out. Interspersed were photographs or artist renditions of windows, even cartoon drawings. Dozens of them. All carefully clipped out. Some still had the remnants of magic markers circling them.

"Zeke, what were you doing?" Jeb whispered.

He tried to group them in some order across the bedspread. A final suicide note perhaps? Or maybe a final letter to his son?

He glanced at the lock a second time and thought back to Mary Tully's reference to the metal box where Zeke kept the hand gun. Was this the lock he used to keep it secure? Where was the key?

He checked the envelope again, turning it upside down to see if there might be something more inside. A thin plastic bag dropped out. Inside was what looked like dried grass or leaves.

"Holy shit," Jeb said. "If this is weed, I gotta another problem. Damn it, Zeke." But it didn't look like any marijuana he could remember from college. "What is this stuff?" He studied it more closely.

He uncrumpled the Porsche article and considered the sections that had been excised. It was just a mundane article. Why take the time to clip out portions?

Maybe the scissor work was simply a way of dealing with the alcohol or the drug withdrawal—therapy for the shakes or whatever maladies afflicted a life-long addict. A simple little game he could play with his boy.

The air conditioner suddenly rattled to life, and the blast of cold air sent the papers flying across the bed. Jeb cursed and dropped to the floor to retrieve them. He adjusted the faded thermostat and the frigid air subsided.

But the picture he was looking at was different now. The Porsche article had been turned over. Staring back at him was a buxom brunette in a skimpy blue bikini. She invited the reader to join her in a multi-million dollar payout for some type of sweepstakes contest. She carried a bouquet of large colored balloons, two of which had been neatly cut away and sat seductively positioned on a large treasure chest. A large, poster-size check was spread across the trunk. But specific numbers had been cut away.

"What the hell were you doing, Zeke?" Jeb murmured.

The paper with the words glued to it—he remembered seeing it, but it wasn't here. He picked the manila envelope back up. Peered inside. It lay at the very bottom. Untouched. He pulled it out. There were three pages, not one. And across each page, the same three words were pasted in different sizes and different print. Carefully glued to each page.

Place. You. Killed.

Joe called it the ticket. The ticket for the car. His Towel Seed ticket. A ticket for a car. What the hell did that mean?

He flipped bikini girl back over. The Porsche article had a date on it. It was the latest issue, or maybe last month's. So in the last days of his life, Zeke Andrews took the time to clip magazines and newspapers.

Jeb sprang from the bed and sprinted in the direction of the hotel lobby. Maybe, just maybe, he would be in luck.

CHAPTER FIFTY-TWO

"Don't really keep much of a stock of magazines, Mr. Mason." Earle the desk clerk smiled. His lugubrious manner and hanging jowls reminded Jeb of Walter Matthau. But Earle was two speeds slower than the actor.

"Where's the closest place I might be able to find a *Car and Driver?*"

"Well…we can just call you a taxi cab for that, Mr. Mason." Earle picked up the phone book and began to patiently thumb through the yellow pages.

"No…it's a magazine, Earle. A magazine. You think there's anywhere around here I could buy a magazine like that?"

"Well…" Earle scratched his jaw solemnly and began. "I'd say you got three choices there. Ya got your Wal-Mart. Now, it ain't one of them super stores, mind you but…"

"Got it, Earle," Jeb interrupted him. "Any other places?"

"Why sure. Ya got your K-Mart and that new Target store. Bet you a biscuit one of them will have it for sure."

Jeb guessed he could have driven to each in the time that it took Earle to recite the choices.

"Thanks, Earle…" he spun and headed out the front door.

"Say, Mr. Mason…" Earle dully called after him. "Is that like a hot rod kind of a magazine?"

"No…not exactly, but thanks."

"Reason is…my nephew, Kenny, he subs for me sometimes. Course he don't do much but read these old things." Earle reached behind the counter and produced a large stack of car magazines. "Maybe it would be somethin' you could find in one of these."

Six magazines down he found it. A pristine copy of *Car and Driver*. He thumbed over to the Porsche article.

"Earle, I owe you a steak dinner, my man! I'll bring this back to you." Jeb disappeared out the door.

"Them Chicaga boys get a hankering to read, they really get a hankering," Earle mumbled as he picked up the remote and restored the volume on the portable TV that was mounted in the corner of the small lobby. The Braves were just coming to bat in the bottom of the fourth.

CHAPTER FIFTY-THREE

Jeb laid out the intact magazine alongside the dissected slips of paper from the envelope.

Whoever had cut sections out was not working on the Porsche article. They were extracting portions of the advertisement. He pulled a highlighter from his briefcase and began to highlight those pieces that might have been removed. There was a pattern there. But what was it?

His fingers ran across the page. The balloon that had been removed. It was the July balloon. The others, though shredded, were still there on the bed. But the July balloon was gone.

The original ad had Roman numerals across the bottom of the page, each designed to stipulate a different level of award. Jeb found his hand began to tremble as he compared the cutout with the full advertisement.

Several numbers were gone. He flipped through the pieces that were spread across the bed. All could be accounted for except for one. He checked again. Then a third time. He felt the sweat beading on his forehead.

He studied the piece of paper that had been left behind. Crumpled into a corner and discarded.

Place you Killed.

He laid the yellow balloon beside the word.

July

Then the one Roman numeral he could not account for. The one that had been carefully clipped away.

VII

July 7. The Place You Killed

"Merciful God," Jeb whispered.

• • •

"Jeb, he's not here. I know he had to run some errands before we picked you up at the motel. Is something wrong?" Brenda Gardner's voice grew a bit more urgent. "Is everything OK?"

"He's just...not answering his cell. Had something I had to run by him. That's all." Jeb struggled to sound calm but guessed he wasn't quite pulling it off.

"Oh, he never answers that silly thing. You know that."

Jeb remembered the attempts to reach him from Chicago. "Just... have Andy call me when you hear from him. Would you do that, Brenda?"

He hung up and stared down at the papers on the bed. What in the hell was going on?

Then he noticed a partial piece of another page. The paper appeared to be the same quality as bikini lady. Could it be the same magazine?

The article was a retro piece. Nineteen sixty-six Ford Mustang. He checked the table of contents from the *Car and Driver*. Page eighty-four. There it was. He quickly compared the circles removed and then again turned the page. Another ad. This time for an upcoming Formula 1 race. A young kid screaming about the greatest race he ever saw. He held his father's hand and they were watching the cars go speeding by. Once again, the words were large and in bold print. He circled the same cutouts and compared.

As he worked, he found his pulse begin to quicken. He underlined the two words he could not find. Then double checked his work a second time. There was no mistake.

Saw You

He picked up one of the window cutouts and gently fingered its corners.

The buxom bikini girl looked up at him and implored him to pick the winning ticket.

"He said it was his daddy's ticket..." Jeb whispered the words.

• • •

The dispatcher at the sheriff's office advised the caller that Roy Yates was out. If there was an emergency, she could dispatch a deputy. The caller declined. Instead, Jeb left his name and telephone number and asked the dispatcher to please ask the sheriff to give him a call. She politely declined. Calls of a personal nature could not be handled through the dispatcher. The caller insisted. He indicated he was returning a message from the sheriff. She grudgingly wrote down the name at last and placed it on a pink memo pad. The name "Jeb Mason" was not familiar.

Jeb glanced at the digital clock beside his bed. It read 4:15. The Gardners were to be by in less than an hour to pick him up. Outside, the first large drops of the promised storm had begun to plop down against the hot asphalt of the motel parking lot. Steam rose up to greet the rain.

In room 398, Shauna Spencer was wrapping a preliminary report on the Steadman investigation. The paperwork was always hers to complete. Mac Boller was not the most meticulous when it came to the administrative aspects of the job. But in this case, putting down on paper the progress on the investigation was a chore she welcomed. A simple inquiry into a fire on state property had mushroomed into a full-scale arson and murder investigation. It had attracted attention in Raleigh. Shauna welcomed the challenge.

But the motel phone proved a welcome distraction. Since almost all her calls came on her cell, she guessed it was the front desk wanting to know if they could clean her room the next morning. More often than not she left a "Do Not Disturb" sign on her doorknob. She was wary of strangers pilfering through her room. She could get towels and bed sheets from housekeeping on her own.

But the voice didn't sound like the old fellow at the front desk after all.

"Ms. Spencer," Jeb began. "You probably don't remember me, but..."

CHAPTER FIFTY-FOUR

The restaurant at the Dogwood Inn consisted of fourteen tables, each decorated with the same faded floral tablecloth that at one point might have been yellow and lime.

At 4:45 in the afternoon, dining traffic was already at its apex. Four of the tables were occupied.

Shauna accepted her second cup of coffee from the matronly waitress and again considered the kaleidoscope of paper strips and cutouts that were spread out on the table in front of her.

She looked up at Jeb and smiled. "OK, Mr. Mason. Let me get this straight. You're telling me that thirty years ago, you and two of your buddies snake some house..."

"Right...a harmless prank. Kids playing."

"And why does that even remotely relate to any of this?" she gestured toward the papers.

"Because I think my friend saw something that night...something that changed him."

"And what is it you think he saw, Mr. Mason?" she studied him closely.

"I know what he saw," Jeb said. He studied her blue eyes. "He saw a man die."

"I'm not following you. What do you believe he saw?"

Jeb pushed back from the table. Glanced over at the other patrons in the restaurant as if each might be quietly listening.

"We chose the Thompson house for a reason. He was maybe the most famous—or infamous—man in this town. Kind of a feared figure, I guess."

She nodded.

"And so...we came up with the idea of soaping a few of his windows. That was the plan, anyway. Zeke was not quite ten, and it was the Rite...a sort of challenge of manhood. I know it sounds silly now, but it was a big deal to three kids in a small town."

"I'm following you," Shauna said.

Jeb's mind suddenly swirled back to that night. "Zeke...he had just started when..."

"When what?"

"Not sure...something went wrong. Zeke, he stood up. Right in the light of the window. Like he'd...I don't know. Seen something."

"Seen something." She repeated the words. "And that was..."

Jeb leaned forward. "What he saw...was Judge Thompson die. He died that night."

"And how do you know that?"

"Because the next morning, we hiked back home. When we got back...all hell had broken loose."

"Meaning""

"News was all over town. Judge Thompson had been found dead at his home. Heart attack."

"So...you're saying that you believe your friend, Zeke, may have seen the body?"

"Or something worse."

"And what was that something worse?"

"That we killed him, Agent Spencer. That we killed him."

CHAPTER FIFTY-FIVE

"Look, we were *kids*. An old man, late at night...couple of dumbass kids. He's by himself. Sees someone at the window. Freaks out. Not impossible to think our being there that night..." Jeb's words trailed away.

"Possible, I guess. Bit of a reach," Shauna said.

"Not when you're a kid, it's not. And Zeke...Zeke was beyond a basket case. Crying. Hysterical. That night...It was terrible."

"You're telling me he went into shock?"

"Thinking back now. I'd say that's exactly what happened. He couldn't talk. Couldn't stop crying."

"So, what happened?"

"We ran until we finally caught up with him. Got lost. Panicked."

"What did you think your friend had seen?"

"We didn't know. But Zeke wasn't the kind of kid who would react that way. He just wasn't."

"And how did you find out what had happened to the old man?"

"Like I said, when we got back home that next morning all hell had broken loose."

"Meaning?"

"That was the night of the floods. Yadkin overflowed that same night. Hell, our parents didn't even know we went camping. They would have gone nuts if they knew we were within three miles of the river."

"So, nothing was ever said?"

"Zeke was quiet—really quiet that next morning. We hiked back into town early. The news was everywhere about Judge Thompson dying. Then we knew."

"What your friend had seen?"

"Right. All of a sudden we realized that Zeke must have been look-ing in the window. Maybe Thompson saw him. But we knew he saw him die."

"And so, you never told anyone?"

"No…" Jeb looked down at his coffee cup. "We really didn't know what to say. We were scared kids. We were at the scene of the death. Our buddy had gone 'bye-bye' and couldn't talk about it."

"So…you *never* talked about it?"

"We pretended that night never happened." Jeb said. "We were afraid for Zeke. We were afraid for ourselves."

"I'm not following…"

"Hey, we have a kid at the window of the most well-known citizen of the town at sometime after midnight. That citizen suffers a fatal heart attack."

"So, you assumed you were in some way responsible?" she asked.

"Well, I guess you could say we just didn't know. It was pretty clear Zeke could not, or would not, talk about what he saw."

"And you and the other boy, what was his name again?"

"His name is Andy Gardner." Jeb suddenly wondered if he was now ratting out his friend as well as himself.

"You just put this thing away. And never talked about it…ever?"

"Not exactly," Jeb said. "We never talked about it again…until last night."

"You're kidding me, right?" Shauna smiled, and Jeb noticed again how pretty she was.

"No. I'm not kidding."

"And why after thirty years, do you decide to bring this back up?"

"Because…the person we thought we were protecting…no longer needs protecting, I guess."

"I'm not following again, I'm afraid."

"Zeke Andrews is dead."

Shauna's eyes softened. "I'm sorry," she said. And Jeb believed her. "But what you're experiencing seems pretty normal, I think. I mean, your friend is gone. It's natural to discuss things in your past in situations like—"

"No, Ms. Spencer, you're really not following me," Jeb interrupted.

"So, Mr. Mason, help me to understand."

"I believe that maybe...we were wrong. I think Zeke saw something very different from what we thought that night."

"And that would be..."

"I believe someone else was there that night."

"OK. Someone was there," she said. "Why does that become suddenly so important?"

"I don't think Judge Thompson just died," Jeb began. "I think he might have been...murdered."

CHAPTER FIFTY-SIX

Shauna Spencer considered the man sitting across the table from her carefully. He seemed intelligent and very well spoken. He was a corporate executive. He appeared level-headed, and, if she could take it at face value that he had returned to this small town to bury an old friend, was not without compassion. Maybe a tad impulsive and too macho for his own good, as in the failed break-in attempt, but not recklessly so.

But her two interactions with him had been of a most unusual nature. During the first, she almost shot him. During the second, he presented her with an unlikely story of murder.

"I think...Mr. Mason..."

"Please, Ms. Spencer...I would appreciate it if you just called me Jeb. I mean, after all, you did almost arrest me." He smiled and reached across the table to slightly brush her wrist.

"All right...Jeb." Shauna felt herself slightly blush. "I'm just not sure what to make of all this. This is something that..."

"You believe I'm 'certifiable'."

"No. I think you've run across some information here that could be explained any of a number of ways."

"OK. Give me some of the possible explanations," Jeb said.

"Well, my point is, just because you've developed a suspicion about this doesn't make it valid."

"I understand that. But you have to admit, what we're looking at here is more than a little bit odd," Jeb said.

"Odd does not equate to murder, though."

"Agent Spencer..." Jeb began. "I have several pieces of paper on which three words have been pasted...'place you killed'."

She nodded.

"We know he clearly clipped out pictures and numbers to spell out the date of July seventh," Jeb continued.

"Possibly…possibly," Shauna said. "This is something less than scientific proof."

"Point taken." Jeb went on. "And then we add the pictures of windows."

"Which may or may not have been in some way added to the earlier words you believe your Mr. Andrews pasted onto a sheet of paper," Spencer said.

"But isn't it clear that he was in some way building some type of note…a message that at least alluded to the date of July seventh? That at least alluded to something he saw? And then we have the words 'place you killed.' I mean, that's *something* right?"

"You have some information that suggests your late friend and his son liked to clip pictures and words, and possibly then paste them to blank pieces of paper." Shauna shrugged. "But not much more than that."

"But I believe it does."

"Then you need to turn it over to local authorities and explain everything you've explained to me," Shauna said. "I think you've run across something unusual, I'll concede that."

"But I think it means he knew something…something he never revealed. Something that he himself didn't want to reveal. Until he had no choice."

"No choice?"

"He was desperate. He was broke. He was alone," Jeb said.

"Meaning what…"

"Meaning he meant to make up for what he didn't have." Jeb paused and looked carefully at the page in front of him. "I think all of this was practice for something else."

"Practice for something else?" Shauna studied him closely.

"I think he finally put together a letter. I think he sent that letter to someone he saw in the house that night. Someone that he saw kill Judge Thompson."

For a brief second Shauna Spencer felt like the air had been sucked out of the room.

He was serious.

"You're telling me your friend might have been trying to extort a payoff...from the killer?"

"Yes, Agent Spencer. That's exactly what I'm saying."

"I would tell you that you're following a very weak evidentiary trail, Mr...Jeb, a very weak trail. And, besides, if your friend has passed away, without a lot of luck, trying to re-establish that line is almost impossible."

"Agent Spencer, if I'm right, then I believe we have a much larger problem," Jeb said.

"And what's that?" she asked.

"If I'm right, then there is a very good chance that the circumstances...of my friend's death are not what people have assumed."

Shauna folded her arms and leaned forward. "Jeb, just how did your friend Zeke die?"

"Officially? Officially, they say he committed suicide."

"Your friend...your friend was the jumper?"

"He was my friend, Agent Spencer. But no, I don't think he was a jumper."

CHAPTER FIFTY-SEVEN

"You think...your friend...was murdered." Shauna Spencer waited for Jeb's response.

"I think there is a possibility of that."

"But from what I've heard about that situation, the victim was a longtime substance abuser. Was sick. Had attempted suicide before..."

"All true." Jeb nodded.

"We need to go ahead and get your local law enforcement to take a look at this," Shauna said. "I think it might be best if we return all of this...material...to the envelope you held it in."

Jeb's expression brightened. "So you think there may be something here?"

"Honestly?" Shauna looked at him and, not for the first time, found herself wondering if Jeb Mason had a significant other back in the world he lived in. She quickly pushed the thought away. "I don't think any of this will turn out to change much of anything. But I believe it needs to be investigated."

Jeb's smile faded and he shook his head. "OK...so it's a long shot, I know that."

"Let's allow your local authorities to tell us that. I would suggest you call the sheriff or maybe the police department..."

Jeb's mind flashed back to Benny Greer. He knew who he would *not* call.

"Jeb. It's not my business, but I think you are doing the right thing."

Her tone softened and once again he found himself staring at her. He could lose himself in those eyes.

"Well, I appreciate you listening to me. I know...you have a few other things to occupy your time." He gestured toward the waitress, and she glided over and left them a check. "This has nothing to do with why you're in town. I hope everything goes well with the fire investigation."

She smiled in return. The conversation was coming to an end. "How did you know I was involved in that?"

"*Stacey Star* can't seem to talk about anything else...and there was a picture that looked like you and a few others in one of the snapshots."

"Small towns. Big stories. Very sad situation." Her mind flashed back to the facts of the case. This one wasn't speculative. It was murder. It was a badly-botched arson cover-up. It was a vicious act of violence that had been perpetrated on someone that, to the best of their knowledge, was truly an innocent victim. And she couldn't afford to invest too very much more time working on what might be a fantasy tale. She glanced briefly at her cell phone. Mac Boller would be calling soon. They were to debrief that evening.

"If you saw me in one of the photos, you are very observant. I didn't even see it." She stood to leave.

"What happened to the red ones?" Jeb asked.

"The red ones?"

"You wore red running shorts the first night I saw you. I like these though." He gestured to the light blue shorts she had not bothered to change out of when she had received Jeb's call.

Now she really did blush. "Well, I guess I didn't consider our date to be too formal." Was she flirting with this guy?

"I'm glad. You...look...good. In running shorts, I mean." Jeb flushed. Was he hitting on her? She was a government agent. And he would never even see her again.

"Thank you, Mr...Jeb." She shook his hand, and when she smiled Jeb felt his breath catch. He watched her walk toward the restaurant door in her blue shorts and tan legs and wondered if he had ever seen a better pair of shorts in his life.

She turned just before she got to the door and looked back at him. He didn't even attempt to pretend he hadn't watched her walk away. She smiled and walked back.

"Just out of curiosity, what did you say the boy called the ticket?"

"He called it his daddy's ticket for a new Corvette."

"No, didn't he call it by name? You called it by name."

Jeb paused. "He called it his Towel Seed ticket. Or something like that. Why do you ask?"

"Have any idea what that might mean exactly?"

"Not in the slightest. Do you?"

"Just a thought…he said his daddy was going to get a lot of money and had a ticket for a car. Right?" Shauna asked.

"Yeah…I think that's right." Jeb wondered what she was getting at.

"Jeb, would you like to come with me to my room? I have something I would like to try."

He didn't have to be asked twice.

CHAPTER FIFTY-EIGHT

"Directory information for Tallahassee, Florida, please." Shauna Spencer placed a hand over the phone. "This is nothing but a shot in the dark, but Towel Seed may be what the little boy heard. Sounds a little bit like Tallahassee to me..." She removed her hand. "More than one? Yes, please." She scratched a number onto the legal pad that sat beside her on the bed.

She placed the phone on speaker setting, and she and Jeb waited for the call to be connected. The salesman who finally took the call was named Tommy Yoder. He seemed hurried and had little interest in a phone-call inquiry. As "Mrs. Smith" made clear her interest in purchasing a black Corvette, his mood softened.

None available on the lot, but he would do a data search and get back to her in a few hours at most. The option package might make it more difficult, but it could be done.

"How often do you sell a black one?" she asked, and Jeb thought he detected just a hint of a flirtatious tone in the question.

"Dunno, Mrs. Smith," Tommy Yoder answered. "And by the way, everybody calls me Boo. Popular color. Good month, maybe three or four. Can't always guarantee a custom order will be on the lot, but like I said, I can get it."

"I really appreciate the help, Boo," Shauna answered, and her voice took on an even deeper tone. "I really do." She looked at Jeb and grinned. "Boo" suddenly sounded about as sexy a name as he had ever heard.

The effect was equally strong in Tallahassee. "Yes ma'am, yes ma'am. I have your number and I will be calling you very, very soon." Jeb guessed this was one callback that he would be anxious to complete.

"Thank you, Boo…" Shauna started to end the call.

"Mrs. Smith? Mrs. Smith?" Boo's voice came back over the speaker. "Look, look, if you think you're really interested, we might have a beauty available in the next several days. T-top. Sports package. Luxury leather interior. The ZO-6. Top-of-the-line car, ma'am…top-of-the-line." His pace quickened and Jeb could imagine him panting on the other end of the phone.

"Why, thank you, Boo…I'll have to get back to you. I was just hoping there might be something already there…"

"You see, ma'am…we might have a buyer backing out. Haven't been able to raise him, and…"

"Well, like I said…" Shauna answered.

"Midnight-black metallic, too. Just sitting here."

She paused. "You mean it's there…on the lot?"

"Yes ma'am…but we can't release it. We received the down payment on her, but the guy was supposed to pick it up a couple of days ago and hasn't shown yet. We're not obligated to hold it more than five days. I mean, if he backs out…"

"You said he made a down payment."

"Two thousand, but these big money guys…I've seen 'em walk before. Backing up on 'em…the money I mean. They got so much they don't know what to do with it all, I reckon." Boo paused to take a breath. "But he's still got to show with the rest of the dough."

"Do you happen to have the buyer's name?" Shauna asked.

"Can't really give that out, ma'am…I mean, not s'posed to, anyway."

"I see, but…"

"Damndest thing. Never even met the son of a bitch…oh, I'm sorry, ma'am. What I mean is…he never even came down and looked at the car. Called up and ordered it. Didn't even have to put down two thousand dollars. Five hundred would have held it."

"He sent you a check, Boo?" Shauna looked over at Jeb. Her expression had changed.

"No ma'am. He sent hundred-dollar bills. Damndest thing…er, sorry, ma'am…I ever seen. Got the receipt right here somewhere," Boo clucked.

"Let's see. Yup, here she goes…Ezekiel Andrews of Stacey, North Carolina. Never heard of Stacey, have you?"

CHAPTER FIFTY-NINE

"Mac, I'm just saying that it is very, very odd." Shauna looked over at Jeb. She had spent the last fifteen minutes briefing her senior partner on her cell phone. "We need to go ahead and get this to the locals and ask them to begin to sort it all out." She waited. "I'll meet you in the lobby...say, twenty minutes."

She clicked the phone shut. "We'll meet him downstairs. Go over this again. Would be worth our while to invite the sheriff to join us. You know there's every possibility that your friend could have saved the money."

"He couldn't pay his electric bill...he couldn't afford cab fare," Jeb said.

"He could have stolen it. He could have been into drug trafficking. There are endless possibilities. You understand that, right?" But she did not sound convincing.

"I do. And I left a message for the sheriff before I called you," Jeb said, and he checked his cell. There were no messages.

"OK, let's do this. I'm going to change out of this...and I'll meet you and Agent Boller in the lobby. If we can round up the sheriff, all the better," Shauna said as she stood up from the bed. She paused. "If you don't mind," she smiled, "might be better if you...gave me a little privacy."

"Yes. Right!" Jeb's face reddened, and he found himself briefly scanning her body almost involuntarily. "I will...just step down to my room. Sorry. Wasn't thinking..." his voice trailed away as he hurried toward the door.

Shauna's face suddenly grew darker. "You know, Jeb. The night I met you...the break-in attempt..your room."

"Hey, I'm going...you don't have to pull your gun again." Jeb raised his hands in mock surrender and walked through the open door.

"No...that's not what I mean. You know, there was something that was wrong about that. It just didn't make sense then. It doesn't now."

"OK....I'm listening. But now I'm confused...."

Shauna paused. "Look, I think...we may want to consider...if your friend was in some way involved in an extortion attempt. And I'm saying *if*..."

"Shauna, I think he might have been. I do."

She hesitated, working it through in her mind, and then she said, "If this Zeke Andrews was witness to some type of crime...a murder, and if he was, in fact, killed because of it..."

"I know...I know. It all is probably nothing but a wild theory."

"No...no. I'm saying that if any of this *is* true..." Shauna worked it through in her mind carefully, "then it is possible that you could even be at risk. You and your friend...Gardner."

"What? How do you figure?"

"You told me your friend was not alone that night...at the Thompson house, right?"

Jeb nodded.

"Again, assuming any of this is true. If we make ourselves assume that. Then we must assume that a killer who has believed he was not seen that night might now realize...that he *was*..."

"All right...and?"

"You believe your friend was trying to extort money from a killer. A killer he saw commit the act." She paused, turning it over a second time. "How difficult is it to believe that now he wonders who else might know?"

"I don't recall anyone taking a shot at me over the last several days," Jeb said.

"No. But you did have someone try to break into your room," Shauna replied.

"Agent Spencer, you don't believe..."

"That was not a garden-variety break-in, Jeb."

"Wait a minute...wait a minute. This is crazy..."

"Can I ask you to go to the bathroom?" Shauna asked.

"You want to run that by me again?"

"Why don't we just check this out a little more closely? It couldn't hurt. I'm going to change clothes and since I don't really want to just strip in front of you, I'm asking you to please wait in the bathroom? Would you do that?" Shauna said.

"No. I mean, I appreciate the offer, but if you think I'm going to huddle in a bathroom. I'm sorry, you can forget that."

"Look, I know you're Mr. Macho. But as a favor to me I'm asking you to just humor me." She placed her hand on his wrist. "It's a very nice bathroom."

Jeb's cell phone buzzed. He glanced at the number. Local. "This is Jeb Mason."

Static on the other end. "Mason...is this Jeb Mason?"

The voice sounded familiar but not quite.

The voice continued. "Mason, you are Andy Gardner's friend. Is that right? Mason, this is Sheriff Roy Yates."

"Yes, Sheriff," Jeb nodded toward Shauna. "Thank you for returning my call. I've come up with something that I would like to discuss..."

"Hold up, Mason. I'm not returning a call, sir."

"Excuse me?"

"Said I'm not returning a call..." More background noise filled the phone. It sounded like Roy Yates was standing in the middle of a construction zone.

"Well, I was trying to touch base with you about Zeke Andrews..." Jeb rose, hoping to talk over the blare of the noise. He walked out onto the outside landing, hoping the reception would improve as he spoke.

"Calling you about your friend..." the sheriff's voice again, fading in and out.

"Yes...yes. I'm saying I've come up with something that I need to show you, Sheriff."

"...an accident, Mr. Mason. I'm afraid it's a bad one..."

Jeb suddenly caught the words. What was he saying?

"We don't have a lot that we can say at this point..." The sheriff continued, his voice clearer now. "Looks like he lost it in a curve. It is a critical situation. I can't offer a lot of hope."

What in the hell was he talking about?

"Mr. Gardner is en route to Carolinas Medical Center over in Charlotte. They had to fly him out. The family is on the way. From what we could tell from Mrs. Gardner, they were planning to meet you this evening. She is pretty shook up, so…"

"Andy? Andy was in a wreck?" Jeb yelled into the phone. "You're saying he was in a wreck?"

"Yes, sir." Yates answered. "Like I said, I'm sorry to have to give you this kind of news…"

"What caused…what happened?" Jeb struggled to comprehend what he was hearing. Shauna walked closer, intently watching Jeb's reaction.

"Just can't say yet. Right now we're still trying to clear the scene. By himself. Single vehicle accident. We'll know more in the next several hours."

"Where are you, Sheriff?" Jeb asked. "I need to talk to you."

He listened for another moment before he ended the call. He then turned to Shauna, his face pale with shock.

"Andy…something has happened to him." He shook his head, hoping to shake the image from his mind. "I'll leave you to change. I'm going to check my room. I'll see you and Boller in the lobby."

"No…no," she grabbed her travel bag a second time and reflexively felt for her firearm inside. "I'm going with you."

"No…I don't need a bodyguard. I appreciate the offer. I'll give you some time. I need to make sure I have my things together in the room, anyway."

"I'm not your bodyguard. And I'm going with you so I can change in your room, if that's all right."

"Agent Spencer, your room seems perfectly fine for changing…"

"My name is Shauna. I'm going with you. And I am going to change my clothes because a T-shirt and jogging shorts are not going to be appropriate attire for a hospital, OK?" she smiled. "Now if I have to do that in your sleeping room, in your bathroom, or in the motel lobby… I'm going with you. And I do have a gun. I will shoot you if I have to."

CHAPTER SIXTY

The crumpled mass of metal smelled of oil and gas. Steam spewed from what was once the in-line six engine. The lights of two highway patrol cruisers created an eerie blue glare around the scene as Shauna's car eased around the portly deputy sheriff guiding traffic at the crash site. Roy Yates squinted against the glare and frowned as it approached.

"Don't need no more vehicles in here, buddy. Pull it on around." He struggled to recognize the unfamiliar driver.

"Agent Spencer, what brings you out here?" Yates looked over and recognized her passenger for the first time. "Didn't know you two knew one another."

They pulled the car to the rutted curve on the other side of the highway and slowly got out to see the twisted remains of the blue BMW. The car lay on its side, but it was easy to see by the long tears across the body that it had rolled a number of times before coming to rest against a large pine tree. What remained of the top had been peeled back like the top of a sardine can.

"Jaws-of-Life," Yates observed. "Only way they could have got him out."

"How bad?" Jeb asked, and then dreaded the answer.

"I'm not a doctor, Mr. Mason," the sheriff said quietly. "But I believe it is pretty bad. The EMTs seemed awful sure of that, anyways."

"Do they know what might have caused it?"

"Those highway patrolmen are working on that right now." Yates pointed to a tall, rawboned officer who was running a tape measure along a skid mark in the center of the highway. "Reckon they'll be able to tell us more in the by-and-by."

Shauna Spencer was quietly surveying the scene as well. It was a long and flat stretch of highway, with a slight hint of a curve some two hundred yards before it straightened out again. High pines on either side of the road and a narrow shoulder. A driver that lost control, particularly at a high rate of speed, had little room to maneuver back onto the highway. A minor mistake, a lapse in attention, a cell call...all could cause even an experienced driver to make a potentially fatal error.

"I'm guessing your buddy drove this road about a million times. It's a damn shame something like this could happen," Yates said. He shook his head and reached down to pick up a small lug nut that had most likely rolled across the highway from the crash site. He tossed it back and forth in his hand, and they watched a slew of officers walk gingerly around the vehicle, studying it as they might if it were a spaceship from another planet.

"How many times are you guessing it rolled, Sheriff?" Shauna asked.

"Ma'am, it's hard to say really. Judging by how beat up the body is...and this is just me talking, of course, I'd say four or five times at least. Your friend had a kind of heavy foot, Mr. Mason."

The fire truck across the highway slowly began to pull away and they could see the yellow lights of a wrecker as it began to wind between the patrol cars, moving closer to the carcass it was to tow. The harsh bark of multiple radios blared from the officials on-site.

"Something kind of funny about all this," Shauna said, and she walked closer to one of the skid marks and bent down to examine it.

Yates and Jeb walked over and stood behind her.

"Sheriff Yates...you got a minute?" said a rangy patrolman, who was standing at the car. A second man, shorter and with wire-rim glasses and what looked like a bad comb-over, was talking to him. "Comb over" was pointing to something on the body of the car and the patrolman seemed to be listening intently.

Yates left Jeb and Shauna and walked over.

"What's funny?" Jeb asked, turning to Shauna.

"I'm not an expert, but this is kind of strange." She gestured again to the skid marks. "Very short skid pattern...too short, in my opinion. Like he tried lightly pumping the brakes and then thought better of it."

"Does that make sense to you? I mean...why would he not hit the brakes hard if he were losing it?" Jeb asked, and he too studied the marks left on the highway.

"There's a lot of possible reasons…thought he had control of the car. Maybe another car coming in his direction, I guess…but it's almost as if…" She fell silent again, intently studying the highway.

"Yeah, yeah…as if what?"

"As if he didn't want to brake…or maybe the brakes themselves didn't want to brake."

"What does that mean exactly?"

Sheriff Yates began to walk back to them. "Well, we're going to have to impound the car. State boys want to take a real close look at this thing," he said. "Get a load of this. They're saying the brakes might have been faulty…might have even been tampered with. Now don't that put a new wrinkle in your bonnet?"

Jeb stared at the remains of the BMW for a few long seconds. "Sheriff, I believe we need to talk," he said.

"'Bout this wreck, Mr. Mason?" Yates glanced over at Shauna. Her expression was equally grim.

"No…about Zeke Andrews," Jeb answered. "I have a story to tell you. I've waited a long time to tell it."

"Son, we get this straightened out," Yates glanced over to Shauna Spencer briefly, "be happy to talk to you about the Andrews boy."

"Sheriff, might be important to talk to you as soon as possible."

"You sound pretty serious, Mr. Mason."

"We're going to head over to the hospital, Sheriff. You think you might be able to ride over with us?"

Roy Yates's leather brow tightened. He looked over his shoulder, acknowledged one of the patrolmen with a nod, and clambered into the backseat of the Crown Victoria.

• • •

On the drive to Carolinas Medical Center, Jeb explained his discovery of the papers at Mary Tully's, then his recollections of the summer night so many years ago. Yates listened quietly, only occasionally asking questions to clarify his understanding. Shauna drove without offering opinion. She watched the sheriff closely through the rearview mirror for his reaction.

Jeb ended his story just as the first large skyscrapers of Charlotte came into view. Roy Yates sat silently for a while. He quietly considered a large passenger bus as it pulled up alongside them at a stoplight on the outskirts of the city. The bright panel on its side blared the local prominence of a Carolina Panthers call-in radio show host.

"So it was you three? You, Zeke Andrews, and Gardner who were outside the Thompson house the night he died?" Yates asked.

"That's right. Andy and I were in the trees. Zeke was at the window."

"You have any reason to believe then that he had seen something like that?"

"No, Sheriff. But we were kids. And we were scared."

"Yes sir, I imagine so. I imagine so. You ever tell anybody about that night?"

"No."

"How 'bout Gardner? Reckon he ever talked about it?"

"Can't say, Sheriff. I doubt it, though. Wasn't something any of us wanted to dredge up."

"You got them papers with you? The cutouts and such?"

Jeb held up the brown envelope that lay beside him on the front seat. "Yeah...I've got them."

"Ms. Spencer, I'm guessing some of your people could help us with this. Some expert analysis might not hurt right now," Yates said.

"I believe we can do that, Sheriff. We'll need to get Mac Boller involved early tomorrow."

"Mind telling me again 'bout that break-in over to the motel?" the sheriff asked.

Jeb related the story a second time, up to and including his introduction to his fellow passenger, just as they wheeled into the parking deck at Carolinas Medical Center.

"Sheriff, you think any of this could be related? Even Andy's car wreck?" Jeb asked.

"Can't say, son. Can't say." Yates opened the rear door of the car and glanced warily around the parking lot. "Why don't we go and check on your friend right now?"

The three walked toward the stairwell. The sound of their footsteps echoed against the concrete walls.

CHAPTER SIXTY-ONE

Brenda Gardner sat in one corner of the ninth-floor Intensive Care Unit waiting room. A throng of people milled around her, and Jeb watched an older woman kneel and whisper into her ear. Several men stood quietly talking in another corner of the room, occasionally glancing over toward Brenda. A television sat on a single table, and an older man sat huddled in front of a *Gunsmoke* rerun. Festus Hagan sauntered merrily across the screen, his spurs jangling in rhythm with his stride.

Jeb drifted toward Brenda. She glanced up blankly, then recognizing him, stood, and they embraced. He could feel her sobbing as they hugged.

"It's bad, Jeb...it's so bad." She struggled to catch her breath.

"I know, Brenda. But Andy's a tough guy. He'll pull through." But he realized how stupid a suggestion that was. He had no idea of his condition. What else could he say?

"Do you know...what happened?" Jeb asked.

Brenda shook her head. "No...an officer came to our house. Only that he's been in an accident. And that he's badly hurt." She wiped her bloodshot eyes as another arrival to the waiting room embraced her.

Over the next hour they would learn the situation was just as grave as Sheriff Yates had earlier described. Andy Gardner's injuries were significant. His condition had been listed as critical, with extensive internal trauma. He was unconscious but breathing on his own. The physician who appeared in the wee hours of the morning spoke privately with the family. He was decidedly cautious in his assessment of Gardner's chances for recovery.

Sheriff Yates quietly expressed his sympathies, mingling easily with the people who moved in and out of the waiting room. His presence was not of an official nature, but Jeb could see that many of the visitors were friends, not just neighbors.

Shauna waited in the doorway. She spoke quietly into her cell phone. Jeb caught her eyes once. She flashed the feint hint of a reassuring smile. He returned the favor, glad for some strange reason that she was there. At one point she slipped over and exchanged a few quiet words with Brenda Gardner. Jeb watched them embrace silently.

A few moments later he eased out the waiting room door, hoping to find a vending machine or someplace far away from the stifling tension of the ICU. He lingered in the hallway until Shauna fell in beside him, and they made their way to a small canteen on the first floor. The hospital seemed almost surreally quiet, as if the sick and injured had been tucked away for the night.

"Can I buy you a cup of coffee?" Jeb asked, dropping quarters into a coffeemaker. They watched the Dixie cup drop into place and the hot stream of java follow.

"No, thanks. Reached my limit couple of hours ago," Shauna answered.

Jeb dropped heavily into the chair beside her. A janitor, his shoulders bent with age, pushed a mop on the far side of the canteen so slowly that one might guess it weighed a hundred pounds.

"So, what do you think?" he asked. The coffee tasted as old as he guessed it probably was.

"I think it's been a hell of a day for you," she replied. Her eyes locked on his. "And I'm really not sure of what to think yet."

"You know, if any of this is true..." Jeb glanced back in the direction of the ICU. "I mean, it just is possible that..."

"Yes. It just is possible that your friend was not just an accident."

"Sheriff said it looked like the brakes might have been tampered with."

"He said they *might* have been tampered with," Shauna said. "And I do believe that the accident did not look right."

"The skid marks?"

"Among other things. Too short. Straight road. Familiar highway."

"So it is then possible that someone was trying to kill him...right?"

She paused for several long seconds. "Yes, Jeb. I believe it is possible."

"Mother Mary," Jeb whispered. "What the hell have we stumbled into?"

Shauna tapped her fingers idly on the hard metal table in front of them, her mind lost in thought. "I just don't know, Jeb. But we have some very strange pieces that may be linked together. I believe some funny things happened with your friend before he died. I think there is sufficient evidence of some type of activity that may or may not be related to extortion. There is some suggestion it might be connected to the incident you described when you guys were kids. It's clear he got a lot of money, at least by his standards, shortly before his death." She paused.

"And...?" Jeb waited.

"If...if any of this is even partially accurate, and I'm not saying that it is, then it is entirely possible that Mr. Andrews's death wasn't a suicide. And it *is* possible that the individual or individuals responsible for his death would be very eager to make sure that the information he had..." Her voice trailed off.

"Would be very interested in making sure it never comes to light," he finished her thought.

"Yes. Very interested. But it is an incredibly bold move to try and kill someone in broad daylight. If we find that the brakes were tampered with...or that your friend was actually run off the road, it might mean that the killer is getting desperate."

"Shauna, there's something else. Another aspect to all of this I need to tell you about."

He related the story of the near-miss with the transfer truck the evening before.

"You're telling me someone tried to *kill* you the very same night of the attempted break-in of your room?" Shauna's voice rose and her eyes grew wide. "Why are you just getting around to telling me this?"

"It seemed crazy. I really didn't think it was important. Some drunk on a deserted country road..."

"You said the car just sped up and wouldn't let you pass?"

"Didn't appear to want to, that's for sure."

"And when you slowed, the car slowed."

"Seemed like it. But it all happened so fast. Could be that the driver was trying to slow at the same time I was to avoid the head on collision."

"You buying that?" Shauna's big blue eyes studied him closely.

"No. Not really."

"And when I suggested back at the motel that you could be in some degree of danger, you weren't even going to bring this up?"

"I am not, by nature, a conspiracy advocate. Just didn't see them as being related."

"Damn it, Jeb. You are lucky to be alive." Shauna angrily slapped her hand against the table.

"But I can't be at any risk *unless* Zeke's letter is real. Unless he really did see something that night. Right?"

She nodded. "You should have told me. It might have made it easier to pull all the pieces together."

"I'm not too accustomed to being in the middle of one of these things, OK?"

"Will you promise me to tell me everything from this point on? I mean everything."

"Shauna, I'm not going to hide behind the law on this. If Zeke was involved in something, I am going to find out what..."

"That's law enforcement's responsibility, Mr. Mason." Shauna's voice grew harder.

"And I intend to help law enforcement in that undertaking," Jeb answered.

"Law enforcement does not need..."

"Law enforcement *failed* to recognize Judge Thompson's murder or my friend's. I came to *you* with evidence, Shauna."

"Look, Jeb, I understand how you..."

"No, Shauna, you don't," Jeb interrupted her.

"You are the most stubborn human being." She glared at him. He grinned back at her and the moment of tension suddenly fell away. She tried to stifle a smile but could only look away. "I should have arrested you when I had the chance, you know."

"Do you realize what we're saying here?" Jeb leaned back in his chair and studied the panels of the ceiling, his eyes falling on the sprinklers that were scattered overhead. "If this turns out to be accurate, we have someone who murdered thirty years ago, then again in the last several days."

"We have a lot more than that, Jeb," Shauna answered. "We have someone who also may have attempted two other murders in the last week."

"Two murders, two attempted murders…over the last thirty-plus years?" Jeb could scarcely believe his own words. "Is that possible?"

"It is definitely possible, Mr. Mason," Sheriff Yates answered. He stood at the canteen door. "But I'm thinking it may be a lot more than just two murders. A *lot* more."

CHAPTER SIXTY-TWO

It was almost one o'clock on Tuesday morning before Yates, Shauna, and Jeb left the ICU waiting room. There had been no further updates from attending physicians around Andy Gardner's condition. Only a small contingent of friends remained. Brenda Gardner had curled into a ball in a corner of the room and begun to doze. Someone had dimmed the lights.

Across the street from Carolinas Medical, a dark sedan was parked on a tree-lined residential street, diagonal to the CMC parking lot. There were no streetlights for another fifty feet or so. The solitary figure inside could remain unnoticed until daybreak if necessary. The man watched the three get into the Crown Victoria on the third floor of the parking deck. The exit was no more than one hundred yards from where he was parked. Spencer's car pulled out onto the city street. He slowly pulled out behind.

They were almost out of Charlotte before anyone spoke. Traffic had lightened to the point that only a few cars were left on the road. Shauna had already briefed Mac Boller, whose grumpy demeanor at being woken up at such a late hour had been only modestly ameliorated by the nature of her call. He promised to meet them at 7:00 a.m. the next morning.

"So, Sheriff," Shauna glanced into her rearview mirror at Yates, "you have our undivided attention."

Yates watched a battered pickup pass by in the left lane as they left the city lights of Charlotte behind. "What do you think the chances are that we could learn anything much from the papers Mason found?" he asked.

"I don't know," Shauna answered, "we need to talk to the boy, of course...at best, we could get prints, probably only from Andrews, but we could establish a tie there. Possibly we could get a sense of what the message was he was trying to put together...but we have fragments of a letter he may or may not have ever sent. Circumstantial evidence. Nothing more."

"Sheriff, do you believe this is real? That Zeke might have seen something that night?" Jeb turned to look back at Yates.

Roy Yates looked out the window, vacantly watching the fields pass by in the darkness.

"Sheriff Yates?" Shauna asked.

"I believe," Yates began, "that something happened that night. Something that none of us could even begin to understand...until now."

"So you believe we may be dealing with a homicide in the Andrews case?" Shauna looked at his dark silhouette in the rearview mirror.

"Yes ma'am, I believe the possibility is there. Yes ma'am, I do."

"Sheriff, you said 'more murders.' What were you talking about?" Jeb asked.

"Son, I'm going to tell you both a story. One that you know nothing about. Maybe I shouldn't. Maybe I should just sit on this for a while. But I'm guessing it's one you ought to hear. We got an hour to Stacey. It's a good time for a ghost story, I reckon."

CHAPTER SIXTY-THREE

Highway 73 was a two-lane that cut through cotton and soybean fields as it headed east. A crescent moon bathed the land in a silvery glow as the car made its way toward Stacey. Except for an occasional car headed in the opposite direction, the road was theirs alone.

"I remember that summer for a lot of reasons," Yates began. "I mustered out of the service in May of that year. Piddled around down in Havelock for the better part of a month after I got my papers, partying with some of my old buddies who were in 'Nam with me. Woke up one Sunday morning at a little flea bag of a motel not more than a stone's throw from the guard gate' to Cherry Point and said to myself, 'Roy, it's time to go home."

"Been sixteen years in the Corps by then, two tours in Vietnam. Had no plans, just wanted to do something else. Got on the bus. Came home to Stacey. Back then, jobs were fairly plentiful around here, even for an old jarhead like me. And wasn't too much resentment toward servicemen either. Not like it was in other places, anyways.

"Second night back in town, went down to Brady's Pool Hall, a little shack that used to be out west of town, close to where Floyd Lewis's Citgo Station is today. Played pool 'til one or two in the morning. Won me forty or fifty bucks from a few of the local boys. I was just getting in my Uncle Leon's pickup when a sheriff's car pulls up alongside."

"Sheriff Sam Nunnelly was driving. He up and offers me a job right then and there. Remembered me from Sunday school and baseball and such. Just offered me a job! I remember he said to me, 'Yates, you got a little smarts in ya, the marines made sure you got some tough, how'd you like to be a deputy?'

"I accepted on the spot. Hadn't even put in an application at one of the mills yet, and I already had a job. It was probably two or three years before I knew my Uncle Leon and Sheriff Nunnelly were old card buddies. Didn't make any difference to me anyway."

"Sheriff, what exactly..." Shauna interjected.

"Getting to it. Getting to it. So happens my first few weeks of deputying was pretty much "'learn as you go.'" Back then, there were only three deputies anyways, so we sort of divided the county up. They gave me the western part, which tended to have a few more problems because Lancaster County was wet. We were dry. Lots of drunks coming home on Saturday nights. I'd park beside the big JP Stevens's billboard and pull 'em over, sometimes as many as ten in one night.

"Saturday night, July seventh, was like a lot of other nights, busy for the most part. Around 5:30 the morning of July eighth, I got a call from our dispatcher, requesting I respond to a call at 619 Grissom Street. The call came from next door, 617 Grissom, from a neighbor, a fellow by the name of Henders. Seemed he was to meet his neighbor, Judge Thompson, at five o'clock that morning for a trip to Lake Norman—bass fishing.

"It was a trip they made once a month. The Judge owned a boat he kept at the lake. Well, this morning, Henders couldn't raise him. He got worried. Thompson was an old man, heavy. Had a heart attack a number of years before.

"I got there by 5:45 or so; the sun still hadn't come up, I remember. Tried the front door, found it locked. No signs of life in the house. Curtains weren't drawn. There were lights on. Something didn't feel right, though. Couldn't exactly tell you what, but for some reason, I was kind of spooked.

"Old man Henders, he stood out on the sidewalk in front. Wouldn't come back on the porch. Reckon he was thinking the worse, too.

"I finally went around back. Big old house, three-story. There was a garden area, as I recall. Maybe a little overgrown. I remember how strange it felt to be creeping around back there, still dark and all. Halfway thought about pulling my pistol. There was a big bay window, lights were on. I went up and looked inside.

"He was laying across a big wingback chair, sprawled, more like it. I could tell he was dead. His face was puffy already. Big man, ruddy.

Looked like he had been reading a newspaper when he suffered the heart attack.

"I had seen my share of dead people, but for some reason, this one kind of shook me. Couldn't say why. Without even going in the house I got on the radio to the sheriff. Before you knew it, all kinds of law enforcement were there. City, county, even a few highway patrolmen. The judge was a mighty influential man. News of his death traveled fast.

"Me being a rookie and all, I never got that close to the situation. The coroner pronounced him dead at the scene. A few of the boys examined the room. From what I heard, it was open and shut. They got his wife on the phone. She was down in Savannah visiting family. The old man had a history of health problems. Type A personality in a high-profile job. I don't believe they even did an autopsy. Back then, state law didn't require it. Family didn't seem interested in pursuing it."

"So, that's it?" Shauna asked. "Local civic leader drops dead. No questions asked. Gone and buried?"

"No reason to question it, Ms. Spencer," Yates answered. "But it always kind of bugged me a little, I reckon. Can't say why. Just did."

"Sheriff, forgive me, but I'm not following you. Why does this have any bearing on any of this?" Shauna asked.

"Because of what else happened that night, Ms. Spencer. Because of what else happened."

"And that is?"

"Mr. Mason, do you remember anything else about the night of the seventh?" Yates looked to Jeb.

"Can't say that I do, Sheriff…I mean, other than what we've already talked about…"

"Remember the Glasser boy?"

Jeb paused. "Yeah…I do…the boy that drowned."

"Make that the *boys* that drowned down on the Yadkin," Yates said. "The very same night."

CHAPTER SIXTY-FOUR

"Sheriff, I'm not following any of this. Who is the Glasser boy and what does his death have to do with Zeke Andrews?" Spencer asked.

"Mr. Mason, you mentioned that when you and the other two got back to Stacey that next morning that all hell had broken loose in the town. You remember much about the drownings?"

"Not much." Jeb struggled to reconstruct the memories of that morning. "But I know the town was in an uproar..."

"That might be putting it mildly," Yates said.

"Sheriff, please forgive me, but what in the hell are we talking about?" Shauna asked.

"Agent Spencer, on the morning of July eighth I had another call. Probably 8:00, maybe 8:30. Late in my shift. I remember that. Billy Glasser lived out on Carthage Road. His boy, Matt, had gone camping with two of his buddies the night before. Matt had a lawn cutting business with his older brother, Caleb. Seems they were due to cut the grounds at St. Timothy's Presbyterian bright and early that Sunday morning, way before church services, say around 7:00 a.m. The minister wanted it cut early on account of some big city guest that was in town. Can't say why Saturday afternoon wouldn't have worked, but it didn't. So anyway, the boy doesn't show. The older brother goes off alone, bellyaching the whole time. But Billy, he's worried. Calls in. Says his son never slips up on his yard cutting. Asks if we can send somebody by to round them up." Yates grew quiet, thinking back to the events of that summer day so long ago.

"I knew the area pretty well. Camped down on the Yadkin a lot when I was a boy. So I head down to the river. I had just parked my car and was headed down this little trail to the water when I spotted something, hanging in the branches of a big old oak that swung out over the river. I got closer and could see it was a boy's windbreaker—dark blue, soaking wet."

"The sandbar most everybody camped on was still a half-mile away upstream, and the trail went right alongside the river. The water was high, real high. And fast. You could tell there had been a big storm the night before. Lots of sticks, debris."

"I saw him, half-way lodged up underneath a tree on the other side of the river. Could tell he was dead. His arms were all contorted. Even from a distance, his skin looked more like a fish's than a person's. Oily white. Like the underbelly of a fish. That was Joe Keyes. They didn't find the Clover boy, believe his name was Paul, until noon. Matt Glasser's body was almost four miles downstream."

"Wait a minute. Are you saying three children drowned…on the same night?" Shauna asked. "My God…how?"

"The official verdict was that they had camped too near to the Yadkin. Violent storm had raised the river's waters in a matter of minutes. Sleepy little river becomes a raging wall of water. Three kids huddled in their tents. Maybe asleep. Probably didn't know what was happening until they were swept away."

"The official verdict…" Jeb interrupted.

"Yeah, the official story. I didn't believe it then. Don't believe it now."

"Why, Sheriff?" Shauna continued to periodically glance through the mirror at the dark image in the backseat.

"I found what was left of the campsite. Most of it was washed away. Few stakes, what looked like a rope-line. But something didn't set right with me, wasn't sure why for a long time. Then it occurred to me when I watched them fish the last boy out. Shoes. He had tennis shoes on. Fully clothed. Even a jacket."

"I'm not following you," Shauna said.

"Well, Ms. Spencer, the official theory was three boys camped on a river bank, a sandbar, get caught in rising waters and swept away."

"Yes…I understand that but…"

"So why are they wearing tennis shoes? Why are they wearing their jeans, a jacket?" Jeb interjected.

"That's right. Didn't look to me like they were tucked away in sleeping bags."

"So kids don't wear shoes in sleeping bags?" Shauna asked.

"Not normally, no. It was a relatively warm night. Why the jackets?" Yates continued.

"Maybe they got caught in the storm. They're soaked. They jump in their tents. Zip up the bag, trying to stay warm," Shauna continued. "Isn't that possible?"

"Yes ma'am, it is," Yates answered. "Funny thing, though. We only found one of those sleeping bags...a few miles downstream. Still bundled and tied."

For a few moments only the sound of the road responded. They rode together in silence, Shauna and Jeb factoring Yates comments carefully.

"So, what happened?" Shauna finally asked.

"Nothing. I told Sheriff Nunnelly that I wondered about all this. He said there was no other rational explanation. Certainly nothing that warranted an investigation. Families were hurting. Best thing we could do was get these boys back to their families. Put them at peace."

"So...nothing happens. You have three dead kids. You're doubting the circumstances surrounding their deaths. And *nothing* happens?" Shauna's voice rose higher.

"Ma'am, it was thirty years ago. I was a six-week rookie. What could we do? Conduct an autopsy? Talk to witnesses? Those boys were still dead."

"But you had doubts..." Jeb again.

"Yes. Or maybe questions. It didn't sit right."

"So...that's it?" Shauna asked.

"No ma'am. I spent Monday morning, the day after we found the boys, looking for something, anything."

"And...?"

"Found what looked like a campfire pit, only pitched on the bank, well up from the river. Everything else had been pretty much washed away by the rain. But it made me wonder. What if those kids weren't camped on the sandbar at all? What if they were well up on the bank?"

"What if they were?" Shauna asked.

"If they were...if they were, then there's no way three boys, all of whom had been camping for years, wander off into the dark and happen to fall in the river. Doesn't make sense."

"So what did you think?" Jeb asked.

"Mr. Mason, I thought then the same thing I've thought ever since. That something else happened to those boys. What, I can't say. I couldn't imagine, didn't want to, that someone could have deliberately drowned them. But something was very wrong."

"It ended there? The judge is buried. The kids, too?" Shauna asked.

"It ended there. Over the years, people forgot. The town moved on. Some of the families moved away. Time passed. But I never forgot."

Yates tapped his index finger against the car window, staring out at the dark trees that bordered the highway.

"There was one more thing. A little thing. The next morning when I went back, to the river, I mean...it was early, very early. I was down on the very same sandbar, just seeing if there was anything I could find. I heard something or maybe just sensed it. Not sure what. But I'm sure there was someone else there. On the bank. In the trees. Watching. I called out. Even drew my pistol. Never found anybody. But somebody was there."

"Sheriff, are you saying there might be a connection between the deaths of the judge and the three kids?" Shauna asked.

"No, at least not directly. I accepted Thompson's death for what it was announced to be. Heart attack. But not the boys. But I couldn't come up with any reason for them to have accidentally drowned either. Didn't want to consider that a monster lived in Stacey that could have just killed three of our kids. No motive. No evidence."

"No motive?" Jeb asked.

"Mr. Mason, that's what bothers me. If, just *if*...your friend did see something that night. If he did see something in that house that he shouldn't have...then there's every chance *someone* could also have seen him. Someone who couldn't afford to be identified. Someone who gave chase."

For a time, only the steady thrum of the dark road and the tires filled the silence. The fields had given way to tall pines, and the moon's light grew into even deeper shadows as the car sliced through the trees.

"My God..." Jeb whispered at last. "Someone who saw three boys vanish into the darkness..."

"Someone who saw three boys running. Running west," Yates said.

"Toward the Yadkin River," Jeb continued.

"Yes," Yates answered. "Toward the Yadkin River."

CHAPTER SIXTY-FIVE

It was ten minutes past two o'clock when Spencer's Crown Victoria pulled into the parking lot of the sheriff's office. Except for the dispatcher, the building was quiet. Yates's car sat in a dark corner of the lot.

"I'm going to be seeing the both of you at seven, then?" the sheriff asked as he leaned over the driver's window.

"Sheriff, we'll be happy to meet you here. Might be easier to do that than to meet at the motel," Shauna said.

"No...let's stick with the motel right now, if it's all the same to you, Ms. Spencer. Might be better to talk off-site, if you get my meaning."

"I'll have Agent Boller with me," Shauna said.

"I appreciate you're letting me join you, Sheriff," Jeb added. "I know there's no obligation to include me."

"Mr. Mason, kind of figure we're trying to sort this all out right now. And unless I'm wrong, you seem to be the only one that's still able to do that."

The comment hung in the humid night air.

"You know, Mr. Mason, it's none of my business...but I'm going to suggest you make sure to lock up tight tonight. I got a deputy I'm going to send over to the motel, too. Seems to be a pretty good idea right now."

"Thanks, Sheriff, but I'm fine."

"Mr. Mason may turn out to be a material witness in a murder investigation, Sheriff. That is a very good idea. Thank you," Shauna answered for him. "We'll make sure to check the area ourselves.

"You gonna be a lot better off listening to this lady. This thing is starting to look mighty serious," Yates said.

Jeb nodded.

"Reckon might be a good idea for me to take possession of that envelope, too." Yates said. "You agree with that, Agent Spencer?"

Shauna nodded as Jeb pulled the envelope out from underneath the front seat of the car and handed it over to the sheriff.

Yates grinned. "You thinking you have to hide this thing?"

"There's a packet in there. Not sure what's in it." Jeb answered. "Might be marijuana, but can't say…"

"Well, then. All the better that law enforcement has it."

The sheriff watched Spencer's car pull out of the parking lot and head back in the direction of the motel. With only four hours of sack time ahead of him, he would spend tonight in his office. A few moments later, he settled behind his desk and poured his first cup of coffee. He reached behind him to the large filing cabinet and pulled out the bottom drawer. In the very back, wrapped with kite cord, were the first spiral notebooks he ever used as a deputy sheriff. Each had been carefully sorted by month. He cut the cord with his pocket knife and pulled out the month of July. Then he began to go back to a summer night thirty years before.

•   •   •

Just as Sheriff Yates opened the notebook, Shauna and Jeb pulled into the Dogwood Inn parking lot. She insisted on double-checking Jeb's room despite his objections. Everything appeared in order. It was in the same general disarray he'd left behind when he had first called Shauna.

"You should try and get some sleep. We're going to have a long day tomorrow," she said, standing in the doorway.

"Not sure I'll get a lot of sleep tonight," Jeb said. He wiped his forehead and looked over the room as if none of it seemed familiar. Only a few hours before he had been sorting pieces of paper on the bed and wondering about why Zeke Andrews's last days were consumed with cutouts. It seemed like a dream.

"We start trying to sort all of this out tomorrow, Jeb."

"Shauna…I came back here because I believe I owed a debt to an old friend. I had no idea how much I really owed."

"I know all of this is very overwhelming. But we will figure this out. I promise you."

"I may have gotten my friend killed. I may have gotten three innocent children killed..." His voice drifted away.

"You didn't get anyone killed, Jeb. Do you hear me? You may have stumbled into something terrible...but you didn't get anyone killed."

He smiled and looked out over the few cars parked in the lot. "You want to try telling that to Joe Keyes...or to Matt Glasser's family or..."

"I want you to listen to me." She placed her hand against his chest. "Victims don't commit the crimes. They just have to deal with the consequences of the perpetrators. If a murder was committed, everything that's happened since was to cover that up. You cannot assume the guilt for that. Do you hear me?"

"I hear you, Shauna."

"I need you clearheaded tomorrow, Jeb. We have one thing now that we have to do. We have to figure out if there was a murder...or murders...and we have to identify who committed them."

"And we will do that."

"Yes. We will do that." She smiled at him and he felt his pulse quicken. She slowly removed her hand and for the briefest moment he wanted to draw her closer.

"Give me your cell phone," she said.

"Are you confiscating it?" He managed a smile.

"No, I'm entering my number into your phone. And yours into mine." She glanced up at him. "Will you promise me to keep this door dead-bolted? And not to go on any late night jogs or drives or vigilante searches?" She handed him back the cell.

"So, huh, if I hear something, should I give you a call?" his tone was teasing. "And does it have to be of an official nature?"

She glanced over her shoulder as she walked away and flashed a winsome smile. "You can call me anytime you like, Mr. Mason...and no, it does not have to be of an official nature."

He watched her walk the length of the balcony and then onto the wing that completed the L-shape of the hall. He didn't close his door until she had climbed the next flight of stairs and was inside her room. She waved and made an exaggerated demonstration of locking the dead bolt a final time. He returned the wave and as he closed his door, noticed the deputy sheriff's cruiser that was now parked in a far corner of the lot. A uniformed officer stood leaning against the hood, casually smoking a cigarette. He was looking in Jeb's direction.

•   •   •

That night, Jeb dreamed he was walking across a narrow ridge high above the boiling, black waters of a river. He was alone and the darkness swelled around him as he scrambled over rocks and through brush until he came to the highest point of a great cliff. A solitary figure stood there, his back to Jeb. The figure looked out into the abyss.

Fear welled up in Jeb, wrapping around him with the gloom. He recognized the boy.

The figure slowly began to turn, and Jeb looked into the dead eyes of Zeke Andrews.

"You killed me, you know," Zeke said.

Then he turned and stepped into the abyss, into oblivion.

CHAPTER SIXTY-SIX

The first hour of the breakfast meeting was devoted to debriefing Agent Mac Boller on the developments of the previous day. Though Shauna had offered a thumbnail sketch, both she and Sheriff Yates wanted Boller to have the opportunity to ask Jeb questions and to gauge the evidence, or lack thereof.

Boller listened quietly for the most part, and managed to down two ham and cheese omelets along with a side of bacon and three pieces of heavily buttered toast as he did. He carried with him the Steadman arson investigation file which Sheriff Yates thumbed through quietly. Though they had planned a formal meeting with Yates and Police Chief Greer at some point over the next several days, Boller thought a bit of professional courtesy might be a good idea. He had spent the better part of a career trying to work with local law enforcement. A few bones tossed in the right direction could go a long way.

Shauna stuck with a bowl of cereal and declined the coffee. Jeb managed a few pieces of dry wheat toast. His appetite had left him. He noticed Sheriff Yates did not eat, and by the look of his eyes, he hadn't slept much either.

"So you're saying that only one of you, Andrews was it, actually saw what took place in the house that night?" Mac Boller drained his coffee cup and looked toward Jeb.

"Only Zeke."

"And you never tried to find out what happened?" Boller's tone was sarcastic. "I mean, damn, somebody died in there."

"I know that. And no, not after the first morning. We were scared. We'd never seen anything like that. Zeke was almost catatonic that night."

"So you're saying you three just ran into the night? Found a dark corner and waited out the storm. That right?"

"That's right."

"And the next day you just walk out?"

"We walked out. No one knew until we got back to Andy's house that Judge Thompson was dead."

"What was your friend's…this Andrews boy…reaction?"

Jeb paused. "I don't know. I mean, I don't remember. I know Andy and I were scared. I can remember we walked Zeke home. He wasn't really talking. We told him to stay cool. That we didn't do anything. Later on, Andy and I talked about it, of course. But we both pretty much thought he had seen the judge have a heart attack. We knew the less said, the better."

Boller considered his response quietly, never taking his eyes off of Jeb. Roy Yates continued to thumb through the file Boller had given him.

"Sheriff, you say there was never an autopsy conducted on Thompson?" Boller asked.

"No sir. It was determined to be a death by natural causes. Heart attack. Maybe heart failure. Can't really say for sure."

"Was there a physician called to the scene?" Boller asked.

"My guess would be that it was Dr. Harrison Carter. He's retired now, but he was county coroner. I'm pretty sure he pronounced him dead at the scene. His nephew does the same job now. Prominent family," Yates said.

"Were there any questions about that at the time?" Boller picked up the empty coffee pot and shook it, then glanced warily toward the kitchen.

"Not that I recall," Yates answered.

"You say Thompson was married? Where was his wife?"

"Again, my recollection is that she was in Savannah. Sick sister that she was taking care of."

"Where's the guy buried?"

Yates shook his head and frowned. "He isn't. The body was cremated."

"Damn." Boller picked up a pack of cigarettes that sat beside his plate. He started to pull one out, and then stopped himself. "How about the Andrews's deal? Any evidence of foul play?"

"No. But I think it's worth a second look. We had a lot of people up on that ridge. I'm not saying we missed something...but given what Mr. Mason has run across...we need to look again," Yates said.

"Have we impounded the BMW? The Gardner vehicle?" Boller asked.

"Highway Patrol has it now," Yates answered.

"And the Andrews boy. The one who had all these newspaper clippings. Have we got anyone who has talked to him yet?"

"I think that's you or me, Mac. And the sooner the better," Shauna piped in.

Boller looked toward Roy Yates. "Sheriff, you have the envelope Mr. Mason here believes indicates this thing was a murder or something?"

"Got it. Tried to take a look at it last night but don't want to monkey with it much. Figure your people will want it now?"

Boller sighed and looked toward Jeb. "Guessing might be a good idea if we have our evidence experts take a look at it. See what they see as regards letters or symbols or secret codes or whatever..."

Sheriff Yates nodded.

"But it doesn't prove anything," Agent Boller continued. "This guy could have fantasized about blackmailing some rich bastard as a way of escaping his own miserable life. Doesn't prove a damn thing." He looked back to Jeb.

"No. It doesn't prove a damn thing," Jeb answered.

"You mentioned some drug paraphernalia?"

"I don't think it's drugs," Sheriff Yates interjected. "Looks to me like Andrews or the boy just yanked up a handful of the front lawn, stuck it in a bag..."

"Well, we can verify pretty quickly. Find anything in the search of his residence that suggested he was using?"

"No, but wouldn't be surprised if we did," Yates answered. "He had a prior on drug possession."

"So, even if this is part of the front yard, could very well be drugs involved with all this."

"Could be," Yates said. "But the only thing we found when we searched his trailer were some syringes in the refrigerator."

"Syringes?"

"He was a diabetic. Insulin. Appears he didn't take it often, but he did occasionally inject."

Boller glanced toward Shauna. "You have a feeling about all of this, don't you?"

"Yes, I do," she said.

"Mind if I ask why?"

"I don't know. Just a feeling."

"Well, we got more than enough to take a closer look at the Andrews death. I just don't know how much we can dig up on the judge's death… or those young boys who drowned. That's going to have to be some of you local folks, Sheriff," Boller said.

Yates did not look up. He was carefully reading a page from the file Boller had carried with him to the breakfast.

"Sheriff?"

Yates looked up. "Sorry, Agent Boller. Just reading through this Steadman thing more closely. Run it by me again."

"We're going to need the local authorities to help us with any information that might still be available about the death of the judge…or of the children."

"We'll see what we can find. I just don't know."

Boller nodded. "Shauna, I can get some help from Raleigh on the Andrews papers." He turned back to Jeb. "You said that lock you found might have come from his trailer, right?"

"Can't say, but his ex-wife said he used to keep a gun under lock and key. The lock I found might have been the one he used."

"But no gun?"

"No gun."

"And the key?"

"Wasn't there. Just the actual lock."

"What kind of lock is it?"

"I don't know. Just a simple lock," Jeb said.

"It's a padlock. Garden variety. And definitely no key," Yates interjected. "Went through those papers. Couldn't find it."

"What do you think about the gun?" Boller asked.

"Could be it's somewhere up on that ridge. Maybe down by the river. Or in the river, for that matter," Yates answered.

"All right, we can cordon off his trailer home and the spouse's residence. We ought to be able to start running down the dollars that were sent to Florida for the car. That might help us with some leads," Boller said.

"We can also get official records on Thompson's death certificate. Not sure it will offer us a lot," Shauna answered.

"Seen a thousand of 'em. Won't give us anything." Mac Boller waved the empty coffee cup and glanced again in the direction of the kitchen. "And we'll need to get a court order to exhume the Andrews body."

Jeb groaned at the thought. The Lebo boys would be getting paid double-time this week.

"Agreed. It's at least a start," Boller said. "Damnedest thing I've ever heard of, I'll tell you that. I'm sitting here trying to figure out what would compel someone to kill again after thirty years. If, in fact, that's what happened."

"How about the fear of being caught?" Shauna asked.

"I'll grant you that someone still walking this earth thirty years later would probably go to extraordinary lengths to silence someone who carried evidence against them."

"And we have the added ingredient of what might be an attempt to kill Andy Gardner...and maybe the same thing with Jeb...Mr. Mason here," Shauna added.

"Agreed, agreed," Boller answered. He studied Shauna as he spoke, then again inspected the empty coffee cup.

"There's one more thing...didn't think about it much at the time," Jeb said. "The morning after our little "deal" at the motel, the break-in attempt...Andy said his home had something several days before. The alarm went off...security company was alerted." He watched the others exchange glances.

"Do you know if they actually entered the home?" Boller asked.

"I don't. Just know Andy acted as if nothing like that had happened before."

"Yeah," Boller said quietly.

"Still no guarantee he knows who else was there that night though," Jeb offered.

"No guarantee," Shauna said. "But if you and Gardner paid for Andrews's funeral..." She left it unsaid.

Boller turned toward Yates. "Sheriff, you're pretty quiet. Something on your mind?"

"Motive," Yates answered simply.

"Well, I think we could say that if extortion was involved, we might have motive right there...at least as regards to Andrews," Shauna answered. They paused as the waitress returned to the table with a fresh pot of coffee.

"No ma'am, I guess I wasn't being clear," Yates shook his head. "I mean for my friend...Bump Patterson." He waved the Steadman file in the air.

CHAPTER SIXTY-SEVEN

"Sheriff, if it's all the same to you, I would like to stick to one investigation at a time," Boller said. "Not sure we can handle two of them. Jesus, are we going to get some questions on this one."

"'Bout that," Yates said as he laid the file down beside his plate. "I've been thinking about that since last night..." he paused and ran his fingers down one of the pages. "Got something to run by you about the Steadman fire. Maybe it's important. Maybe it's not."

The two agents turned their attention on Yates. "Mr. Mason," Boller said, "Thank you for stepping forward with this information. Either the sheriff or the SBI will be talking with you further. If I could ask you to excuse us now, we have a case we're working on..."

"Agent Boller, I think maybe we want to invite Mr. Mason to stick around a little while longer," Yates interrupted.

"Say what?"

"Yes sir. Maybe just a mite longer," Yates answered.

Mac Boller refilled his cup and did the same for Jeb's and the sheriff's. "Well, Sheriff, you got our undivided attention. Though I can't understand why we need to include Mr. Mason here in a conversation around the fire at Steadman."

"I don't know..." Yates began. "Let's say Zeke Andrews really was involved in a little blackmail scheme. Trying to soak somebody for a few bucks over something everybody else had long since forgot about. Maybe there was even a little payoff. He got the two thousand dollars somewhere. Maybe after he provided proof of some kind, or maybe as a show of good faith from the other party."

"The way I figure it, Andrews had no way of knowing about the three boys drowning and its connection to any of this. Hell, we still don't know how they died, but if the actual perp learned somebody out there had seen them that night…" Yates left his statement unfinished.

"Assuming that is possible, at some point, the killer had to realize…" Shauna said.

"That the three kids they killed that night…were the wrong kids," Jeb finished her sentence for her.

"That's right," said the sheriff, "the wrong ones. But that also meant that they could have missed one or more than one. They may have missed on all three. So suddenly they have to assume that more than one person knew about all of this. Had remained silent, but knew."

"What are you thinking, Sheriff?" Shauna asked.

"Let's say thirty-plus years ago, you pulled off the perfect murder. Or so you thought. Then one day a letter comes that says, *I know what you did.* You panic. You suddenly realize that a coupla kids saw everything. That the cover-up murders were a terrible mistake. What do you do? You begin to wonder, who else knows? Maybe you set up a down payment to the blackmailer, with a final meeting to take place later. But you're crafty. You set it up so you can kill this guy too. Maybe it's a coupla minutes. Or, maybe you have time to get the other names out of him before you kill him. What do you do if you don't?"

"I give up, Sheriff. What do you do?" Boller asked.

"You try to find out who else could have been there that night."

"All right. Let's say you've only got one name, Zeke Andrews. There's no guarantee they even knew his name, but we'll assume they do. That's a pretty big haystack to try and find someone in," Boller said.

"So, where would you go?" Yates answered, looking at each of the people seated around the table. "Where would you go?"

"You mean to find out who else might have been out there?" Boller asked.

"Yeah…if you suddenly find out someone saw you. And you know for a fact they were not alone…how would you go about finding out who else knows?"

The table fell quiet. "Sheriff, I don't know any way how you find out something like that three decades later…I mean who keeps records for that kind of stuff?" Boller answered. He fingered an unlit cigarette and watched the sheriff closely.

"Maybe health department records, I guess. Maybe the county courthouse, but that wouldn't give you viable leads. If the perp didn't know Andrews or his family, I can't see how finding out where his family lived that long ago would help very much," Shauna offered, shaking her head slowly, "I can't think of anyplace that would be of much help. You can't run an ad in the personal columns."

"No ma'am, can't say that would help. But you're scared now. Who else knows? Who else was there that night? Who were the other two boys you saw running away?" Yates asked.

"Just aren't a lot of leads that carry you back thirty years. Short of asking people around town, which you can't do," Boller answered.

"Yes, you're right. I've given it a lot of thought. Where would I go to find out about a kid that was ten or eleven years old when they were peeping through my windows? A small town kid, a local...I mean after all, who keeps a record of kids?"

Shauna exhaled softly, looked closely at the sheriff. Jeb exchanged glances with her and then turned back to Yates.

"I'm thinking a school might," the sheriff said. "I'm thinking a school might."

CHAPTER SIXTY-EIGHT

"If it was me," Roy Yates said, "I'd go to Steadman Elementary." He ran his finger down the list of materials in storage there, pausing when he came to student records. He pushed the page forward for the others to view. "I'd dig through those old student records. Try to find something, anything pertaining to Zeke Andrews. I would hope to get lucky. Hope to find a clue to who this kid was. Classmates, friends, you name it. It's the only lead I had."

He paused and searched the eyes of the other three. "I would go to the storage room right off of the administrative offices. I would find where they keep information on students from those years."

"Sheriff, do we know for a fact that student records were stored there?" Shauna asked.

"Yes ma'am, believe we do," Yates answered.

"This could be a long shot," Boller growled, but his eyes were focused on the materials list even as he spoke.

"And we know that teacher evaluations of students were a part of those records," Yates continued. "And from what I can tell, they had something like twenty years of old files."

"Sheriff, are you suggesting..." Boller began.

"Just saying, if it was me, I would pick a time late at night when no one was around. When I had time to work. When I could go through every file one-by-one."

"Where you would have all the time in the world," Shauna said, "unless an old janitor happens to get a call about picking up a grill at the school, and walks right into the hands of a murderer."

"Yes ma'am…an old janitor who inconveniently walks into the hands of a murderer." Yates ran his hand down his bristled jaw. "Like I said…motive."

CHAPTER SIXTY-NINE

Blaine McQuinn watched the reporter from the *Charlotte Observer* warily and then checked his watch a second time. Local authorities, namely Police Chief Greer and Fire Chief Hampton, had notified the media of the press conference late the previous evening. To no one's surprise, it was twenty minutes past the appointed hour and there was no sign of either.

McQuinn had hoped more would develop around the arson investigation than what had. He also recognized that the best sound bites were long past. Follow-up work, truly investigative reporting, was more the domain of the print media. His producer had asked that they film a short segment then head back to Charlotte later that morning to cover a series of robberies at local convenience stores. McQuinn was ready to go. Small-town stories flashed by and quickly slipped onto the back burner.

Approximately a half-dozen members of the media were on hand with twice that number of production crew personnel milling around them. The steps of the courthouse became jammed when there was a finally a rustle of activity from inside the building.

Police Chief Benny Greer stepped to the mike. McQuinn involuntarily flinched as Greer's eyes swept past and then returned to him, a hint of recognition there.

"Fire Chief Hampton and I would like to take this opportunity," Greer's cigarette-stained baritone blared into the microphone," to give the general public an update on our continuing investigation of the Steadman Elementary fire and the resulting death of Arthur Patterson. At this point, we have established the fact that the fire was started by gasoline, an accelerant that was probably already on the premises.

It's equally clear that we have a homicide investigation. We received a report late last evening from the State Bureau of Investigation confirming that Mr. Patterson suffered a series of blows, although none were fatal prior to his death. The actual cause of death was due to injuries sustained from the fire. The body was apparently wrapped in blankets before being set on fire. The gasoline that was used to start the fire was also spread throughout the storage room and administrative offices. We believe this was done to cover up the cause of death for Mr. Patterson. We are currently pursuing every possible lead in our investigation. That's the extent of our statement. If you have questions, we'll address them now." The Police Chief folded the notes from his prepared comments and looked out at the reporters.

"Chief Greer, are there any theories you're pursuing around the motive behind Mr. Patterson's murder?" the *Observer* reporter's question was first.

"No sir. The obvious answer is to cover up a robbery or a break-in. We believe Patterson was in the wrong place at the wrong time. But we have a lot more to find out," Greer answered.

"Are you in search of more than one person?" asked another reporter, one who McQuinn didn't recognize.

"Don't know," Greer's response was terse.

"Chief Hampton, Chief Greer said "cover-up." Can you say more about that? How can you tell a fire is a 'cover-up?'" asked Suzie Holley. She was a WSOC beat reporter and Channel 9 was McQuinn's number one competitor in the Charlotte market.

Brett Hampton stepped to the microphone, ran a hand through his curly gray hair and said, "The individual who set the fire did a poor job of hiding their tracks. As Chief Greer pointed out, clear they simply used a common accelerant and flung it around. Struck a match. Might have thought they could have hidden Mr. Patterson or his injuries but anyone who knows anything about fires knows you don't get temperatures that are high enough to do that. Would take a fire of maybe 1500 degrees or higher to break down a body. And for several hours. Not going to get that in a typical building fire."

"Chief Greer, so what can you say about the robbery? What evidence do you have of a crime outside the arson? What's the motive for killing the man?" The reporter who asked the question was from one of the newspapers. McQuinn guessed it was the Fayetteville Constitution.

"Like I said, we don't know. We believe the individuals were already in the building when Patterson arrived. We don't know that, however. If he walked in on them, could be it was easier to kill him than try to build an excuse."

"Chief, what would anyone want to steal from a school that's closed for the summer?" McQuinn asked. He watched the massive Greer shift his weight. He glared down from the microphone.

"I can't say. Machines, maybe, AV equipment, maybe, computers…"

"What was missing?" McQuinn's question interrupted Greer's response and he smirked. His dark eyes glared at the reporter.

"We're building an inventory of what we know was on-site. At this point, we can't say for sure, exactly, what might be missing. We may never know."

"Chief, can you comment on the method of break-in?" asked another out-of-town reporter from the back of the group. He was a rotund, red-haired man.

"Nope. Again, the damage to the building was severe. We did find jimmy marks on a side door, but the school had been broken into before, so there's no way to tell if we have evidence of another one."

"Are there any suspects?" McQuinn again.

"Yeah," Greer said, "a whole town full."

CHAPTER SEVENTY

The news conference lasted all of twenty minutes. There was little substantive information, at least as far as McQuinn was concerned. He nodded to his camera man and they began to store their gear. The convenience store caper waited an hour away.

The last of the reporters' vans had left the parking lot by the time Blaine McQuinn pushed the final piece of camera equipment into the back of the truck. He was sweating and his charcoal suit was matted to his back. He looked up to see Sheriff Yates's car turn into the lot, followed by what looked like an unmarked patrol car. He recognized Yates, but the others he was less sure of. The red-faced man in the wrinkled dark suit he recognized from the Steadman investigation. The same for the cute brunette.

There were two other men in the second vehicle. Their demeanor was business-like and their stride purposeful as they entered the police station. McQuinn watched them go and then made the decision to make his second visit to the Stacey Police Department.

Benny Greer was just as surprised by the visit of such an official-looking entourage. He and Brett Hampton had just sat down over two cups of coffee when Yates knocked at his door.

"Well, now, Sheriff Yates," Greer's voice boomed, "to what do I owe the honor of a visit from Stacey's most tenured public servant?" Greer did not stand but instead leaned back in his chair, a huge smile on his face. He paused in mid-gulp as he noticed Boller and Spencer in the hallway behind.

"Hello, Benny," Yates answered. "You got a minute to chat?" The sheriff smiled at Brett Hampton. "Hamp, how are you?" The Fire Chief stood and they shook hands.

Benny Greer leaned back even further in his chair. "I can take a minute. See you got your state boys with you there, Sheriff...no wait excuse me, 'state persons' with you." He glanced at Shauna. "Got 'em working with you on another big case?"

"Matter of fact, I do, Benny." Roy Yates could not bring himself to address Greer with his official title.

"Let me introduce you all around here. Police Chief Benny Greer, Fire Chief Brett Hampton, this is Agent Mac Boller and Agent Shauna Spencer of the State Bureau of Investigation. Back in the back here is Taylor Fletcher, he's also an agent, just down today. And last is a young man by the name of Jeb Mason. Jeb's a visitor in our fair city, but a former resident."

Greer assessed the group warily. He grinned at the introduction of Shauna, as if the oddity of a female law enforcement agent was on a par with a poodle that had been taught to dance. She felt his eyes sweep over her and resisted the urge to smack him. Greer didn't bother to stand. Brett Hampton did, offering her his chair. She politely declined.

"What's up, Yates?" Greer took another swig from the large mug labeled "Southeast Softball Sectionals 1987."

"We've had some developments around the Steadman fire, Chief Greer," Boller answered. "It's a good time for us to bring you up to speed."

"Bring me up to speed." Benny Greer repeated the words, as if their very sound was contemptible. "Yeah, why don't you just do that?"

In the waiting room in the lobby, Blaine McQuinn was carefully studying a complaint report on a brown clipboard. He'd asked the lady at the front desk if he could fill one out, and after a few perfunctory questions, she'd handed him the form. As he pretended to weigh the questions, he watched through partially closed blinds the events unfolding in Greer's office with great interest.

There was clearly something of some significance taking place. The two SBI agents appeared to be doing most of the talking, but Yates took the floor on occasion. He was most interested in the response of Benny Greer, who had gone from what appeared to be aloof and indifferent to rapt attention in only the first few minutes of the meeting. The same was true for Fire Chief Hampton, who stood several times and paced back and forth to the window that faced the parking lot.

The female agent carried several files that she carefully laid on Greer's desk. They became the focal point of continued discussion. At one point there seemed to be a debate taking place, but McQuinn couldn't be sure.

"Excuse me, sir. You had a complaint you were filing?" McQuinn looked up to find a young black male smiling down at him. McQuinn looked back vacantly.

"A complaint. Our desk sergeant said you had a complaint. Maybe I can help you." Officer Bobby Patterson recognized the man, but he wasn't sure from where.

"Uh, no, I don't...don't think so. I guess maybe not." McQuinn looked back at the meeting. The discussion was clearly an intense one.

Patterson looked back over his shoulder, saw the group in Greer's office, and turned back to the man.

"You're Blaine McQuinn. Channel Three News. I know you!" Patterson grinned. "You thinking you might have a story in there, Mr. McQuinn?"

"No, not really. I just wanted to fill out..."

"'Cause I hope you're not filing a false complaint. We take a pretty dim view of things like that 'round here. You weren't going to do that, were you, Mr. McQuinn?"

"Not at all, Officer..." McQuinn read the nametag. "Not at all, Officer Patterson. In fact, I've decided not to file a complaint at all." He handed the clipboard to back to the young man. "No relation to Arthur Patterson, I guess?"

"Well, as a matter of fact, my uncle. The family appreciated how you handled all this stuff with your report and all. My Aunt Ilene wanted to see if she could get a copy of the videotape. Think that's possible, Mr. McQuinn?"

"Why sure it is, sure it is. I'll talk to the station."

"Much appreciated. Is there...anything else the Stacey Police Department can do for you today?"

"No. Just on my way, Officer Patterson."

McQuinn stood to go.

"Are there any leads on your uncle's murder?"

"Not that I'm aware of, sir."

McQuinn looked over Patterson's shoulder a second time. Bobby Patterson followed his gaze. Both men stared into the room.

"I have a feeling that there may be one now, Officer Patterson," McQuinn offered. He reached into his pocket and pulled his notepad out.

CHAPTER SEVENTY-ONE

"Gawd Damn...have you people lost your fucking minds?" Greer roared. "With everything else I got going on you come waltzing in here with this shit?" He had listened, for the most part, as the agents laid out the evidence they had compiled around the circumstances of the Zeke Andrews's death and then begun to build the possible link with the Steadman Elementary fire and Bump Patterson's death.

"Architectural blueprint, miscellaneous accounting bills, equipment...and old student files." Shauna read the list slowly, looking at each of the people gathered around Greer's massive desk as she did.

"I don't give a shit if they had the Library of Congress in the damn school, Missy. There is no damn way you can convince me somebody goes into that school to look for information about some murder that never happened." Greer spat the words.

"My name is Spencer, Chief Greer. You may refer to me as Agent Spencer or Spencer if you want, but you will not call me Missy. Are we clear on that?" she glared at Greer and they could see the wave of anger flash in his face.

"I don't give a damn what your name is, Missy..." Greer hissed. "What you got here is a pile of shit...nothing more."

"Actually what she has here, Greer," Agent Boller interjected, "are some very interesting developments that lead us to believe we may have more than an arson and murder investigation." He returned Greer's glare with his own.

"You see what you get for us when you contact the state boys, Yates? Gawddamn stupidity." Greer barked.

"Stupidity comes at all different levels, Benny. You know that."

Greer laughed and looked over to Brett Hampton. "Hamp, looks like your little fire ain't no fire at all. It's a fucking conspiracy. Hell, I guess if we look long enough we'll find Jimmy Hoffa buried there somewhere, too."

Brett Hampton did not answer.

Yates spoke up. "Look, Greer, suppose this Andrews boy saw something that night, something the killer never suspected. He's a three-time loser and he decides to make 'em pay for the knowledge. Only along the way, he gets hisself killed."

"And you're basing that on a bunch of cutout pictures, right?" Greer asked.

"No…but it is unusual. That, plus the fact that this old boy couldn't get two dimes to rub together, and he puts a two-thousand-dollar payment down on a new Corvette."

"Could have stolen the money," Greer said.

"And he decided to pay for it five hundred miles away. In Tallahassee, Florida."

"*Stolen money*. Not going to spend it here."

"Yeah, but you don't go four states away, either. He had the car reserved, Benny. He wasn't planning on dying. He was scheduled to pick up a new car," Yates continued.

"All right, so our jumper might have got himself involved in something. I ain't buying some damn murder deal, but let's just say *something*. That ain't got nothing to do with this Steadman thing."

"Chief Greer, if we can assume there was an extortion attempt being made we have to assume it wasn't for a long-standing shoplifting case." Boller said. "And if that part is true, then we have to also assume Andrews did not commit suicide. If we believe he was murdered, we must believe the someone who did it was prepared to cover their tracks…completely."

"And you are sitting there and telling me that the only way to do that was to break into the school and kill the janitor?" Greer frowned. "Dog don't hunt, Boller…that dog don't hunt."

"What we're saying, Chief Greer," Shauna interjected, "is that there is enough evidence that seems to be linked that makes it possible that the Steadman fire, the Patterson murder, and the Andrews death are all connected."

"How in the hell is anybody going to know they keep student records at the elementary school? I didn't." Greer's look was still skeptical.

"Not too hard," Shauna answered. "I took the liberty of calling the school board this morning. Told them I was with the university continuing education system and needed to verify the academic background of a student. Could they help me? Spoke with an Emily Melton—" she glanced at her notes "—and she said it shouldn't be a problem. All the records for students in this county were maintained at a central location. Local elementary school. Notes and records pre-1984, before computer files, were still kept in hard copy form at Steadman. She said she wasn't sure at this point if they were damaged by the recent fire or not, but that she could get back to me.

"I asked her if I wanted to do a background check, references, etc., would it be difficult...her answer—" she glanced at her notes a second time "—'No ma'am. They don't throw away anything over there. I expect we can tell you what they had for lunch in third grade if you want to know.' She did say we would have to produce a signed-records release for them to share any information, which I was somewhat relieved to hear,"

Shauna continued. "I'm not sure what the legal issues are here, but it would appear the Steadman file program isn't necessarily unprecedented. A number of rural systems keep copious records, only because that's what they've always done. It consumes a lot of space, oftentimes is warehoused, but dozens of small towns have exactly the same process. And the records systems in North Carolina were very manually intensive. There were student appraisal forms that were completed four times a year."

She pulled a folded paper from her black leather carry bag and slapped it on Greer's desk.

"*Every* student who passed through the educational system in Richmond County from 1952 through the mid-eighties had one of these filled out on them and placed in their permanent file. No exceptions."

Greer did not look at the paper.

Shauna continued, "This county did not have an active system-of-records review until the last several years, at least not one commonly adopted. No audits. No removal of dead files. Nothing." She paused. "Teachers would just complete the form, along with the report cards, drop them into a file. At some point, somebody comes along, boxes it all up."

Greer growled his words. "So you're telling me some nut kills the judge thirty years ago, gets away with it, or so he thinks, until he sees a couple of snot-nosed kids running away. He follows. Murders all three. Then discovers he killed the wrong ones and re-starts the process all these years later? Along the way, our janitor gets in the way, so he pops him, too. Is that about right?"

"There is a little bit more, Chief," Boller said as he glanced over at Fletcher, the one agent who had remained quiet. He continued, "At this point, we may or may not have an unusual string of circumstantial evidence. But if we accept the premise of the original murder, then the events since could suggest someone has been desperately trying to cover their tracks. The suspicious death of Andrews, the discovery of materials that suggest an extortion attempt, the break-in attempt at Mason's room, and last night's accident involving Mr. Gardner."

Greer responded, "Andy Gardner has been hot-rodding around this town for years. I've warned him a number of times about revving that little blue sports car. It's a wonder he hasn't already been killed."

"Maybe so," said Boller. "Taylor?"

Taylor Fletcher was a tall, raw-boned man with high cheekbones and piercing blue eyes that seemed to never blink.

"I've been over to Monroe's Garage this morning to take a closer look at the Gardner vehicle. There's no question that the brakes have been tampered with. The lines were tapped. Pretty amateur job, at that. I've got a couple of technicians breaking down the overall apparatus now, but there's not a lot of question."

"Shit," said Greer, pushing his bulk away from the desk, "shit."

"Chief, the most important thing right now is that we coordinate our resources and make sure that the investigation moves forward efficiently," Boller said. "I hope we can count on you and your department to do that."

"So what are you telling me? That the state is heading this investigation? Is that what you're telling me?"

"Chief Greer, we're saying we have definitive evidence of at least one murder, conducted on state property," Boller began. "And we have proof of arson. We have circumstantial evidence that suggests a recent death may have also been a murder. Your jurisdiction. Your case, along with Sheriff Yates. But if there is ample evidence that previous murders were also committed, no matter how long the time frame, murders that can perhaps be tied to the Steadman incident, then yes, you have a state investigation."

CHAPTER SEVENTY-TWO

In a far corner of the police parking lot, Blaine McQuinn sat in his red mustang with the sun visor pulled down. He watched a car pull to the front of the building and an officer hustle inside. At the same time, another uniform ran down the stairs on a sprint to a cruiser. The whole building seemed to be coming alive.

His last glimpse of Benny Greer had confirmed the good chief was clearly pissed, and McQuinn figured he generally reserved the worst behavior for his subordinates or others he could look down on. This time the attitude seemed more real.

He guessed the four people with Yates were state agents, and the fact that the number had doubled was not without significance. The unannounced visit from the sheriff had also raised a few eyebrows. He'd heard an officer commenting on that very fact as he left Bobby Patterson. Those two didn't exactly swap birthday cards to begin with.

It had to be an update on the Bump Patterson case, and one that Police Chief Greer was not pleased by. The front door of the station opened and the three men, along with the female, walked out. They got into the same unmarked cruiser they'd arrived in. He watched the car pull out, headed east on DeKalb.

McQuinn cranked the mustang and followed. The cruiser continued out of town on Highway 73 with McQuinn following at a safe distance. He watched it turn into the Dogwood Inn and come to a stop in front of the office lobby. The woman, along with one of the three men, the most casually dressed of the trio, disappeared into the motel. McQuinn followed the car as it pulled back out onto the highway. He picked up his cell phone and placed a call to Steve Coombs.

Neither Jeb nor Shauna noticed the second car. Shauna was involved in a cell-phone call with Raleigh. Their discussion with Chief Greer had overstated the degree of official interest in the Stacey case, but she wasn't going to say that to the asshole. As far as he was concerned, a fleet of agents were descending on the metropolis of Stacey.

The simple fact was that SBI Deputy Director Bill O'Flynn's response was guarded at best. There was a great deal of speculation, but no solid proof, so not enough to release additional agents or to invest more resources. Taylor Fletcher was a "gimme"—he was stationed locally and had expertise in mechanics. The case was limited to Boller and Spencer until someone could present tangible evidence that the Bump Patterson case was in some way linked to the other murders.

• • •

While Mac Boller dropped Taylor Fletcher off in nearby Asheboro, Shauna Spencer and Jeb Mason had a far different assignment. They were going on a little hiking trip.

"Sheriff says this is the best map we're going to find of the Yadkin River and the general area around it." Shauna spread it out over the console of Jeb's Camry. She sat in the passenger seat. They both studied it carefully.

The Yadkin River ran north and west of town, a snaking ribbon of water that flowed gently across the northern tier of the county. The river was flanked by thick forest on either side as it ran north of town, but as it neared the far western corner, miles of rolling pastureland began to border it. Many years before, the Yadkin had been a source of power for much of the area, and at least two mills had at one point been located on its banks. Both had fallen into disrepair many years before.

Shauna guesstimated the distance from the Yadkin to the Thompson house to be at least four miles, maybe farther. An hour to cover that much ground, minimum. Maybe longer if the terrain was difficult, and most certainly closer to an hour and a half in the dark, regardless of the panic factor. They had pinpointed the locations where each of the three boys' bodies had been found. Jeb could not be sure of the exact location that he, Andy, and Zeke had camped, but he believed he could find it. At best, it was no farther than a half-mile from where at least one of the deceased was found.

"You up for a walk, Jeb?" Shauna looked at him.

"I don't think I've ever been more ready," he answered.

"OK, our plan is pretty simple here. We want to give you the opportunity to walk us through exactly what happened that night with as much detail as possible. Try to remember what you said, what you did, what everyone did...OK?" She smiled at him.

"It's been a few years..." Jeb said. He looked out over the parking lot, lost in thought.

"You OK?"

"Yeah...just thinking about something."

"You going to let me in on it?"

"Something your partner said when we were talking about the Steadman fire...the Patterson murder. Probably nothing."

"What was that?"

"He said you couldn't go around asking people if they knew who Zeke Andrews's friends were. Remember?"

"I do, but I'm not following you, Jeb. Are you saying someone might have?"

"No. But can't help but wonder if they ran across a name...if they might ask a question or two...discreetly, of course."

"You think that could have happened?"

• • •

A few minutes later Shauna's cell phone buzzed.

"You want to do that *now*?" she asked. She listened for another moment. "We'll be at your office in five. Oh...and Sheriff Yates, have you ever heard of a local citizen by the name of Clarence Parker?"

When she hung up the phone moments later she turned to Jeb and said, "Yates says he'll swing by and have a chat with the Parker man, but he's sounds doubtful. Seems he also wants to make a house call before we head to the woods. He's invited us to join him."

"A house call?"

"The sheriff suggested we join him for a visit to the Thompson house."

"Does his family still live there?"

"His widow does apparently. She's elderly but Yates says she's lucid," Shauna said.

"But what do we gain from that?"

"It all happened there, Jeb. I want you to see it...in the daylight this time. So does Sheriff Yates. Maybe it will jog something..."

"Holy shit." Jeb glanced down at his cell. "Had this thing on mute since we left for the hospital last night."

"What? What is it?"

His voicemail box was full—the same for his text messages. He opened the last message and read its simple line aloud. "Where the f r u??????"

"You were supposed to be back in Chicago?"

"Not only back in Chicago, but I just blew off a teleconference with our president," Jeb cursed quietly.

"You need to make some calls?"

"Just one," Jeb answered. They pulled onto the highway and headed back toward town.

CHAPTER SEVENTY-THREE

The initial game plan was simple. Mac Boller had agreed to hand-deliver the Zeke Andrews papers to evidence experts in Raleigh. He would make the two-hour trip that very day to also debrief with forensics experts on the results of the Patterson autopsy and the Steadman arson investigation.

A few calls had already been made around the money transfer with the car dealership in Tallahassee. The money had been sent in a series of one hundred dollar bills and by mail. There was some question whether the money now sat in a safe at the car dealership and could potentially be traced by the serial numbers, or if it had simply been deposited.

Deputy Director O'Flynn wanted a "sit down" around the phone call he'd received from Shauna, and he wanted the meeting today. Boller would play point on that meeting, while Shauna stayed back in Stacey and attempted to get some of the answers they both knew O'Flynn would demand.

Boller didn't mind the latest turn of events at all. The loose ends would carry him at least through the next day. And a night at home with Dottie seemed to be more appealing with every passing year. Retirement and fishing off the coast of Holden Beach was one day closer. He'd had his fill of the slime balls of the world. The only surveillance he wanted to be involved in a year from now was of a can of Budweiser and the Atlantic Ocean, and in that order. He allowed himself a few moments to daydream as he drove through Asheboro and glanced at the sign for Raleigh.

Less than a mile behind, Blaine McQuinn followed, wondering whether he was just on one long goose chase.

• • •

Grissom Street was a sleepy, tree-lined avenue in the northwest corner of Stacey. Most of the houses were sprawling colonials, ante-bellum designs that might remind a visitor of Charleston and the Old South. Beautiful perennial beds of red lilies and snow white roses dotted the well-manicured lawns. Shading the street were towering oaks, sentinels to the few pedestrians that were walking the quiet sidewalks.

Yates pointed out the elderly lady in the light blue floral-print dress and the large, floppy straw hat as she walked toward the backyard of the Thompson house. She wore heavy work gloves and was carrying a small spade and a wicker basket. She seemed oblivious to her visitors until Yates hailed her.

"Well hello…" she drew closer, "Why, Sheriff Yates! How are you?" She smiled warmly.

"I'm fine, Mrs. Thompson. And how are you?" Yates removed his hat and shook her hand enthusiastically. "Let me introduce you to some friends of mine."

"And where are you from?" Mrs. Thompson directed her attention to Shauna after the introductions were complete.

"I'm from Alabama, ma'am. And my friend is from Chicago."

"Alabama and Chicago. My goodness. My goodness. Well, welcome to Stacey. Are you going to be able to stay long?"

"Well no, we're just in town for a short time…"

"Well you are a beautiful young lady. Are you married?"

"Uh, no ma'am, I'm not married…"

"Well, you should be, a pretty young thing like you," she looked toward Jeb, "is this your young man?"

"No ma'am," Jeb spoke up, slightly embarrassed. "We're just friends."

"Young man, are you feeling all right?"

"Excuse me?" Jeb asked.

"You better start looking at this young woman. Just friends… rubbish."

"Mrs. Thompson, we were just driving by. We really can't stay." Yates glanced over to Shauna and Jeb and stifled a smile.

"These are lavender irises. Aren't they beautiful?" Mrs. Thompson said as she snipped two stems and daintily placed them in her basket. "Just a beautiful, beautiful flower…"

The backyard of 619 Grissom was indeed a meticulously landscaped panorama of brilliant color-azaleas, hostas, and various perennial beds of flowers wrapped over long brick walls. Boxwoods lined the back of the house. An ornamental birdbath, its patina a golden shade of green, stood some fifty feet away, a circle of yellow day lilies framing it like a Monet masterpiece.

Still farther back were the large poplars Jeb remembered from so long ago. His eyes lingered there.

"Oh, and my zinnias…" Marie Thompson paused, gently pushed the soil around one of the plants, and then moved on to the steps that led to the back porch, "and my oleander." She pointed to a luscious red plant in a pot beside the back door. "I need to prune that."

"Mrs. Thompson, I was telling Ms. Spencer and Mr. Mason how you've been a widow for a long time now," Yates said.

"Yes, yes. For a long, long time." Her face grew somber. "But Judge Thompson loved our gardens, too. Known him to spend the whole day in the garden. Yes sir, the whole day." She looked out over the courtyard and grew quiet.

"How long has your husband been dead, Mrs. Thompson?" Shauna asked.

"Oh, so long. His heart just gave out on him…just gave out." She paused and looked back toward Yates.

"Maybe we ought to be going now," Yates said, "appreciate you talking to us, ma'am." He glanced toward Shauna and Jeb and nodded slightly.

She led them down a long corridor toward the front door. They entered a large foyer. A cherry wood secretary desk stood to their left. Through double French glass doors they could see into a music room to the far right. A massive grand piano stood prominently in a corner, a large crystal vase with white peonies atop it.

"Mrs. Thompson, what a beautiful piano!" Shauna exclaimed.

"Oh, it is, isn't it? Franklin gave me that. He loved music so."

"Do you play?" Shauna asked.

"Oh, at times." She walked over to the piano, reached down to a red flowering plant that rested in a pot to the side. She plucked a leaf.

"They dry out so...they're used to a more humid climate, you know." She smiled and walked back. "Oleander was Franklin's favorite, so pretty...reminded us of Savannah. Have you been to Savannah?" She looked at Shauna.

"No ma'am. Have been meaning to...just haven't gotten around to it."

"Just beautiful...just beautiful. Oh, dear me..." she looked through the open door out onto the front lawn, "I need to spray those roses." She ambled past. They followed her into the front yard. "It's aphids, oh my dear."

"Mrs. Thompson, it was good seeing you. We'll be off now." Yates put his hat back on..

"Yes...yes, and please come again, won't you?"

"Yes ma'am. We will." They waved goodbye as they clambered into the cruiser, leaving Marie Thompson to do battle with the aphids.

CHAPTER SEVENTY-FOUR

"It's going to be somewhere...up here." Jeb pointed into the trees directly ahead. They had left the highway several miles back, and the Camry followed a winding dirt road that appeared to have washed out innumerable times over the years. Twice it seemed to disappear all together before Shauna or Jeb managed to make out a clearing in the trees that signaled its re-emergence.

"How can you tell where we are?" Shauna asked. "It all looks pretty much the same."

"River's just through there." Jeb pointed through the trees. "This road was used for timbering back in the twenties. We used to use it as a trail. I'm guessing we're less than a half-mile away from the Yadkin. You want to run this all by me again?"

"Nothing new, Jeb. Returning to the scene of the crime has been a part of investigative work since Day One."

"Shauna, we're talking almost thirty years here."

"Don't care if it's fifty. We want you to experience the same sights, the same smells, the same feel of the place...that you did before."

"And what is this supposed to accomplish?"

"You had a traumatic experience...one neither you nor your friends were prepared to discuss afterwards. You emotionally put it back in a dark corner of your psyche. We're going to pull it off that shelf."

"Are you thinking there's something I could have forgotten?"

"Don't know," Shauna said as they pulled the car under a towering maple. "But we'll find out, won't we?" She patted the holster of her gun instinctively as she started to open the door. They had changed clothes back at the motel, and they could feel the heat of the day rush into the car now that the air conditioner was no longer running.

"Shouldn't that mean we do this at midnight then?" Jeb asked as he shouldered the day-pack they had been given by Sheriff Yates. "I mean, after all, the stimuli in the day would be a lot different...right?"

"We may do just that. But for the time being, I want to understand...and see exactly what you three did that night. And I don't want to go stumbling through the darkness yet if I don't have to. I am not that fond of camping." Hard woods towered over them, and with the car's engine off, they could clearly hear the river's rush through the thick foliage. Shauna watched a bumblebee dart by her, return to her eye level, consider her for a split second, then disappear in a blur.

"OK, Jeb. Let's make sure to stay close together. I don't want to find myself lost in the wilderness, if you don't mind."

"Agent Spencer, you ever done any camping?"

"No, Mr. Mason, I haven't. Does that make any difference to you?"

"Not at all. Just want to know if I'm dealing with an experienced person or a babe in the woods."

"Well, Mr. Mason, I guess that makes me a babe then, doesn't it?" she said as she headed in the direction of the river. "Do you care to lead the way?"

The path wound around massive trees and thick foliage. It paralleled the water for a time, and they could catch glimpses of the river through the branches. It was a relatively clear trail, deeply shadowed by the trees, but as they drew closer to the river, it narrowed, and the limbs snagged at their clothes. They ducked and swerved as they made their way. Jeb set a steady pace, confident in the direction he was taking, sliding under the wayward branches with the learned step of a veteran. Shauna didn't fare as well.

"Want to hold up there, Daniel Boone?" she muttered after some twenty minutes. "I think I may have missed walking into one of those branches back there."

Jeb turned and smiled back at her.

"So how you doing, Agent Spencer?" he looked at her appraisingly.

"Well, I remember now why I never pursued the Forest Service as a career option, if that's what you mean." She ducked below the willowy arms of an oak, only to entangle herself in the creeping limbs of a hanging vine overhead. "Yuck!"

"I think that could be the Forest Service's loss, if you ask me." Jeb worked to extricate her from the grip of her molester. "We're at a place that might be good to stop at, anyway. Here."

He grabbed her by the hand and led her into a clearing that pushed up to the river. They were looking out over a flat expanse of grass that emerged onto a long sandbar. The river was narrower there, no more than forty to fifty feet wide. It rambled over a series of rocks, smoothed by the waters over the many years. Across the way, the trees were much thicker, and the bank grew into a hill that rose at least one hundred feet.

Jeb stood there for several long moments, taking in the scene carefully. He still held Shauna's hand. She made no attempt to release his grip.

"I think it was here." He pointed at the wide plain in front of them. "This is where the Glasser boy, the others...This is where I believe they camped that night."

"You're not sure?"

"No, anything but."

"You knew them?"

"You knew everybody in a town this size. But I think Clover was homeschooled, and the Glasser kid was a year older than me. Not sure about Joe Keyes," Jeb answered.

"No, I mean did you see them that night?" Shauna asked.

"No, but remember, we packed in late that night, and we could have walked right past them unless we saw their fire...and I don't remember seeing a campfire."

"Then how can you be sure they camped here?" she asked.

"Lot of us camped here over the years. Flat, so you wouldn't slide down in your sleeping bag. Easy to build a campfire in the sand. Plenty of water. Not a tough hike out. Perfect spot," Jeb answered.

The water rolled by, burbling a melancholy backdrop to Jeb's story, oblivious to the tragedy that had happened so long ago.

"Course everybody knew about the chance of flooding. Hell, it was drilled into everyone's head long before we got to camp out alone."

"From what Sheriff Yates said, do you think they could have set up camp here? Then just been surprised by a flash flood?" Shauna asked.

"Guess so. I mean, it's a lot more probable than what we're thinking about."

"The sheriff said when he came back; he thought someone else might be there. In the trees. Watching." Shauna glanced over the water to the tree line beyond.

Jeb followed her gaze. "I can only guess, but I would assume he meant across the river...there."

A brief wave of unease swept over them. It would be easy for someone to stand there, no more than fifteen feet from shore, and remain virtually invisible. Both stared deeply into the darkness, almost expecting to make out a figure all these years later. Shauna tightened her grip slightly and each looked down, realizing for the first time that they were still holding hands. Neither spoke.

Shauna felt herself blush slightly, though she couldn't be sure why. She walked to the edge of the water, picked up a small stone, and chucked it into the river.

"How far was your camp that night, from here, I mean?"

Jeb looked to his left. "Another mile or two, and on the other side, farther north. We crossed farther upstream I think."

"And the Thompson house?"

"Across the river, headed back toward town." He waved in the general direction to his right.

"How long to get there from here, would you say?" She watched him consider her question carefully.

"A hard sixty, maybe more."

"Is there a place we can cross? I mean...easily?" she looked at the water.

"We're there," Jeb answered.

"How deep?"

"Waist high, probably. Maybe a little higher."

"Damn it," she whispered softly.

"It's OK. It's just going to be cold," Jeb warned, walking toward the water's edge.

"No other way, huh?" She watched him wade in, gasping at the suddenness of the chill, a sensation he had forgotten long ago. Now it was his turn to mutter underneath his breath. He waded farther, then carefully turned, making sure to negotiate the smooth stones on the river bottom.

"Care to join me, Shauna?" He extended his hand. She laughed and plunged into the cold, yelping as it washed over her.

They emerged on the other side sufficiently frozen, both giggling like school kids. The water was faster than both realized, and they found walking against the current more treacherous than they guessed. The sun's warmth was a welcome relief as they trudged up the bank.

"If I had known this was going to be a safari, I would have at least worn jeans." Shauna offered. The khaki walking-shorts were not the best protection against the plant and insect life, or the biting cold.

"Should have warned you. Sorry." Jeb appreciated his denims all the more. "The right clothes are pretty important out here."

"Tell me about it." Shauna smiled between quivering lips. Jeb found himself glancing quickly at her shapely brown legs and realized for a second time that her choice of apparel was just fine with him.

"Want to head toward the Thompson house?" he asked.

"Yes. Let's do that first. I want to get some sense of the distance and of the terrain. Is this the path you took that night?"

"No. We came straight from where we camped. We'll intersect the way we went that night, but it's probably a mile or more."

Shauna stopped and considered Jeb's comments.

"Maybe we should go to your camp first, then. I would like to start exactly where you did that night. Then, if you could walk me through everything you did, it might help us reconstruct the evening of July seventh."

"All right, the going's going to be tough for a little while, though. We've got to crest this hill, then head due north alongside the river. Probably twenty to thirty minutes of scratchy walking."

"Why am I not surprised?" Shauna smiled, and then fell in behind him. She was anxious to find sunlight unencumbered by trees somewhere up ahead.

"Jeb, why did you take me here...first, I mean? You guys didn't camp here. It wasn't on your route that night."

Jeb continued to plow through the underbrush.

"You're partially right. We didn't camp here, and it wasn't the way we came..." He stopped and looked back at her.

"But on the way back...from the house that night, I mean...we lost our way. We ended up a long way from camp. We crossed the river too far downstream. We finally ended up curled up underneath some trees, sopping wet and scared to death. Not even sure of where we were."

"So you didn't make it back to your camp at all?" Shauna asked.

"No...we ended up under some hemlock pines. Huddled together like scared puppies. First hint of daylight we found our camp, gathered our things, and got the heck out of Dodge."

"How far, Jeb? How far were you from the sandbar when you stopped that night?"

Jeb turned and pointed back to where they had stood.

"I don't know. Maybe a half-mile."

Shauna looked back in the direction of the river, already obscured by the trees. Three boys running into the darkness, toward the Yadkin River. Somewhere behind, someone follows. A storm is building, flashes of lightning overhead. Enough to see them, even in the distance? Finally they collapse, huddled in a dark corner. The pursuer, anxious, uncertain, misses them. Continues toward the river. Crests the hill. Plunges down it. Suddenly bursts into a clearing. The river. And there, across the water, he sees three boys.

"We led him straight to them, didn't we?" Jeb was looking in the same direction as Shauna. "I think we may have led the killer right to them."

CHAPTER SEVENTY-FIVE

Five miles upriver, Sheriff Yates carefully traversed a narrow ridge that overlooked a wider expanse of the Yadkin, with a far more panoramic view. Darby Ridge rose several hundred feet above the river and then plunged spectacularly to the rocky flats below. The only way to get to the top was via a long abandoned lumber road that snaked around the ridge to within several hundred yards of the precipice. The remaining ground could be covered only on foot.

Yates's Crown Victoria had protested the hilly, rock-strewn trail that led up Darby, threatening on several occasions to become mired in one of the many holes and gullies, or to become wedged in one of the cutbacks so severely that it could never be moved. The road was too narrow to turn the vehicle around, necessitating an even more harrowing backing down the mountain, which Yates didn't relish attempting a second time in one week. The decision not to bring a deputy along had been arrived at with some thought. He preferred the tranquility of conducting his own investigation first. He could bring others in later, if there was sufficient cause. He did not expect to find meaningful evidence anyway.

For the first half-hour, his theory proved correct. Thick ground cover eliminated any possibility of footprints. There were no tire tracks on the lumber road when they first arrived at the scene a week ago, but heavy rains had fallen the night of Andrews's death. A tank could have come up the mountain with no discernible imprint left behind.

Yates stood on the point of Darby Ridge, cautiously peering down at the rocky base where Zeke Andrews's body had been found. He thought back to Dr. Carter's coroner's report. The official verdict was that Andrews had died sometime in the wee hours of the morning, but his body was not discovered until some eight hours later. Yates was one of the first arrivals shortly before 11:00 a.m. on the morning of the thirteenth. He glanced down at the rocks and pictured the dismal image again.

He stayed there for a time, looking out over the river. It was a peaceful place, high above the rest of the world. At the ridge's point lay a huge, flat, granite boulder that many had visited over the years. There were a few beer bottles scattered in the brush, final remnants of picnics or teenager make-out visits. The drop from that point was dramatic.

He could remember two deaths that preceded the Andrews tragedy. In the late 1950s, a visitor from up north had slipped and gone over the edge. The same thing happened again in 1994, when a scout troop on a day-hike had rested there. One of the boys, attempting to prove his manhood, had wandered out too far and lost his balance.

It was an idyllic setting at this time of day, but at night, that was very different. It would be difficult to find the path, even more challenging to stay on the ridge. You could just as easily march off into space.

"What were you thinking, Andrews?" Yates said aloud. "What were you doing way up here alone?" He gazed out over the river and the thick trees beyond. He could see most of the county from where he stood.

The night of July twelfth was cloudless, with a quarter- moon, so visibility was limited. No flashlight was found on the body or at the scene. There was no evidence that anyone else was there that night. Zeke Andrews's dilapidated 1987 Dodge pickup was found some two hundred yards away on the timber path. The keys were still in the ignition.

Yates carefully walked the area a second time, his mind running through the facts of the case. He paused to thumb through his spiral notebook again.

"Need to talk to me now, son," he whispered.

He walked back to a large maple that rested in the baked clay beside the point. The mammoth tree reached out over the cliff, part of its root structure bared by the years of erosion. Quite a resting place, and with one hell of a view, Yates thought to himself. He sat down, his legs dangling over the edge.

He pulled a cigarette out, lit it, and tossed the match off the side, then took a long drag and watched the smoke drift out into the open air above the valley. Across the way, the river ran from left to right, and from his vantage point he could see patches of trees and pastureland on the other side. There was a boat landing, broken down with age farther upriver and on the opposite shore. It protruded out of the trees and out into the water. Yates could make out the dirt road that led up to it.

The Slayton road was an old field path that had never been paved by the state. Its traffic was limited to locals; fishermen mostly, though more than a few farmers could be seen driving their tractors on it at any given time. It ran almost twenty miles, and actually reached into Yancey County to the north, but it was a poor alternative to the county road system. Farmers preferred it because it was a safer thoroughfare for farm equipment and had a number of tributaries that connected to the highways. You could easily follow the Slayton road for miles, either north or south. Yates made a note to remember the landing. Not a bad place to fish. The river was wide there, and relatively deep. Bump Patterson would have loved it. The sheriff smiled as he considered the thought.

He breathed in the Salem and let the smoke out slowly. He glanced down to make sure his match hadn't ignited the brush and then paused. Below him, caught in the snare of a bramble bush, was a pack of Marlboros. Scattered throughout the bushes were matches, at least thirty, maybe more. The area was heavily eroded and the root system of the maple wrapped around parts of the scrub brush. Yates looked back and surveyed the far shore a second time. He paused, and then glanced directly below him again.

"Gawd Almighty," he rasped.

He flung the cigarette away and started to climb down the face of the cliff.

CHAPTER SEVENTY-SIX

Yates's pulse pounded as he made his descent. Below the roots were a number of scrub trees and weeds that grew almost horizontally from the side of the cliff for some twenty to thirty feet. Beyond that the soil gave way to a solid rock wall. If he lost his grip and began to slide, his next stop would be almost the same place that Andrews had landed, several hundred feet below.

The dirt was loose and Yates clung fiercely to part of the large tree's root system. He reached the empty cigarette pack, wedged himself against the side of the hill and pulled out a handkerchief. He delicately grasped the Marlboro pack and placed it in his front pocket. Then he began to pick up each of the used matches and do the same. He scoured the bank a second time. Some four feet below, deep in the folds of another bush, laid another Marlboro pack.

Yates grunted, said a quiet prayer, and then started to climb down. He was at the end of the maple's large roots. He felt for a foothold, a place to brace himself.

He had at least two to three more steps down before he could reach the second pack. His sweat made his hands wet, and he felt the small pine sapling he held with his left hand begin to slide through his fingers.

"Oh shit…" he gasped as he struggled to gain a better grip, hugging tightly to the mountain, his face pressed into the brush.

Suddenly the rock he had planted his right foot against shifted, and then fell away. He heard it bounce against the rock wall below and then bound into the emptiness beyond.

"Please, God…" Yates groaned as he began to slide.

CHAPTER SEVENTY-SEVEN

Benny Greer watched Fire Chief Hampton walk back across the steaming parking lot to his car. He sat back in his leather chair and took a final gulp of the cold coffee. A cigarette lay smoldering in the ashtray in front of him. The office was empty now.

There was no case file on the Judge Thompson death. But he sent an administrator downstairs to look for one anyway. "Patterson still out here?" he yelled to no one in particular.

"Yeah, Chief. Want me to get him?" A young officer popped his head around the corner.

"Get him," Greer barked.

Bobby Patterson arrived several minutes later. He found Greer gazing out the window, lost in thought.

"Need me, Chief?"

"Yeah, Patterson. Want you to ride out toward Yanceyville, Highway 9. There's a Billy Tully out that way, few miles beyond Big Pete's... here's the address." He handed him a slip of paper. "You're gonna pull in there, keep 'em company for a while."

"Sir?"

"That's it, Patterson, pull in there. Park in the front yard. The SBI people are telling us they want surveillance, so that's what we'll do. Tell 'em they got an SBI agent coming by later to talk to them. They'll explain things. You got that?"

"Yes sir," Bobby Patterson said as he backed out of the office. "Chief Greer?"

Benny Greer turned.

"Are there any leads...anything new on my uncle's death?"

Greer looked at him vacantly.

"My uncle...Bump Patterson."

"Oh yeah...I forgot you two were kin," Greer said. "Hell no, no leads. Only a snot-nosed agent and an old man with too much time on his hands."

Patterson stood at the door, waiting.

"You going to stand there all day?" the chief growled. "Hit the road."

CHAPTER SEVENTY-EIGHT

Blaine McQuinn cursed his stupidity at following the SBI agent. The drive to Raleigh had been without event, and for the last two hours, he had sat in a scorching parking lot watching state employees wander in and out of the SBI headquarters without any sign of his man.

He had learned that the agent was Mac Boller, a veteran investigator, and that his assignment to Stacey was a direct result of the Steadman fire. The burgeoning homicide investigation had apparently taken a new twist in the last twenty-four hours, but in what direction was very much an unknown.

A third agent, Taylor Fletcher, had become involved very recently. That same Fletcher had also been involved in some type of official call on a Monroe's Garage the previous evening. The visit had involved the wrecked automobile of a local resident named Andy Gardner. Gardner had been seriously injured in a car accident the previous day.

The other on-site agent, the good-looking female McQuinn remembered from the Steadman investigation, was also on the go. Apparently she had been dropped off with the third man, still unknown, at the Dogwood Inn, where McQuinn had continued his tail of Boller. Shauna Spencer was believed to be actively pursuing a new lead in the case.

That Blaine McQuinn had learned this much while camped in a sweltering parking lot in downtown Raleigh was not remarkable. Like any good reporter, he had learned years ago the value of networking, and of informants. Most journalistic investigation involved building contacts, establishing relationships.

The chain had begun by first calling his camera man, Steve Coombs. McQuinn described what he had seen at the Stacey Police

Station. Coombs then called a friend in Charlotte's police department, who made another call on his behalf. Twenty minutes later, the desk sergeant on duty at the Richmond County's Sheriff's office received a call from the State Forensics Department in Raleigh, attempting to reach two on-site agents who had called earlier that day. Could the desk sergeant connect them? The matter was urgent. Five minutes later, Coombs called McQuinn back with the cell phone numbers of Agents Mac Boller and Shauna Spencer. He had no number for the agent from Asheboro.

Coombs had a few more tidbits to share. His haircut at the Stacey Barber Shop late that morning had plenty of updates from the locals. An SBI agent had come in from Asheboro to examine Andy Gardner's wrecked BMW. Petey Lawson, the proprietor's oldest son, whose balding pate didn't seem to merit a visit to any type of barber establishment, said they had found evidence of brake tampering, and they had impounded the car. The agent's name was Taylor Fletcher.

McQuinn began to write down names and questions on his notepad. He asked Coombs to find out what he could about Andy Gardner. What is his connection, if any, to Steadman? He also needed to find out more about the mystery man, the one who had accompanied the agents and Sheriff Yates to Greer's office. He ended his call with Coombs.

He then placed a call to the Dogwood Inn, the same motel he had called home for the last few days. Earle answered on the second ring.

"Earle? Blaine McQuinn here. How are you today?"

Even Earle brightened at the sound of McQuinn's voice. By his reckoning, Mr. McQuinn was probably the most famous guest they had ever had at the Inn. Everybody in the county recognized Channel Three's intrepid investigative reporter.

"Earle, I could use your help on a story I'm working on."

He could hear the old man's chest expand over the phone. "Why, yes sir, Mr. McQuinn. I would be happy to help," Earle gushed.

"I need to get in touch with an SBI agent I've been working with. Shauna Spencer. Is she in right now?"

"No sir. I'm afraid she's not. I can leave a message for her though..."

"No, no. I don't want to do that. It's too sensitive a subject, if you understand."

"Certainly, certainly. Can I leave her a number?" Earle's voice dropped an octave, taking on a conspiratorial tone.

"No, we better not. Earle, you wouldn't have any idea where she might be right now, do you?"

"Why sure I do, Mr. McQuinn. Sheriff Yates dropped her and Mr. Mason off a couple of hours ago. Saw 'em walk right through the lobby and get into Mr. Mason's Camry. Drove off together."

"Didn't say where they were going?"

"No, no they didn't. But they did have a couple of hiking packs though. You know, them Boy Scout sacks. Asked Mona in the kitchen if she could fix 'em up some sandwiches and soft drinks to toss in there. She did, too. Course we had to charge 'em two dollars a sandwich, fifty cents for the pop. That's not a bad price when you..."

"Earle, did they say how long they would be gone?" McQuinn interrupted, fearful that Earle would advance his theory of food pricing ad nauseam.

"No sir, no sir," Earle answered. "But I reckon it can't be too long. Mr. Mason's done got two calls from his business up in Chicago. I reckon he was supposed to be home by now."

"Do you have that number, Earle?"

"Yes sir. Right here it is." He read the number off and continued, "It was his secretary...said he needed to call as soon as possible. Ain't that like a big city feller? Meets one pretty gal and forgets to come home..."

"Who's the pretty gal, Earle?" McQuinn interrupted again.

"Why, Miss Spencer of course. Now that's a mighty pretty young lady if you ask me..."

"Earle, how long has Mr. Mason been a guest of yours?"

"Well, let's see. He checked in on the fifteenth. Coulda got him a better price if I'd known he's gonna stay all this time. Got us a week-long special, you know."

McQuinn noted that the Steadman fire occurred that same day. Out of town guest. Suddenly very involved with local law enforcement. Suspect? Witness? "Do you know the time he checked in? Do you record that, I mean?"

"Naw, Mr. McQuinn. We don't do that sort of stuff around here. But heck, I can tell you when he checked in. I was working the desk. It was just after the eleven o'clock news got underway, I'm guessing. I'll always remember that night. I betcha he hadn't been in more than ten minutes before Bob Nicholson broke in on Channel three with the news of the big fire. I ran out front. You could already see it lighting up the sky. That's a night I won't soon forget."

CHAPTER SEVENTY-NINE

"Brenda, I'll call you back in a few hours." Jeb's voice was low. "Andy's going to be OK, you know that, right?" Shauna watched his face as he listened to Brenda Gardner. "My cell is about out of battery... but I'll be there tonight. You hang in there." He clicked his phone off.

They stood in a small thicket of pine trees at the edge of rolling pastureland. The hike from the river had taken a half-hour and both had found the chill of the water quickly replaced by the grimy perspiration of midday. A slight whiff of breeze was welcome relief.

"It was here. I'm pretty certain of it. We camped here a couple of times. Hasn't changed that much." Jeb looked around at the trees as if they were long lost friends. They were at least a mile from the river, and the pasture was surrounded on all sides by thick woods.

"It was a perfect spot. High ground. You could see some of the lights from town from here. It was a great place to see the stars. Beautiful sky up here." He looked back at Shauna.

"So this is where you left your sleeping bags? Your tent?"

"No tent...but yes, I think this is where we set up camp anyway."

"And where did you actually end up that night?"

"Can't be sure...my guess is that we came close to it over the last half-hour. Like I said, a couple of big hemlocks. Closer to the river, for sure."

Shauna gazed back in the direction they had come, and then turned to consider the first hint of rolling pastureland that headed back toward town.

"Is that the direction of the Thompson house?" she pointed toward the rolling terraces.

"General direction, yes."

"So, if I've got it right, as you three ran back that night, you simply overran your camp. Came in farther south than you wanted. Is that about right?"

"I think so...I know that by the time we reached the big trees we weren't completely sure where we were. And to find the camp...this place, we would have had to backtrack. We weren't going to get Zeke headed back in the direction of the house...and we weren't planning on doing that, either."

"Jeb...*were* you were being followed?"

Jeb paused and looked out over the pasture. "I don't know. I can safely say we felt as if we were being pursued. But I can't honestly tell you I remember seeing anyone...if that's what you mean."

"Back in the car. You talked about the nightmares," Shauna said.

"Oh...I've had those off and on for years." Jeb blushed despite his best efforts. "Maybe just a flashback or something."

"Would you mind telling me about them?" she said, her tone softened.

"It's nothing, Shauna. Just a...a vivid recollection. I'm sure it's my mind playing tricks on me."

"OK then, tell me about it." She sat down on a deep bed of pine needles and patted the area beside her. "I love a good story."

He sat down beside her and told her about the dreams. Walked her through their approach to the house, the gathering storm, the first hint of trouble, and the panicked retreat into the night. It was the first time he had ever discussed them, and he found his pulse begin to quicken as he described the night air and the tension as things began to go wrong.

When he finished, he felt a thin sheen of sweat across his forehead. Shauna was watching him closely.

"Sound pretty kooky?" he asked.

"Sounds like a traumatizing kind of event. But I'm not an expert."

"I think Zeke's reaction was traumatizing. Never saw him that way...never."

"You heard music?" She asked.

"I...don't know. I'm not sure if what I recall is the dream or what actually occurred."

"And you said that there was someone...something in the shadows."

"In my dreams there was…"

"And the image…at the window?"

"That's the part I just can't be sure of, Shauna. In the dream, I clearly see an image at the window. And it's pointing at us."

"And in reality?"

"I don't know."

"But in your dream, you believe you're being pursued?" Shauna whispered.

"Yeah…in my dream, we are running. Whether we're running from the event or our perception of the event, I don't know."

"Does…the dream…always end the same way?"

"No. Not exactly."

"How so?"

"Sometimes we're running. Other times…"

Shauna shifted toward him and waited for him to talk.

"Sometimes I hear Andy screaming 'We have to help Zeke'…"

"And you. What are you doing then?"

"Sometimes I can see him there. See someone reaching toward him. But…" he paused. "It's like I can't move. I can't help him."

"Jeb, did you believe all these years that you and Zeke and Andy… did you believe you were responsible for the judge's death?"

"I…I think that had something to do with the nightmares."

"But it sounds like you knew—at some level, anyway—that there could be something more that happened, right?" Shauna laid her hand on Jeb's arm as she spoke.

"Guess Freud would love this, huh?" Jeb said.

"I don't know. But it's been my experience that dreams do have meaning. They might not always be absolutely accurate, though." She scanned the distant horizon. "Which direction did the rain come from that night?"

Jeb pointed back toward the river. "Most always come from the west…from the mountains."

"So when you three ran that night…"

"Yeah," Jeb said. "We ran right into the storm."

CHAPTER EIGHTY

"Tell me something. As an experienced hiker and camper, do you actually plan to eat, or are we just carrying these packs to look cool?" Shauna asked.

The pair had hiked another half-hour, and the sun they had longed for after the river had become less of a comfort than they had hoped. A thin line of pine trees offered an ideal resting spot.

Jeb's mood lightened. "I was thinking both, actually."

"Well, are you going to invite me to have dinner with you or not?" Shauna asked, and she curled her lips into what might have been a pout.

"Does this...count...as a date?" Jeb asked.

"Only if you want it to," she answered. "But I think Mona packed this as a picnic."

"Wouldn't want to upset Mona, now would we?" Jeb laughed and began to tear into the first of the backpacks. "You have a choice of ham or turkey or what looks like a combination of the two."

They devoured the sandwiches quickly, both surprised at the hunger they had built up in such a short time. The oatmeal cookies Mona had slipped in without charge was a special treat. Jeb was glad he had remembered extra water bottles. In the shadows, buffered from the heat of the day, it seemed peaceful there. They ate in silence, enjoying the quiet.

"So tell me a little about you, Jeb Mason. Outside of Zeke Andrews and the investigation, I don't know anything about you," Shauna said.

"Is this an official question, or a personal one?" He grinned at her.

"Hmmmm." She pursed her lips as if in deep thought. "I guess we'll say a little of both."

"Well, if that's the case, I'm compelled to answer. I'll be forty-two in September. Married once. Divorced. No kids. No immediate prospects for re-marriage. Current mistress of choice is Tolliver Medical, where I am Vice President of Sales. We're medical equipment—syringes, lab supplies, gowns, tongue depressors, a few devices...you name it. Over twenty years in the business. I've lived in Chicago for four years. Love the city. Travel quite a bit. It's a pretty competitive industry. My hobbies include working out, dining, occasional opera, dancing, and spending time with friends."

"You sound like a bio for a re-make of *The Dating Game*," Shauna laughed.

"Well, this was my attempt at being concise. You know, just the facts, ma'am."

"And your ex?"

"Remarried and quite happy from what I understand."

"It happens, Jeb. Sometimes people are not meant to be together."

"It happens. But the truth be told, I wasn't ready to be married."

"Meaning?"

"Meaning I was too in love with my career. Rising up the corporate ladder. Trying to prove myself."

"And now?"

"Now, I would like to think I'm at least a littler wiser."

"Your parents?"

"My dad passed away when I was nineteen, freshman year in college. Massive heart attack brought on by years of attention to his job and no attention to his health."

"Sounds like it might be hereditary."

"What, cardiovascular disease? I'm as healthy as a horse..."

"Disproportionate attention to career."

Jeb smiled. "But curable."

"Was it his job that brought you to Stacey?"

"Yeah, he was a manufacturer's consultant. He worked with the big textile mills on their system's production, stuff like that. We moved pretty often."

"How long were you here?"

"Three, three and half years. But this was the place I most remember. The best friends. The best times."

"Your mom?"

"Alive and well in Portland, Oregon. She remarried fifteen years ago. Great guy. Retired doctor. They have a good life together...they're happy."

"And how about you, Mr. Mason? Are you happy?"

"Official question?"

"Official question."

"Yeah. I'm happy. Good shape financially. Lots of friends. Busy, but it's the life I asked for. Worked for."

"But...?"

"But nothing. It's a great life, Shauna..."

"Why does your answer strike me as wistful?"

"Not wistful...nostalgic maybe. Melancholy."

"Why?"

"I don't know. Probably just coming back here. Seeing people, a place from my past. Remembering a simpler time. The past is a comfortable place...sometimes."

"Not as comfortable a place as you remembered, though?"

"No, not exactly." Jeb smiled.

Shauna pushed the pine needles into a tiny pile. She looked out over the rolling pastureland.

"OK, my turn. Beautiful girl with a big gun. What's your story, Agent Spencer?"

Shauna smiled and almost blushed at the compliment. She'd heard similar lines a hundred times, but it felt different coming from Jeb.

"Is that an official question or a personal one?" she asked.

"Completely personal."

"Well then..." Her smile grew larger. "I guess I better answer. I really am from Birmingham. But I left Alabama a long time ago. Went into police work because, I guess, criminal behavior fascinated me as a little girl. Never thought about it that much. Got into the Agency five or six years ago...met up with Mac Boller, and we've been a team ever since."

"So you started out..."

"Walking a beat, or riding one, anyway. Was recruited into the academy."

Jeb whistled in appreciation.

"Not that impressive. There are quite a few women in the SBI. It's not quite the good ol' boy fraternity it once was," Shauna said.

"I guess you meet some fascinating people in your line of work."

"Sure. But it's not quite what you might expect. It's a lot more like a business than the movies make it out. I've hardly ever even drawn my weapon."

Jeb mimicked a frown, and Shauna laughed at him.

"OK, you were the exception."

For a brief second the quiet swept over them. Their eyes met. Lingered there.

"Ever married?" he asked quietly.

"No...never quite worked that out."

He nodded, and then smiled back at her.

"It's beautiful up here," she said.

They watched a hawk circling high above.

"We used to spend a lot of time up here," Jeb said. "It's funny...I think of this place often. This spot, I mean. Tucked away in the trees. You could see for miles from here. Could see the whole world, it seemed."

"What was he like..Zeke Andrews?" Shauna asked.

Jeb smiled. "Let's see...rambunctious, precocious. A little Huck Finn and a little Dennis the Menace." He grew quiet again. "Zeke's home life was only OK. Not like mine. My dad was the neighborhood hero...when he was home, anyway. Always playing ball in the backyard, running with the kids. Zeke's dad worked at the mill...didn't hear about him much."

"So Zeke spent most of his time with you guys?"

"No, he spent *all* of his time with us." Jeb turned. Looked back somberly at Shauna. "He was my responsibility, Shauna."

"Jeb, you were what...twelve years old?"

"No, I was old enough to know that I had to look out for him. That anything I said, he would do. That he needed me..."

"And I think you did look after him."

"That night was my idea. The Rite...the Thompson house..." He turned away.

"You couldn't have known, Jeb. It was a childhood prank."

"I should have looked after him." Jeb felt his face warm.

"You did, Jeb."

"No. I got him back home. But then I turned the page. I went on with my life."

"That's what you were supposed to do," Shauna said.

"No…I left him…maybe not that night, but I left him all the same…"

"We'll find out what happened to him, Jeb. What happened to Zeke, I mean." Shauna took his hand as she spoke.

"He wasn't a bad guy, Shauna. I know everyone thinks he was. He was troubled. But I knew him, knew what he was. He didn't die the way they say. He was more, he was a lot more than people give him credit for being."

"You know the story behind your Steadman Elementary, Jeb?" she asked.

"The story?"

"Did a little research as background for the investigation," she began. "Seems Steadman is named for P. Titus Steadman. He was a revolutionary war captain."

"I'm not following you, Shauna…"

"In September of 1780, Captain Steadman led a group of rebels…a few professional soldiers, a lot of volunteers…against a Loyalist brigade of General George Cornwallis. Steadman was one of the first true guerilla fighters. Story goes that he learned at the shoulder of General Nathaniel Greene."

"And that's important because…"

"They encountered Loyalists somewhere near the Yadkin River… probably right around here." She gestured toward the fields. "On the evening of the twenty-third of September, the militia attacked and captured or killed a majority of the brigade. Steadman was the architect of the attack. Two weeks later, Battle of Kings Mountain took place west of here…effectively crippled Cornwallis's plans. A year after that, British forces surrender at Yorktown…and the rest, as they say, is history."

"Are you saying that we now attack the town?" Jeb deadpanned.

Shauna giggled. "If there had been no Battle of Kings Mountain there would have been no United States of America. I'm just saying that had we lost those battles, P. Titus Steadman would be a footnote in our history…a terrorist, nothing more."

"But because we won…"

"It's the winners who write history, not the losers," Shauna said. "Isn't always the objective recount we expect it to be…always dictated by those who came out on top, never those who didn't."

"Meaning what exactly?" Jeb asked.

"I don't know…maybe your friend's life was, I don't know, influenced by someone who came out on top."

"So you're saying we get a chance to do a rewrite, Shauna?"

She smiled. "Winston Churchill once said, 'History will be kind to me, for I intend to write it.'"

He grinned.

"My undergraduate minor was in World History. Don't look that impressed," she said.

"All right, Mrs. Churchill." Jeb stood. "Let's get started."

CHAPTER EIGHTY-ONE

Roy Yates knew the last moments of his life were slipping away.

He frantically grabbed for something, anything, to stop his grinding slide down the cliff face. His fingers dug into the loose clay. He was losing it.

Dirt filled his eyes, and he prepared for the free fall to come, when suddenly his hand wrapped around the gnarled roots of a dead tree.

One hand desperately holding to life.

He felt the side of the mountain, locked onto a second pine sapling. It held. His feet dug into the rocks and gained a place there. He heaved a deep breath. Then steeled his courage to look out over the drop-off.

"Merciful lord," he gasped. The rock face was only inches away. Far below, he could see the jagged rocks on which they had reclaimed the body of Zeke Andrews. They seemed like tiny pebbles from this distance.

The Marlboro pack that had almost killed him lay tucked into the brush to his right. He painfully edged his arm closer. He wrapped his fingers around it, and then drew it closer to him.

He looked up. He was at least fifteen feet below the ledge, and he was already exhausted, but he had no choice but to climb. He couldn't hold on there for long, and it would be hours before anyone thought to check on him. Then that many more before anyone found him there.

"Linda, darling," Roy Yates whispered, "I may be coming to join you here in a few. If I do, I hope you'll put in a good word for me." He began to painstakingly pull himself back up the side of the cliff.

Thirty minutes later he edged himself over onto the ledge. He laid face-first, his heart pounding into the dirt. He smelled it.

The soil, the grass...life.

When he found the strength, he rolled over and checked his watch. It was 6:30. He would have guessed it was much later. He propped himself back up against the maple, looked back over at the river below. Felt for the Marlboro packs in his breast pocket. Gave a long sigh.

"Andrews," he said in a low voice, "guess you were trying to tell us something after all."

CHAPTER EIGHTY-TWO

"I want you to tell me again, Jeb. Tell me everything you remember about the house. About what you saw that night," Shauna said.

They stood in the middle of the pasture, looking at a small patch of trees to the east. Peeking out in the middle of the trees was the back of the large, three-story antebellum house.

The Thompson house.

They were a quarter of a mile away. A few large homes dotted the landscape, each separated by lavish lawns and towering magnolias.

"Damn, seemed like it was so remote back then," Jeb whispered. "Those houses around it. I'm sure they weren't there then."

"OK, so tell me about the night. What can you remember?"

"I'm not sure what else I can tell you, Shauna. It was very dark. We walked single file to somewhere around there." He gestured toward some of the large oak trees some fifty feet beyond. "We could see the lights of the house through the trees. We checked, made sure Zeke had all the stuff. Soap, shaving cream. He may have had spray paint, I'm not sure."

"How did he carry it?"

"He had a backpack."

"Did he have it the next day?"

"I'm not sure. I don't remember seeing it."

"Could he have lost it?"

"Yeah. I guess it's possible. I don't know. Never thought of it."

"Could it have carried any identification?"

"No. I remember it was old…he brought it when we camped."

"But you never saw it again? You're sure of that?"

"No. I'm just not sure. We grabbed our stuff the next day and got out of there. Nobody was really looking to make sure we had everything."

"What else, Jeb? What else do you remember?"

"I remember light. Lights from the house. Zeke was by himself, moving toward the house. Andy and I were behind. Watching from those trees. We didn't think he could do it. But he went straight toward the house. A lot of light was coming out of the large bay window in the back. Zeke stayed in the shadows."

"What were you and Andy doing?"

"We just watched. I remember whispering to Andy, "The little SOB is going to do it." We were laughing but we were scared to death."

"What else?"

"Nothing else."

"Are you sure, Jeb? Are you sure? Were there cars on the street out front? Car horns? Could you see people inside, activity of any sort?"

"Nothing, Shauna…" Jeb paused.

"What, Jeb…what else? You've got to make yourself think."

Jeb paused. "The music…there *was* music. I remember it now. It wasn't just in the dream."

"What kind of music, Jeb?"

"Not sure. Old-fashioned. I remember thinking it was like Big Band, but it was so long ago. Seemed sort of haunting, scary-like. But I'm not sure why."

"What made it scary?"

Jeb shook his head.

"I don't know, Shauna. I can't remember the tune. I'm not sure why, but it seemed…it seemed haunting."

"Where were you? Where was Andy?"

"There." Jeb pointed to three towering trees near the back of the property.

"Could you see the house clearly?"

"Yes."

"Could Andy?"

"Yes."

"Certain?"

"Yes, certain."

"What else?"

"Nothing. Like I said, Zeke started soaping the windows. Maybe thirty seconds. Could have been longer. Then suddenly, he stopped. It was like he was frozen. He started backing up. He backed right into the light. Andy and I started to panic then. He could be seen. Then all of a sudden, he started to scream."

Jeb took a step closer to the house, trying to recreate in his mind what happened.

"Shauna, it was like it didn't come out of Zeke. It sounded, it sounded like a primeval cry, another world kind of scream. We freaked. We all freaked. It was like the panic just swept over us."

"What happened then?"

"I don't remember running. I don't think I knew we *were* running. Somewhere back there—" Jeb motioned in the direction of the river "—we caught up with Zeke. He couldn't talk, couldn't breathe. So we ran some more. Until we couldn't run anymore. By then, the storm had started. We were lost. We had hit the river, made it across without drowning, but had no idea where we were. Andy pulled Zeke over to a tree. There was a lot of undergrowth. We crawled up underneath it. There was lightning exploding all around us."

"Tell me what you remember. Did you see anyone?"

"I remember thinking the woods were haunted, that there was someone, something out there."

"Why, Jeb?"

"I don't know why. Maybe because we knew someone had to have seen Zeke, or at least heard him."

"But did you see anyone?"

"No."

"Are you sure?"

"Yes."

"Did you hear anything?"

"No."

"Jeb...are you *sure*?"

"Yes...I think so."

"You think so...Jeb, I want you to think back. Did you hear anything at all that night?"

"I remember the thunder. The lightning. It was all around us. Like the trees had a current running through them. Zeke, Zeke was crying. Andy was trying...trying to get him calmed down."

"And where were you?" Shauna asked.

"We were under the branches of the hemlock. The others were against the trunk. I sat a little out front, watching…but still covered. But we were way back in the underbrush, so I couldn't see far. I fell asleep, slumped over there."

"You said you thought so…when I asked you if you heard something…what does that mean?"

"It was like a nightmare, Shauna…the storm, the darkness, Zeke…" Jeb stopped. His eyes suddenly grew wide.

"Jeb…what is it?"

"Sometime in the night…I woke up. The storm was right on top of us…I was jerked back…suddenly wide-awake. I couldn't be sure…not at first…but then I heard it again."

"What? What did you hear?"

"Screams, Shauna," Jeb whispered the words. "I heard screams."

CHAPTER EIGHTY-THREE

Yates arrived back at his office, bruised and exhausted, at 7:30 p.m. Mac Boller had already called twice, and the last sticky note the administrator had left on his desk read "Urgent—please call immediately." Yates punched in the number for Boller's cell phone. He answered on the first ring.

"We have news, Sheriff. I think it could be of some significance. I've already spoken to Agent Spencer. She is coming out now. Sheriff, is this a secure line?"

"I'm sorry, is this a secure line? Is that what you asked?" Yates was confused by the question.

"Yes sir, is it a secure line?"

"Mr. Boller, it's secure in that it is my private line. Beyond that I can't say how secure..."

"But no one can tap into the call? Pick up a phone someplace in the station?"

"No, they can't do that, but why...?"

"Sheriff, I want to walk you through a couple of updates. Once I've shared this, we may want to decide who is made aware and who isn't, OK?"

"Fine, fine, what is it?" Yates pulled out his notepad and began to write.

"First, the Gardner car. The brake line was definitely tampered with. Our people say there is no mistaking that. Botched attempt at murder is what we're guessing. Further corroborates the theory that we have a perp who is after the people that were closest to Andrews."

"Second, the blackmail papers have Andrews's prints all over them. No surprise there. We're speculating he built the letter or letters several times before sending one along. The best we can say is that he clearly spent a lot of time with his little project, but no clear proof can be established on what he did with the final product, or to whom he sent it."

"How about the little bag…was it drugs?"

"The bag?" Boller hesitated. "Oh hell no. Just as we figured. The lab guys laughed at that. Let's see…here you go, said it was primarily, let's see, Trifoleum, or trefoil, part of the leguminous pea family. Can pull it up out of any untended yard in this state." A car horn blared in the background. "All right, I got to watch the road here, or I'm going to get killed trying to read and drive."

"Fingerprints?" Yates asked.

"Yup. All over the papers and already matched to Andrews. Along with another set that are smaller, most likely the boy's. Same for the lock. Said it could be matched to a number of standard keys, but again, no key in the envelope. No telling where it might be or why or how the lock was used."

"Still guessing he kept it on that lockbox for the gun that Mason told us about. Believe he was carrying when he went tumbling off that ridge."

"Maybe. No way to tell, Sheriff. No weapon was found with the body. Didn't up and vanish," Boller said.

"Yeah, but it goes to somethin'."

"We have got to get over to talk to the Tully lady and to the boy, and we need to do that soon. At this point, the boy is the only person we can point to that even had an idea of what Andrews was doing. Given the track record of the perp and his or her mindset, we need to also make sure we have provided some form of protection for the boy."

"Thinking now he may be in danger?" Yates asked.

"Yes sir, I do. We're beginning to put some things together." Static came over the other end of the phone. "…paint a pretty bleak picture. Forget what happened thirty years ago for a minute. In the last week, one definite murder, one possible murder, one, maybe two murder attempts, arson…one very probable break-in attempt related to all of this. I'd say we need to take every possible precaution. I think we may have a very dangerous person somewhere..." Again, static filled the line.

"Greer already has a car over there."

"Say again," Boller said.

"Said Chief Greer already has a car over there...at the Tully residence where the Andrews boy is..."

"You sure about that?"

"Well, no, I'm not sure. But he said he would..."

"Think you could send one of your cars over right away?"

"Yeah. I can do that." Yates's voice was uneasy. Why the sudden concern?

"Good. Third, we're pursuing the Tallahassee dealership thing. *Nothing* about that makes sense. Typical down payment to hold a car like that, even top of the line, is five hundred, one thousand dollars tops. Andrews plunks down two thousand. Hard cash, Sheriff. Sends it in an envelope through the U.S. mail. I talked with the sales rep at Bingham. That's the dealership. He tells me that Andrews called him approximately two weeks ago. Expressed an interest in a black 'vette. Sheriff, they closed the deal over the phone. Twenty minutes, max. The guy I talked with...let's see, a Thomas Yoder, tells me he was suspicious, particularly when Andrews indicated he would mail him the down payment. Yoder tells him seven-hundred and fifty would have held the car, but Andrews insists on sending him two thousand. The envelope came with twenty one-hundred dollar bills. Yoder said it was the damndest thing he had ever seen."

"Agent Boller, are you thinking the two thousand dollars might have been a down payment of a different type?" Yates asked.

"Well, Sheriff, I would recommend we take a real close look at any financial records we can get our hands on for Mr. Andrews. Court order, if necessary. There is an outside chance he could have a few dollars tucked away, I guess."

"Not likely," Yates answered.

"I would agree.

"You guessing Andrews gets a 'good faith' payment, puts it in an envelope, buys himself his dream car?"

"I think we have a pretty good reason to consider that," Boller answered.

"Any chance they still have the money, or the envelope?"

"Looks like they might have deposited it that day."

"So that's it? Nothing else?" asked Yates.

"I think we need to ask ourselves why Andrews chose Tallahassee, Florida, of all places, That's gotta be what, four hundred miles away?"

"Farther, and I wonder about that too," Yates said.

"Possible assumption might be that once the last payment is collected, Zeke Andrews is long gone," answered the SBI agent.

"After we visited with the Thompson lady this morning...Mason mentioned one other thing about Andrews and the visit he and his ex made to his trailer," Yates said.

Boller waited.

"Seems there was only one thing this Mrs. Tully hoped to reclaim. But it wasn't there. Couldn't find hide nor hair..."

"What was that, Roy?"

"It was a suitcase." Yates again fingered the notebook in his pocket. "Seems she had given him one a few years back."

"Makes you wonder if our boy was maybe packed somewhere and ready to skip town, doesn't it?" Boller said.

"More we look, more we seem to find, Agent Boller."

"Still leaves us with the question of why he meets his end way up in the back end of nowhere. I don't think he was an Einstein, but to be lured there, where he can just be tossed off a mountain, makes no sense," Boller said.

"He didn't," answered Yates.

"What do you mean?"

"I spent the better part of three hours up there today. Found something interesting. When we recovered Andrews's body he had nothing on him but a pack of cigarettes...Marlboros, to be exact. I took a close look at the ridge where we assumed he jumped. Nobody noticed anything the first time around. Or if they did, it didn't register. Just below the point, I found two empty Marlboro packs, dozens of used matches. Even after the storms, they were still there."

"Meaning..."

"Meaning I think Zeke Andrews was on that ridge for some time. But not to meet anyone. He had made himself comfortable. He was conducting a little surveillance."

"Of what?"

"Across the river is a small dock, a boat landing. There's an unused dirt road over there. From the point on Darby Ridge, you could see for miles. You could just make yourself at home. Wait for your delivery at a safe distance. Have a smoke. Enjoy the scenery."

"Lots of people smoke cigarettes, Sheriff."

"Found a pack of Marlboros on the body, Agent Boller. And his ex-wife gave me a list of Zeke Andrews's possessions. Not much to it." Yates scanned the inventory Mary Tully had provided. "But she called out Marlboro cigarettes. Guess when you don't have much, even a damn cigarette counts for somethin'."

"We dusted the packs for prints?" asked Boller.

"Your people will have to do that."

"So you're guessing Andrews was caught by surprise?"

"Yeah, Agent Boller, I am."

"Could have been there to meet somebody…maybe a drinking buddy…maybe even a drug deal."

"Going to bet you the only DNA anybody will find on those cigarettes will be Andrews's," Yates began. "And I think he was doing a little recon."

"How do we prove that, Roy?"

"Not sure we can. But like I said, I think he was there for a spell. And I don't think he hiked all that way just to grab a smoke…or to admire the scenery. And if I was going to meet somebody, I sure as hell would find an easier location."

"So what? You're saying he goes all that way to stake out a drop zone for the payment?"

"Yes sir, that is exactly what I'm saying."

"Well…" Boller said grimly. "I think you're right."

"We got one hell of a mess down here in Stacey, don't we, Mac?"

"Yeah, Sheriff, I'd say we do," Boller began. "There's another thing. I've spent some time trying to pull up court records from your county for that time period. First to get some sense of whether or not your Judge Thompson could have been involved in anything that could have gotten him killed. I've got one of our researchers working on that. I also had her do a search for all arrests and convictions for your county from 1976 through 1983 for breaking and entering, burglary, theft, assault; pretty much anything that could have gotten you cross-ways with the law. She's in the process of cross-referencing with your latest census reports to get an idea if any bad guys who were around then might still be out there today."

"Agent Boller, I like the way you think."

"Thank you, Sheriff Yates. Can I ask you a question?"

"Shoot."

"Why is it you were reluctant to involve Chief Greer in this investigation?"

"Not necessarily reluctant. Greer just likes chasing headlines or throwing his weight around…"

"That why the first meeting you and Agent Spencer and I had didn't involve him?"

"Like I said…"

"In fact, Ms. Spencer told me you made no mention at all of the police chief when you first discussed all of this. I can't say I got the warmest reception when I suggested a sit-down."

"Greer is an asshole, Mac."

"He's also a convicted criminal, isn't he?"

"Yeah, I believe he is."

"You know Benjamin Weylan Greer was arrested on at least four occasions during those years, once on an assault charge, once on simple battery, and twice on breaking and entering?"

"I didn't remember the particulars…"

"Is that the reason you didn't want to get him involved in this investigation, because when Thompson died he was a low-life himself, or is it for a simpler reason? Plain old country politics?" Boller asked.

"Greer is a prick, Agent Boller…"

"So, it's politics?"

"No…it's not politics," the sheriff answered, his tone low.

"Sheriff, when this happened, would Chief Greer have been considered a viable suspect himself?"

There was no answer on the other end of the line.

"Sheriff?"

"There were a handful of locals that I could have suspected would have been involved in a break-in. Forget murder. Just a simple break-in. Of those, maybe half who I could have said I would suspect in a violent crime…Benny Greer met the criteria on both."

"And the rest?"

"Not sure any of them are still around here. But your cross-reference should help us confirm that."

"Roy, Franklin Thompson's widow...You visited her today?"

"Yeah. Marie's at least eighty now. Mac, she never remarried. Still lives in the same house. Gets about pretty well...shit, this is going to be a helluva shock for the old lady."

"Leaving Raleigh now. We need to talk to Mrs. Thompson. And soon."

"First thing tomorrow too soon?" asked Yates.

"Don't think so. What do you think about Shauna handling that?"

"Pushing me out a little bit there, Mac?" asked Yates.

"Not at all, Sheriff. But we have a pretty volatile situation here. And it might come best from another female."

"Message received. I'll step aside."

"Appreciate it, Roy. There's another aspect to all of this. If Franklin Thompson was murdered, we have to consider all the possible suspects."

"Meaning?"

"Most logical suspect in any homicide is an immediate family member."

"So you're saying this lady killed her husband, killed three boys, killed Zeke Andrews and Bump Patterson. Pretty damn active if you ask me."

"Agreed, but she could be involved in some way," Boller answered.

"Which makes it even more important that Ms. Spencer conduct the interview with Mrs. Thompson?"

"She's the best, Roy. If the old gal knows something, anything, Shauna will get to it."

"So what have we got here, Mac? Is this all paranoia, or do we have something bad, awful bad?" asked Yates.

"Two things, Sheriff. First, I think yeah, we may have something very bad...maybe worse than we even know at this point," Boller paused. Yates could hear him breathing heavily through the phone and imagined him taking a long draw on his cigarette.

"Second, we have got to keep a lid on things. Right now our best advantage is that the killer or killers doesn't know what we know and what we don't know. Because of that, they may try to get this whole thing resolved by eliminating any shred of evidence. We continue our investigation, and we hope that he makes a mistake. Roy, we need to keep this tight. We don't know who our suspects are. No department briefing. No media. For all they know, the investigation is of the Steadman fire, nothing more. We get a break or two, we might figure this thing out."

There was a silence on the other end.

"Sheriff, you still with me?"

A pause, then Yates said, "Sorry, Mac...just thinking through my notes for a second."

"Something else?"

"Something Mason said that day we rode to the hospital...see about Gardner after the accident and all."

"Yeah...."

"It's just that Mason said he went by that stale house out on the highway. Place Andrews worked at last."

"He mentioned that when we talked to him at breakfast. Said he just up and quit the job," Boller said. "Not sure much there to go on..."

"Not just that-he said he was acting jumpy."

"OK...so?"

Yates paused and Boller could hear him shuffling through the pages of his notebook over the phone.

"Here it is. Wrote it down just as he told Agent Spencer and me that afternoon in the car. He said the guy Andrews worked with out there said Andrews asked him about a car in the parking lot. When Mason asked him what he thought might be going on, this co-worker said, 'I thought he was worrying about being busted...that maybe he was on the look-out...for the law.'"

CHAPTER EIGHTY-FOUR

Blaine McQuinn glanced down at his speedometer. He was pushing eighty and was now less than fifteen minutes from Stacey. He wanted to get to this Jeb Mason before anyone else, and to do that he might have to camp out at his door. Earle was to call him on his cell if Mason got to the motel before he did. He checked his watch. It read 7:35 p.m. Maybe an hour and a half of good daylight left, but that was a guess. His heart was racing.

He double-checked the map that was spread unevenly over the passenger seat and struggled to trace the highways with his finger while keeping the Mustang on the road. A pickup passed going in the opposite direction, honking its horn loudly. He was straddling the middle of the highway. He yanked the steering wheel sharply to the right.

"Where is it?" he muttered, glancing back and forth from the highway to the crumpled map. There. Darby Ridge. Just outside of town. Highway 51. The turn-off was just ahead.

He ran through a mental checklist of what he had learned in the last few hours and felt his palms sweat even more.

Jeb Mason was an executive with a major medical supplies company in Chicago. McQuinn had learned that he was once a resident of Stacey in the late 1970s and early '80's. He had returned for the funeral of a childhood friend, Ezekiel Andrews. Andrews had recently made local news—a suicide. The circumstances around Andrews's death seemed vague. Local residents were convinced it was either a suicide or an alcohol-induced tragedy. Andrews's past was "colorful."

Mason had been contacted by one Andy Gardner. The funeral had taken place the day before. Friend dies, friend buried, should be end of

story. But something else had happened. There had been renewed interest in Andrews's death in the last day. Interest that had captured the
involvement of both local law enforcement and state agents. McQuinn
believed it might connect to the Steadman investigation, but he couldn't
be sure how.

He knew that Mason had unexpectedly extended his stay and that
even his personal secretary wasn't clear on the reason why. Bonnie Collins
had been reluctant to offer information when she realized she was speaking to a North Carolina reporter. She did confirm the Andrews's funeral
and the contact by Gardner, but little more. Yes, Mason had lived in
the area in that time frame, but he'd had no contact in the years since.

The next call had been even more intriguing. Arvin Monroe at
Monroe's Garage provided a veritable fountain of information. The
Gardner vehicle had, in fact, been impounded for the purposes of examining the brake system. Gardner had been seriously injured shortly after
the Andrews funeral, and authorities suspected the accident was related
to vehicle tampering. Why state investigators, though?

McQuinn had called Carolinas Medical Center. He was unable to
talk to a Gardner family member but did speak to a neighbor who was
in the ICU waiting room. Gardner's condition was critical, but stable.
A uniformed Charlotte police officer had joined sometime during the
night after a short meeting with family members. Gardner's family was
now sequestered in a separate waiting area.

Though no one could verify, there was some speculation that
Gardner was perhaps under the influence when the accident occurred,
and an investigation had been launched. The rumor had gained additional momentum when a second officer was stationed in ICU. This had
created quite a stir among the various friends who had arrived to sit
with the family.

But the police officer had requested a list of the visitors, and some
type of sign-in sheet was being arranged with hospital staff, limiting
visitation. In the last hour a buzz had swept through the waiting area.
Andy Gardner was under protective guard at the request of Sheriff Roy
Yates in Stacey. There were rumors that someone may have tried to kill
Gardner, perhaps even shot at him, forcing the accident.

McQuinn listened carefully. Jotted down the name of his "infor-
mant"—Rufus Linton, a neighbor and friend of the Gardners. He bal-
anced what Linton knew with what he had already learned. Official

investigation of the Gardner vehicle. Suspected brake tampering. Police protection of the victim at the request of the local sheriff. Victim's strong tie to Zeke Andrews. Similar tie to the newcomer, Jeb Mason, who was talking to authorities, namely SBI agents. Those same agents were the principals involved in the murder investigation at Steadman Elementary.

He hung up the phone and placed another call to Earle at the Dogwood Inn. Moments later, he was searching for the 51 turn-off, his mind swirling around the information that was almost overloading it. Why would SBI and locals suddenly shift attention to Andrews? He was guessing now, a dangerous step for a reporter. But there was a connection there. He was sure of it.

Much of this seemed to swirl around the jumper. Steve Coombs read the news story of his death and the recovery of the body to McQuinn over the phone. He died at Darby Ridge.

And Spencer and Mason, according to Earle at the front desk, were going on a hike...

It was time to gamble a little bit. He made the turn onto 51. Four miles later, he spotted the washed out dirt road Coombs had described as leading up to Darby Ridge.

He wheeled in, leaving the asphalted highway behind.

CHAPTER EIGHTY-FIVE

"Are you sure, Jeb? Are you sure?" Shauna asked. They stood together on a small knoll that looked out over the Thompson house.

"No, I'm not...not completely. I'm not sure about anything that night. But I believe...there...were...screams. Damn, Shauna, how could I not remember that?"

"You won't be the first to repress portions of your memory because of a trauma, Jeb. It's not uncommon."

"It is for me. Jesus, I think maybe...I always knew. But it was just part of the nightmare. I mean, I just pushed all of it away. I never associated it with those kids drowning..."

"Nobody would expect you to." She placed her hand on his shoulder. He looked down at the house, shook his head slowly.

"I wonder if there's anything else I could have forgotten."

"Maybe...but remember, it doesn't prove anything. You could have also heard a kid being swept up in a flash flood, not necessarily struggling against a killer. There is something else that makes me wonder, though..."

"Which is?" he turned and watched her closely.

"Let's say we have a pursuer that night. They lose you guys in the darkness but run across the other three kids. They're scared, maybe panicked. A storm is either underway or ready to break on top of them. The killer is desperate."

"OK, the killer is desperate..."

"But the three boys, they were ages thirteen, thirteen, and twelve. Yates said the boys were fully clothed, even had their shoes on. Let's say they weren't in their sleeping bags. Maybe they see the killer coming...

or the killers. Assumption number one is that they don't, and he or she is able to summarily murder them, one by one. What do you do? Do you just sneak up, pull them out into the water and hold them down until they drown? These are healthy, rambunctious young boys. How easy can that be? I mean it's possible I guess, but hard to imagine pulling it off."

"All right, so assumption number one is problematic," Jeb said.

"But assumption number two is even more so. Let's say they see the killer or killers. What do they do? Sit patiently by the water while they wait for their turn to die? Jeb, I would think they would fight, yell, run, whatever it took. But I just can't come up with any scenario that seems completely plausible."

"Meaning what? Back to assumption number one?" Jeb asked.

"I guess so," Shauna sounded unsure, pensive, "but it doesn't jive well with Yates's description of how the bodies were found fully clothed. Doesn't sound like kids bedded down for the night, does it?"

"No, but maybe there are a couple of other possibilities..."

"Which are?"

"The first, and the more obvious I guess, is that there was more than one murderer...and they overwhelmed them. Drowned them before anyone could get away."

Shauna nodded, considering Jeb's answer quietly. He looked beyond her, to the house in the distance.

"But the second, the second possibility could be something else. And it scares the hell out of me."

"Which is?" Shauna asked.

"That they didn't consider the killer a threat."

"What?"

"That they didn't consider the killer a threat. The killer was someone they knew. He could have walked up. Maybe offered to walk them across the river, or to help them make it through the storm. Whatever. Brought one or two out into the river..." Jeb fell quiet. He contemplated the image.

"It's possible, I guess."

"Shauna, have you guys decided on follow-up with Zeke's family yet? I mean SBI...police......sheriff's department...who does what?"

"I don't follow you, Jeb. The only follow-up right now is through us. Yates was going to take a second look at the Andrews crime scene.

Mac is touching base with Raleigh. There are no more steps. Not until we decide exactly what we have here."

"I'm not so sure of that, Shauna," Jeb interrupted. She turned and followed his gaze.

A Stacey Police Department car was cruising on the street in front of the Thompson house. It came to a stop. From their vantage point, they could make out the bulky figure of Benny Greer as he climbed out and slowly walked toward the front door.

CHAPTER EIGHTY-SIX

"Malcolm? This is Roy Yates. Look, I'm sorry to bother you, but I need to touch base with you on the fire investigation."

"Damn, Roy, Sally and I were just sitting down to dinner. Can't it wait?" the Steadman principal's exasperated tone didn't invite a telephone conversation.

"No, Malcolm. It can't."

"All right, all right, all right...Sally, go ahead, Hon, I'll be a minute," his voice louder, "wait a minute, Roy." There was a pause of several minutes on the other end. Malcolm Lindsey picked up a second line. "I don't suppose I should expect steak biscuits as restitution this time?"

Yates chuckled. "Not hardly, Malcolm. We're making some progress here, but I need your help."

"You got it, Roy. What's up?" Lindsey's voice grew serious.

"First, the storage room. It's my understanding that dated student files were kept there. We think there's a good chance the murderer may have been after some of them."

"Student files? Why the hell..."

"Malcolm, do you remember Zeke Andrews?"

"Zeke Andrews? Not off the top of my head, no."

"Remember the suicide over at Darby Ridge?"

"Yeah, OK. The drug guy?"

"Yes, the drug guy. He was a student at Steadman years ago. We believe the killer was trying to find some information on Andrews..."

"Roy, our fire happened after Andrews jumped, as I recall. Why in the world does someone want...?"

"Malcolm, listen to me. There's a good chance they're related, OK? Now I'm going to depend on your confidentiality on this."

"All right, Sheriff."

"Malcolm, the break-in. We're under the impression that old student files were housed in your administrative storage. Is that correct?"

"Roy, I guess so. I can't say I spent a lot of time in there, but yes, I'm sure we had old files back there."

"Would you have kept files as far back as the late seventies, early eighties?"

"I'm guessing, yes."

"Who had keys to those files, Malcolm?"

"Well, other than me, I'm not sure. There's duplicate keys all over a school building. Who has them? I can't say."

"All right, who had responsibility for the files, I mean, did anybody have to maintain them or anything?"

It was Lindsey's turn to laugh now. "Roy, you kidding? No one gave a damn about those files. I don't think anybody ever even looked at them."

Yates sighed. "So anybody could have pretty much waltzed back there and taken a look at them?"

"Afraid so, partner."

"Malcolm, did you have any type of security during the summer months at the school?"

"No, I mean nothing other than the police drive-bys, if you want to call that security. Greer set it up."

"Greer set it up? When?"

"Oh, I don't know. Let's see. I saw him at a city council meeting back in April sometime. He mentioned beefing up patrols. We had that break-in last year, you know. So he put together twice-per-night drive-bys. Even gave him a set of keys for his officers."

"Greer ever touch base with you on this? You know, ask questions about school property, expensive materials?"

"No, not that I recall...well, come to think of it, he did ask me once...maybe a month ago, about what we kept stored in there."

"And?" Yates tone changed.

"Told him same thing I told you...computers, books, records... stuff like that."

There was a long pause on the other end.

"Anything else?" Yates finally asked.

"Only thing I can think of is I believe he asked about employees on site during the summer. Said he wanted to know if there were any people that were supposed to be there. You know, if a patrol car happened to run across somebody."

"I see, and what did you say?"

"I told him he might run across the janitor sometimes during the day. The vice-principal or myself. But that's about it. And only during the day. Nobody should ever be there at night."

CHAPTER EIGHTY-SEVEN

"Still not getting the sheriff." Shauna snapped her cell phone shut. "Not convinced he even uses a cell."

"You think he knows about Greer going over to visit Mrs. Thompson?" Jeb asked.

"Don't know, but he's going to hear about it. That fat bastard could blow the whole investigation if he goes stumbling into the middle of things."

"Why, Shauna..." Jeb grinned. "You have some piss and vinegar in you, don't you?"

"Just a little bit." She returned the smile. "When the occasion warrants."

"I know...I remember."

"You ready to lead me back to the car?"

"Sure. I was thinking you might want to go ahead and knock on the Thompson house...find out what's going on."

"Last thing I would want to do. Want to understand a little more about what's going on. Talk a little more with Mac and the sheriff. Worst thing I could do would be to add to the problem by walking in after Greer."

"Well, that being the case, let's head back to the Yadkin."

They turned and started back along a path.

As they walked over the terraces of the field, Shauna successfully connected to Mac Boller on her second try. She quickly related Jeb's recollection and the Greer visit to Marie Thompson's house.

"Son of a bitch..." Boller growled. "Have you got through to Sheriff Yates?"

"No, tried a couple of times."

"Look, Shauna. I'm headed back after all."

"Mac, you're fine where you are. Dottie wants to see you. Take the night. I'll see you tomorrow."

"No...Shauna. I'm already on the road." His voice had grown hard. She could recognize it when the edge was there.

"Mac, what's going on?"

"There's a reason the sheriff was reluctant to share any of this, Shauna."

She waited.

"Ran a felony list for the area. Discussed that list with Roy Yates in the last hour," Boller said. "One of the hits was our friend Benny Greer."

"What? You're telling me Chief Greer is a convicted felon? Is that possible?"

"In a small country town anything is possible. You know that."

"OK. I'm going back to the Thompson house." Shauna stopped. Jeb turned to watch. She was looking back in the direction of town.

"No you're not, Shauna. You're going to accompany a civilian back to your vehicle. You're going to raise Sheriff Yates on the cell. You're going to report what you've learned this afternoon. And then we're going to see where we are in regards to this investigation."

"Mac, what if the perp is going back to the scene of the crime? You want me to just stand here?"

"We don't have one shred of a clue that Greer, or anybody for that matter, is a suspect."

"Mac..."

"Listen to me closely, Agent Spencer. I am still your senior. We aren't playing *Cowboys and Indians* right now. We are gathering evidence. We are conducting an investigation. Is that clear?"

Shauna groaned and spun around in frustration. "Crystal clear, Agent Boller. Crystal clear."

"Good. Now do me a favor. Take care of yourself and take care of that young buck you're with."

Shauna looked at Jeb. He stood less than ten feet away, but he was watching her intently.

"I plan to do that, Mac."

"Shauna...I believe you were right, you know that?"

"In what way?"

"Something very bad happened in that town. If it's as bad as I'm thinking, we don't have one murder. We have six. Six innocent people."

Shauna found herself scanning the horizon, searching the trees, as if somewhere in the shadows, a murderer lurked.

"If this son of a bitch has killed six people, Shauna, he won't have any problem killing a few more. Especially if he's gotten wind that we're closing in."

"I understand that, Mac."

"Going to have Yates get a cruiser out to this Tully house ASAP. I believe the Andrews boy is at risk. When you're out to your car, would appreciate it if you get out there and have a talk with him too. OK?"

"Agree...I can be there in the next hour or two."

"Shauna, you need to be on guard. You know that, right?"

"Of course I do."

"My point is...you stay glued to the hip with your friend, Mason, you hear me?"

"I plan to do that...and what gives you the idea he's my friend? He's a possible witness in a murder investigation." She was lowering her voice but she still glanced toward Jeb again. For some reason she didn't want him to hear.

"Bullshit, Shauna."

"Excuse me..."

"You heard me...bullshit."

"And what is that supposed to mean?"

"I've worked with you too long, little lady. I knew someday someone would come along that would flip your buttons. Never guessed you would meet him through your gun sights..."

"I'm going now, Mac."

"OK, OK...just be careful, hear me?"

"You're full of it, you know that?" Shauna whispered. She knew her face was flushed. She knew Jeb was watching her. And she knew Mac was right.

CHAPTER EIGHTY-EIGHT

They forded the river just as the shadows of the trees had begun to deepen. The humidity of the day had begun to give way to an eastern wind that carried the promise of thunderstorms to come. Much of their march back had been in silence. The pace was at too great of a clip to allow for much conversation. And each was lost in his or her own thoughts.

"Why didn't you tell me to wear long pants?" Shauna mumbled as they stepped from the water and onto the sand bar. They were both shivering. The water seemed even colder the second time around.

"Because I'd forgotten how cold this damn water was, that's why... or it could be I just like you in shorts." Jeb held her hand, helping to steady her.

She looked up at him. "I'm sure I am a vision of beauty."

"Yes...you are, Shauna."

The first low rumble of thunder rolled through the trees as he drew her closer.

"I look like a drowned dog." She giggled even as she fell into him.

He kissed her just as the wind began to pick up and gust through the branches. It was a deep kiss, long and so passionate that both felt the ache of the cold slip away. And then the rest of the world did as well. She pressed against him tightly and they explored each other's lips with a hunger.

The first crack of lightning overhead startled them back to the Yadkin River, jolting them into the reality of the moment.

"I...shouldn't have done that," Jeb whispered. His lips ran over her face, gently biting at her ear. "I took advantage of the moment."

"Is…that what you think?" She purred the words.

"No, I don't," he whispered.

The first drops of rain began to slap against the sand, creating biting pocks that splattered all around them. For several long minutes they clung to one another, allowing the rain to blur the world.

"Need to get you back to the car…" Jeb muttered. His face was wet and he blinked as the rain began to come harder.

"Yes…we have business…a case…to attend to." Shauna wiped her eyes with her sleeve and smiled back at him. She felt light-headed.

"Gets dark in these woods pretty quickly," Jeb said. He stepped back and peered through the trees just as the thunder exploded overhead. He glanced up at the boiling, black clouds.

"Are we far? From the car, how long?" Shauna followed his gaze.

"Just a few minutes. If we can keep from getting killed, I mean."

Shauna stared at the cauldron overhead. "This doesn't look too smart, Jeb. Think there's any low place we can get cover?"

"Not likely, Agent Spencer."

"Then lead on, Mr. Mason. Lead on!" Shauna yelled over the sudden roar of the storm.

"Lightning at night's twice as dangerous," Jeb whispered, as he took Shauna's hand.

"What's that?" she asked.

"Nothing." He smiled. "Just something I heard once."

He began to clear a path in the direction of the car.

CHAPTER EIGHTY-NINE

"Jeb, when we get back...I'm going to need to drop you off at the motel for a bit." Shauna spoke between the branches that they ducked and swerved around in the growing shadows. Fifteen minutes of steady hiking and they were finally drawing closer to where the car was parked.

"Kind of guessed that." Jeb spoke over his shoulder. The darkness was closing in quickly now. "Does it have something to do with Joe Andrews?"

"Mac thinks we may have a handle on something. It's very important that we get to him...and soon."

"Why?" He pushed a limb out their path, held it so Shauna could pass safely underneath.

"Because there's a chance he could be in some danger," she answered. "Mac's guessing that the killer knows now that we have some evidence that could implicate him. The same evidence that got your friend killed."

"Why would he know?"

"Can't say just yet. But we have reason to believe..."

"Whoa..." Jeb wheeled and faced her, "what do you mean you can't say? Is it can't say or won't say, Shauna?"

"Won't say." She gazed at him, her tone emphatic.

"Why not?"

"Because Jeb, this is an official investigation. There are guidelines around confidentiality. We are in an investigation...period. It's not for public consumption."

"So I'm the public. That about right?"

"Look, Jeb. You've been critically important in all of this, but you have to understand I have a responsibility as a state agent. I can't involve you...no matter what personal feelings I might have," Shauna gripped his hand tighter, "or anyone for that matter, in an *official investigation* unless we know what we're dealing with..."

"Gotcha, Shauna. I'll go home, sit by the phone. Are you going to call me when it's safe to come back outside?"

"Jeb, that's not what I'm saying..."

The bullet whistled by them a split second before the sharp pop of the rifle's discharge. It bore into a large oak just behind them as they dove for the ground. A second shot exploded into the earth just in front of Shauna's head, sending the dirt and grass into a cloud that choked the air.

"Roll!" Jeb's voice, grabbing her by the hand. Her eyes were filled with debris but she was already pulling her weapon from its holster, drawing it into a firing position.

"Move, move, move." He was pulling her over and they were tumbling over roots and grass. She tried to answer but her mouth was caked with grime. She couldn't see and could scarcely breathe.

Couldn't be sure that she hadn't been hit.

A third shot that seemed closer. In the mass of brush and twigs she could barely make out where it had been fired. They rolled; one over the other, another five to six yards, then suddenly fell over a steep bank and were sliding head-first down it. They grunted in tandem as they pounded against the foot of the bank, a mass of arms and legs.

She instinctively pulled herself to a kneeling position, desperately tried to see to find a target. Her hair was matted with leaves and sticks and her eyes burned.

"Get ready!" her brain screamed to her. "Locate your target."

A hand suddenly encased hers, tightening its grip around her fingers. She tried to pull away. It pressed against her harder. Her pistol fired into the darkness above. She began to flail against this new antagonist, unsure of what was taking place. She kicked violently. A powerful arm suddenly wrapped around her, pulling her head closer. She squirmed, tried to push it away.

"Shauna," Jeb's voice, low. "Shauna, it's OK, I'm with you. It's me."

"What are you doing?" she spat the words, unsure.

"We have to let them know we're armed. They were moving in to finish the job. Now they can't be sure." His voice was calm, she thought to herself.

"He's near the car. He was waiting there. Whoever it is has a high-powered rifle. They were waiting for us just like a hunter. But he missed the kill-shot," Jeb whispered.

"How far? How far away?" she gasped, spitting parts of the forest from her mouth.

"Seventy yards, maybe less."

They fell quiet. Nothing. Only the faint sound of the river behind them.

"Did you see anything?" She strained to make out any hint of movement ahead.

"No..." His voice was barely audible above their heavy breathing. "But it was an ambush...would have been successful if they'd waited another ten feet or so."

A sound, a breaking branch, somewhere up above.

"Can you see? Can you see to fire?" Jeb whispered.

She wiped her brow and rubbed her eyes frantically. Blurred perhaps, but she could see. They were in a gully, surrounded by small saplings and a variety of briars and underbrush. A perfect trench, she thought to herself.

"I can see." She lay on her belly, her weapon at an arm's length in front of her, poised for anyone that suddenly looked over the edge.

They lay there in the quiet of the looming darkness, waiting for the killer to come.

CHAPTER NINETY

Roy Yates checked his notebook a final time as he pulled the cruiser to the side of the street.

Clarence Parker, 16 Poplar Glen. This was the right address.

The old man who eventually answered the door was bent with age. He welcomed his guest warmly and invited him in for iced tea. Yates politely declined. Parker carried a rolled up copy of the *Stacey Star*.

"Mr. Parker, I wanted to talk with you just a minute about a fellow named Mason," Yates said.

"Mason, yes Mason."

"You remember talking to someone by that name over the last several days?"

"Why sure I do...sure I do, huh?"

"Believe he used to live at this address. You knew that, right?"

"That's what he says, all right...used to live right here. Nice young fella." Clarence swatted at a fly that buzzed around them.

"Wanted to find out about someone who might have been asking about Mason. You remember anything about that?"

"Nice young fella. Ain't sure if he's kin to Nate or not. Can't be sure about that." Clarence looked out over the yard in the direction of a sprinkler several houses down the street.

"About that visitor..."

"You going to ticket them about that sprinkler, Sheriff?"

"What's that?"

"Going to ticket them for that water on the sidewalk down the street?"

"Ticket them? No sir. Mr. Parker, did someone else come by and talk to you about a Mason family living here?"

"That other feller, that other feller with the badge." Clarence gestured toward the sprinkler.

"Other feller?" Yates stopped.

"Yeah...I thought he was going to ticket 'em, but he didn't."

"Mr. Parker, who was that?"

"Can't say, can't say..." Clarence paused. "You tell Mason hello for me won't you?"

"I'll do that, sir...and thank you."

"Tell that other feller the same."

Roy Yates stopped at the foot of the steps. "Mr. Parker...was it that other officer that asked about Mason?"

"Yes sir." Clarence grinned. "Seems like everybody in this town knows Mason, huh?"

CHAPTER NINETY-ONE

Blaine McQuinn was standing high on Darby Ridge when he heard the shots. He flinched involuntarily then yanked to his right, trying to see downriver. But the water took a sharp turn a half-mile down stream.

Three shots in succession. He recognized the rifle fire. Once, in his first year with the television station, he'd been on hand for a hostage situation over in Belmont. You didn't forget that sound. But the fourth shot was distinctly different. Higher pitch. A handgun of some type. Then silence.

Hunters, perhaps, but deer season wasn't for another few months. More likely locals engaging in a little target practice on the river. Guns and beer proved a pretty popular entertainment source out here.

He looked down from his dizzying perch at the jagged rocks far below and stepped back. He never particularly cared for heights. By his estimate, this was where Andrews jumped, fell, or was tossed. More and more he had begun to believe there was a tie between this incident and the Patterson murder. He needed to talk to someone live. But who?

Suddenly another shot rang out. The rifle again…and then again. Maybe just a couple of drunks out shooting at the moon. But he had a bad feeling.

He tried to gather his thoughts. Another shot. Then a car horn began to blare, its sound wafting through the hills and up the river.

It was getting dark now and from this vantage point McQuinn could see the last glimpses of the sun setting in the west. The clouds were clearing and the sky was a brilliant orange, mixed with shades of deep crimson.

For the first time he felt a rush of fear sweep over him. He was standing there totally exposed. He looked at the black waters of the Yadkin as they flowed downstream. He wondered what might be happening there in the darkness.

Somewhere far below, the horn continued to moan.

CHAPTER NINETY-TWO

Roy Yates checked his cell phone as he pulled his cruiser into the Tully yard. He waved to the Stacey Police Department vehicle parked in the driveway. Benny Greer's one concession to the investigation had been to send a car over to the Tully house as security for the Andrews boy. Yates watched Officer Bobby Patterson climb out and approach his car.

He'd known Patterson for all of the kid's twenty-four years. Yates would have liked him even if he wasn't Bump's nephew, and had quietly supported his hiring by the city, which paid more than his county staff received. Chief Greer had been encouraged by City Council members to enhance his racial diversity over the last five years. Bobby had been the fourth minority hired, a positive step for the good ol' boy network that was Stacey law enforcement. The fact that he was a damned good officer was an added bonus.

"Everything OK here, Bobby?" He slipped the cell into his front pocket. He could check messages later.

"It's fine, Sheriff. Can I ask you what's going on?" Bobby asked as they shook hands.

"Not sure that I know myself, Bobby. We got some funny stuff happening. Looks like there's a chance Zeke Andrews was murdered."

"You're kidding!"

"Nope, sort of wish I was." Yates looked around the yard. A faded blue bike, its front tire removed, sat propped in a far corner against what looked like a rolled-up section of chicken wire. It was almost 9:45 now. The distant rumble of thunder could be heard far away to the west.

"The SBI people think the Andrews boy could be in some danger. They're saying he may have run across something his old man had gotten into that got him killed."

"Damn," Bobby sighed and looked back at the house, "must be some deep shit."

"Yeah, I'd say you're right. Anybody come by since you got here?"

"No sir. Been quiet."

"You checked? Everybody's OK inside?"

"Soon as I got here, Sheriff. Just the lady and the boy. The old man's out on a trip. He's a trucker, I think. The chief's instructions were for me to introduce myself. Advise them that I was being dispatched to their house as a precautionary measure only. That an officer would be by later to talk with them further."

"And what was Mrs. Tully's reaction?"

"I think she's scared, Sheriff."

"Reckon I would be too," Yates answered. "For the time being, at least, that's how we're going to need to leave it, though. Got an SBI guy coming in to talk with her. Like I said, we got some funny stuff going on."

Yates knelt down, plucked a long blade of grass and stuck it in his mouth. He thumped a small ant mound with his hand, watched the occupants come pouring out in a black hoard.

"Bobby, Greer tell you anything about any of this?"

"No sir, he didn't."

Yates drew a deep breath, grabbed up a handful of grass and weeds even as he studied the ants' march closely. "You need to know, we are exploring the possibility that all of this could be connected to Bump's death."

"What?"

"Like I said, we're not sure what's happening. But I'm guessing the same thing that got this Andrews fellow killed might have got your uncle killed, too."

"Sheriff, my uncle didn't even know this man. I can't see how…"

"I know he didn't, Bobby. But it's looking more and more like this Andrews fellow had the goods on somebody in this town. Somebody who wanted very much to shut him up and finally did it. We're guessing that after he killed Andrews he decided to make a late-night visit to Steadman to find out more about Andrews and his friends. It's a long shot, mind you, but we have some pretty good evidence pointing that way. If we're right, the killer was going through files the night Bump came up on him. He couldn't risk being identified. So he sets the fire, kills Bump."

"Sheriff…I don't understand. You don't just go and kill somebody just because they come up on you."

"No, you don't…and I don't. But there are people out there who might. You know that, Officer Patterson." Yates stood and considered the assortment of dry grass, weeds, and clover he still clutched in his hand. He guessed the "drug bag" Zeke Andrews had stuffed in an envelope probably came from this dry and barren front yard.

"Are we close…do we know who the suspect might be?"

"No, we don't. But I'll tell you one thing, Bobby…" Yates face was grim, and for a second his voice broke. "We're going to find the son of a bitch that killed Bump. We're going to find him."

"Does my aunt know anything…about any of this?"

"Son, at this point I don't know what we could tell her." Yates considered the Tully home as he spoke. "Bobby, who kept the Steadman keys at the police department? Did it rotate, or were they assigned to one officer?"

"Sir?"

"Who kept the keys, for your drive-bys at Steadman Elementary?"

"Sheriff, we didn't do any drive-bys at Steadman."

Yates looked up, a puzzled expression on his face.

"You guys did drive-bys at the elementary school, didn't you?"

"No, I mean, we might occasionally cruise by if we were in the neighborhood. No formal assignment, though."

Yates stood, looked closely at the police officer.

"Bobby, you sure?"

"Course I'm sure, Sheriff. I have the western part of town; work the night shift every other week. We have designated points that we're asked to closely patrol, but Steadman wasn't one of them."

Yates's radio blared to life. The dispatcher was trying to reach him on the emergency frequency.

Sheriff Yates reached into the open car window and snatched up the radio. "I'm here, Barbara. What's up?"

"Sheriff, you've had a call from SBI Agent Boller. He's requesting your back-up at 619 Grissom. He believes there could be a domestic disturbance of some type there."

Yates read the address back: 619 Grissom Street—Judge Franklin Thompson's address.

"Barbara, he wants back-up *now?*"

"Yes sir. He declined when I suggested Stacey Police Department assistance. I tried to explain jurisdiction, Roy, but he wasn't interested. Said to get you on the squawk box ASAP. There's something else, Sheriff. Here," she scrambled for her notes, "He said Agent Spencer called. She indicated Police Chief Greer was already on-site. Wonder why he's got to have all of you there?"

"Barbara, can you reach Agent Spencer?"

"Negative, Roy. Tried a few times, but I'm guessing the cell phone has poor reception. Agent Boller said something about her being out in the woods or something."

Yates knew where she was supposed to be. Taking a hike from the Yadkin to the Thompson house. "I'm en route to 619 Grissom, Barbara." He signed off.

CHAPTER NINETY-THREE

"Too quiet," Shauna whispered, "too quiet." She and Jeb lay in the blackness of the gully, listening for some type of activity above.

"Might have left. He missed with the first attempt," Jeb answered, "but I haven't heard a car."

Shauna felt for her cell phone, pulled it out, and quickly punched in the numbers.

"Dammit. Doesn't work. I think I broke it when you decided to play tackle football," she whispered. "Jeb, I'm going to try and move into a better position. If we can't see, he can't see. It's not going to be easy to get a clean shot at us."

"Wait a minute. You're not moving without me," he replied.

They quietly crawled toward the rim of the trench, some ten feet to the right of where they had gone over the side. A gun sighted on where they had disappeared might not easily pick them up in the deep shadows of the trees.

Shauna glanced at her watch. It was now 9:47 p.m. Darkness. She slowly peered over the edge, into the night. Nothing. The trees surrounded them. No sound. Jeb slowly began to rise. She clutched his arm.

"Wait."

The shot pierced the night. The bullet tore into Jeb's shoulder, knocking him backwards. He fell into the trench, the pain burning through him like a branding iron.

Shauna ducked. She scrambled down the hill. "Jeb, are you OK, are you OK?" The sound of her voice shocked her. She held the gun in a firing position, while she frantically reached for him.

"Yeah" he gasped. The wind had been torn from him. He felt for his shoulder and the warm flow of blood coursed between his fingers. His entire side was numb. "Have...have I been shot?"

"You've been shot. Lay still, Jeb. I want you take your good arm and press down here with your hand. Just press down." Shauna felt herself fighting against the panic. She could not even attempt to assess the wound, but even a glancing shot could be deadly from a high powered rifle.

"Son of a bitch must have great eyes." Jeb moaned and tried to sit up.

Shauna felt for him in the darkness. She breathed a sigh of relief when she felt him grab her arm and then squeeze it.

"I'm OK, Shauna." But she could tell the pain was already beginning to seize him.

"Jeb, we've got to get closer to the river. Can you move?"

"Yeah, yeah." He was rolling over.

"We can't stay here. He's...getting nearer."

"Shauna, listen to me. If we move toward the river, we'll have to give up our position. He can't get a clear shot here because of the terrain. We move toward the river, we're sitting ducks. He has the high ground, but we're protected here..." Jeb groaned as the pain coursed through him. He knew he was losing blood quickly.

"But he's some distance away, Jeb. I just can't tell how far by just the sound. We could maybe outrun him, hit the water."

"No, Shauna. I know the area. You don't. Whoever has the gun knows the area too. They'll pick us off."

Shauna's mind raced back to her training. Pinned down under rifle fire with only a handgun. Civilian in her care. Wounded. Unfamiliar terrain. No contact with the outside world. Unknown number of assailants in a superior position. Not the rosiest of situations. And this perp clearly had a hell of a view to their location.

Too good of a view.

"Oh, my lord," she whispered.

"What?" Jeb wheezed. "You need to use the potty?" He laughed through the pain and wondered if he might be going into shock.

"No this guy has more than just good eyes, Jeb. He was waiting for us to move on him."

"Yeah...so?"

"It's why he fired too early. He didn't expect to get both of us, probably one, tops. He waited for the night, wanted to slow us until it was like a tomb out here," she whispered.

"Why would he want the night?" Jeb groaned the words.

"Because he's at an advantage in total darkness, Jeb. He has a night vision scope on his weapon. He can see in the dark. He knows we can't."

"You sure, Shauna?"

"Pretty sure. Too good a shot at that distance, Jeb. He saw you clearly. Waited for you to stand. He waited to begin his hunt."

"What are our options?" he whispered, searching to find her face in the blackness.

"Jeb, he'll be moving in soon. He knows we can't see him but he can see us. He's holding the cards."

There was the sound of something, a rustling in the brush somewhere to the right. Closer. They moved together, wounded animals awaiting the predator.

"He's going to try and flank us." Shauna's voice was low now. She struggled to find movement to their right but couldn't.

"What's your chances of clipping this guy if you can get an angle on him. If you can see the rifle fire, I mean?"

"Probably none."

"But we can't just wait for him to circle us, get a shot." Jeb knew his voice was getting shakier. The pain was starting to throb through him. "If you knew the general area he was in, you'd have a chance, right?"

"What are you asking?" Shauna asked, suddenly confused.

"If you see the rifle fired, there's gotta be combustion, a discharge or something. Right?"

"No, Jeb. If you're suggesting we try to draw his fire, it's suicide..."

Another sound. Closer now. The hunter was moving toward them.

"Shauna, we've got to try. Honey...when I break for it, it will draw fire. Look for where the weapon is fired. He's close enough that you could get him..."

"No, no. Goddamn it, Jeb, you can't do that..." she felt him draw nearer. For a brief second his lips pressed against hers, lingered there.

"Get him, Shauna. You get him." He grunted as he staggered to his knees. She grabbed him, but he was suddenly strong and pushed her away. He bolted into the night, running headlong into the blackness.

Shauna screamed and then rolled instinctively upright, her gun pointed.

The first shot screamed through the gloom like an avenging angel, its lightning stabbing the night. Somewhere in her consciousness, Shauna believed she could see the bullet. She could taste it as it swept through the trees in front of her. Time slowed. She could feel it. She raised her weapon, scanned the trees. Searched for the discharge flame.

There, a vague hint of the rifle's fire. Watched it explode a second time. Steadied her gun. She pulled the trigger. Then again, and again, and again.

CHAPTER NINETY-FOUR

Mac Boller slowed his car on the street in front of the Thompson house. He checked his watch. Greer's cruiser sat in front.

There were lights on inside, and he could hear music playing. He recognized the melody. It was a concert piece of some kind. Dottie would know. She knew every waltz ever written. He pulled his car to the curb and sat quietly in the darkness. There was no sign of activity in the house.

Boller picked up the cell and started to punch in the sheriff's cell number, then decided against it. This was a state investigation and no matter what his opinion of Yates was, or of Greer for that matter, it clearly no longer was a local case.

But there was no solid evidence in any of this, he told himself. Not at least in regard to Andrews or Judge Thompson. Police Chief Greer was not a definite suspect but was under suspicion. Yates clearly did not respect the man and had played his cards very close to the vest in regard to his opinions.

But Greer was a lawman, for Christ's sake. And he had been briefed on an emerging investigation. He might be guilty of bad judgment in initiating his own side investigation, but nothing more.

Boller opened his car door, walked up the sidewalk to the wrought iron gate that fronted the Thompson's front yard. He pushed it open slowly. Listened to the creaking hinges announce his arrival. He contemplated drawing his weapon but second-guessed himself.

"There's an eighty-year-old woman inside, probably discussing her husband's death with the Chief of Police." He thought to himself. "Calm yourself, Mac."

As he climbed the porch steps, he saw for the first time that the front door stood slightly ajar. He pushed it open slowly and stood back to allow it to swing open. He reflexively stepped back and away from the doorway.

He was looking into a large foyer illuminated by an enormous crystal teardrop chandelier. Beyond that there was a long circular stairwell with a deep crimson oriental runner. Boller could see double French glass doors to the far left leading into a darkened room. He waited. Only the sound of the music. He walked inside, his hand instinctively resting on his holstered weapon.

"Mrs. Thompson? State Bureau of Investigation, ma'am...Mrs. Thompson?"

He heard the sound of footsteps slowly approaching from the larger room. A small elderly woman appeared in the hallway. She stood there watching him.

"Mrs. Thompson? My name is Mac Boller. I'm an agent with the State Bureau of Investigation. Is Chief Greer here?"

She didn't move, only stood there. The music seemed to grow louder, though Boller couldn't be sure. He took a step forward.

"Ma'am?"

She looked at him, unblinking.

"Are you OK, Mrs. Thompson?" There was a faint movement to his left. He saw her eyes dart briefly in that direction, toward the double glass doors.

Boller pivoted. Something was wrong. He faced the darkened room to his left. He began to draw his weapon. There was movement, and his eyes suddenly swept over the silhouette of a figure in a high-back chair in the far corner of the room. He was raising his pistol when the first shot exploded, spinning him around with the impact.

The second was entering his chest as he squeezed the trigger of his nine-millimeter Glock. He screamed as it ripped through his pectoral muscles and tore into his left ventricle, exploding his heart.

His mind flashed an image of Dottie as he slumped to the floor, a last psychomotor response to a fatal injury.

CHAPTER NINETY-FIVE

Shauna emptied her weapon, reached for a new clip, and snapped it into place. Silence. She waited, and then rose to a crouched position, both hands on her gun.

"Jeb!" she screamed his name, not daring to look in the direction he had run. "Jeb! Are you all right?"

Seconds passed. She felt a first tinge of panic and swallowed hard against it.

"Jeb…can you hear me?" She continued to look straight ahead, expecting the roar of the rifle to cut through the night at any minute. "Jeb Mason, you answer me!" She felt her eyes begin to burn.

"I'm here…Shauna." Jeb's voice from somewhere in the murk.

"Stay there, Jeb. I'm not sure if I hit him. I need for you to maintain your position," she called back.

She advanced slowly, desperately trying to sight something, anything in the blackness. There was a noise somewhere to her left. The perp? She swung her gun back and forth, trying to gauge the threat.

"Moving, Shauna. Don't just shoot, OK?" Jeb's voice was twenty to thirty feet away.

"Damn it, Jeb," she barked, "You can't move. I don't know if I hit anything."

"Gotcha, Agent Spencer." He was moving quickly now.

"So damn thickheaded." She hissed the words. But she continued to move on a parallel path as they closed the distance to the car.

When they emerged in the clearing, they could make out the dull image of the Camry. Some ten feet in front of it a dark object lay sprawled in the dirt. They approached it cautiously.

"Show me your hands!" Shauna yelled. The man was lying face-down. There was no movement. "Show me your hands!"

She advanced quickly, kicking the rifle that lay beside him. Jeb rolled the body over with his foot. They bent down closely and could smell the blood hemorrhaging from the chest wounds.

Shauna gasped. They were looking at the man they had met with the day before, though not the one she had expected.

Fire Chief Brett Hampton's lifeless eyes stared back at them.

CHAPTER NINETY-SIX

"My God," Jeb heaved the words as the pain suddenly swept over him again. "It's Hampton. Why in the hell was he trying to kill us?"

"I don't know." Shauna knelt down, looked closely at the body, checking for vital signs. "But he was definitely trying to kill us."

She picked up the rifle, checked to confirm it was loaded, then handed Jeb her firearm.

"Hold onto this," she said. She set the rifle against her shoulder, assumed a firing position.

"Wait a minute. Who are we shooting at now?" Jeb whispered.

"Nobody hopefully. But now we have the night scope. Let's take a look around." She began to carefully scan the area, slowly surveying the landscape in a full 360-degree turn. Nothing but trees, no sign of life. She started a second sweep.

"Jeb, are you OK?" she asked, not daring to devote her attention to checking his condition until she had some assurance the area was secure.

"I'm wonderful," he whispered, but she knew it wasn't so.

"If you can, check Hampton to see if he has car keys on him." She continued to peer through the scope, searching for any indication of movement.

Jeb knelt down and could feel the pain grab him and shake him with its burning grip. He fought a sudden wave of nausea. He had to stay in the game. He had to get Shauna out of there.

"Nothing. I got nothing." He double-checked Hampton's pockets a second time, rolling the body over.

"Pat down his legs, Jeb. Make sure."

He complied. Hampton's body was still warm. He half expected him to open his eyes.

"Nope. Nothing, Shauna."

"I was afraid of that," she sighed.

"I don't follow you. We have a car. I don't think Hampton is going to need his anyway," Jeb answered.

"It means someone left him here, Jeb. Or, possibly, that he parked a good distance away and left his keys with the vehicle. Of the two, but I'd bet door number one. If I'm right, that same person could be returning for pick-up service."

"All right, we get in my car and we get some people out here," he said.

"I've got a feeling your car isn't going to work," Shauna answered.

Jeb pulled his keys from his pocket, opened the Camry's driver door. He turned the ignition. Nothing. Tried a second time. Only the click of the switch. He banged the steering wheel with his good arm, involuntarily shuddered when the pain reminded him that sudden movement wasn't a good idea. He laid down on the horn. The sound reverberated through the darkness.

"You're pretty good at this, Agent Spencer," he said. He could see her outline in the darkness as she continued to look through the scope.

"I try…" she answered, and for the first time they could both almost smile.

"Jeb, I want you to listen to me now." Her voice was calm. "You're bleeding. We are in a very dangerous situation. We have to move."

"I'm right with you. It's a nice night for a walk."

She pulled the rifle down, walked toward him. She flashed a small penlight toward his shoulder.

"I need to take a look at the wound, Jeb." She flinched when she saw that his chest and left arm were already soaked with blood. "We've got to get the bleeding under control." The bullet had sheared his shoulder, tearing through the edge of his deltoid muscle, and exited with a gaping hole in the back. Shauna shuddered. Thirty-ought-six high-powered rifle from less than one hundred yards. Two inches farther and it would have literally torn his arm off. The bullet grazed him. And it could still kill him.

"You've lost a lot of blood, Mr. Mason." Her tone was upbeat. She wanted to keep it that way.

"Tell me, doctor, what are my chances?" he teased.

"I would say pretty good. But you'll need a lot of care," she replied as she rigged a makeshift bandage that circled underneath his arm from one of the bandages she carried in her knapsack. He groaned as she adjusted the arm.

"Jeb, I'm going to have to leave you for a little bit. I'm going to walk in the direction of the highway to get some help. But you're going to need to stay here…"

"Forget it, Shauna. Not going to happen. I'm not going to let you go off by yourself in these woods…"

"Jeb, listen to me. You're too weak. You've, you've lost a lot of blood. We can't risk your—"

"Didn't you say there's a good chance we got someone else out there, maybe coming back to pick up Hampton?"

"Yeah, I said…"

"So what? You're going to just walk out to meet them? Shauna, you don't know if they aren't just sitting out there, waiting to pick you off."

"I've got to take that risk…"

"Shauna, you don't know these woods. I do."

"Jeb, listen. I know that, but you're hurt. Maybe badly hurt. We can't risk you trying to walk out of here."

"And I can't risk you getting shot, Shauna. We go together or we don't go at all."

"Damn you, Jeb Mason," she sighed heavily. "I am a law enforcement agent. I am ordering you to stand down. You hear me?"

"I know that, Agent Spencer. And a damn good one." He reached out and pulled her to him with his good arm. "But I have a lot of reasons for making sure we both make it out of here alive…I guess you'll have to arrest me again."

His lips found hers in the darkness, and for a brief moment they left behind the terror of the night.

CHAPTER NINETY-SEVEN

Roy Yates could see the door was standing open at the Thompson house as he drove slowly down Grissom Street. He identified SBI Agent Mac Boller's car a half-block away.

Benny Greer's cruiser was parked directly in front of the house. Yates slowed as he passed by it. To his left he could see a man walking hurriedly toward his car. He unbuckled his holster. Something didn't feel right. The man was moving quickly. Yates stopped the car and pulled his .357 magnum from its harness.

"Sheriff, Sheriff Yates..." the man's voice was agitated. "I called at least ten minutes ago. I heard shots..."

Yates peered into the darkness. He recognized the voice.

"That you, Carl?" he asked.

"Yeah," Carl Lester answered, "I heard shots over at the Thompson house, couple of them. Thought it was fireworks at first, but now I'm thinking it was gun shots, you know."

"All right, all right," Yates answered calmly, "Reckon I better take a look, don't you?"

"Better you than me, Sheriff," the portly silver-haired man responded. "When I saw the police car over there I figured I better call somebody."

"Well, you were right, Carl," Yates answered. He stopped his vehicle and slowly got out. He pulled his radio to hail his dispatcher.

"Barbara, this is Sheriff Yates, you read me?"

"Got you, Roy." The radio crackled.

"Barbara, I'm over here at 619 Grissom Street, the Thompson address. I've got Carl Lester here with me. Carl reports shots fired over here a little while ago. We got Chief Greer already on-site. Barbara, I want you to send me some back-up over here. Will you do that?"

"Yes sir, Sheriff. Consider it done," Barbara answered.

"Carl, I'm going to ask you to head on back home now. I'll take it from here." Yates's tone was calm, measured. "Tell Patty I said hello, will you? Ask her when she's going to bring another one of those deep-dish apple pies to the Shriners' cookout. Damn, those are good." Yates was watching the Thompson house closely, making small talk as he began to walk down the sidewalk.

Carl Lester could sense Yates's intensity, even in the darkness. The sheriff held his pistol at an arm's length, pointed down, as he moved toward the gated entryway.

"I'll, I'll do that, Roy…" He began to back away, "she's off on that Ladies' Club trip to Raleigh right now…" His voice trailed away. "I'll tell her," he said to no one in particular. He began to walk quickly back in the direction of his house.

Yates's eyes scanned the front porch, swept the windows, lighted to the right, darkened on the left. He heard the music for the first time, a gentle, almost melancholy refrain he had heard before but couldn't recognize. The second and third floors were dark. If someone was sitting there, watching…he moved on, through the gated entry, his senses at full alert.

In the distance, the rumbling sound of thunder rolled across the land, signaling a new summer storm. Yates paused at the front porch steps. He knew the importance of waiting for his back-up. He didn't dare take his eyes off the front door.

Yates started up the steps.

He could see clearly into the foyer as he ascended the steps, through the house and into the large main room beyond. The wind had begun to blow harder, and the smell of the coming storm grew stronger.

He stepped onto the porch, and then froze. He could see a man's feet laying on the floor just inside the door and to the right. He crouched, moved closer to the left side of the doorway. Glanced in quickly, and then drew back. Then a second time. His eyes fanned the room, his pistol at arm's length in front of him. He looked down on the third sweep. Recognized Mac Boller. His body was covered with blood.

"Agent Boller." Yates's voice was loud, commanding, his eyes still sweeping the room, "This is Sheriff Yates. Are you all right?"

No response.

"Agent Boller, I have back-up on the way," he said even louder, "I have back-up on the way. Can you tell me what happened?"

There was no sign of life from Mac Boller. Yates glanced down and in that split second, knew the SBI agent was dead.

"In the house," he barked, "I want you to come out with your hands raised. Do you hear me?" Only the music answered, a long haunting refrain that seemed to mock Yates's entreaty.

It was a chest wound, maybe two. He could see the blood gurgling from Boller. The agent was facing to the left. Yates was on the left side of the doorway. The shooter could be in the music room, which was to Yates's back. It meant he didn't have a clear field of vision, but then neither did the shooter. He contemplated holding his position, waiting for additional officers. Cursed under his breath, moved quickly to the right side of the doorway, pressed his back against the house, and breathed deeply.

A clap of thunder suddenly rocked him, so startling that he almost wheeled and fired his weapon. His heart pounded in his ears. He struggled to collect himself. Then he moved.

He swung out quickly, his weapon aimed into the darkened music room. Then back. If the killer was there, they had just missed an opportunity. Exposed enemy, unsure of his location. A second sweep but crouched low this time. A different target area if the shooter had zeroed in the first time. He swept the area, looking for movement or a figure. Nothing. Leapt back to his left and against the house. A third time and into the foyer. Ready to fire.

There, sprawled across a high back chair in the right corner of the room. An object.

"Hold it!" Yates screamed the words. Totally exposed now. If there was a gunman above on the second story landing or behind him, in the parlor, he was a dead man. He couldn't risk moving his attention away from the figure in the chair.

"Show me your hands! Get your hands in the air!" Yates yelled as he advanced slowly, straining to make out what was in front of him.

"I say again, mister, get your hands in the air!" Yates was walking quicker now into the darkened room. Couldn't risk trying to find a light switch. The figure wasn't moving. Less than ten feet away now, his finger pressed against the trigger.

A jagged flash of lightning burst across the room, the thunder exploding with it simultaneously. Yates could see the bloodied head of Benny Greer, a gaping wound in his forehead spilling its contents into his eyes and down onto his massive chest.

Yates moved closer, reached down, felt for a pulse in Greer's fleshy neck. There was none.

The rain suddenly burst against the windows, and the wind swept through the open doorway and into the house. Its suction slammed the glass doors behind Yates shut.

The storm had arrived.

CHAPTER NINETY-EIGHT

Blaine McQuinn was gambling. By his reckoning, he had managed to stay one step behind everything since the very beginning. The Steadman fire investigation fizzled quickly. The Andrews death was all hearsay. The tail on the SBI guy was a bust. The same for visiting Darby Ridge. But something was happening. Something big. Something bigger than perhaps he had ever encountered. But he felt like the guy who was on the other side of the Titanic rearranging the deck chairs when somebody yelled "Iceberg."

He turned onto what looked like an abandoned logging road, overgrown with weeds. He could tell it led back in the direction of the river, but nothing more.

The Mustang's headlights framed the trees in a juggled panorama as the car bounced along the ruts. Absolute darkness ahead.

McQuinn cursed himself. What was he doing? Driving headlong in the direction of where he heard shots fired in the middle of nowhere. He should turn around, get back to the main road.

He rounded another bend, and then screamed when the headlights suddenly illuminated a blood-soaked man standing in the middle of the road. He was holding a handgun pointed straight at the car.

McQuinn slammed the brakes hard and the Mustang veered sharply to the right.

"Run him over!" McQuinn told himself. "Don't just give up your car to some madman with a gun." He started to press the gas pedal to the floor. Better to at least struggle than to be murdered out here in the middle of nowhere. Maybe he could run him down.

He didn't notice the tapping on the driver's window at first. When he did, he turned and stared right into the barrel of the rifle that was pointed at his head.

CHAPTER NINETY-NINE

McQuinn was too frightened to see the badge that suddenly appeared beside the rifle barrel. Nor did anything register when he heard the female voice that yelled out "State Bureau of Investigation."

"Keep your hands where I can see them! You do not even move a muscle, you hear me?"

Blaine McQuinn had no intention of failing to comply with that direction.

The door was flung open. The reporter, his eyes locked with the rifle, could see the badge now but couldn't make out what it read. Somewhere out there in the darkness was the lady connected to the cannon that was pointing at him.

The man he had first seen suddenly appeared at the door. He held a tiny flashlight, used it to peer inside the car, blinding McQuinn.

"Shauna Spencer, State Bureau of Investigation. What is your name, sir?" the female again.

"Blaine McQuinn. Channel Three News," he stammered, surprised to hear his own voice.

"McQuinn, what brings you out here this time of night?" Shauna asked.

"I heard shots. Thought it might be something..."

"Are you usually out here in the woods, Mr. McQuinn?"

"Now wait a minute, lady." McQuinn stuttered. "I'm working on a story. I've been on Darby Ridge this evening. It's the same case you're working on if I'm guessing right..."

"Mr. McQuinn, are you carrying any weapons?" She cut him off.

"No, of course I'm..."

She patted him down as she spoke. The flashlight panned across the interior of the car.

"Sir, we are going to have to commandeer your car. It's an emergency." her tone had changed.

"I've seen him on the news the last several days, Shauna. He's who he says he is," the man's voice. It was raspy, breathless.

"What...the hell happened to you?" McQuinn looked from one to the other. "Are you...Jeb Mason?"

Spencer was beside Mason, underneath his shoulder, struggling to get him into the backseat. He groaned as he clambered in.

McQuinn jumped out, helped her lay him down, and gasped when he saw the extent of the blood that seemed to cover his entire upper torso.

"Mr. McQuinn, I am commandeering your vehicle, sir. Would you please get in on the passenger side?" Spencer asked. Her tone didn't invite debate. McQuinn moved around the car quickly.

She climbed behind the wheel, shoved the car into reverse. The tires sprayed dirt as the vehicle suddenly burst to life, rapidly backing down the trail.

"McQuinn, do you have a cell phone? Could you please dial 911? Alert them that we have a shooting out on the Yadkin River, somewhere off of the Gibbons trail. Mile marker twenty-seven. Advise them that SBI agent Shauna Spencer is currently transporting one of the injured parties to...damn! Where is the closest hospital?"

"Richmond County General, approximately twelve miles," McQuinn answered as he dialed the phone.

The car bounced along the rutted path as Shauna skillfully steered, finally bursting onto the highway in a cloud of dust and gravel. She said a quiet prayer to herself as she shifted into drive and punched the gas pedal to the floor.

"How did you know his name?" she asked McQuinn, her eyes focused on the darkened two lanes ahead.

"I've been investigating the Steadman homicide. Got further information around the Andrews thing...found out who you were. Same for Mason. I know it's not the place for it right now, Ms. Spencer, but I got a whole lot of questions to ask you."

"Mr. McQuinn, right now I have got to get our passenger to a doctor, and soon. I also need your car for a while longer. You promise me your undivided help, I'll promise to answer all your questions…eventually. Deal?" She turned and looked at him.

"We have a turn-off about two miles from here, Agent Spencer. We need to start looking for it," McQuinn answered.

CHAPTER ONE HUNDRED

By the time they pulled the Mustang into the Emergency Room area of Richmond County General Hospital, a myriad of events had already begun to unfold.

State Highway Patrol cars were there to greet them, as were a variety of uniformed local officers. In the blur of lights, Shauna recognized two Richmond County sheriff cars, as well as at least one Stacey police department vehicle. McQuinn had, at Shauna's request, phoned Yates's office and advised the dispatcher of the events on the Yadkin River, requesting immediate back-up.

There was something akin to bedlam taking place at the sheriff's office, however. Apparently there was another shooting that had taken place in town. One or more officers were down. An alert had gone out to county and state law enforcement advising them of a possible standoff in Stacey.

McQuinn's call had further incited the crisis. A phone message on behalf of an SBI agent involved in a shootout tended to create that type of effect.

Shauna was able to put that much together in piecemeal fashion. Her attention was focused on Jeb, who was immediately surrounded by a throng of emergency personnel before the car eased to a stop in front of the ER.

He was in a semi-conscious state as a husky technician strapped an oxygen mask over his face, lifted him onto a stretcher, and began to wheel him quickly inside. Shauna ran alongside.

"Agent Spencer?" a tall, powerfully built highway patrolman was addressing her, "ma'am, I was asked to escort you..."

"What? I don't need an escort, officer. I'll be with you in a moment." She turned, ran to catch up with the stretcher as it rolled through the double doors. A gangly man in light blue scrubs was already running to meet them, pointing to a curtained treatment area. Two other officers were standing inside, one of them speaking into a mobile phone.

She noted the unusual level of law enforcement presence and unconsciously tied it to what she had heard outside. Things were exploding, but in what way she had no idea. For the time being, she didn't care.

One of the attendants began to pull her away, explaining the need for medical personnel to focus attention on the patient. Shauna knew it, understood it, but she shoved the woman away.

"No! I need to stay with him!" For the first time she could feel the tears begin to well up.

Jeb was surrounded by physicians and attendants. He rolled his head, searching for her. Their eyes met and he smiled. He weakly tried to raise his hand but couldn't. He was trying to speak.

A physician gestured to Shauna. She approached the examining table as they cut away his clothes, the smell of alcohol permeating the room.

"We did OK, didn't we, Agent Spencer?" he whispered. She grabbed his hand, squeezed it.

"Yes, we did, Mr. Mason. We did just fine," she said in a low voice, bending over him.

"You got work to do, Shauna. I got things under control here." He managed a weak grin.

"I have no doubt that you do." And then she began to cry. "You know, I'm guessing you saved my life at least twice tonight, Jeb Mason."

"Not bad for a private citizen…" His voice was growing weaker. He was losing consciousness.

"Not too bad." She smiled back.

"Say, while I'm thinking about it, when I get out of here…you think you and I…"

"Oh, I would say most definitely," she answered.

He smiled and closed his eyes, surrendering to the anesthesia pulsing through the IV.

"Works every time," he whispered.

CHAPTER
ONE HUNDRED AND ONE

Roy Yates stood on the front porch of the Thompson house and looked out over a sea of flashing emergency lights. A Charlotte SWAT team vehicle was parked on the front lawn. At least a dozen emergency vehicles lined the street. Both ends of the block were shut off to traffic by parked police cruisers, their blue lights washing the street with a surreal pulse of color.

Some two dozen uniformed officers were on-site. Another dozen SWAT team members were completing their search of the house. Two ambulances had transported the bodies of SBI agent Mac Boller and Police Chief Benny Greer to Carolinas Medical in Charlotte. Both victims were CODE BLACK, dead at the scene. They would be delivered directly to the morgue, where the state Medical Examiner would complete the autopsies.

Somewhere inside, an SBI agent was talking to Marie Thompson, trying to get some sense of what had occurred here this night.

Roy Yates already knew.

A state highway patrol car was coming down the street, its emergency lights flashing. The sheriff watched it roll to a stop. Shauna Spencer bounded out the side door. She walked quickly toward Yates. He could see the blood smeared across her vest.

"Mac? Is he...?"

Yates shook his head slowly. "I'm sorry, Ms. Spencer, I'm afraid so," he said.

"Oh God...oh God, no." Shauna sagged. Yates wrapped an arm around her.

"Greer?"

"Same. Best I can tell it, Greer was waiting for him here, started shooting just as Boller walked in the door. Your partner returned fire..."

Shauna gasped and felt her knees buckle." Has anyone called Dottie?"

"You've got one agent on site, two more en route. It's my under-standing that one of the agents in Raleigh has contacted the family." Yates turned, looked down the street, shaking his head.

Shauna sat down on the front steps, trying to grasp the reality of it all.

"Should have been me...I should have been the one to call her," she mumbled. "Don't want her to have to find out this way." Her mind suddenly raced to Dottie and their daughter, Stephanie. The numbness settled into her.

"You know about what happened at the river?" She looked up at Yates.

"Yeah. I can't believe this. Brett Hampton was one of my oldest friends. He was a good man. I know that. It had to be Greer that kept him involved. Had to be."

Shauna stood and looked into the house. She watched a SWAT team member descend the staircase. His helmet shield was raised. He held his weapon at his side. The house was secure. No more bad guys.

"So it was Greer and Hampton all along? Thompson's murder? Is that possible? My God, Roy..." Shauna's voice trailed away.

"There's another team down at the river, examining the scene. They're going to want you back there," Yates said.

"I know, I know," she answered softly.

There was a stir at one end of the street. They looked to their left and could see a number of people milling about. Brilliant white lights suddenly came to life. The press had arrived with a flourish.

"Can you imagine what type of attention this is going to create?" Yates asked. "Damn, I've spent my whole life trying to uphold the law in Richmond County. Now this..." He watched the chaos emerging at the police blockade and could see the television cameras pointing in their direction.

"You did what was right, Sheriff Yates. You solved a mystery that was thirty years in the making. You did your job," Shauna whispered.

"How many dead, Ms. Spencer? Eight? Eight people dead. Gawd Almighty, it's a heavy price to pay for bringing criminals to justice, ain't it?"

"I guess it is, Sheriff." She looked down the street at the handful of people that would splash this story across America over the coming days, "I guess it is."

"How is Jeb Mason? What's the doctor saying?" Yates asked.

"That he's very, very lucky. They're doing surgery now," Shauna said. "I'm going back there...I want to be at the hospital when he wakes up, Sheriff."

"That sounds like a mighty good idea to me, Ms. Spencer." He looked back at the house. "They're going to have the homicide team going through this house with a fine-tooth comb the rest of the night. I'm guessing we'll be talking to investigators for the next three days."

"Yes sir," Shauna answered, "I would say you're right. Maybe by the time we're finished, maybe we'll understand what's happened ourselves." A cold fatigue had begun to descend on her.

Yates smiled and shook his head. "I hope you're right, Shauna. Dear God, I hope you're right."

CHAPTER

ONE HUNDRED AND TWO

"Agent Spencer?" A well-dressed gray-haired man appeared at the door. "Ms. Spencer, I'm Bill O'Flynn. I believe we may have met at some point in the past."

Shauna recognized the Deputy Director of the SBI, though she seriously doubted he remembered her. With over three hundred agents, she was just one more face in the crowd, though he had presented her with a commendation after the Paine serial murder case.

"Hello, Director O'Flynn. Yes sir, I do remember you, sir."

"Agent Spencer, we have several agents who should be arriving in the next several hours from Raleigh. They are going to be joined by FBI agents who are flying in tonight as well. I think you can guess that there will be a great deal we'll need to discuss around this case."

"Yes sir. I understand. I'm prepared to provide a full report."

O'Flynn smiled. "Agent Spencer, are you hurt?" He looked down at her blood soaked vest.

"No sir. My...a civilian who was with me this afternoon at the river was injured in a gun battle with one of the perps, sir."

O'Flynn raised his eyebrow and frowned slightly.

"I'm aware of the incident over at the river. His condition?"

"Don't know yet, sir. He's been taken to the hospital."

"Suspect we will have a great deal to talk about, Agent Spencer, a great deal. Sheriff Yates…" O'Flynn turned toward him, "the same investigators will be meeting separately with you."

Yates nodded.

"Agent Spencer…I'm very sorry. Agent Boller was a very good man. You know that."

"Yes sir…I know that," Shauna said.

O'Flynn grimaced and shook his head. "I have already had a preliminary briefing from another of our agents, Taylor Fletcher. From what I can tell, this is going to be one for the record books."

He turned, began to walk back inside, and then stopped.

"Agent Spencer, if you have a moment, perhaps you could join me?"

Shauna followed O'Flynn into the house. They walked around the chalked outline of where her partner fell. The blood blended with the deep crimson of the Oriental rug, forming an obscene mosaic of Mac Boller's murder. Shauna flinched as she stepped around it.

She glanced at the music room. The grand piano in the far left corner, the crystal vase atop it twinkling in the light. Beautiful red blooms that seemed to mirror the ghastly scene in the far right corner. The winged-back chair was streaked with dark stains that pooled on the seat, dripping over the side onto a second rug. Benny Greer's blood.

They passed by it through the open French doors into the den. Shauna could see a young female sheriff's deputy on one knee. She knelt in front of a second winged-back chair, this one a deep burgundy that faced a fireplace. She was handing a cup and saucer to the old woman who sat there. A male officer stood behind the chair watching the proceedings. Beyond was the large bay window.

"She was here when all of this came down. I understand you've met her." O'Flynn nodded in the direction of Marie Thompson. "Are you up to talking to her now? My sense is that she's out of it…when the first law officers got here, they found her there."

Shauna nodded. They approached the chair.

"Mrs. Thompson?" O'Flynn's voice grew gentler. "Ma'am, this is Agent Shauna Spencer. She's been working with us on our investigation."

Shauna rounded the chair. She looked down at the frail, white-haired lady, who was quietly sipping from the saucer she had just been handed. She was dressed in a lavender dress with a cream colored shawl. What looked like knitting rested on her lap.

She smiled up at Shauna.

"Hello, dear," she said, "would you care for some tea?"

"No, thank you, Ma'am," Shauna answered. There was no hint of recognition from the old woman.

"Mrs. Thompson. I was wondering if you would mind if Agent Spencer spent a few minutes with you to go over what happened here tonight. Would that be all right?" O'Flynn asked.

"Yes, yes, that would be fine," the old lady answered. Her hands trembled slightly as she sipped her hot tea. She looked out the bay window.

A gentle rain had started to fall.

CHAPTER

ONE HUNDRED AND THREE

Roy Yates felt tired. More tired than he had ever felt in his sixty four years.

He had devoted his life to protecting his county, to preserving its dignity. He was not a brilliant man. He knew that. But he had done his best. He'd gone home every day for the last thirty years believing that he had done some good. All that was gone.

Stacey, North Carolina was about to become known as the capital of police corruption. And there wasn't a damn thing that he could do about it.

He walked across the yard, out the front gate, and down the street to his patrol car. Two of the sheriff's deputies spoke to him as he passed the taped crime barricade. He didn't hear them.

How could so much bad have come to his town? He suddenly thought of Linda and how much he wished she were here now. For a brief moment he could almost smell the hint of her perfume in the evening air, but the steady drizzle of the rain washed it away, and all that was left was the streaked concrete of the sidewalk and the lights of the patrol cars.

His thoughts turned to Lou as he got into his car. Lou would listen, and she understood. A friendly voice would mean a lot right about now, he told himself. He picked up his mobile phone and punched in her number even as he checked his watch. It read 1:20 a.m.

Her answering machine picked up after the fifth ring. Why wasn't she at home at this time of the night? Then he remembered. Half the women in Stacey were in Raleigh this week for the Ladies' Club Meeting.

Hell, he had already heard that once tonight. Carl Lester had been saying the same thing only hours before. He remembered now. It seemed like a lifetime ago.

He slumped down in the seat and pulled his cap over his eyes. Maybe he would just sleep right here. He was so tired he wasn't sure he could make the drive home anyway.

The investigation file lay beside him and as he began to drift off, his mind began to race over the case, like a recurring nightmare that would not leave him. He intuitively reached for his spiral notebook and patted it inside his shirt pocket. Felt the worn ink pen he used to make his notes and pulled it out. A fragment of grass and weed came with it, a last souvenir of Mary Tully's front yard. He started to scratch a line or two in his notebook, struggling to make out the text in the dim light of the car.

"Tough getting old," he whispered as he pulled on his reading glasses. "Can't see shit anymore."

He wrote down his recollection of the last hour. Now, while it was fresh. Might as well get it down. A lot of people were going to want to know.

Something, somewhere far back in his mind, began to nag at him, poke from the periphery of his consciousness. He tried to fight through it, to the peace of sleep but it prodded him. Something that he couldn't quite put his finger on. It began to grow and then gradually, to take shape.

He looked across the street. Could see the outline of Carl Lester peering anxiously out his living room window at the circus that was unfolding across the way.

Poor SOB is probably scared to death, Yates thought to himself. "Bet he wishes Patty was home tonight..."

Yates stopped. Looked down at the notebook. No...it didn't make any sense.

He picked up the radio.

"Barbara? No...I'm OK...I'm OK." The rapid voice on the other end rattled on. "Barbara, need you to listen to me, will you do that?"

The line grew quiet.

"This is going to sound a little funny, but I want you to look something up for me on your computer. Will you do that?"

Three minutes later, Yates replaced the transmitter.

"Oh my God," he said to no one. "Oh my God."

CHAPTER

ONE HUNDRED AND FOUR

"Mrs. Thompson, is there anything else that you can tell me about what you saw, ma'am?" Shauna bent down in front of the old woman. She wondered if Mrs. Thompson could see through her smile and see how ragged her nerves were. Her partner was dead. Jeb Mason lay gravely wounded in the hospital.

"I'm afraid not," Marie Thompson smiled wanly. "It's as I told you before, my dear."

Shauna played the old woman's answers over in her mind again. As best she could tell, Benny Greer arrived that evening just around 8:30 p.m. He had talked at length to Marie Thompson and had explained that there had been threats communicated against her. He had indicated that he would remain in the music room to provide protection that evening and had fired on an intruder some time later.

"So you did see the actual shooting? Is that right ma'am?" Shauna asked again.

"Oh, yes. I certainly did," she smiled and took another sip of her tea.

Shauna's first thought was that the old lady was beginning to sink into dementia, or at the very least, had become very addled. She could just as easily have spent the evening watching her begonias grow in the backyard.

The SBI agent breathed deeply. She looked back at the music room and considered the tragedy that had unfolded there only minutes before. It was a beautiful room, remarkably unchanged by the gun battle that had erupted. She watched the colors reflecting off the crystal vase on the Grand Piano. The crystal captured the pulsating lights of the emergency vehicles parked outside. It absorbed them and then released them in a dizzying array of sparkling color. A perfect setting for the ruby red flowers that flowed from the top.

Shauna sat back in her chair and looked closely at Mrs. Thompson. She had seemed so remarkably clearheaded earlier. Now it seemed she was growing weary. She still sat gazing out at her backyard, an almost serene smile across her face.

"Sure you don't care for a cup of tea, dear?" The old woman shakily poured another cup for herself. "It's freshly brewed." Shauna watched the old woman. She had begun to close her eyes periodically.

"Ma'am, why don't we make some arrangements to get you somewhere that you can get some rest? Would that be OK?" Shauna asked.

"Certainly, dear." She smiled at Shauna. But there was something about her expression that was troubling.

"Ma'am, may I ask you one more question?"

Mrs. Thompson nodded awake. Seemed to turn her full attention to the SBI agent. She smiled, her eyes sparkled with merriment.

"Is this the chair your husband was sitting in the night he died?"

Marie Thompson's smile faded. For a brief second a look of derision crossed her face. Of hatred. It passed so quickly that Shauna almost believed she had imagined it. There was only a sweet old lady sitting there. Old and tired. She did not speak.

Shauna waited.

"They were so stupid, you know." But the voice did not sound like Marie Thompson's at all. She hissed the words. "Stupid, stupid children." She looked at Spencer, her head slightly swaying.

"I saw him, you know. I saw him." she looked back out the window, into the past. "There…" she raised her withered hand. "I see you!" She screamed the words, her eyes suddenly blazing with hatred.

"You were there that night, weren't you, Mrs. Thompson?" Spencer asked.

The old woman said nothing, only glared at the frightened child that peered in from the darkness of her mind.

"They caught them, though," she laughed. "They caught them."

"You sent them, Mrs. Thompson? You sent them after the children?"

She didn't respond. Shauna watched her head begin to wobble back and forth. She reached down, shakily brought the cup of tea to her lips.

"No matter," she said. "No matter."

Something was wrong. Very wrong. Shauna's eyes swept the room. She came back to Marie Thompson, followed her gaze out the window. Into the darkness. In the reflection she could see herself, seated in front of the old woman, looking on a scene that must have resembled what a little boy had looked in on many long years before.

She studied their image against the pulsating backdrop of the emergency vehicles in the front of the house, watched the colors gather, and then converge in the brilliant prism of the crystal vase that sat atop the Grand Piano. She lingered there, absorbing the scene.

What was it? She paused. The blood red flowers. Different. Not the same as that afternoon. White peonies then. Then the words came back to her, hauntingly... "Oleander...they were Franklin's favorite."

Shauna leapt from the chair. She grabbed the cup from the elderly woman. Ripped the tray away. The teapot clattered across the floor, spilling its contents across the scarlet and gold Persian rug.

"What's in your tea, Mrs. Thompson?" she yelled the words. "Mrs. Thompson? Mrs. Thompson!"

Marie Thompson looked at her through glazed eyes. Could feel death's blessed approach. She welcomed it.

"You sent Benny Greer and Brett Hampton that night, didn't you? You sent them to kill those children, didn't you?" Shauna was standing over her. Several officers had rushed into the room. They watched the elderly woman as she began to smile for a final time.

"Stupid girl," she rasped, "you still don't understand, do you?"

CHAPTER

ONE HUNDRED AND FIVE

Roy Yates pulled his car into the long graveled driveway. His headlights were turned off. He cut the engine and allowed the cruiser to silently glide down the slight grade. There was no sign of activity inside the house. He rolled to a stop underneath a mammoth poplar tree and slipped out, making his way through the darkness of the backyard.

Yates unbuckled his holster as he quietly tread onto the long wooden deck that looked out over the rolling hills of pastureland. The rain had begun to subside now and the planks wheezed slightly as he glided toward the back door. A few dark clouds still streamed by overhead, occasionally blotting out the full moon that streamed down on the countryside.

He was shocked to find the door that led into the Great Room unlocked. He slowly pushed it open, waiting for the inevitable creaking but it swung easily...silently. He stood there in the doorway, trying to adjust his eyes to the dim light before he started to creep into the darkness.

He could make out the vague outline of a couch and two high-backed chairs in the far corner. Somewhere in the house a grandfather clock dully tolled away the seconds.

Roy Yates glided toward the large mahogany desk.

He could look out from this position in the room through a bay window at the pastures behind. A large armchair sat diagonal to the window. Yates glanced at it, and then froze. He could see the outline of someone seated there in the darkness, watching him.

"Hello, Roy," Malcolm Lindsey said.

"Hello, Malcolm."

"No sandwiches this time?"

"Afraid not."

"What brings you by this time of night, Sheriff?"

"Sally still up, Malcolm?"

Lindsey grunted.

"Wasn't sure at first. Had to wake up my Lou to confirm she was down in Raleigh with the rest of the Women's Club. Rode with the mayor's wife as I recall."

Only the sounds of the clock answered.

"When I called you this evening…why did you pretend to yell to her? She's been gone all day."

Lindsey did not answer.

"Funny how the littlest thing gets you to thinking."

"That why you decided to break into my home?"

"Those drive-bys you mentioned that Chief Greer had discussed with you for Steadman. Funny thing, Malcolm. No one else knew anything about that. Not even the officers who were supposed to be patrolling."

"Maybe Chief Greer only claimed to increase the patrols. Maybe he never gave the order…"

Don't think he ever discussed it with you. Don't think there was a separate set of keys for the school either."

"You came here because of a damn set of keys. Please tell me you haven't decided to break the law because of something as stupid…"

"Day after that fire at Steadman. Walked the grounds. Checked every one of those filing cabinets, Malcolm. Nineteen files were locked."

"Fascinating."

"Contents were missing for one though."

"Meaning…"

"Someone emptied it…then locked it back."

"Thousands of explanations."

"You locked it back."

"This is growing tiresome."

"SBI report says half the file cabinets were mislabeled. Someone went through a lot of them. Then took the time to rearrange...obscure."

"Anyone could have..."

"Problem was four of those nineteen cabinets were fire retardant, Malcolm. The files in them have fingerprints."

"I am the principal. If there are fingerprints..."

"Fingerprints superimposed with someone else's. My guess is that would be our late fire chief. Brett Hampton was there with you that night."

"Doubt you have proof of that, now do you, Sheriff?"

"You didn't remove the files from 1983. I'm guessing it was because you just forgot. Maybe didn't have the time."

"You are hallucinating."

"Two years after you killed Judge Thompson. One of your students in that fifth grade class...his name was Zeke Andrews."

"I taught a lot of children."

"Your end-of-year said, 'Distracted, socially awkward, a slow learner.' Wonder how socially awkward you become when you spend everyday looking at a man you saw commit murder?"

"You're insane."

"Found something...handwriting...something that gave you a clue. A clue to who was blackmailing you."

Lindsey grunted.

"Why were you in such a hurry when I called this afternoon, Malcolm?"

"Why don't you tell me?"

"You couldn't afford to be on the phone very long then. You were driving Brett Hampton over to the Yadkin River, weren't you? You knew that Greer would be driving to the Thompson house by then. And that Agent Spencer and Mason would be headed back to their vehicle."

"That all?"

Yates scanned the blackness of the room. "No music tonight?"

"Come again?"

"Music...I paid a visit to the Thompson house tonight. But then again, I think you already know that. That little melody. Couldn't quite place it...then I finally remembered."

Malcolm Lindsey chuckled quietly.

"I heard it *here*. When you and I sat down last Sunday and talked about the break-in. Assumed it was a radio. Something more than that, wasn't it?"

"I believe the music you are referring to is 'Dream of A Witches Sabbath, Symphony Fantastique' by Hector Berlioz. Rather sophisticated selection for these parts, Sheriff Yates."

"Played for my benefit, Malcolm?"

Lindsey shifted in his chair and slowly lifted the shotgun over the edge of his desk.

"Do you know what trefoleum is, Malcolm?"

"Come again?"

"Trefoleum. Common grass…find it about anywhere in these parts."

"Don't believe I do."

"Guessing it's the scientific name…we call it clover."

Lindsey did not speak.

"Zeke Andrews sent you a blackmail letter. Think maybe a couple of them. Told you he saw you that night. Threatened to go to the authorities."

"That doesn't concern me."

"We found lot of miscellaneous stuff…clippings, pictures of windows. Words he pasted together. Guess it was the drawing board for the final notes he sent you."

Yates watched the barrel of the gun slide across the desk. It pointed toward the sheriff.

"We found a little padlock. No key. Found a bag of clover. Thought it might be drugs but no, just simple clover."

Lindsey shifted and the weight of the chair creaked as he did.

"When I left the Thompson house tonight…sitting in my cruiser. One little clover fell out of my notebook." Yates gently patted his shirt pocket. "Kept it for good luck. A four leaf clover."

"Luck can be a wonderful thing."

"It's what finally told me what none of us could see for ourselves. There was a reason we couldn't find that little key. There was a reason Andrews kept trefoleum. Sent you one, didn't he?"

"Get on with it."

"A key…a clover…and one other item. One simple, worn pair of glasses."

"And…"

"Very same glasses I handed you the other day…right here in this room. Remember thinking they didn't quite fit someone as meticulous, as neat as you, Malcolm."

The words lingered there in the darkness. For a time only the steady beat of the clock answered.

"Zeke Andrews's glasses…bad diabetic and his eyes were going on him. But he still wrapped those glasses and sent them along. Prescription glasses, I'm guessing. But not *your* prescription…you strained to read that list I handed you. But you know, I've seen you read dozens of papers at school board meetings with no problem."

Lindsey raised the gun off his lap.

"Watched you read that newspaper at the barbershop without even blinking."

"He sent you a *symbol*…a sign just for you that told you he knew you killed Judge Thompson. He knew you killed three boys that same night…a key, a clover, and finally glasses….Joe Keyes, Paul Clover, and Matt Glasser."

"You believe you can prove that…after all these years?"

"Did Marie Thompson know? Was she involved in the murder of her husband?"

"My God, Yates. How blind can you be?" Lindsey began to laugh and said, "Everything that night…was her idea."

CHAPTER

ONE HUNDRED AND SIX

"Are you saying…"

"She hated him. Had hated him for years. I was a convenient and much younger lover. Nothing more."

"You're telling me she planned to kill her husband?"

"We waited there that night…I was hidden away in a second story bedroom." Lindsey paused, as if the memory of July 7th suddenly became strong again. "They'd gone to bed…the old man and Marie. Sometime around midnight she got up. Came downstairs. Brewed the hot tea. He joined her there after a time."

Yates could see Lindsey smile in the darkness.

"Sat there with that stereo playing and waited. The same little tune you heard at Marie's tonight. Sort of our song, guess you might say… the old man was an incurable insomniac. She often made him something to help him sleep. Oleander is a powerful toxin, did you know that, Roy?"

Yates shifted but did not speak.

"It was his second cup before he knew. Of course, by then it was too late. It's when I walked out and sat down beside Marie on the couch and watched the show." Lindsey gestured toward the window and said, "We sat there and watched the panic in his eyes…when he knew his beloved had poisoned him. You know, she talked to him as he began to slip away…told him about the two of us…how much she despised him."

Lindsey shook his head and looked back to Yates and continued. "Then the strangest thing happened. The judge reached toward the window... pleading. I remember we laughed at that."

Lindsey voice grew quiet and he said, "And then we saw him...one frightened little boy. Staring into the window. All alone."

"Zeke Andrews."

"We didn't know that then."

"Greer...Hampton?"

"Pardon?"

"Were they involved then? Or did that come later?"

"Benny Hampton was nothing more than the same slow witted flunky he is...or was...today. Loved to get drunk. Tag along."

"You're telling me Brett Hampton was there that night?"

"Very much so."

"Greer?"

"Sheriff Yates, Benny Greer was not involved in any of this...not then, not now."

Yates could feel the air suck out of the room. "You mean he never..."

"No, Roy. I'm afraid we've manipulated your little investigation all along the way. Our late fire chief was very helpful in that regard. I'm sure it never occurred to anyone that our fire department's response to the Steadman fire was late, even by their questionable standards. When Hampton and I left the school under somewhat hasty circumstances I instructed Brett to make sure that the keys for the lead engine would be conveniently misplaced for some ten minutes or more. Enough to make sure that our janitor was sufficiently dead..."

"So you killed Bump?"

"I had no choice, Sheriff. He walked in when we had papers spread across the floor. Hampton and I were both there. We couldn't risk questions ever coming back."

"So you chose to burn him alive."

"I can't say if he was *alive,* Roy. I hit him hard enough with the baseball bat to kill him, I'm sure."

"You had to burn him?"

"Expeditious, nothing more. Destroy the evidence. And make it look like a botched robbery. Believe me, even Hampton could have done a better job of starting a fire than that. We made it look, shall I say, untidy."

"You made it untidy for a reason, didn't you?"

"Of course." Malcolm Lindsey smiled in the darkness. "Make it look like we were trying to mask the murder. That was the last thing on our minds, I can assure you."

"And the night you killed the boys?"

"Oh, that." Lindsey paused and looked out through the bay window, as if he were reaching back to that summer's night long ago. "Can't recall all of it, of course. Didn't see the boy. Then he was just there... standing in the light. I walked toward the window and he screamed... then started to run. I couldn't see him well. But I could tell it was a young boy. Marie panicked. She sent Brett and me out to catch him. But he had such a head start, after all." He shook his head at the memory.

"Didn't stop you though, did it?"

"Well, of course it couldn't, now could it, Sheriff? I could see them in the field, well ahead. Three of them. I thought we had them when we got to the river. I remember when we came on them there. The Keyes boy even recognized me. I didn't even speak. The first two were easy. The third ran. But this time...*no one* got away. Stupid children. Led them out into the water. Simply held them down...until they were dead."

Lindsey paused and then said, "The storm had started by then. It was so convenient. It...pardon the pun, drowned out the screams. Took us almost an hour to catch up. Three minutes to take care of things."

"And Marie Thompson?"

"She waited for us to get back. We were soaked to the bone. Exhausted. But there was work to do. Brett drove Marie back to Savannah. Her sister was bedridden anyway. No one was the wiser. I stayed behind. Made sure there were no telltale clues. I was still in the house at 4:30 that morning when the alarm clock rang. I didn't expect that. Fortunately I made it out before the attention was focused on the house. But just barely."

"You're a sick bastard, Malcolm."

"Not really, Roy. My little indiscretions have served me well. Marie was quite helpful over the years with teaching positions, the assignment to principal. We shared quite a bond."

"And Brett Hampton?"

"Oh, we discussed ending our relationship with him on a number of occasions. But he was useful, in his own way."

"He fed you information on our investigation."

"From the beginning, Roy. He was trusted. If you recall, he phoned you about the fire, not Greer."

Yates shifted, keeping his eyes on the shot gun barrel.

"And I used him to fan the flames of hatred in Chief Greer. From the time the arson investigation was initiated through your last debrief with him. Hampton was my go-between. Greer was the foil."

Yates thought back to his conversation with Clarence Parker. The "officer" who asked about Mason. He assumed it was a police officer. He assumed it was Benny Greer. He never dreamed that someone with a badge might be confusing to an old man.

"You sent Hampton to wait for Agent Spencer and Mason?"

"Of course."

"And Greer?"

"After your meeting with the SBI people and Greer, Hampton called me. Explained everything. I gave some thought to the possibility that you might actually someday find I was at the center of the web, so I put a little plan in place."

"Which was?"

"I encouraged Hampton to call Greer and suggest he call on the widow Thompson, to get the jump on the investigation, before the competition so to speak. He had nowhere else to turn. He trusted Hampton. A master stroke really. Marie and I had the visit totally choreographed. She began to put together quite a tale for the chief over tea."

"Poisoned tea?"

"Oh, yes, the same blend that we used a few years back. I was there waiting. When he was near death we drug him into the study, where we propped him in a chair."

"And when Agent Boller arrived?"

"Afraid it wasn't totally a fair fight. I shot as he came in the door. Oh, he got a shot off, but it was into the body of a man who was already near death. I added a head shot from Boller's revolver to make sure."

"And Zeke Andrews?"

"Same perfect fool who stood at the window thirty years ago. He sent me three blackmail letters, you know, which I followed to a tee. Even made a ten-thousand-dollar down payment on a hundred-thousand-dollar charge. All the time I was coming closer to finding out who he was. You were right incidentally, about the envelopes. They were handwritten!" Lindsey laughed out loud. "Can you believe it? All that work cutting and pasting and he hand-writes the envelope and sends them through the mail. I knew the approximate age of the sender. The handwriting...I had an idea early on, let's say."

"Is that how you found out who your blackmailer was?"

"We had the same drop instructions for each of the payments. A small boat landing on the Yadkin. Hampton and I followed the instructions. I knew we were being watched." Lindsey sighed and said, "Then the night came when I happened to catch the slightest glimpse of a cigarette burning...high on the ridge and across the river. He waited there in the dark. The night of our last "installment"...it was time for Mr. Andrews to pay for his transgressions."

"Did you kill him?"

"Why did you come here tonight, Roy? Was it to find something? The glasses, maybe?"

"I figured you kept something. The files, maybe something else... sociopaths generally keep a memento or two."

"Sociopath is such an ugly word." Lindsey laughed and tossed a dark bundle toward Yates. "A souvenir for you, Sheriff."

Yates caught the dark lump. He struggled to make it out. Stopped when he realized he was looking at a boy's backpack.

"It's the only link that remains, Roy. I couldn't bear to part with it," Lindsey said. "Well, one of only two."

"And the other?"

"I believe we both know the answer to that, Roy. That would be *you* of course. I simply have to tie up the loose ends. I had hoped Brett Hampton would be killed tonight, actually. Suspected that he would. With Greer, the likely co-conspirator, fatally injured in a gun battle with the SBI, I almost had it wrapped up."

"Then why were you sitting here waiting for me, Malcolm?"

"Because I am *very careful*, Roy. I don't make mistakes. I gave you the benefit of the doubt. There was an outside possibility you might stumble onto me."

"You're a very bright man, Malcolm. But you made mistakes before, didn't you?"

"In what way?"

"The night of the first murder."

"The boy at the window? Stupid misfortune, Roy. Nothing more."

"Zeke Andrews saw you, Malcolm. And he ended up telling us everything. Just took him a long, long time to do it."

Lindsey raised the shotgun and cocked it, then placed the butt-end against his shoulder. The barrel pointed directly at Yates.

"An intruder, shot in the dark. So unfortunate to hear that our sheriff was involved in the same sordid affair as our chief of police and our fire chief. It will make headlines." Lindsey hissed the words.

"You never know who's watching, Malcolm. Always someone there…watching in the darkness."

Yates nodded to his right.

Lindsey turned slightly, glanced to his left. Could see the outline of a figure silhouetted in the rain. He screamed and swung his weapon as the first bullet crashed through the large bay window, sending glass exploding across the room. It struck Lindsey in mid-chest, and he was knocked back into the chair. The second bullet had almost the same entry point as the shotgun fell from his hands and banged against the hardwood floor.

Officer Bobby Patterson stood outside in the gentle rain, his gun still pointed at the figure sprawled in front of him. He remained in that position as Malcolm Lindsey drew his last breath.

CHAPTER

ONE HUNDRED AND SEVEN

Jeb sat quietly in the passenger seat of the car as Blaine McQuinn pulled the Mustang into the Stacey City Park. It was not an all together unpleasant hour-and-a-half drive from Charlotte, one which he felt honor-bound to take.

The last four days had unfolded in a thunderclap of attention on his old hometown. Only now, days after the events, was the total picture beginning to unfold in newspapers and magazines around the country. The anticipated influx of electronic media had been even greater than feared. Every entertainment, public interest, or crime-oriented program in the world seemed to have found their way to the Richmond County Courthouse, where media briefings were conducted throughout the day.

At first the conversations with the press had been terse, official statements of progress in the homicide investigations involving the local chiefs of police and fire departments and the elementary school principal. But as more information came to light, and the other murders became public knowledge, the amount of media attention had become blinding. *Newsweek* and *Time* both had seven-page layouts on the emerging investigation. Each of the major networks was on-site.

Earle and the Dogwood Inn had become something of a celebrity hangout, a development that was not displeasing to Earle. He began to depend more and more on his nephew to cover the front desk while he held court in the restaurant, thrilling his listeners with tales of turkey sandwiches and SBI surveillance.

The internal investigation of Agent Shauna Spencer and the shooting of Fire Chief Brett Hampton lasted less than forty-eight hours. Her actions were deemed appropriate and in the line of duty. Stories of a beautiful and intrepid female SBI Agent had begun to percolate amongst the press corps, but no actual interviews would be conducted until the investigation was complete.

The death of Agent Mac Boller was the focus of even greater scrutiny. Early reports of a standoff with local law enforcement had been retracted over the last two days. Local citizen Malcolm Lindsey had been identified as the shooter. He was also named as the likely culprit in the murder of Police Chief Benny Greer. Even that was still under a veil of controversy, since a State Medical Examiner Report from Charlotte had been released the day before. It indicated the presence of a very powerful poison in Greer's system. The press, of course, had a field day with each latest development.

There was emerging information from state investigators that both Lindsey and Hampton would be named in a series of murders that dated back to the early 1980s. A press release the previous day credited SBI agents Boller and Spencer, and local sheriff, Roy Yates, with ultimately breaking the case.

There was also mention of an unnamed private citizen who played a key role but who would not be identified for several days. The mystery man immediately became the focus of an intense media search. One of the more skilled researchers had run across Mason's name by checking ER admissions over the past week. Gunshot wound, admitted by a Shauna Spencer to Richmond Memorial, and subsequently transferred to Carolinas Medical Center in Charlotte. The pursuit was instantaneous. Security was tightened at CMC, though one of the more imaginative investigators made it to Jeb's fourth floor room by disguising himself as an orderly.

At 11:05 that Friday morning, Jeb had donned a similar disguise and with the help of a doctor, two nurses, and a most accommodating security officer, had walked quietly out the back door of a loading dock for purchasing and into a waiting Ford Mustang driven by local reporter Blaine McQuinn.

McQuinn's day had already been a busy one. He had spent much of the morning in a private home twenty miles west of Stacey with

Richmond County Sheriff Roy Yates and SBI Agent Shauna Spencer. He enjoyed an exclusive interview that would propel his career into the stratosphere and, if logistics could be finalized, would be the center-piece of a prime-time exclusive two nights later. He had promised to chauffeur Mason back to Stacey in exchange for the missing pieces of the story, a fare he considered infinitely low.

Two hours later, they pulled into the gravel parking lot of the city park and parked underneath the shade of a towering oak tree.

"Jeb, you sure this is where you want me to drop you off?" McQuinn looked out at the swings and teeter-totters across the way. A few small kids were at play, their parents chatting nearby.

"Yep. Thanks, Blaine. Good luck with the national thing."

"You sure we didn't spring you too early? It's a serious wound…"

"Doctors say I'm fine. They pumped enough IVs into me to fill a water tank. I'm good to go."

"You know, I guess it's none of my business, but when I did the full background on your friend Zeke Andrews," McQuinn said. "There were a lot of problems…a lot of things that… could have contributed to his…problems."

"Not sure if I get your meaning."

"His dad was a chronic alcoholic. Left the family by the time your friend was fifteen. Zeke started getting in trouble before he was eighteen. Ran with a rough crowd and all."

"Yeah?" Jeb studied him.

"Just saying…there was a lot that went wrong for him." McQuinn tapped the steering wheel with his index finger. "Lot of things…lot of things."

"Thanks, Blaine," Jeb said. "I mean that."

McQuinn nodded and looked out over the playground to the base-ball fields beyond. It was a beautiful summer's day, maybe even a tad cooler than the past week. He could hear a lawnmower somewhere in the distance and could smell the freshly cut grass. A butterfly flittered by and landed briefly on the hood, then continued on.

"You ever play ball on those fields?" McQuinn asked.

Jeb smiled.

"Good memories huh?"

Jeb nodded, looking back into summers long past. "Yeah…good memories."

The Crown Victoria slowly pulled into the far side of the parking lot. It cruised over to a shaded corner, where it parked beside a mammoth pin oak. Mason did not look in its direction.

"You know, the night you were shot. All hell broke loose," McQuinn said.

"So I've heard."

"Stayed up all night trying to get the story put together."

"Sounds like you did a pretty good job."

"I just wanted to tell you. That next night. Must have been eleven or twelve..." McQuinn started. "Well, I thought I would run by and check on you."

"Well, I appreciate that."

"No...no, that's not what I wanted to say." McQuinn paused. "They had run everybody home by then. Everybody out of the ICU waiting room. Even Mrs. Gardner and all of Mr. Gardner's friends."

Jeb smiled. "She needed the break. Everybody did."

"*She* was there," McQuinn said. "Guess they couldn't make her leave."

"I'm sorry, who was there?"

"The ICU nurse came out. She kind of politely ran me off when she found out I wasn't another agent."

"Another agent?"

"She was curled into a ball in a straight back chair in the corner of the room. You didn't come out of surgery until late that day and was out of it the whole night. The charge nurse said she refused to leave. I could see her there. Sound asleep," Blaine McQuinn said. "Ms. Spencer wasn't going to leave you."

Jeb nodded. He followed McQuinn's gaze over to the cruiser.

"I would just as soon that not come out. Shauna is..."

"None of my business, anyway." McQuinn looked away from the other car and back to Jeb. "I just wanted you to know...off the record, I mean. She wasn't going to leave you there."

Blaine McQuinn extended his hand, and Jeb reached over and offered a partial handshake with his good arm, grimacing at the stiffness in his left shoulder.

McQuinn left him there. Mason walked unnoticed across the playground. A middle-aged man with what looked like a broken arm out for a quiet walk in the park on a beautiful July day.

Shauna waited for him.

"You seem to be moving pretty well for a crippled corporate executive." She smiled and Jeb remembered again why just looking at her was the best therapy of all.

"Doctor says my chances of playing in the NBA are going to be compromised."

"Poor baby," she cooed. "There's always Major League Baseball. I understand your precious Cubs are always in need."

"Did your meeting with Mr. McQuinn go well?" Jeb asked.

"Remarkably. I actually like him...I mean, as far as the press goes."

"Funny, so do I." Jeb turned and watched the Mustang round the corner and head back into town. "Guessing Blaine McQuinn will be splashed all over the news in the next couple of weeks."

"So will Stacey...and so will you...and so will this whole thing."

"No, not me," Jeb said. "I am officially going on medical leave."

"You're kidding me. Mr. Hard Core Business is actually going to take time away...I thought you'd be dying to get back to the desk."

"I was actually thinking about finding a quiet corner and healing up."

"I think that is a very good idea."

"A few weeks away might be good...for both of us," Jeb said.

"I see. For both of us. Tell me more."

"You're wrapping this up. And we've both lost people that were very close to us." He stepped closer to her and placed his one good arm around her waist. She nudged closer, her face inches from his.

"I'm listening, Mr. Mason," she whispered.

"I know we need to stay close...but maybe not *so* close. I was thinking maybe somewhere other than the Dogwood Inn...though it is a beautiful vacation spot."

"A beautiful vacation spot," Shauna agreed. "I do have a very nice condo in Raleigh. I have no problem taking on a boarder."

"When I was a kid," Jeb said. "My dad used to rent this cottage up in the mountains. Rustic little chateau. It was on the water. Quiet and peaceful...little town called Lake Lure. It seemed like it was a million miles from anywhere."

"Tell me more..."

"It's maybe three hours away. Easy drive," Jeb said. "Still have it pictured in my mind. Red A-frame. Pier that ran out over the water. Nothing but blue sky and mountains."

"So…are you inviting me to go with you on some exotic retreat?"

"Yes, Shauna Spencer. I believe I am."

"Then I believe I'll accept, Jeb Mason. You know your little piece of heaven might not even be there any more." Shauna smiled. "I mean, a few years have passed since then."

"It's there. I made the reservations this morning for the two of us for two weeks. Beginning tonight."

"Hmmm…you're pretty sure of yourself aren't you?"

"I'm pretty sure of *us*. And I know I don't give a damn about going back to Chicago right now. Not unless you're waiting at O'Hare when I land." And then he kissed her.

"Jeb," her voice was breathless. "This could be complicated. I'm not going to be able to…I don't want to think about you…going back to Chicago."

"Would you rather I stay?" he whispered into her ear.

"I can't tell you that. I just met you. I don't have the right to just…"

"Shauna…there's no commitment there. Simply asking, would you rather I stay?" He pulled back, his blue eyes burning.

"Yes," she said quietly.

"Good." His voice was husky now. "So do I. I told Tolliver that I would take a six-week leave of absence. And there was a good chance I wouldn't be coming back."

"Are…are you kidding me?" Shauna's eyes grew wide. "Cause if you are, this is *not* funny, Jeb Mason…it's not funny at all."

"No, I'm not kidding you, Shauna."

"But I know how important your career is. You can't just up and toss all of that out the window…can you?"

"Was a window that led me here, Shauna. Guess it's a window that will lead me out."

"We hardly know each other. Are you sure?"

"I'm sure I found my friend when I came back here. I'm sure I found you. Maybe I even found a little bit of me."

"Then I guess now we'll see if we find each other," Shauna said, and as she did, a tear began to roll down her cheek. "You think you can just cold-turkey this career deal?"

"Thinking it's time I focused on the life deal."

She nodded, and he was certain her smile was the most beautiful thing he had ever seen.

"We won, didn't we, Shauna? I mean…Zeke, Mac Boller, Bump Patterson…but, we tried to make it right. Didn't we?"

"We did what we were supposed to do."

"We'll keep telling ourselves that."

"Sheriff Yates called me this morning. Said there was an envelope left in a safety deposit box they've located. The envelope is in the name of Joe Andrews. Opened it up. Found eight thousand dollars inside. No note…nothing. Wrapped with a single rubber band and Joe's name on it."

Jeb smiled and said, "What happens to it?"

"Hard to say. This investigation will have a lot of loose ends."

"He went back, you know. Zeke went back to where it all began that night…to help his boy. I know that." He looked out over the park and to the fields beyond. "Maybe he can be at peace now."

"Maybe you can too, Jeb." Shauna turned and followed his gaze. She nodded and said, "You have an engagement to keep."

He saw them near the largest of the old oaks that surrounded field number three. Just as agreed. A thin, brown-haired woman with a small, freckle-faced boy. They both smiled as they watched him approach.

"Hello, Mrs. Tully," Jeb said.

"Hello, Mr. Mason," Mary answered. Her eyes welled up. "Thank you…thank you so much." She hugged him.

"Hello, Joe." Jeb grunted as he knelt down stiffly and shook the boy's hand.

"Hello," Joe said quietly, glancing back quickly at the ground.

"I hear Mr. Gardner's going to be getting out of the hospital any day," Mrs. Tully offered. "That's good news."

"Talked to him this morning, Mary. He's so ornery they're going to throw him out."

She smiled. "And you?"

"Fine, fine. 'Course I won't be doing any pole vaulting for a while longer."

The boy grinned.

"I just want to thank you for, you know, making people see that Zeke didn't just…" She paused.

"Zeke was my friend, Mary. He will always be my friend."

Jeb looked down at Joe.

"I'll be dropping him off around seven, if that's still OK?" Jeb asked.

"I think it will be just fine," Mary Tully answered. Jeb extended his hand. Joe took it.

• • •

Shauna sat quietly in the Crown Victoria. With the windows down, the late afternoon breeze wafted lightly through the car. From her vantage point she could look across field number three to the bleachers on the other side.

She could see them there, relaxing from their exertions on the merry-go-round and the swings. They each carried an oversized snow cone. She guessed Joe's was grape.

The man and the boy took a seat on the third row of the faded wooden bleachers. Looking out on a dusty field, underneath a beautiful azure sky, Shauna Spencer watched as the older one told the boy about another summer's day many years before.

About a baseball game with the Asheboro All-Stars deadlocked in the bottom half of the last inning. And about the hush that came over the crowd as Zeke Andrews stepped to the plate.

THE END

ABOUT THE AUTHOR

Tim Cole grew up in western North Carolina, where much of his family still resides. He has been a part of the health care and pharmaceutical industry since graduating from the University of North Carolina over 30 years ago. His career has encompassed positions in sales, marketing and multiple management and leadership roles. Along the way his family has lived in a number of areas throughout the country. This is his first novel. He and his wife Nancy live in North Carolina and are the parents of two sons.

MEDIA CONTACT
Tim Cole
Email: info@timacole.com
Phone: (704) 661 3862
Website: www.timacole.com

REVIEW COPIES AND INTERVIEWS ARE AVAILABLE